Prologue

North Wales
February 1795

I N THE UNCERTAIN LIGHT FROM the candle guttering on the mantelpiece, the clock read four. Sophie got up, drew the amulet out from under the pillow and took it with her through her dressing room and Émile's to his bedroom. Here, the lingering smell of his and Georges' cigars was strong to her and she had to fight back nausea.

In the dim glow of the embers she saw Émile, face down on the bed. He was stripped to the waist, but still in his breeches. He slept heavily though the room was chill. Even now, the sight of the fine muscular definition of his back, arms and shoulders sent a tingle through her. This equalled the thrill of her nerves as she stole up to him, in terror that her approach must surely rouse him.

He seemed to sleep on.

As she bent to slip the amulet under the pillow, his hand shot out, seizing her arm.

He was glaring at her, fully awake in an instant. "What are you about now, my girl?" Anyone would think she devoted her life to annoying him.

They both looked at the amulet. Sophie felt as she had at eight, when her older cousin caught her 'borrowing' some of her rose water.

He snatched the amulet from her. "Superstitious artefacts!" He jumped up.

Sophie thought her voice sounded whining as she pleaded, "If it be so, Émile, then could you not humour me and endure it?"

"You officious little human! This thing stings me even now." He tried to tear it between his talons. Sharp as they were, he failed. He loped to the fire and threw it on, snatching up the poker and thrusting it down amongst the glowing coals. Flames shot up, and an acrid smell brought tears to Sophie's eyes even before they welled up through her disappointment. She blinked them back.

Then a dart of jealousy stabbed into her as the sudden blaze illuminated the skin near his upper ribs and she saw scratches.

He threw a log on the fire and turned about, managing to look self-righteous. "I suppose I may thank *ma petite* Katarina for this latest attempt."

She managed to say, "We only do it because we love you, Émile."

"No, you do not love what I am become, whatever your protestations. Hours since, you and Agnes berated me for trying to make you truly mine by force and attacked me with your poison, yet now you use sneaking methods to change me back to a human. What difference is there between my use of force and yours?"

Her nausea from the cigar smoke tormented Sophie as much as her anguish. She swallowed. "This, Émile; as your real self – whom we dreaded that we must lose – you desperately wished to stay human."

"I will see about asserting some control over you women later." Émile said haughtily, getting back down on the bed and stretching out again. "Do try and refrain, *Madame*, from another attempt. Trying to surprise me is a waste of time. I must take some rest in order to go and submit to Kenrick's orders so as to protect you human ingrates." He shut his eyes, and she found the closing off of their strange glitter a relief.

You submit to the orders of Mistress Kenrick too! Sophie forced back a sob.

This time, the woman had only marked him in a place not generally noticeable, high up on his right ribs. Sophie never scratched him herself; if her pleasure became too great, she chewed the pillow.

THAT SCOUNDREL
Émile Dubois

OR
THE LIGHT OF OTHER DAYS

LUCINDA ELLIOT

AN HISTORICAL PARANORMAL ROMANCE SATIRE

I would like to thank my family and friends for all their generous help and support. Particularly, I would like to thank the outstanding writer Jo Danilo for her invaluable support and advice and for those brilliant suggestions on rewrites – not to mention the book cover and her delight in my characters. I would like to thank Liese Szwann for her help and advice, Jayne Cooke for her unshakeable belief in my writing, Doris Martin and Lisa Edwardes for their support, Tara of Cornerstones Literary Consultants for her encouraging professional critique and many other writer friends for their enthusiasm for my book, too.

Finally, I would like to express my thanks to Jonathon Ferguson, the Firearms Curator of Leeds Armoury Museum for giving me the benefit of his expert knowledge on flintlock pistols.

Part One

Chapter One

Château des Oliviers
Near Avignon
Provence

August 1789

MONSIEUR DUBOIS STOPPED HIMSELF FROM boxing his oldest son's ears. At nineteen and now six inches taller than his father, Émile was too old for that or to be sent for a whipping. *Monsieur* Dubois showed his outrage in his tone.

"I do not take orders from my son. It would be absurd to send the youngsters away." Seeing the anguish in those normally veiled light green eyes, he burst out, "Why, you are afraid!"

Contemptuous, he went and stood staring out to where the breeze sighed through the olive groves.

Émile said softly, "*Bien sûr,* you say rightly. I do fear for them, *Monsieur.*"

Monsieur Dubois snorted a while. "This is hardly the first time the peasants have been restive." He turned, laughing sourly. "All will be well; *après tout,* your mother is with the cleric even now, praying for them to be brought to a better state of mind."

Émile – though far from devout himself – didn't laugh. Perhaps he resented the jeer at his mother's expense. "This is different."

Something moved in *Monsieur* Dubois' eyes. "They are safer here than elsewhere. Why must needs you come *poste haste* from the university with your tales of alarm? I hope you do not think to prate again on the sorrows of the peasants? I do not forget the failure of the olive crop; we suffered from it too. That is my last word on the matter."

As Émile went on arguing, he made a dismissive waving movement. Émile bowed and stalked across the great room. He said to the footman who flung open the door, "Please see if you can find Georges and send him to me."

Upstairs, the Nurse, stout and elderly, got up to curtsey, but Émile kissed her. Nine-year-old Marguerite, slight and brown haired, was standing at the great window of the inner chamber, staring down at the olive groves as her father had done, while singing some ditty and swinging a wooden doll. Hearing Émile, she jumped down and rushed to him.

He swung her through the air. "Have you been keeping Bernard and Charlotte in order?"

As they chatted, she began to look disappointed. "Have you brought sweetmeats?"

"Forgive your remiss servant, *Mademoiselle*. I shall seek to remedy matters by braving the dragon and swimming the moat to procure you some." The nurse was clicking her tongue at Marguerite. Émile turned to her, rubbing the bridge of his freckled nose. "I think I must stay here a while."

Émile found his other sister Charlotte and his younger brother Bernard playing chess together in the gloomy panelled library. Their appearances contrasted; Charlotte was tall and fair, like Émile and their mother, Bernard stocky and dark, like their father. Their being together at this time of day was unusual.

Charlotte jumped up to greet him, while Bernard wanted to know, "Have you been sent down at last?"

"No, I return expressly to ensure your game improves. How go matters here?"

Bernard shrugged. "You picked a poor time. The feeling between *Madame* and *Monsieur* is worse than usual. He has a new mistress."

Charlotte shook her head, but Bernard snorted. "Why pretend?"

"Then we shall have a happy dinner." Émile stood looking at the chess game a while. Finally, he spoke casually. "I wouldn't have you worry too greatly, but there may be some unpleasantness over the next few weeks. It is scarce to be wondered at; things have gone hard with the people."

"There's been unpleasantness already," Charlotte picked up her bishop. "Someone in the fields threw a stone at *Monsieur Notre Père's* carriage, and cracked the window."

Bernard laughed. "He was furious, railing of what our forebears would have done."

Émile was still there days later, though his father called him a fool. He and his valet slept on couches in an ante room off from the passageway leading to Charlotte's bedroom, which was only two corridors from the nursery.

If *Monsieur* Dubois knew where Émile and his valet Georges spent their nights or that they had pistols and swords with them, he said nothing. He and his wife continued to pay calls and to keep up appearances.

Georges was muscular with curly hair, flashing dark eyes and a devastating profile. During those nights in the ante room, Émile shared cigars with him and their conversation was light.

Georges lay back on his couch, his cigar glowing in the dark. "Young Bernard was after the wench too, but he couldn't prevail against me. I stole out to sing at her window every night."

Even in the uncertain light he could see the twinkle in Émile's eyes and added, "With your voice, such an approach must lead to a dousing in cold water."

Émile laughed, then for the first time, spoke seriously. "This is good in you, Georges."

Georges snorted. "I am ever game for a little excitement."

The tapestries, dry with age, were catching light one after another, collapsing and hurling flames across the passages. Already, the smoke felt unbearable and the noises were terrifying, while the heat increased each minute.

Georges hauled Charlotte along while she coughed; he swore at Bernard, who tottered ahead, seemingly about to fall. They were only steps from the open window. Through it they could hear the shouts of the rioters; once, a head poked through to be jerked back at once, as though startled at the inferno inside.

Émile came out of the corridor leading off, his youngest sister Marguerite over one shoulder, dragging along their old Nurse. Even through the smoke, Georges noted her livid colour. He felt no surprise when she dropped. As Émile stooped over her, another tapestry fell just behind them, the flames darting forwards. Marguerite's squeals sounded over the other noises.

"Leave her–" Georges was coughing too much to go on, eyes streaming so he could hardly see.

Émile turned her head, made out the glazed eyes through the smog and staggered up.

"Cover your face!" he spluttered to Marguerite, starting forwards again, bent double to breathe the better air near the floor. As he jerked up his head, trying to see how far it was to the window, his pupils dilated.

An older version of himself was materialising in front of him.

This Émile – a man rather than a youth who thought of himself as a man – seemed to be straining to reach out to them, mouth open as he shouted, yet no sound came.

Georges and Charlotte saw the apparition too, even pausing a moment, streaming eyes dilated.

The figure was gone as suddenly as it came.

The younger Émile started, then, choking, stumbled on through the smoke to the window, where Georges was bundling out Charlotte. Émile thrust the struggling Marguerite after her and she landed on Bernard as he lay in a heap on the leads.

Émile and Georges hid the others in an outhouse while outside the din of the riot and the blazing *Château* raged on. Émile explained how he and Georges must go for horses. For Charlotte, the terrors of the night coalesced in that visit from the wraith like form of her older brother. She hung on to him with one arm as she held Marguerite with the other and begged him between coughs, "Saw you that spectre? It boded ill."

"Calm yourself, Lottie. It was some illusion merely. We will be back betimes. Come, Georges."

Chester*
Six months later – February 1790

"*Monsieur* Émile showed himself to be a resourceful young devil from what poor *Mademoiselle* Charlotte – you may imagine how distraught she is – has been able to tell My Honoured Correspondent. Perforce they journeyed further and further north to evade capture. On their way to Calais they had many narrow escapes, during which *Monsieur* Émile bribed peasants and outwitted officials. Poor *Mademoiselle* Charlotte is now safely in England and their noble cousin, His Lordship the young Count of Ruthin – another relative of ours, as you know, Harriet dear – at once travelled down from Wales to see *Mademoiselle* Charlotte to try and bring her comfort."

John de Courcy wandered about the drawing room, clutching the letter from the grand and distant relative who shared their name. Sophie guessed it would be shown all about his whist circle.

Harriet, his fiancée, smiled. "I gather that is typical; Lord Ynyr seems altogether so charming and thoughtful a young man." She giggled. "And near as handsome as you, dear."

John de Courcy smiled too, while pretending not to notice the compliment. He turned to his sister. "What ails you, Sophie, you are flushed?"

Sophie looked up from the bonnet she was making up for Harriet's trousseau. "I am merely warm. So now they are in England?"

John smiled. "*Mademoiselle* Charlotte is safe in England. Seemingly, their adventures culminated in an unseemly fight at Calais involving cutlasses between *Monsieur* Émile, his man and a group of treacherous sailors who threatened to go to the authorities. *Monsieur* Émile emerged victorious, if cut, to hand his sister over to a woman confidante. But he would go back to find their Honoured Parents, his servant, one Georges, with him. Entirely proper, if rash, given the dangers."

Sophie bit her lip. John paced again. "Yes, it is distressing enough.

That the outhouse roof should collapse after they escaped from the *Château*! But *Monsieur* Émile is in God's hands now, while their young siblings are in Heaven. Sure someone must have turned those peasants' weak heads for them to dare to torch the *Châteaux!* Riotous, illiterate masses must comprise the greatest threat to civilisation."

He paused, impressed at his own eloquence. "I think I must write to the papers on those lines. Harriet, dear, I do not like my pen, and nobody mends them like you."

Harriet jumped up. "I'll about it at once, John."

Sophie murmured, "I do wish *Monsieur* Émile was safe."

Harriet clicked her tongue. "So do we all, Sophie dear! Are your eyes tired, for you have not taken a stitch these five minutes?"

"No, they are quite rested." Sophie went back to working on the bonnet, worried about how things might be when Harriet took over as mistress of the house. When she and John were first engaged, Harriet made pretty speeches about how happy they all would be together. Since then her tone had changed. Sophie knew Harriet to be economical, and with John's income being so limited, she began to fear Harriet might find her a burden.

Plas Uchaf*
Famau Mountain*
North Wales
Over four years later – June 1794

The girl who showed Sophie up to her room at Plas Uchaf (Highest Hall) had bold brown eyes and a confident air. Sophie, tired by the journey and overwhelmed by the grandeur of the Manor, found it difficult not to return her smiles. Still, she heard Harriet's voice: *'No servant will respect you if you allow familiarity.'*

Sophie wasn't confident they would respect her anyway. Still, she made an effort and pulled a prissy face as the maid said, "I'm Agnes, Miss. I am to be your maid. You will like it here. They are very nice, generally."

When the girl opened the door to her room, Sophie stared about, amazed. Instead of a room under the lofts, fireless and cramped, the Dowager Countess had given her one of the guest suites, complete with dressing room off. There was a wonderful bed with gold brocade hangings, a walnut writing desk in the window alcove, a blazing fire (it was a wet, chill evening) and tapestries on the walls.

Sophie stared wordlessly, unable to take in the girl's words. How could she have a maid of her own?

The girl smiled again. She was pretty; her mob cap set upon thick glossy brown hair serving almost as a decoration. "I hope you will forgive my familiarity, Miss, but you and I are going to be friends, despite differences in rank. My cards say so, and they are Never Wrong. I knew you would have fair hair. You came up as the Page of Coins, too young to be a Queen, an earth type, kind and fond of babies and animals. Some say the Coins people is dark, but I say otherwise."

"Cards?" Sophie was lost.

"Tarot cards, Miss Sophie. My *Nain* (Grandmother) showed me how. I read them last night. It's so exciting, what they say. Begging your pardon, Miss, I must tell you. There are two young men coming from across the water and the dark one is for me, the fair one is for you. You must watch out for a dark woman with bad intentions, though, and – I hope you will not be shocked by this – dark forces unleashed by a man who has suffered a loss." The girl's eyes were sparkling.

Sophie fought back laughter. Here was an example of what happened if you listened to too many Gothic tales. She put on the prim tone Harriet used when scolding a maid. "Really, Agnes, this is shocking. Reading Tarot cards is unChristian."

The girl dimpled. "Maybe, Miss, but as I say, my Tarot cards is Never Wrong, which is more than you can say for the Vicar, saying as we would have a good harvest if we prayed more and then we had the wettest summer in years."

Sophie felt her lips twitch. "Gracious, Agnes, such a tale you have concocted! Regrettably, the most exciting thing likely to happen to me will be to tea with the curate if I am lucky. Now, I must dress, for it would never do for me to be late to dinner on my first evening."

Dinner was served by many footmen in what was known as 'The Little Dining Room'. This was at least four times the size of the drawing room that was John's pride back in Chester.

Lord Ynyr, the young Count of Ruthin, was affable, just as John and Harriet said.

Sophie saw his mother the Countess tried to unbend, but her manners being so stiff, it was difficult. Sophie had been told how the late Count's widow wished to be addressed already as 'The Dowager Countess', though the young Count wasn't yet married. This had made her seem the more forbidding a prospect to her future companion, yet now Sophie thought her eyes kind.

Miss Morwenna, her niece by marriage, took little notice of Sophie beyond a formal welcome. She was striking; tall, statuesque and dark, her eyes a flashing hazel.

Lord Ynyr – Sophie supposed attempting to put his Poor Relative at ease – smiled on her. "Is not this a cosy room, Miss Sophie? We always eat here when by ourselves, and we trouble not about formality, talking across the table."

That was no easy matter, for the table would make two of the bedroom to which Harriet had moved Sophie back in Chester.

Sophie was startled at how good looking he was, besides affable, as Harriet said. If this was a novel, he would fall in love with her at once, viewing her lack of money and position as nothing compared to her beauty and pretty modest ways. As it was, he was being kind. She shifted uncomfortably in her chair, for her bottom – though well padded – was stiff from the seemingly endless jolting journey from Chester, especially the last bit up the *Famau* Mountain.

She thought how unlucky it was that she was ordinarily pretty, not exceptional. Her teeth were good enough for her to be happy to show them in her smile. "That is nice, Sir."

He was slim and upright, with chestnut hair, clear grey eyes, regular features, with nice teeth himself. Sophie wondered Agnes hadn't made him, Count as he was, the romantic figure in the tale she had dreamed up rather than inventing an admirer from abroad. Perhaps even she realised Lord Ynyr was unlikely to fall for his mother's companion when all the local young ladies of family must be fighting over him. Even now, Miss Morwenna was beaming on him.

The Dowager Countess, silver haired and elegant, smiled in agreement about this informality. Bolt upright as she was, she looked no more likely to talk across the table than to push peas into her mouth with her knife.

Of course, though now in Britain so long she had only a faint French accent, she was a Dubois; Sophie had heard how the older Dubois were terribly proud, and before the revolution, visitors to *Versailles*.

Now, the Dowager Countess' brother and his wife were facing execution as enemies of the state*, *Mademoiselle* Charlotte was in a decline in Brighthelmstone* and *Monsieur* Émile was said to be in hiding somewhere in Paris, trying to get his parents out of their prison. Sophie prayed for him every night.

She was trying not to stare at the grandeur of her surroundings – the intricate decoration of the magnificent fireplace, the cathedral like ceiling, the tapestry, the furniture antique and priceless. Harriet would be overwhelmed by the army of footmen. She might have been surprised by the ancient butler, though Sophie guessed if he worked still, it was through choice.

Sophie made a good dinner from the roasts, the side dishes, the selection of puddings and the choice wines. For days past, she had dreaded her future at Plas Uchaf too much to have an appetite.

She followed the Dowager Countess and Miss Morwenna from the table, leaving Lord Ynyr sitting alone to enjoy his port (did he tell himself coarse jokes?).

In the drawing room, the Dowager Countess asked, "Miss Sophie, are you skilled with your needle?"

This is where I shall be told how I can make myself useful. "I hope so, Your Ladyship."

"The baby's gown I am working on for the Poor Box has somehow got itself into a Sad Tangle. I hope you may be able to right it for me?"

"I am sure we may speedily mend matters, Ma'am."

Meanwhile, Miss Morwenna took up a book. The Dowager Countess clicked her tongue. "Morwenna, are you still reading that nonsense about '*The Vampyre's Curse*'?"

Morwenna smiled. "Yes, Ma'am, I have nearly finished it. By the by, I note there is a book of old vampire lore on the shelves here."

"Someone – was it young Kenrick? – presented it to the Dear Late Count, knowing of his interest in myths. Still, I consider this modern fascination with the so-called 'Gothic' unhealthy."

"For sure, Ma'am, but there is a dreadful appeal to such tales." Morwenna began to read.

The Dowager Countess hadn't exaggerated about tangles. Sophie had only finished righting matters when Lord Ynyr bounced in to beam on them. "I trust you are happy with your rooms, Miss Sophie?"

"They are delightful, Your Lordship. I was quite overwhelmed to be given such luxurious apartments."

He waved this aside. "You play and sing, Miss Sophie?"

"Yes, Sir, but I fear I am sadly untutored." When Sophie's family were better off, before the death of her father, she'd had music tutors. Then, as her family's funds had gradually dried up, so too had the music lessons. Everyone used to say she showed promise, and she loved to play and sing.

"Perhaps you could play something for us now, Miss Sophie? The instrument is lately tuned, and Miss Morwenna has a sore throat today."

Sophie was shy as she went over to play. She chose, '*All Through the Night*' as appropriate to Wales. At the end, Lord Ynyr broke into applause. Miss Morwenna clapped twice. This was too energetic for the Dowager Countess, but she smiled. "Why, *ma chére*, you have a delightful voice. But I think with tuition it could be still improved. Your playing, too. We must organise tutors for her, Ynyr."

Miss Morwenna looked disapproving, but the Count was enthusiastic. "I will do so tomorrow, Madam, if Miss Sophie is agreeable."

Sophie stammered, "I should like it above all things, Your Ladyship, Your Lordship. Thank you!" She was scarcely able to credit her luck. To be given a lady's maid to herself, such rooms and now music lessons was astonishing.

Sophie expected more forward behaviour from the maid as she readied her mistress for bed. So it proved.

As Agnes unlaced Sophie, she made a noise of approval. "Miss has a neat waist, for all she is so well built. The gentlemen do like that."

Sophie put Harriet's voice. "Agnes, that is impertinent."

She girl's eyes danced. "Beg pardon, Miss."

She was going out with a candle as Sophie knelt down for her nightly devotions. Sophie recalled her. "Agnes, I hope you say your prayers nightly?"

"Oh, yes, Miss, when I remember!" the girl went out cheerfully.

Left alone, Sophie's own prayers included the one she never forgot: "Please spare *Mademoiselle* Charlotte and *Monsieur* and *Madame* Dubois in the prison, and please protect *Monsieur* Émile wherever he is in Paris."

Perhaps he was dead already, but remembering the lanky boy she had met the one time with the freckled nose and the twinkling green eyes, she couldn't endure to think of that.

"It is good in you to take this calling upon the afflicted in the village upon yourself, Sophie, when sadly I am not able for it. *Alors*, so many babies are being born at the moment that one wonders how it comes about."

Sophie hid her unmaidenly smile. Surely the Dowager Countess, who had given birth to five children herself (of whom only Lord Ynyr survived) couldn't mean that?

Sophie liked visiting in the village. She had time enough, her duties being so light; she was in charge of the flowers; she did work for the poor box and she played for the company in the evening. Of course, at some point during every day the Dowager Countess would discover: "*Alors*, how comes my embroidery/sewing/tapestry work/crocheting to be in so sad a tangle?"

The contrast between how Sophie was treated at Plas Uchaf and what she dreaded as she had left Chester, blubbering, was astounding. She had thought to have to do endless domestic chores and be grateful, as at Chester. She had expected to have to drone endlessly, 'Yes, Your Ladyship' and 'Thank you, Your Ladyship, You are Very Kind'.

Instead, the Count of Ruthin and the Dowager Countess treated her more as a valued guest than as a dependant.

The Dowager Countess insisted on buying her new clothes, for, '*If we expect you to come about with us, Sophie, then we must have you suitably equipped*'. She had ordered made up for Sophie new dresses, matching bonnets, gloves, shoes, and other things, including a fur lined cloak in readiness for winter on the *Famau* Mountain.

Then there were the delightful singing and music lessons.

Whereas, as soon as Harriet became mistress of the house in Chester, she made it clear to Sophie what a financial burden she was. Sophie had tried to be useful, particularly in helping to look after the babies as they started to arrive, but it never reconciled Harriet to her presence.

Finally, there was that incident some weeks back when Sophie had fallen down on her bed, remaining comatose for several hours. She awakened to Harriet's voice. *'Yet she went out earlier, for the room was empty! Whatever ails her? Does she walk in her sleep? If she is going to turn into an invalid as well, it is too bad.'*

Sophie's long period of unconsciousness was inexplicable when she hadn't felt ill. It was then John had written to Her Ladyship asking if she would consider taking Sophie on as a companion who was handy with her needle, musical and who knew how to make herself useful about a house.

Sophie's new life at Plas Uchaf would be too good to be true, if it wasn't for Miss Morwenna. She treated Sophie more as might be expected.

The girl was now looking out of the window at the view over the foothills of the Famau Mountain to the green and gold patchwork quilt of the Clwyd Valley below. The red roofs of Plas Cyfeillgar*, the nearest great house, caught her eye. "Do you know, Ma'am, they say Mr Kenrick is to return with the second Mistress Kenrick?"

The Dowager Countess clicked her tongue. "I am glad Goronwy Kenrick has remarried, for by all accounts he was devastated at his first wife's tragic accident. Of course, his new wife has known bereavement herself, her own husband dying so recently, hmm…Kenrick is a clever young man, but from what the Late Count used to say, his ideas are become misguided. As for those mischievous investigations into the myths of Transylvania! Sure it is an irony it was His Late Lordship – whose ideas were exemplary – interested Kenrick in such matters. At one time, he instructed Ynyr, Émile – Ah, *zut,* I do so hope he anyway is safe, the rumours from France are terrible – and Kenrick at one time. It seems only yesterday."

Statuesque Miss Morwenna swished to the glass to primp her glossy dark hair. "Don't trouble yourself, Ma'am. Émile will outwit the Jacobins, you will see…I do remember Kenrick from those days, and he is much changed. I met him and Mistress Kenrick when I was down in Town for the last season. She is quite a beauty, but he – Ow!" She fell over Sophie's feet, seemingly having forgotten her presence on the sofa.

Sophie forced herself to say, "Beg pardon, Miss Morwenna. I trust you did not hurt yourself?" One of Sophie's own feet, which were much smaller than Miss Morwenna's, hurt from the trampling.

Morwenna wandered away, waving away the apology.

Some people might say the Dowager Countess and the Count spoil me so that I am in danger of forgetting My Place and I should thank Miss Morwenna for reminding me of it.

"I suppose that we must visit." the Dowager Countess sighed as at a great effort. "Unfortunately, my own health will not permit me to call, though I shall send Ynyr." She made it sound as if he was ten. Perhaps that was how she still thought of him.

Lord Ynyr at that moment opened the door. He looked pale, his eyes wide. "Madam –" he stammered. He held a letter, and they guessed the news at once.

Chapter Two

Paris

WHEN THE GROUP OF SHOPMEN seized an intellectual to hang him from a *lanterne,* yelling he was a Royalist, he cried out how he'd had a sheet printed at his own expense: '*The Dawn of Liberty and Fraternity*'.

This didn't stop them from stringing him up. There he struggled, jerking his legs like a frog, his face puce.

A long, lanky fair man ran up yelling. He kicked one of the group, punched another and gaining the *lanterne,* pulled out his knife to slash at the rope, half severing it. The tortured man swung violently, but didn't come down.

Someone warned, "It's Gilles Long Legs!"

The group members drew back. Their leader, a burly, red faced man whose brother owned the *charcuterie,* was so outraged that despite Gilles Long Legs' knife, he aimed a kick at his stomach.

Gilles Long Legs jumped sideways, grabbed the man's leg and tipped him over. Meanwhile the victim's face became ever more bloated and discoloured and his kicks slowed.

Then another man, wild-eyed and piratical, was amongst them, cutting through the half-severed rope with one slash.

The intellectual thudded to the ground. The crowd began to melt away. The red-faced man scrambled to his feet and Gilles helped him on his way by kicking him in turn. Then as he knelt down by the victim to cut the remains of the rope loose, the dark man shouted after the fleeing group. "Murderous bastards!"

A voice came back in feeble defiance, "Murderer yourself, Marcel Sly Boots!"

Marcel made a threatening movement as if to give chase, but it was only a feint.

A woman ran from the café over the road with some wine. "Here, Gilles, Marcel!"

They poured the wine into the man's gaping mouth between his tortured gasps. They knelt looking at his slate coloured face and the deep mark about his neck. "We'll leave him in your place if you don't mind." Gilles spoke with a southern accent.

"He's a sight to lose me customers." She shrugged. "Oh, put him in the back, then."

Giles Long Legs took the man's shoulders, Marcel Sly Boots his feet. They lugged him into the café, lying him on a table in the back.

"*Alors, ma chère,* take this for your trouble." Gilles dug in his pocket, but Marcel Sly Boots forestalled him in giving the woman some coins.

They quickly covered the short walk to where they were staying. Marcel's strutting walk moved him almost as much from side to side as forwards, while Gilles' endless limbs gave his gait a bouncing vivacity.

"Disgusting swine." Gilles' slanted light green eyes flashed and he rubbed the bridge of his freckled nose. "He's no Royalist. It was some of his outpourings about Equality and Fraternity our Professor Felix was reading to us the other day."

"He did?" It seemed to have made no impression on Marcel Sly Boots. He had an easy solution to the mean spirited attack. "Poor sod, eh? *Alors,* that *charcuterie* is not so far from our workroom. We'll call there tomorrow."

They paused by another *lanterne* to discuss some further business. The girl Françoise came out of the house with her pail, heading for the nearby pump.

Seeing them speaking, she stopped. She stood watching them, keeping too far away to hear what they were saying. She was discreet, though *Les Messieurs* – as her *Grànd-mère* called the ruffianly lodgers –

trusted her with their safety. She knew Marcel Sly Boots' workshop was a useful blind for the authorities. *Les Messieurs* had been clever, too, in evading the *Levée en masse** so far (no doubt they used a bit of judicious bribery) but she wondered if – with all these informers about – their luck could last much longer.

Grànd-mère could have got into trouble herself for using a formal term like '*Les Messieurs*' but she wasn't even scared of the Committee for Public Safety*.

After a minute *Monsieur* Marcel swaggered off somewhere. Gilles went over to the pump where, pulling off his waistcoat and shirt, he began to wash.

Françoise stood watching his muscular frame as he stood at the pump. Quite the gentleman, he never went to his dinner with blood on his hands. He turned and smiled at her as she came over with her pail. "*Ça va, Françoise?*"

She spoke suddenly. "Gilles, it does not do to think too much about people who have gone out of your life, I know myself. That Sophie girl was downright mean to go away without a word and you should trouble yourself no more about her."

He looked startled and resentful. "Why think you I trouble myself about her, *ma petite?*"

Françoise had to laugh. "We women can tell these things."

The Sophie Episode had taken place a couple of weeks since at one of *Les Messieurs* parties. They were young and high spirited; in good weather, they liked to hold dances out in the street where everyone could forget the daily struggles of existence. Marcel Sly Boots would play his violin; if his cough wasn't bad, Professor Felix would bring out a funny little whistle he said an Irishman gave him.

Gilles had brought a blonde *Anglaise* to this party. His besotted attitude towards her drew people's attention even more than her nationality. He'd had various good looking girls, his status as one of the leading scoundrels in the area guaranteeing that, and he'd treated them gallantly, but never acted as he did towards this one. This girl – whom Françoise thought nothing like as good looking as, for instance, Lola – he devoured with his eyes.

Then, the girl disappeared. Gilles Long Legs – who faced sudden death every day with equanimity – seemed as near distraught as anyone had ever seen him. He'd spent most of the night looking for her, sending some of his cohorts to search too. They'd all failed; she had vanished without trace.

After that, Françoise noted how Gilles went off his soup. Also, while *Les Messieurs* would drink all day every day, they never allowed themselves to get downright drunk; not, naturally, through any objection to excess, but because they had always to be ready to defend themselves. One night, though, Gilles Long Legs came back falling-down drunk.

Françoise was going up to bed when he staggered in to collapse on the floor. It was lucky *Grànd-mère* was already abed, or she would have kicked him until he woke.

Now, Gilles looked at Françoise thoughtfully as he pulled his shirt back on, still damp as he was. He came over to pinch her cheek. "If only I knew she was safe, I would trouble myself no more about her."

Françoise cast her eyes down. "Are you ready for the soup?"

He carried the heavy pail for her back into the building. He tended to do such things without thinking. Their accommodation had been a café and was palatial compared to how most people lived.

Grànd-mère's sharp eyes lingered on them as they came in together. Then, hearing her enemy neighbour come back, she bustled out, leaving the door open. When Françoise had given Gilles his bread and soup with some wine to wash it down, he said, "Sit down, Françoise; I want to talk to you."

Françoise recoiled. When a man said that to a girl, he wanted to talk about one thing only.

But *Grànd-mere* never missed anything; she called through the open door, "Be polite to *Monsieur* Gilles, girl." She was in a mood to give Françoise a clip on the ear if she disobeyed. Françoise sat down.

Gilles went on breaking up the bread with long fingers that must have done awful things today. "You are a Southerner like me, are you not?"

He didn't look much like a Southerner, with his fair hair and skin, strange green eyes and the band of freckles across his nose that gave him an incongruously innocent look. Still, his accent was unmistakable.

Grànd-mère came in. "Yes, and I don't want you to think my girl is like some of these Parisian sluts. She's a good steady girl."

"I know." Gilles Long Legs took a sip of the wine and then looked at it with dismay, as though for a moment he had expected something better. He chewed some more bread, musing.

Grànd-mère pounced. "She'd make anybody a fine wife."

"*Grànd-mère!*" Françoise's face was red with humiliation.

Gilles Long Legs smiled, unperturbed. "I am sure Françoise wants a steady young man, not a villain like me."

Just then they heard a yell from their neighbour. "Only see what the terrible old woman has done to my washing!" There was a clattering noise and *Grànd-mère's* eyes glowed as she rushed out, shouting about cheek. Françoise and Gilles were left looking at each other.

There was another metallic sound. Gilles looked out of the window and smiled at Françoise. "*Madame* has kindly given us a ladle. It should be useful."

As the angry voices tangled together outside, Françoise forced a smile in return. He looked thoughtful again. He went on with his soup, and then stopped. "From your words at the pump, Françoise, I'm wondering: did you leave a sweetheart back home?"

She coloured. "It's no good, there's no money. We had hoped to take a small farm, but...Perhaps after all this time he has found someone else, though it would not be like him."

"Hmm." He swallowed the rest of the wine. "How much money would need you, Françoise, to do so?"

"Only the moon and the stars, as far as I am concerned."

He removed his knives to dig in one of his pockets and more instruments to dig in others. He assembled a number of bills and handed them to her. "Will that do? Will you go and marry your old sweetheart?"

"I couldn't take that!" She stared at the fortune longingly.

"I don't want anything in return. Put it away and tell not your *Grànd-mère* of it, eh?" Gilles wandered off as if he had almost lost interest in the matter.

She asked nervously, "But how can I ever repay you?"

He smiled reassurance. "You need not."

Her jaw dropped. Yet his insane generosity was only an exaggeration of that of some of the other ruffians they knew in Paris, who would do some dreadful violence to make money before giving away half of it to somebody to whom they took a liking.

She had only just put the money away, beginning to stammer her thanks, when the door crashed open.

Marcel Sly Boots swaggered in, blades in his boots, roaring a song, pausing to pinch hers cheek. Professor Felix came in soon afterwards. They wanted their bread and soup, so she was kept too busy to think for a while.

Marcel Sly Boots was full of murmured plans for the next day. "We've got a good chance to do it good tomorrow. I'll tell you why. There's some Southern *Monsigneur*, one Dubois and his missus going to meet their maker earlier than was arranged. I heard it from a direct source at the gaol. Everyone'll be watching so we can do it easy."

Gilles Long Legs sat down suddenly. His face was a nasty greenish colour, the freckles across the bridge of his nose standing out. He looked ill. Perhaps he was, for like all the others, he drank shockingly, while – apart from the one time – never allowing himself to become helplessly drunk. He began every day with a good swill of wine before going on to chew a bit of bread for breakfast.

None of the others took much account of his queer turn. They were sometimes taken that way themselves. Marcel Sly Boots surmounted a ferocious hangover every morning; Professor Felix wasn't strong anyway; he had a chronic cough and the purple shadows under his eyes never went.

The others were trying to get him to go away to the country, but he put it off. Preserving their health wasn't something important to *Les Messieurs*. None of them expected to reach thirty.

The others went on talking for a while, shouting each other down.

Gilles Long Legs suddenly jumped up. "I'm going out."

Felix looked at him in surprise. "I wouldn't, *mon ami*. You don't look good to me."

"I have to go." He moved quickly towards the door before they could stop him, and was gone.

They never saw him again.

The most likely explanation must be Gilles Long Legs had met with some enemies, who threw his weighted body into the *Seine* some time later that night. Françoise felt sad: he'd given her the money for her escape, and she'd never even thanked him properly. On the third evening, when it became obvious he wouldn't come back, she burst into tears. "Poor Gilles! I never –" she broke off, for *Grànd-mère* was in the room.

Grànd-mère turned on her, cursing. "Never what, girl? I hope you never considered lying down for that young ruffian without a respectable payment first? I don't want any to have to keep any bastards!"

In private, *Grànd-mère* told Françoise the world was one murderous ruffian the less. She wouldn't have said so in front of *Les Messieurs*, who might have taken offence and their rent elsewhere.

The others mourned for him and it came out, of course, as anger. They went round bristling with threats and got in to several more bloody fights than usual. Still, they couldn't find out what had happened to him.

Professor Felix was of the opinion – and this suggestion roused the others to paranoid rage – that the blonde girl he'd so taken to at the party was some sort of spy from a rival group who subsequently lured lanky Gilles Long Legs to his death.

He had last been seen leaving a café down the road in the company y of a scoundrel from that group. Handsome, strongly muscled Southern Georges was an appalling fellow who was said to have seduced half the girls in his area. He had vanished likewise. Perhaps they'd killed each other.

Françoise confided to the others about the gift. She knew they, being honourable ruffians, wouldn't steal it. She could tell they thought that Gilles Long Legs must have been her lover, though they didn't say so. They packed her back off to the South before *Grànd-mère* could get wind of the money.

Her old sweetheart was still waiting for her and they took a small farm. Françoise couldn't tell him the truth about how she came by the money. He wasn't suspicious, but even he would never believe that a man had given it to her for nothing.

Every week, she lit a candle to say a prayer for poor Gilles Long Legs to shorten his stay in purgatory. Once, he even came back in a dream to tease her about it.

Chapter Three

Famau Mountain
North Wales
July 1794

L ORD YNYR SANG AS HE opened the gate to the lane down through
the foothills of the *Famau* Mountain to nearby *Llangynhafal.*
He led Sophie's horse, while the groom was leading the Count's
magnificent grey.

On this summer's morning of loud birdsong and lambs calling, the
icy winds that buffeted the mountainside in winter were unimaginable.

Sophie hadn't seen the Count so happy since before the older Dubois'
execution. At Plas Uchaf, all the family were in mourning, though as a
distant relative Sophie wasn't expected to wear full mourning herself.

She smiled at Lord Ynyr now, knowing how people admired her
dimples. She was pleased to see him cheerful because she liked him.
Besides, naturally she was working at encouraging his liking for her. You
never knew where it might lead. She smiled so on all eligible bachelors.
She didn't need John's recent letter to remind her of self interest.

> *'...I am rejoiced, my Dear Sister, to hear that you are happy*
> *with the Illustrious Benefactors amongst whom Harriet and I,*
> *in despite of our Natural Affections, felt it wise to place you. I*
> *am sure you now comprehend the wisdom of our decision. I am*

confident that I do not need to advise my Good Girl to endeavour on all occasions to be agreeable to her Noble Relatives, for with a correct approach to Duty, what might not be achieved?...'

If Sophie felt ashamed of her mixed motives in the bereaved household, she must take into account her own helplessness. Her situation at the Manor might continue as happy until Lord Ynyr married; then – surely – his new wife must resent a Poor Relative being as indulged as Sophie was, especially if Miss Morwenna happened to be that new Countess of Ruthin.

It was up to Sophie to find herself a husband before that. This mightn't be easy, with her one hundred pounds a year.

She tried to make herself delightful company for the young Count. She encouraged him to talk of his interests. These included experiments with herbal draughts and scientific work in the laboratory built by the late Count. These were largely incomprehensible to her. Of course, she always laughed at his jokes, which by contrast were obvious.

Naturally, she always made sure she looked as pretty as she could in his presence. She batted her eyelashes at him when his mother wasn't nearby.

Throughout, she combined encouragement with maidenly bashfulness. It wasn't easy to balance the two. At twenty-one, she began to see why most unmarried woman over thirty gave up trying to attract a mate. If Sophie herself was still single then (hateful thought!), she supposed she would be worn out with the effort.

"You are in spirits this morning, Sir."

"I am indeed, Miss Sophie." He smiled on her so guilelessly, she felt ashamed of her artfulness. "I received a letter this morning from Mistress de Courcy – from your side of the family, of course – who has been caring for my poor Cousin Charlotte. It gave both good and sad news. The heavy news was expected. Poor *Mademoiselle* Charlotte is sinking fast..."

Sophie bit her lip, thinking of the girl she'd met years before at a family gathering so huge that even the *déclassé* de Courcy's were invited.

Mademoiselle Charlotte had been standing with her older brother

Monsieur Émile, who lounged in his finery, coaching their cousin Ynyr in walking on his hands along with their younger brother Monsieur Bernard.

As Sophie approached, Monsieur Bernard ignored her, but the lanky, fair-haired Monsieur Émile turned on her a lazy smile. She was overcome at this honour from a boy years her senior, thinking he looked wonderful in his crimson velvet and silks. Just then their small sister Mademoiselle Marguerite staggered up to hand Monsieur Émile a flattened, hair-encrusted cake which she must have picked up from the floor.

"Thank you, ma petite, I will enjoy that." he smiled. Sophie thought him the kindest of older brothers. John would have sent her on her way with a sharp word. When Marguerite was gone, he gave it a look of incredulous disgust. "Who danced on that?" He opened the window and hurled it out with a whistle to accompany its flight.

This struck Sophie as uniquely funny, and she giggled until she feared she might wet herself. He honoured her with another smile of acknowledgement, and she changed her mind about people with freckles. From then on she drew the heroes of legends, Theseus, Achilles and Robin Hood, too, with just such a band of freckles across the nose.

Mademoiselle Charlotte took a different view of the boys' fun. "This is silly," she told Sophie as Lord Ynyr came towards them upside down. "Let us do something more interesting." She took Sophie's hand, leading her up to a great nursery, where there was a magnificent dappled rocking horse. They took turns riding on it until some more children demanded a turn. Sophie had been overwhelmed at all this casual friendliness from the younger members of the great Dubois family.

Now, Lord Ynyr went on, "But Émile has turned up safe in England!"

Forgetting her riding terrors, Sophie clapped her hands, nearly losing her seat. He caught her arm. "Excuse me, Miss Sophie." He had such perfect manners he made it seem as though he were at fault in saving her.

"Thank you, Sir. So he is alive, after all!" She beamed on him. He was a delightful aristocrat. Still, everyone, even the nose-picking groom, was delightful in the face of such news. Only the Count's horse snorted cynically, disappointed about being led rather than ridden.

"Yes, he has written me from Brighthelmstone, where he stays with

Mistress de Courcy who has been taking care of poor Charlotte. Her Ladyship and Miss Morwenna are overjoyed, for Émile has ever been a favourite with them. I could scarce read his handwriting in places, but it is scarcely surprising. What he must have been through!"

"Yes, indeed, Sir." Sophie sighed.

"I have written reminding him how he must treat this house as his second home and we hope to see him soon. We must do what we can to ease his mind."

"Oh, certainly Sir!" Sophie wondered what she could do. She must do something. She could embroider *Monsieur* Émile a pair of slippers, but that would hardly be much comfort to a man who would lose his last family member. At least he had seen *Mademoiselle* Charlotte still alive.

They left invitations for dinner for Dr Powell and the Reverend Smythe-Jones. This done, Sophie wanted to see a young village wife who'd just had a baby. Lord Ynyr insisted on taking her, though he wouldn't go in as it would be regarded as improper for him to enter so soon after a birth.

Sophie was concerned for the baby. She had prayed for him every waking hour since she saw him yesterday, a minute bundle pressed against his mother's breast. He was weak and not feeding properly.

The woman who met them at the low cottage door had no teeth and with her strong accent Sophie found it hard to follow what she said. Lord Ynyr understood better. "Dead?!"

"Yes, Your Lordship. She takes it hard."

In her sorrow, Sophie spoke before Lord Ynyr, a shocking breach of precedence for a poor relative, but he didn't seem to notice. "I am so sorry! Please tell me if there is anything I can do!" She pictured the devastated girl above, who had lost the centre of her world.

Lord Ynyr said, "Yes, do please, let us know if we can do anything. We will not intrude at such a time."

To avoid distressing the bereaved girl further, Sophie had to take back again the things she had brought for this first baby: the shawl she had knitted, the gown the Dowager Countess had added proudly to the basket, the blankets, bonnets and so on, leaving only the nourishing foods for the mother. Lord Ynyr meanwhile stayed outside looking stricken, though for him, of course, proprieties were set aside and he was invited in.

All the way back to the manor, there was a lump in Sophie's throat, so she could hardly speak. Lord Ynyr seemed equally cast down. The groom wiped his nose solemnly upon his sleeve.

Back at the manor, Sophie made her quick thanks and curtsy to Lord Ynyr and hurried to her room. She didn't even notice his look – more intimate in its concern – than any he had yet given her.

She fumbled at the handle of her bedroom door, tears blurring her vision. Agnes came out from her sewing room down the corridor. "Why, how now, Miss Sophie!"

The next moment, the girl took her in her arms. Sophie was startled at how comforting it felt. Still, whose hold was more comforting than her nursemaid's? "Now then, Miss. You are upset about Sian Jones' baby, I take it? I heard this morning, and a shame it is. *Nain* always said that these things happen for a reason we are not allowed to know in this world." She was patting and stroking Sophie as though she were a baby herself.

"He was so tiny!" Sophie thought her own hiccoughing voice idiotic.

"I know, Miss, I know. But it will be all right, she will have another healthy one within the year. My cards do say so. Now you will take me for task for speaking of them. Take my handkerchief. Yours is soaked, isn't it?"

Sophie took the handkerchief. In practice, she had already given up rebuking Agnes for her card reading, teasing the girl about her predictions instead. After all, Agnes was now not only her maid, but her tutor in Welsh. Mopping her eyes and nose, Sophie said, "I think I will not take you to task about them today, Agnes."

The girl gave her a familiar squeeze. "Now I will make you a cup of tea. That does make everything seem better."

"I don't know what you will think of me, Agnes."

"There, there, I will think what I have always thought, that you have a kind heart beneath those hoighty-toighty ways of yours, Miss Sophie."

Sophie accepted that she and Agnes must have an oddly democratic relationship for mistress and maidservant; it would be a relief to give up the unequal struggle.

Brighton

Georges took at once to Mistress de Courcy, Émile's distant relative, who had cared for *Mademoiselle* Charlotte since she came to England. Since Charlottes' death her eyes were red and swollen, but she made no fuss.

When she told him how she wanted him to talk to *Monsieur* Émile about his losses, George's response was – for him – gracious. "No, *Madame*. I have no idea what to say. Women know how to talk to people so and comfort them, not men."

"I have attempted to speak to him myself, and he does not respond. Do try, Georges." Rumour had it that the now respectable *Madame* de Courcy's past had been outrageous; it was true she had about her a freedom of manner.

Since Charlotte's death three days ago – the funeral was tomorrow –Émile had been going each day to sit in the room with the coffin for hours. Georges thought this morbid. Besides, Émile had given up talking beyond monosyllables, which in one fond of the sound of his own voice was alarming. Georges had been hoping *Madame* de Courcy might do something about it. The thought of such a discussion with another man – even one to whom he was so close – made him shudder and groan as he went up to the room where Charlotte's body was laid out.

Émile sat not far from the corpse, arms on knees, chin on palm, staring in front of him. At least he was dry-eyed. Georges came to the point abruptly. "What are you thinking of, sitting here for hours?"

Georges had decided Émile wasn't going to reply when he spoke. "I talk to her; I apologise for not saving the others."

"Have you been about that all this time? You could not do the impossible."

Émile sighed. Finally, he spoke lightly, "*Alors*, Georges, one must count one's blessings, as the English say. Should I end up dangling from Tyburn* it will inconvenience nobody but myself."

"I suppose *Madame* de Courcy might object, or even those other relatives of yours in Wales, your cousin and aunt."

"Very likely." Émile got up. "Is it time to dress for dinner?"

"You could think of getting married." Georges watched Émile tie his cravat. This was a long process, for when not *Monsieur* Gilles, Émile was fussy about his clothes. It was as if Charlotte's spirit put this suggestion about marriage in Georges' mouth; he couldn't think of anyone less suited for it except himself.

Émile's eyebrows shot up. "I am in no hurry to resign myself to an appropriate match and a lukewarm marriage bed, Georges."

No doubt he thinks of that blonde girl yet, the poor Devil.

The next day, at the funeral, Émile was more his normal self than he had been before it. Over brandy with Georges in the evening, he grinned suddenly. "My financial affairs are involved, Georges. It will take time to sort them out. *Mon Grand-père* showed prescience in investing half of our fortune in Britain, eh? *Alors,* before the funds become available, I should go and rusticate at Dubois Court in Buckinghamshire, fending off creditors with my tongue. Frankly, that does not appeal. I think I must live as a scoundrel still, and that offer to us about Hounslow Heath lures. Fancy you some experience as a Gentleman of the Road, Georges?"

Georges grinned back. "From what our fellow smuggler said, we should take ourselves to the tavern in that village some ten miles West of London – Brentford – that was it – and ask for one Mr Kit."

Plas Uchaf
Famau Mountain
North Wales
December 1794

Sophie was sighing over a copy of 'Clarissa'. * She added to her pleasure in the story by curling her toes in the warmth of the fire, for the December weather was bitter, the tapestries shifting in the draught. It being Sunday, she should have been reading her Bible. Yet Richard Lovelace enticed and Sophie envied Clarissa her excitement with him (before the awful ending, naturally).

She thought about her own romantic prospects. Lord Ynyr and the Dowager Countess had taken her to some assemblies. There she danced with the Count. Women had looked enviously at the Poor Relation he honoured. Handsome and charming as he was, Sophie should have thought herself lucky.

She was, but she noticed something was missing; she felt no spark at his touch, such as she was sure even prissy Samuel Richardson intended Clarissa to feel at Lovelace's rascally caress.

No doubt that was a shocking, immodest thought. After all, what did she expect? She had heard Harriet and her married friends talking in whispers. *'Men are made so. You just have to put up with it. After all, you do get a baby as a result.'*

On a quiet Sunday afternoon like this Sophie often found herself thinking of things highly unsuitable for the Sabbath; of romance and adventure. She yearned for a dashing admirer to rush into her life and sweep her off her feet. For a Dowager's companion that was as likely as being struck by lightening. Perhaps, up here on the *Famau* Mountain – where thunderstorms were frequent – it was rather less likely.

Agnes bustled in and came to poke up the fire. "Nasty old North East wind there is today, isn't it, Miss Sophie? You are right to wear your heavy shawl in this draught. They are on their way, by the by."

Sophie's mind had drifted to the coming Christmas party for the village children and whether she had made enough dolls. Though the giving of presents belonged traditionally to St Nicholas' Day*, she couldn't resist the pleasure of a surprise present for each of them. "Who?"

"Why, the two young men, the dark one and the fair one, of course."

Sophie laughed. "Agnes, when I first came here you told me we should each of us have an admirer, and they are not here yet! I have been taken in quite. Such tardy dispatch is far from inspiring. Why, by the time they arrive we shall all have grey hair and the rheumatics."

Agnes put out the new blue dress she had just completed. As Sophie rushed to admire it, Agnes admitted, "I am deft with the needle, though I do say so myself…Well, they will be here within the sennight." She looked thoughtfully at Sophie. "I feel I must warn you, though, Miss, they are a pair of rascals."

Sophie was shocked. "Really, Agnes! As if I would encourage the advances of a rascal!"

"Begging your pardon, Miss, you won't be able to help yourself. You will fall for him like a ton of coals being delivered." She smiled with satisfaction.

Since Agnes' comforting her over the death of Sian Jones' baby, Sophie had indulged her maid; they were friends, but now she felt she must take a stand. "Agnes, not another word! Really, you say some shocking things. No more of such nonsense!"

She thought Agnes hid a smile and she hurried on, "This is a lovely dress, you are brilliant with your needle. I must hurry, though, for Mr Kenrick is to dinner tonight, and I want to take one last look at the flowers before Roberts begins to harry the footmen. Ah, I shouldn't encourage you, but Mr Kenrick has been overseas, Agnes, so it is a shame that he is a married man and by all accounts not a romantic figure. Still, I am looking forward to seeing Mistress Kenrick when she arrives, for she is accounted a beauty. Why, you shiver; are you still cold?"

"Only at the thought of him, Miss. I took against him the moment I saw him. He's a bad 'un for a certainty. He came early to look over the Count's laboratory, though for sure he cannot be interested in herbal cures, or anything that might help others. There's talk that he is involved in the Forbidden Arts, and the Cards did warn us of such, for all your joking, Miss Sophie, so you must avoid him all you can. After he grew up, he never did get on with the late Count and the Dowager don't like him neither. "

She began on Sophie's hair. "By the by, Miss, I ran into Sian Jones this morning. Do you remember – the girl whose baby died back in the summer? – Well, she's expecting again. I met her in the shop and I gave her belly a tap. 'Nice work, *cariad* (dear), and this time he will be as healthy as can be, and you'll be having a few more after him, too.'"

"That is wonderful, Agnes! I am so happy for her."

———⁂———

Sophie was still smiling at this happy news when the newest footman flung open the blue sitting room door for her. She saw with dismay that Mr Kenrick was already in the room. He was looking over a book from a side table, glasses perched on his nose; at her entrance he whipped these off. Taking her fading smile to be for himself, he moved swiftly to greet her, his agility startling in a heavily built man.

As he took her hand, she shuddered. He exuded a repellent atmosphere, though there was nothing to account for it, save his lecherous stare. He was an ordinary looking man in his mid twenties, heavily made and tall, with a high colour, glassy eyes and a long nose. The oily smile he turned on her showed startlingly white, sharp, longish teeth.

"Miss Sophie, I believe. I have heard all about you and your Angel's

Voice." He squeezed her hand, and though he ran his eyes eagerly over her, they remained glassy. "Mr Kenrick, your nearest neighbour. Regrettably, Mistress Kenrick has not yet been able to join me."

Sophie tried to be welcoming even as she tried as hard to free her hand. He bent to kiss it, and the touch of his lips was horrible. She felt his teeth graze her skin. His pale eyes met hers, and he let out what she could only think of as a giggle while his saliva gushed out on to her hand.

Horrified, she tried to wrench it away as he mumbled something. He kept a tight grasp on it, and she noticed the alarming strength in his fingers. He giggled again, looking almost pleased at her show of repugnance. Straightening, he made a sort of lunge towards her, still salivating freely.

What he would have done, she never found out, for the door was flung open for Miss Morwenna and Dr and Mrs Powell.

Kenrick took out a silk handkerchief to mop at his lips. His greeting of Miss Morwenna was more restrained, though his look gloated.

Miss Morwenna said smoothly, "Mr Kenrick, welcome back, Sir. I am sure you recollect Dr and Mrs Powell." She was vibrant in yellow silk. Sophie envied her being able to wear it, as she herself would almost have disappeared behind the strong colour, though that would have made little difference to her visibility for Miss Morwenna. Now Miss Morwenna honoured her with a glance, and Sophie supposed she must have seen part of the strange assault.

Meanwhile, Dr Powell talked with Kenrick, though from his look Sophie suspected he had seen too.

She stood quaking, wiping her hand with her own handkerchief. Disgusting! She wondered if that was the sort of thing poor relatives must endure from certain male visitors. Still, that drooling was something she had never overheard Harriet and her friends or the maids mention in their secret talk.

Lord Ynyr joined them, smiling apologies. "Please forgive me, Morwenna, Mr Kenrick, Dr Powell, and Miss Sophie. I was delayed by estate affairs." His being such a conscientious landlord made his tenants demanding.

Dinner, taken in the huge dining room proper, wasn't successful.

The Dowager Countess was stiff and formal at one end of the great table, her son affable at the other. Kenrick was talkative, but strangely cold even as he smiled. Dr and Mrs Powell tried to hide their dislike. Meanwhile, Miss Morwenna, who usually could be relied upon to rally any man between the ages of seventeen and sixty, showed no wish to do so with Kenrick.

There was talk of war news. Lord Ynyr said, "Do you know, a press gang was at work about *St Asaph's**, miles inland?"

"For sure, Your Lordship, they won't find many sea-going men there, but I believe a couple were taken even so." Dr Powell turned to Kenrick, "It is lucky, Sir, you were returned from your travels abroad some time before the outbreak of the war with France."

"Yes, indeed, Sir." Kenrick agreed in his flat voice. He smiled to himself over something. "Since His Late Lordship introduced us youngsters to scientific ideas, I understand Your Lordship has become interested in curing disease through the use of plants?"

"If I could defeat one of the major diseases that cause so many deaths, I would be sufficiently proud."

Kenrick didn't look as though he gave a fig for such deaths. Sophie noted how the Count made no enquiries about Kenrick's own scientific experiments; she remembered Agnes' talk about his dabbling in black magic.

Morwenna's eyes sparkled. "Never mind, Ynyr, you did wonders for Her Ladyship's maid's bunions, which is a beginning." While Sophie managed to keep her face straight, Morwenna gave the low-in-the throat laugh Sophie envied. "Gracious, Ynyr, I am an ingrate indeed, for you cured me of a sore throat last spring."

As often, Lord Ynyr beamed on her so that Sophie thought that it was well how she took a modest view of her own chances with him. "You may be an ingrate all you please, Morwenna, for I would forgive you much."

The Dowager Countess spoke mournfully, "The Dear Late Count became first intrigued by herbal cures during a stay in my native Provence."

"He made great progress upon them, Ma'am, and I have used his recommendations as a basis for all of my cures." Lord Ynyr turned to Kenrick. "You have been to all sorts of exotic places, I believe, Kenrick.

I suppose you came across some intriguing cures in Transylvania?"

For the first time, Morwenna looked at Kenrick with interest. "Transylvania, of course! How widespread is the vampire legend there, Sir? Do tell, for I hear you made some investigations into it during your time there."

The Dowager Countess clicked her tongue, possibly thinking that Kenrick's wife having died in Transylvania, these references were tactless. As Kenrick smiled emptily on Morwenna, Sophie thought with such teeth, it was a wonder that he hadn't been taken for a vampire himself. Recalling those teeth grazing the skin of her hand, she shivered.

At the moment, Kenrick was gazing at the trifle the footman spooned out for him with the same hungry interest with which earlier he had gloated over Sophie.

He said, "Their beliefs vary according to area – some more, please, my man! – though all agree that the best form of protection from the vampire

is –" he paused, looking disgusted, "Garlic. As I am allergic to the weed, I suffered accordingly and was regarded with suspicion." He let out a sudden shout of laughter that contrasted oddly with his former giggling.

The Dowager Countess looked stern. "The Dear Late Count held that such tales arise through a combination of empty minds and active tongues. We have sufficient foolish legends of our own here in Wales such as the Black Dog."

Morwenna was determined on one more question. "But what if despite the garlic, they are bitten?"

"Then, my dear young lady, they show a touching faith in the efficacy of sundry weeds to prevent the victim from turning into a Half Vampire, the creature halfway between the human and the vampire. His Lordship might be interested in those." Kenrick giggled, in odd contrast to his earlier shout of laughter. "That is, if the bite has not been fatal, in which case the victim's transformation to a full vampire is inevitable. For those who wish to prevent this, the only course is –" He paused again and to Sophie's surprise his ruddy complexion drained of colour before he finished with a shudder of disgust.

"– A series of barbaric rituals."

In the middle of the night, Sophie awoke with a gasp of fear to an odd chill. Mr Kenrick stood by her bed. His lips were pursed for a kiss, and as he moved silently closer she let out a gasp of terror. At this, he stopped and drew back, wrinkling his nose, looking disgusted. His form wavered and vanished in a subdued flash.

Too terrified to scream, head whirling, she stared wildly at the space where Kenrick had stood. She tried to put it down to a nightmare, possibly brought on by the garlic cure that the Count had given her for a sore throat.

It was an hour before she dared to lie down again and a couple more before she relaxed into sleep.

Chapter Four

FROM THE LANDING WINDOW, SOPHIE watched the carriage draw up and the two young men spring out. Agnes would be delighted that one was dark and one was fair.

Sophie rebuked herself for having light thoughts about poor *Monsieur* Émile, so terribly bereaved. Still, it wasn't as if he looked miserable from here as he stopped to joke with two of the footmen. Harriet wouldn't approve of his informality; once he even jumped up on the carriage to help unload something.

Both *Monsieur* Émile and his man looked in excellent condition, though they were so different in build; *Monsieur* Émile was spare and lanky, while his valet was square and stocky with an almost cherubic look.

Monsieur Émile was long legged and fair haired, as she remembered him, though now he was broad shouldered and muscular. He had the sort of fitness which makes a man bounce about as though he were on springs. Both he and his valet were expensively and fashionably dressed. The valet's jacket looked as though it had cost three times the yearly wage of John's footmen.

Sophie smiled as Lord Ynyr went down the steps to wring his cousin's hand. Miss Morwenna followed, all happy animation as he bent to kiss her hand. When Sophie watched Morwenna with others, she could see the charm that she never showed towards herself. Well, Sophie knew already that she must learn a lot more humility to be suited to her position as Poor Relative.

The group moved inside. Sophie thought that she would give them three quarters of an hour for a family reunion before joining them.

When she came into the sitting room, eager and yet hesitant to meet the man she had admired from afar for years, she smiled at the sight of the group standing chatting and laughing by the fireplace. Everyone was animated; even Roberts moved slightly more briskly as he took about a tray of drinks.

"– You must come there with me when we are both next in town, Ynyr. Perhaps we may even impose on Morwenna to join us?" *Monsieur* Émile looked round as the Dowager Countess said, "Sophie: there is no need to be shy! Come and meet my nephew, *Monsieur* Émile."

Monsieur Émile was even taller than she thought. As she'd noted when watching him from the window, he exuded vigour and was magnificently dressed, his fair hair carefully styled to look untidy. He had the same cast of feature, high cheekbones and wide mouth she remembered. He still retained the band of freckles across the bridge of his nose which after meeting him, she used to puzzle everyone by giving to the Greek heroes in her childish drawings. The slanting light green eyes, wide set and acute, were the same. Instead of smiling at her lazily, as when he was a boy, he gawped; his jaw dropped; his eyes dilated, and he froze on the spot.

Sophie glanced behind her; a footman must have entered with a knife between his teeth, say, or possibly a tiger followed her into the room. There was nothing there. She came over to greet him, astounded at his rapt stare.

Had this been a scene from a novel, she would take this gaze as evidence that *Monsieur* Émile was falling in love at first sight with his aunt's companion. Sadly this was unlikely, if only because she had overheard the Dowager Countess complaining in a hushed voice to Lord Ynyr of her nephew's rakish activities in London: *'It is shocking. I realise that Émile has had much to endure, but there is no excuse for Such Behaviour.'*

He was even breathing quickly as he stared at her. Of course, Miss Morwenna noticed. She raised her eyebrows at him in silent enquiry. Sophie curtseyed. "I am so happy that you are here, *Monsieur* Émile."

"*Enchanté, Mademoiselle.*" He bent to kiss her hand, showing remarkable gallantry towards a poor relative. "But surely we have met before, *Mademoiselle?*" His expression was still intense.

"Why, yes, Sir," she smiled, astonished and delighted that he should remember, though she was sure that had nothing to do with his apparent amazement. "We met at a wedding, when I was quite a child and you were possibly twelve, and I remember you advising His Lordship on the art of handstands."

"I do remember that occasion now, *Mademoiselle* Sophie, but surely we met again later?"

"That may well be, Sir." She hesitated. She must be careful to avoid contradicting her social superior. Besides, saying that she didn't remember a meeting between them since would imply he was forgettable, when he showed condescension in remembering her at all. She'd been at a couple of large family occasions at which he might be between that wedding and the outbreak of the Revolution, where she had always looked for him in vain. When could he mean?

He gave her hand – which he still retained – a sudden squeeze. He smiled down into her eyes – he was fully a foot taller than she – before reluctantly loosing hold of it.

The Dowager Countess was saying, "I remember that wedding. It must have been how you came to make sorry holes in the knees of your breeches within an hour, Ynyr. The Dear Late Count was annoyed."

"It would seem then that my instructions were not helpful, eh, *Mademoiselle* Sophie?" *Monsieur* Émile beamed on her. This was extraordinary, yet somehow there was nothing insincere about him.

"I remember that they were quite detailed, Sir." She smiled back at him, hoping he didn't notice how red in the face she was. This wasn't only due to confusion over his strange attitude; it was because, at his touch, her insides had given a melting sort of lurch.

Meanwhile, Lord Ynyr, who fancied himself as the sort of countryman who can predict the weather, went to look out of the window, looking for snow. "It is well that you arrived today, Émile, for I am sure that there will be heavy snow within hours, and the head gardener agrees. It would have made for a difficult journey. By the by, Cousin, with your robust attitude towards settling disputes I suppose that you would have welcomed a confrontation with those highwaymen who have been terrorising the roads out of town?"

Sophie, glancing back at *Monsieur* Émile, saw a momentary look of consciousness before he laughed. "I had no trouble with them, Cousin. They must be taking a break in the country, like me."

This made her uneasy; she wasn't sure why.

Meanwhile, Morwenna was eager to return her long-lost relative's attention to its proper place. "Émile, if it snows heavily, we must go out on the sleigh, if Ynyr will be kind enough to arrange it. Please, Ynyr, with sleigh bells?"

"Of course we must, Morwenna!" Lord Ynyr was delighted.

"An excellent idea, Morwenna. I hope you will come with us, *Mademoiselle*?" *Monsieur* Émile turned his rapt gaze on Sophie.

She murmured, "I would be honoured, Sir." She wondered if he had met her double.

"I must rely on you gentlemrn to do the driving of the sleigh." Morwenna sparkled. "I hope if you take a turn at the reins you do not overturn us quite, Émile?"

"Miss Morwenna recollects my mishap nine years since." He laughed too.

Soon afterwards, Sophie slipped out to check upon the centrepiece on the dining room table, leaving the others chatting. She thought she left unnoticed, but as she crossed the great hall she heard quick footsteps behind. Turning, she was astonished to see *Monsieur* Émile loping after her.

"*Mademoiselle* Sophie!" As she paused, he rushed up to seize her hands. "Ah, *chérie,* I cannot believe my luck!" He bent to kiss them passionately.

She sometimes made up a fantasy where an attractive, rich, dashing young man took one look at her and for some reason best known to himself, fell violently in love with her, once and forever. She never dared dream about *Monsieur* Émile, though, as she knew him and he was out of reach. It would just make it embarrassing should they ever meet again.

She had imagined that the emotion that would quiver in her suitor's voice as he declared himself would stir her likewise to passion. Now, her reaction was horror; this despite finding him attractive, and his having been for so long her hero. She felt like running away.

She must have looked stunned. He went on, "It is a shock to you. I could scarce believe it myself. I had given up hope of seeing you again.

To meet you, my lovely girl, as *Madame ma Tante's* companion! *Alors*, it will not continue so. You shall have my status, anyway. If you will take a rascal like Gilles Long Legs, that is? You look alarmed, Sophie. I hope you are not scared of me? You did not seem alarmed by me back then. Those innocent's kisses that you gave me led me to hope that you forgave me for being a ruffian." He squeezed her hands passionately, meanwhile staring at her as if he would swallow her up with his eyes.

She was speechless. She began to fear that he had been driven mad by his terrible experiences. All she could think of to say was, absurdly, "Oh, gracious!"

"But where did you go, *chérie*? Do you know how I have suffered on your account? I had men looking for you all night, but you were vanished. So many nights since I have been awake till dawn wondering what became of you. To see you here, and in the same dress, too!" He looked at it almost gloatingly. The said dress was a grey everyday dress that the Dowager Countess had ordered made up for her last autumn.

Then he went back to kissing her hands in the most embarrassing, passionate way. At least, unlike Mr Kenrick, he was personable and did not slobber on them.

While in the sitting room his kiss had made her tingle, now she felt nothing. Amongst her whirling thoughts came the memory of Agnes' predictions, which were coming true so bathetically. After all, here was a fair-haired young man from overseas. All she wanted was for him to stop talking nonsense and go away.

"Do speak to me. I suppose you are astounded to see me here as Émile Dubois, and shy too, about how we went on, but what could be happier?" He took hold of her chin and raised it. As she caught his adoring gaze, she felt a pang of dismay, for by the expression in his eyes, even if he was mad, he was sincere. He was convinced of some imaginary, passionate (and improper) encounter.

It seemed that the look in her eyes confirmed his fears. He drew back slightly. "Sophie, I know I have been bad enough, but you gave me the impression that you liked the wicked Gilles Long Legs somewhat. *Alors,* I do not want to be ungallant enough to remind you, but now we meet again, and as Émile Dubois I adore you no whit less, *ma chère*, than I did as Gilles –"

They heard distant footsteps and drew apart. "Wait!" He loped across the hall to the library door to glance in.

"*Viens ici!*" He beckoned to her. She felt like taking to her heels, but that wouldn't do. She followed him into the room.

This great room was so chilly in winter that the family rarely stayed in here long. The fire never had much effect upon the frigid air. It burnt brightly now, illuminating the room with a pleasant glow. The drapes were as yet undrawn. She automatically noted some specks of snow whirling against the great windows, now blue in the gathering dusk. The Count would be pleased. Harriet would have been equally displeased by the fact that two candles were left alight on a table. This waste typified the extravagance at Plas Uchaf.

He took her arm as though he had a right to it, and led her over to the blaze. "We will not be disturbed here. You shiver. Come over to the fire." He massaged the arm familiarly.

"Er, thank you, Sir." She had no idea what else to say. Thoughts whirled in her head. It seemed that the grand *Monsieur* Émile had – incredibly – just proposed to his poor relation. She suddenly realised that John would take the view that Sophie must humour him, deranged or not. What was a little sanity gone astray compared to such an offer?

Monsieur laughed, nervously, she thought. "'Sir?' You did not call me so, back in Paris. It was but seven months since, yet it seems like years." He put his arms about her. "Come, my lovely girl, give me that same *ingénue's* kiss you gave me then. I sound like some imbecile in a novel, but I care not, so as you kiss me." He bent down to her, lips at the ready.

She was roused, not to passion, but to resistance. She struggled and burst out, "I am sorry Sir, but I have to say that – that there is some sort of mistake. I have never been in Paris."

He froze and then slackened his hold. "What? What did you say?" He gasped the words, staring.

"Sir," she thought that her unsteady voice came out as an unappealing whinge, "I am sorry, but truly I do not know of what you speak. I think you – forgive me – confuse me with another."

He gave a laugh both mocking and uncertain. "Come, *Mademoiselle* Sophie! There is no need to take discretion to the point of absurdity.

I make no excuses for what you saw. No doubt I am depraved villain enough. Are you horrified by me? If only you will trust me I will turn my back on my horrible past. "

"But how, *Monsieur* Émile? What can be happening?"

His eyes flashed. He drew back himself and let go of her. "I think you are not acting, and you have no memory of me and that evening. I can scarce believe it, but it is true!" He breathed so heavily and quickly that she thought it lucky that he was so wiry and active, or he might even keel over in an attack of apoplexy. "I am not vain, but I had no idea that I was so forgettable."

He turned away from her to march about, apparently at a loss for words in either French or English. Every now and then, he shot her a look of outrage. If his besotted attitude earlier was unnerving, this was worse.

After a while, during which she could think of nothing to say, he came to a stop. Voice shaking with rage, he berated her some more. "*Alors*, I would have been a cad as well as an assassin had I not done my best for you then. Ah, and I was a jest amongst the others as I fretted over you. I heard them laughing at me over it, 'Poor old Gilles Long Legs has it badly!' But I didn't care – I was tortured by the thought of that innocent lost somewhere amongst brutes. I think perhaps *Mademoiselle* decided that it was time to withdraw as her scoundrel of an admirer was becoming too pressing in his attentions. Sure it was the hardened ruffian who the innocent all along!"

He broke off to aim a furious kick at the logs in the fire, knocking one into the grate. He turned about and loped aimlessly about the carpet for some moments before breaking out again. "Perhaps that little adventure was but one amongst many? *Après tout*, what was an English *bourgeoise* doing in such a neighbourhood, and you would not tell me? Is that why you won't remember? " He glared at her again. By some unfair trick of fate she blushed, though she didn't understand what he meant.

In the face of such bizarre abuse, such wild imaginings, she felt three things. The first was a sense of injustice; she wanted to stamp her foot and scream that it wasn't fair, as in childhood when her friend stole her doll. The second was an hysterical desire to laugh at the absurdity of the situation. A third was an inclination to burst into tears.

She took a fourth course of action, trying to speak calmly. "I have never been in Revolutionary Paris, *Monsieur* Émile. How could I so? Truly, this is someone else of whom you speak."

"An identical twin with the exact same gown? So you are determined to keep up this ludicrous pretence? It is as well that I am disgusted enough by human nature not to be entirely surprised." Yet he went on glowering at her with baffled rage. "However do you come to be with *Madame ma Tante* and Cousin Ynyr?"

She found herself saying ludicrously, "*Monsieur* Émile, you are not acting the gentleman."

"You, *Mademoiselle* Sophie, have invariably acted the lady."

"Yes, indeed, *Monsieur* Émile, to the best of my ability." Sophie's indignation at these vague but intolerable slurs on her character spurred her on to give a speech worthy of one of Richardson's beleaguered heroines.

"I am your poor relation, your aunt's dependant, and you speak to me so. My furthest trip has been to come here and my only adventure has been to live amongst such grand people. I am dismayed at your attitude towards me, Sir, when I have ever wished you well and throughout your vicissitudes I prayed for you every night."

Monsieur Émile – far from being soothed by this speech – looked so angry that she wondered that steam did not burst out of his ears. She'd heard somewhere how Henry the Second suffered from rages so terrible he used to roll on the floor, chewing the rushes. *Monsieur* Émile looked as though he would have liked to do so too, but in the absence of rushes was forced to remain on his feet, contenting himself with marching about. For variety, though, he did some snorting worthy of the Count's horse Boris.

He half turned. "Think you that prissy speech suited to your new role of humility? *Alors*, you do not need to fear, *Mademoiselle*. I am not so mean spirited that I would run tales to my relatives about anything you may wish to conceal, such as your brief liking for the ruffian Gilles. You are at liberty to divulge to them what you wish of my own miserable past." He went over to stare into the fire, arms crossed.

Suddenly, her sense of his distress calmed her. She went over and put a hand on his arm. "I really am sorry. I wish I could remedy matters, but how can I, when I have no recollection of these incidents? Yet truly I am overwhelmed that you –"

He flung off her arm, with a look that exceeded all the others in outrage. "You are clearly a cynic, little Miss Sophie, besides the most accomplished actress and I am surprised that though you evidently have no warm feelings towards me, you should so turn your back upon worldly advantage as to ignore my naive offer for you a couple of minutes since. You might give me your reason."

Being unable to give him the true one – that she thought him slightly mad – she could make no reply, but watched him anxiously.

Suddenly, his eyes flashed as some explanation came to him. "Perhaps you have your eye on Cousin Ynyr and his title? So that is it! To have brushed aside my offer so contemptuously you must be complacent about your chances of success."

She in turn was speechless. Staring wildly at her, he hissed something rude in French, and turning, rushed out of the room, banging the door behind him so violently that some specks of plaster drifted down from the ceiling. She heard his footsteps dashing across the hall and sprinting up the great staircase.

"Oh, dear!" Sophie realised that this was ridiculously inadequate.

The great portraits of the Lords and Ladies of Ruthin seemed to stare down rebuke at her in the glow from the fire. The statues in the alcoves seemed united in disapproval.

She emulated her grand relative, and did some wandering about, though she was too fond of her slippers and too scared of singeing her feet to aim kicks at the fire.

One statue in particular – that of a bald man with a prominent nose – seemed to be looking at her with outrage. She was relieved to see that it wasn't a family member, but a Roman emperor, she forgot who.

Sophie addressed it. "Really, I do not see what I could do. I am sorry for it all, but I did nothing to provoke such an outburst. Poor *Monsieur* Émile's nerves must be out of sorts. He was being such delightful company when I came in, too. It is a shame." She added, more prosaically, "As if I would not give my eye teeth for such an offer, particularly from one I have always so admired, were it made in a sane manner! It is too bad."

Émile rushed into the bedroom, kicking aside a small tapestry stool and swearing horribly. "Oi, Georges! Where are you?"

Georges appeared in the doorway and whistled. "What ails you, Monsieur Gilles?"

"Nothing." Émile paced over to the window, and stared out at the darkening sky. "Get a move on, Georges, I've got to get myself ready for dinner, we're in civilised company now, don't forget." He made another furious snorting noise at some recollection.

"*Alors*, I can tell that this is about a woman. With a man you'd just do what you aristos term 'Calling him out'. Wouldn't coy Miss Morwenna let you take liberties?"

"Hold your noise, you dirty minded rascal, I'm in no mood for your nonsense." Émile came over to sit in a chair, then immediately jumped up to pace over to the fire.

Georges went on teasing. "*Alors*, you'll have my luck with them skirts one of these days. A subtle approach, that is what is needed. I have that. There's some pretty girls here, including Éloise, who comes from France, but it is a *Galloise*, Agnes, who takes my fancy most. I can tell that she likes me already. She is shockingly ignorant about good cuisine and did think that we French only dine off frogs and snails." *I am not sure I could kiss a man as ate them things.*" she told me, lips all pursed up the while, you understand –"

"*Tais toi*! Stop blathering about banalities, imbecile. Where are my clothes?"

"Your pardon, Master, I will fetch them immediately." Georges lounged to the dressing room. "I think it might be best to wear a mask for dinner; that face of yours will sour the wine."

—❧❧❧❧❧❧❧—

Meanwhile, Agnes was lacing Sophie. "Is unaccountable, Miss Sophie. Yet I don't think he is mad, for all that. I cannot see Georges – him and me is getting to be good friends already – working for a lunatic."

Sophie had to smile. "Then *Monsieur* Émile and his valet are the fair and the dark man? I fear poor *Monsieur* Émile must be subject to delusions after his awful experiences. It is dreadful, when he was a real hero." Her eyes sparkled.

Agnes smiled. "He was so, and maybe there is some explanation without him being fit for Bedlam. I was just thinking, Miss, you must take my word for it, but when I did that reading said the young men would come from overseas – and here they are – the timing was all mixed up. Cards which should have come in the positions for the future came in the past and the Lovers was one."

"It is a wonder, Agnes that is not more often so. But as I said, he kept insisting that we met when he was 'Gilles Long Legs' and a 'ruffian'. Perhaps the poor man believes himself to be two people? He rambled strangely. I fear he is outraged at my not recollecting it." She went red, remembering his talk about kissing.

"Georges calls him '*Monsieur* Gilles' sometimes."

Sophie remembered the names underneath a small portrait back in her family home that she used to gaze on so often. "Of course, he's Émile Gilles Gaston Dubois. It is going to be so embarrassing meeting with him again, Agnes, though I have done nothing wrong."

"Your new pink gown for dinner this evening, I think, Miss Sophie, to give you courage. Well, is impossible to think hard of a man as has the good sense to fall in love with you."

"Even in a meeting that never happened? I believe he said in May. That was some weeks before I left Chester."

Agnes worked hard upon Sophie's toilette and finally gave a sigh of satisfaction. "You do look lovely, Miss. Miss Morwenna does think herself such a beauty, but you will outshine her quite."

Sophie thought the new, bright pink dress shockingly low, and tried to pull the neckline up. Still, it was made up according to the Dowager Countess' specifications. Sophie suspected her patroness took the same satisfaction in dressing her up as she herself once enjoyed with her dolls.

"You have done wonderful work on my dress and hair, Agnes. Still, you should know that there is an unspoken rule for Poor Relatives all: '*Never Outshine Your Betters*', though Miss Morwenna is so handsome there is no danger of that."

Agnes wouldn't concede this. "She don't have half the figure or complexion that you do, Miss Sophie, and clomping great feet besides."

"I think you prejudiced in my favour, Agnes, *cariad*, and she is tall, and she could scarce balance on my feet. Wish me luck, dear, for I am terrified of *Monsieur's* anger."

As Sophie entered the room, making her curtsey, she caught *Monsieur* Émile's gaze at once. He was talking with Miss Morwenna (becomingly dressed in green). After one glance at Sophie in her low-cut dress and a nominal bow, he went on joking with Morwenna. Obviously, his form of madness wasn't one where he forgot a wrong almost as soon as he imagined it.

The Dowager Countess was wearing her spectacles and examining her tapestry work in dismay.

Lord Ynyr was in an expansive mood. Apart from this visit from a favourite, long-lost cousin, lately his herbal cures were proving effective. There was an outbreak of a seasonal illness, with ten staff members ill in bed; he had treated them himself with encouraging results.

Sophie smiled at him, touched by his enthusiasm. Then she remembered *Monsieur* Émile's suggestion that her apparent indifference to his own proposal was due to her having an eye to Lord Ynyr's title. She felt her face redden guiltily as Lord Ynyr ran on, "There is the strange case involving Mair Jones from the farm on the top road; Dr Powell confesses himself puzzled. There is shock to the system, though how this happened is a mystery. She was walking back from seeing a friend and claims – perhaps she was influenced by the stories of a ghostly dog who supposedly stalks the lanes of a night, though this was late afternoon – she saw red eyes and remembers nothing else before coming to herself."

"The poor girl! That sounds most alarming, delusion or not."

"It is absurd, but it seems she had odd bites upon her throat, and is convinced it was a supernatural attack. Miss Morwenna will be delighted, I fear, at this similarity to the vampire tales of Eastern Europe. One has to remember that there are any number of biting insects under the trees of an evening, and some may have survived into the winter. She possibly scratched herself in falling or when coming to herself. One of the problems in treating the local community is the poorer members retaining many superstitious beliefs. I am using a cure, but it is a puzzling case."

"Émile, you are dreadful!" Miss Morwenna' clear voice came suddenly. Sophie and Lord Ynyr glanced over to see her smiling encouragement of whatever form this dreadfulness was taking.

As so many of the footmen were ill, Émile's valet Georges was obliged to wait at table for dinner. Clearly, he was outraged. He avenged himself by wearing the livery in which he had been fitted out as though he revelled in its absurdity. Besides this, his position between Miss Morwenna and Sophie enabled him to leer down the cleavages of both. Meanwhile, he wore an expression combining lasciviousness and self-congratulation, as though congratulating himself on the pornographic nature of his thoughts.

Sometimes, Sophie caught Georges' master taking a look at her exposed flesh himself, though more quickly and subtly. *A most unfortunate duo.* She had to smile at this thought. Naturally, *Monsieur* Émile chose this moment to glance at her and his face froze.

Sophie sensed Miss Morwenna picked up the tension between and *Monsieur* Émile and their poor relative; no doubt her elaborately styled head was whirling with speculation. In her surprise, she even glanced at Sophie twice, while she treated *Monsieur* to the same teasing ways she used on Lord Ynyr, attacking him with her fine eyes and lashes.

As so often, Sophie admired Morwenna's vivacity; she wondered Lord Ynyr hadn't admitted defeat and proposed years ago. Watching the exchanges with Émile Dubois, she wondered if Miss Morwenna preferred him, but she seemed scrupulous in how she divided her attention between the two young men.

The atmosphere of the dinner table was lively and cheerful ostensibly, for all the undercurrents of hostility. *Monsieur* Émile told funny stories.

"The lovely primrose shade of Morwenna's gown (Morwenna smiled and batted her lashes) puts me in mind of an absurd thing that happened when I used to call on a friend back in London, for the room was decorated in the same colour. An abusive parrot – a pet of the lady of the house – perched in a gilded open cage. It liked to remind me, '*You are ugly*'.

'One day, it lost patience with me altogether and flew at me, ripping out some of my hair and tearing my jacket and shirt. I had to beat it off without hurting it, and it retired sulkily back to its cage just as Captain Allsopp was shown into the room." He took one look at me, and then drawled: *"By Gad, Monsieur Dubois, I had no idea that the situation of the émigrés from France was so deplorable..."*

Sophie didn't need to force her laugh. She felt more than ever regretful that they had fallen out. She delighted in people who told stories against themselves.

For all *Monsieur's* vivacity, his appetite disappointed his Aunt. "Émile, I ordered all your favourite dishes, yet you leave half of them untasted!"

"Forgive me, *Madame*. I will remedy that at once. This *omelette rustique* is excellent." He picked up his fork again. Sophie heard Georges sniggering.

"Did you know Kenrick is back at Plas Cyfeillgar, Émile?" Lord Ynyr asked. "I believe you met him in Town."

"Yes, Ynyr, he came over at a mathematics lecture at the Royal Society and reintroduced himself. He asked me if I understood the principles, confessing that he hadn't.

'On my saying if so he cannot have found the talk interesting, he said he was hoping to further his own understanding, claiming he had been working upon extending the borders of natural philosophy* to include: '*That branch of knowledge vulgarly known as "magic", Monsieur Dubois.*'

'He was hopeful that he might apply certain mathematical formulas to the use of, 'The *Power of Thought Forms to Effect Travel Through Time.*' I had to hide my smile, seeing an incongruous picture of him in a wizards' crooked hat and starry gown, frowning over some mathematical tome."

Morwenna giggled happily. "How absurd!"

Lord Ynyr laughed, but twirled his moustache, which Sophie had noted was his habit when uneasy. The Dowager Countess clicked her tongue. "Such mischievous ideas, Émile. Whatever would the Dear Late Count make of one of his *protégés* meddling in such matters?"

"*Alors*, he would think it nonsense. Kenrick's combination of outrageous notions and a sharp intelligence add to the amusement of his conversation, Ynyr."

"I confess, Émile, when I called on him I found the atmosphere at Plas Cyfeillgar unpleasant. There is an unnatural quiet there which would no doubt delight you, Morwenna, with your weakness for a ghost story."

Morwenna dimpled.

"A sullen manservant opened the door and a sad little girl from the kitchens served us refreshments. He apologised for it, speaking of staff difficulties, saying that his better staff were away with Mistress Kenrick. I am afraid that Miss Sophie must find this a chilly house, on high as we are, but the cold here is as nothing to that at Plas Cyfeillgar."

Monsieur Émile frowned. "I cannot endure a man who mistreats his staff."

His own servant aimed another hot glance down Sophie's cleavage. The ancient butler noticed and his expression hardened from wood to stone. Sophie tried to pull up the neckline of her dress surreptitiously, and *Monsieur* shifted uncomfortably.

———ᴄᴧᴏ〇ᴄᴧᴄᴧᴏ〇ᴄᴧᴏ———

The men lingered over their port far longer than was normal for Lord Ynyr, while Sophie righted the Dowager Countess' tapestry work and Miss Morwenna played seasonal music.

When they came in, the Count asked at once, "Morwenna, could we have some carols?"

"If you hadn't been roaring with laughter over your own stories you would have heard me singing them this past half hour, for the dining room is directly underneath us." Miss Morwenna had left the instrument on their arrival. "I do hope you are not becoming a couple of topers."

Monsieur smiled at her. "We must apologise for the delay and would be delighted if you were kind enough to indulge us, Morwenna."

"Seeing you ask, Émile – just restored to us as you are – I will submit. What would you like?" Miss Morwenna swayed back over to the instrument, her silks rustling.

When Sophie had to cross the room herself to give the Dowager Countess her untangled tapestry work, she felt hostile eyes on her. After that, she sat as far away from the lively group by the piano as possible, working on a baby's shawl and enjoying the carols.

Then, Lord Ynyr came up. "Miss Sophie, Morwenna wishes to try out some new strategies on my Cousin at chess, so I wonder if you could oblige us in turn? I would so like to hear that song you sing sometimes, that obscure one from one of Handel's operas, '*Ombra* something'."

"'*Ombra Mai Fú*'* Your Lordship? I would be delighted." That was only polite, but Sophie was nervous at singing before the hostile *Monsieur* Émile, who must have heard all the best singers in London. She was scared her voice might wobble with nerves.

To her relief, she was able to hold the long note at the beginning of the song more firmly and sweetly than she had yet. Out of the corner of her eye she saw *Monsieur* Émile pause, holding a chess piece, as though startled. The whole song went well.

Everyone broke into applause when she had finished, even the stunned looking *Monsieur* Émile, while Lord Ynyr called, "Bravo!"

"Why, Morwenna," he laughed as he glanced at the chess game, "You have my Cousin looking like he has been sucking a lemon!"

Morwenna frowned. "Émile, do you think I am still ten, to believe that you missed that trap for your Queen?"

"*Vraiment*, Morwenna, I did. There is no excuse for me. I deserve to lose her."

It was only later that Sophie thought that those words might have been aimed at her.

Now, she went on to sing more pieces, all enthusiastically received. At the end of '*Voi Che Sapete*' from Mozart's '*The Marriage of Figaro*', she heard the Count exclaim, "Morwenna, you have Émile routed!"

"I surrender, Morwenna. I am sorry to have given you such a sorry game, and hope Cousin Ynyr puts up more resistance."

—————⊙⁊⨏⊙⦿⨏⊙⦿⊙⁊⨏⊙—————

"*Alors*, you still have a face like a boot." Georges told Émile, when the Landlord had set down the bottle and glasses on their table. "You may as well say what is amiss. You ain't had much luck with blondes, one way or another, have you? I'd go back to them brunettes you always preferred, like that Lola. She was some woman! I was after her myself for weeks."

Émile downed a glassful in one go. "What do you mean?"

"I sent her all sorts of presents with compliments –"

"No, I mean about blonde women."

They were at the inn in *Llangynhafal*, the nearest village from the *Famau* Mountain, where a group by the fire sang Welsh carols.

"I saw you give that little Sophie de Courcy a couple of filthy looks over dinner, so I suppose she has to do with your foul temper. For myself, I was too grateful for the nice view she gave us to find fault with her. Umm. I shall dwell on them dugs later, and Miss Morwenna's too."

Émile cursed him again for a dirty minded rascal and stared at his drink.

"Then before that there was that blonde little bourgoise back in Paris was robbed and you was looking after, clean vanished from one of them street parties. My spies told me of it."

Émile smiled sourly. "Of course, it would have got back to you."

Georges spread his hands. "Naturally. My spies said you was acting besotted so they tried to find her themselves, reckoning you would pay well to know where she was. Come to think of it, weren't she called Sophie too? It's Sophie's you want to avoid, then."

Émile grimaced. "Georges, would you strongly object to not telling me any more about what your spies told you? It's the same girl."

Georges stared. "What?"

"*Mademoiselle* de Courcy is the girl I met back in Paris. When I saw her here, you can imagine how delighted I was. But when I got her alone, she acted as though she didn't even remember me."

Georges stared. "*Merde*! But it would be even more insulting, had you got further with her."

"Her forgetting is insulting anyway – because – *alors*, it's insulting anyway. I was waiting for a meeting with some fellow at Adeline's with a couple of the others when *Mère* SlapEm came along with a fair-haired *jeune fille* she said was set on by a couple of roughs she would know again. I told Professor Felix to look after the girl, but he reminded me I had a meeting so I stayed behind with her."

Georges snorted. "I would have taken my chances with you rather than *Mère* SlapEm any day."

"So would anyone, Georges. I was put out at first, having things to do. Besides, I didn't trust the girl's story, though if she was acting she was brilliant at playing a lost *ingénue,* and an *Anglaise, too.* Ma SlapEm was no fool and she believed her. Still, you may guess I kept an eye on my pockets as I sat her down and talked to her over a glass of wine. I realised she was a genuine *bourgeoise* and she seemed so innocent. I could scarce believe it.

'Besides, I enjoyed practising my English. We had soup. She didn't let me take her back to where she was staying. That was suspicious enough. She had no money, yet she freely admitted she'd had none before those cowards tried to rob her. It was such things made me sense that I could trust her; so I thought then, anyway.

'She insisted on giving me a sapphire necklace in a ridiculous payment for the food. I put it in my pocket, but only to make her stay; I became ludicrously anxious that she should stay. She said she could explain everything later, only I would scarce believe her.

'Even that did not make me cynical about her. Some couple of times, it was as though she tried to tell me, and she seemed to choke. That did not bode well for her character, *bien sûr*....." Émile sighed and fiddled with his glass.

"We went on talking. I began to feel ever more stupidly happy. I was delighted the man I was meeting didn't come. You may laugh, Georges, but truly, I did not realise what was happening to me, so I never thought to get out of the way, having never fallen in love since I was a boy. *Alors,* I didn't know what it was until it was too late."

Georges wasn't laughing now; he was looking sympathetic.

"I asked her to come with me to the party. You already have it from your spies how things went on there. I still have the necklace. "

"Are you going to give it her back? It seems but fair, as she cannot be well off."

"I suppose I will. Georges, now she denies with wide eyed innocence that she ever met me in her life after we were youngsters, protesting she has never been abroad!"

Georges whistled. "Maybe you acted sudden and she was shy about having carried on with the ruffian as you then were."

"I suggested that myself, Georges. I actually asked for the arrogant minx, and she ignored me!" Émile did some more heavy breathing.

Georges snorted, blew his nose and poured Émile another drink. "I am sorry, *mon ami*, but can she really be the *ingénue* she would have you believe, out alone in those parts with our countries at war? How came she there?"

"If she is acting, she is a genius. It is unaccountable, Georges. If I were on the outside, watching us, I would say that she told the truth."

"I believe you, for if anyone had asked me before hearing this odd tale, I would say she was a guileless creature. Fancy *ta Tante's* companion rejecting your offer! That is a lesson for you, *Monsieur*. You always did consider yourself such a catch. You must talk with the girl again, *du calme*. Tomorrow, I will ask the delectable Agnes about her, but discreet like, for I can see she dotes on her mistress."

Émile said sourly, "You ask Agnes, Georges. Still, I do not know if I shall ever honour the wretched girl with my attentions again. She humiliated me quite! I saw her smiling to herself over dinner, no doubt gloating over her conquest. Perhaps that is what woman are like, if they find themselves in a position of power over you. I never saw that in them before.

'We must stay on here, because of the trouble down south, and it wouldn't be polite to *Madame La Comtesse* to leave betimes, but I detest the thought of having to see her constantly. On top of everything else, she sings like a siren."

"Hoighty-Toighty, *Monsieur* Dubois, as Agnes would say. Perhaps you should go to her dressed as Gilles Long Legs. It may well be she prefers them rough, for it can be so with these nicely brought up, sheltered girls, as I was delighted to find out one day last spring – "

Émile glared. "*Se taire*, Georges!"

A stout, red-faced farmer had left the group by the fire to go and look through the window. Georges turned to look too. "Snowing again. We didn't get that in Provence."

"We saw enough of it in Paris."

"*Mae hi'n bwrw eira eto.*" The farmer pointed to the snowfall.

"*Dim ond Saesnig.*" (Only English*). Georges indicated himself and Émile. He had learnt that much Welsh from Agnes already.

The farmer screwed up his face in his effort to understand; after some moments, he gave up.

Émile poured him a drink. "Please accept that with the compliments of the season, *Monsieur*. You see, Georges? The sight of my happy face spreads festive cheer wherever I go."

Chapter Five

As Sophie waited with the others for the carriage to church the snow was thick on the ground from the fall overnight. She smiled at Lord Ynyr's delight in his accurate prediction – he and Agnes had more in common than they realised – and at the wonderful view of the Clwyd Valley, magically transformed.

He said, "Our ride on the sleigh this afternoon should put us in appetite for Christmas dinner."

Miss Morwenna clapped her hands. "Remember the bells, Ynyr!"

Monsieur Émile smiled agreement, but looked weary and heavy eyed.

The Dowager Countess sighed. "What it is to be young! If you will take the girls out in such weather, I must insist you all wear your furs."

Miss Morwenna dimpled at her boots. *Monsieur* Émile roused slightly: "*Bien sûr, Madame.* We will also ensure any snowballs we might throw have no stones."

Miss Morwenna was kept back by well wishers as they went to their pew; *Monsieur* Émile moved as though manoeuvring to sit next to Sophie and torment them both. Once next to her, he ignored her.

Sophie was distracted from the Reverend Smythe-Jones' sermon on self denial over Christmas by a sudden memory of his eating many mutton chops at a dinner.

Within a couple of minutes *Monsieur* Émile began to doze, and even to sway towards her. She was worried the Dowager Countess might see. She nudged him. His strange green eyes opened, to wander, all at sea, before snapping back into hostile recognition. *"Merci, Mademoiselle."* He drew himself up as though the idea of his falling asleep again was absurd.

A minute later, he was asleep again, beginning to sway towards her as though he thought her a natural pillow. Incongruously, mortifyingly, she had to fight an urge to put her arms about him. It seemed as though that, too, was the most natural thing in the world. She reddened, frightened she might do so.

She remembered now, being disturbed in the small hours by footsteps going up the middle stairs; at the time she had assumed it to be the awful Georges with one of the footmen. Agnes had told Sophie of Georges' shocking drinking, her tone indulgent. This worried Sophie, as seeming to indicate the girl was thinking of him as a possible sweetheart. Now, Sophie suddenly wondered if *Monsieur* Émile might be eccentric enough to go out drinking with his valet. It fitted with other odd aspects of their relationship.

She nudged *Monsieur* Émile. He responded with a startled grunt. She murmured to him, but he dozed on.

She didn't blame him; she had never known the Reverend Smythe-Jones to speak so badly. "It is a time even to permit ourselves a little self-indulgence. Er. Yet, Always…Er…We must look for an opportunity to share…" Sophie fought back laughter. Miss Morwenna stared ahead, but Sophie saw her lips twitch.

As the sermon ended, Sophie gently prodded *Monsieur* Émile – who by some fluke had only leaned his lanky frame on her lightly – awake. *"Monsieur* Émile, please do not think me impertinent, but I think you are in need of some rest." He didn't reply beyond a heavy eyed but inscrutable look. Scarlet faced, she snapped shut her prayer book.

Sophie was standing in the great hall. Back from the village children's Christmas party, she was admiring the view from the windows. Hearing footsteps she recognised, she skipped under the mistletoe nearby.

When the Count came into sight, she looked unaware of where she stood as she gazed through the window. He paused, smiling, more handsome than ever in his liveliness. "Why, Miss Sophie!"

"Such a magical transformation, Sir."

He came over, smiling. "Do you realise that you are putting any passing gentleman to temptation and yourself at risk?" He pointed to the mistletoe.

She followed his gesture and cast her eyes down. "My goodness, Your Lordship, I –" Not liking to lie outright, she broke off and dimpled coyly. "What must you think of me?!"

He took her hand and kissed it gently. "I must think you a delightful addition to our family, my dear Miss Sophie. I have never seen my mother so happy as since you have joined us. My compliments of the season."

There was a slight tingle as his well-shaped lips touched her skin. It was an improvement, anyway.

"Cousin Émile has surfaced from wherever he was in hiding," from his smile Sophie suspected that the Count had seen something of what had happened at church, "And is even now helping to prepare the sleigh bells."

———⁓⊙⊙⁓⊙⊙⁓———

Sophie tried to angle for the Count to hand her into the sleigh. These moments of intimacy could be built upon.

To her disappointment, the aloof *Monsieur* Émile seemed unaccountably to place himself so as to be the one to do so. As he lifted her, her cheeks burnt as she forced herself to look into his eyes – almost as a dare – and they were as cold as she had expected. It was made worse by the way his touch still made her tingle.

Lord Ynyr drove the team first. This being an occasion for the gentlemen to show off their driving skills, Morwenna teased them both about their pride in their horsemanship; she assured *Monsieur* Émile she had forgotten all about that accident years ago; he teased her in turn.

She even honoured Sophie by pointing out a bird of prey up on high. If it hadn't been for Sophie's embarrassment about *Monsieur* Émile – who sat as far away from her as possible, avoiding looking at her – Sophie would have loved the dash through the frozen landscape.

As they rushed along the path which ran level past the home farm, Lord Ynyr exclaimed, "Surely it is Kenrick?" He slowed down as they approached two horsemen.

Sophie found Kenrick – cheeks florid in the cold – even more repellent in the harsh light of the snow. Remembering her dream, she shuddered in her furs. A weedy, dismal looking boy groom was with him. She remembered how Kenrick had been the only local of note not to attend church that morning, though no doubt some had taken in no more of the sermon than *Monsieur*.

Lord Ynyr spoke heartily. "My compliments of the season, Mr Kenrick, and to Mistress Kenrick, if she has joined you."

"Ladies. Your Lordship and *Monsieur* Émile." Kenrick bowed to left and right. Sophie thought his voice oily enough to grease the runners of their sleigh. "Delighted. *Monsieur* Émile, I heard you were here; compliments of the season to you, Sir. It seems so long ago that we were all young pups, agog in His Late Lordship's laboratory. Your Lordship, you must tell Her Ladyship again how I did so enjoy that excellent dinner at Plas Uchaf."

Sophie was sure he had fond memories of the trifle. She might have smiled at the thought, had she not feared *Monsieur* Émile might suspect her of thinking mockingly about him, as she sensed he had at dinner yesterday. Perhaps it was all part of his delusions.

After she had been wakened in the small hours by those footsteps, she had lain awake for some time. She had gone over the astounding scene in the library again and again, feeling both bereft and guilty. She had wished then – and ever since – that she had managed things better, though how she could have avoided upsetting him while being truthful, she didn't know.

The Count and *Monsieur* Émile agreed on behalf of them all that they should call in at Plas Cyfeillgar, while Miss Morwenna looked as doubtful as Sophie.

As they drew into the grounds of the great house, Sophie noticed the deathly hush, the silence from the birds. They had been quiet in the frozen landscape before, but here their stillness was eerie.

They got out of the sleigh by the grand front entrance. Kenrick jumped down from his horse, throwing the reins to his groom, showing again startling litheness in a heavily built man. He hurried forward to help the ladies dismount, but the others forestalled him. Lord Ynyr rushed to hand down Sophie (who was nearest to him) and *Monsieur*

Émile quickly lifted down Miss Morwenna before turning to help the unhappy looking groom to blanket the horses.

Kenrick opened his front door himself. Sophie put off entering until last. She was slightly behind the rest of the party as they walked up the hall. This, despite the long windows, was unaccountably dark close to the walls. It was icy. She saw a movement in the shadows and paused, stunned by the impression of a handsome, moustached man in naval officer's uniform leering at her from their depths, white teeth flashing.

To her surprise, *Monsieur* Émile turned back. "*Mademoiselle* Sophie?" His tone was cold, but he paused, waiting for her. The shadowy figure was gone. With a smile of thanks to *Monsieur* she caught up with the rest of the group.

Kenrick showed them into a great room where a fire made even less impression on the frigid atmosphere than in the library at Plas Uchaf.

He went to ring the bell. "A servant will be along in a minute." He didn't sound confident. Sophie thought the distant tinkle had the desolate noise of a bell fated to be ignored. This didn't seem to match with Lord Ynyr's description of the nervous servants, but perhaps they were elsewhere.

Kenrick looked at Sophie and Miss Morwenna, huddled in their wraps, and laughed. "You ladies are like a couple charming little Baby Buntings in your furs. Let us be grateful that there are no wolves about, sharp teeth at the ready to snap at your soft flesh." He giggled.

The others didn't. The Count frowned, "Why, Sir!" *Monsieur* Émile went further. His eyes sparked: "What do you mean by that, *Monsieur?*" He clearly had no inhibitions about his duties as a guest if he didn't like his host's conversation.

Kenrick smiled. "Do not scowl so on me, *Monsieur* Émile, you have not changed, living up to your reputation as a hot head. Forgive my familiarity. The young ladies do look so charming…Where are those wretched peasants? The insolence!"

He darted to the door, flung it open, sprinted across to a corridor opposite and yelled. From somewhere in the depths of the house, a sullen male voice shouted back.

"Do not raise your voice at me, my man! Come here at once!" Kenrick's voice rose into a shriek of outrage.

The man's voice bawled again in loutish defiance.

Instead of falling into a terrible rage, Kenrick appeared deflated. As he came back into the room, the Count cleared his throat, about to make some protest.

Sophie might have pitied Kenrick in his humiliation had he been less alarming. He spread his hands deprecatingly. "Forgive me. Servants these days are become impossible. The spread of Jacobin ideas, naturally. I scarce need acquaint you, Sir, with the dangers of that." He turned his oily smile on *Monsieur* Émile.

Monsieur said coldly, "*Alors,* it is a day most people celebrate as at least a partial holiday, *Monsieur.* We will not impose upon you further. You will forgive my Cousin and me if we take the ladies home."

The Count smiled. "Yes, please convey our respects to Mistress Kenrick when she arrives if we do not meet before."

There was an indefinable air of threat in the room, and Sophie was still alarmed by what she thought she had seen in the hallway. Perhaps *Monsieur* Émile wasn't alone in suffering from delusions.

They left with thanks for Kenrick's defective hospitality. He assured them, "Mistress Kenrick will soon have the staff in order."

As they went through the corridor again, Sophie once more saw the shadows stir. She wondered if Lord Ynyr and *Monsieur* Émile did, too, for they automatically formed a sort of phalanx on either side of the girls.

"There is an odd trick of the light here merely." Lord Ynyr murmured to Sophie. She suspected him of reassuring himself as much as her. Meanwhile, Miss Morwenna had tight hold of *Monsieur* Émile's arm.

It was a relief even to be in the grounds with their unnatural hush. Lord Ynyr said, "For sure, there was little enough seasonal goodwill in there! Émile, we owe the ladies an apology for subjecting them to such an unpleasant visit."

"Do forgive me, *Mademoiselles.* I will just see about tipping that wretched boy."

Émile was striding over the frozen snow round the side of the house to the stables when a small figure darted up some steps and hurled itself against the front of his greatcoat. Startled, he realised it was a scrawny young girl. He laughed. "Careful, *ma petite!*"

Then he saw she was sobbing frantically, her face soaked. "What ails you, girl?"

She wailed in an unfamiliar accent, "She beat me! I go!"

It was starting to snow again. As the girl made to pull away, he took her wrist. "In this snow? Have you family nearby?"

She burst out, "They are dead!" This seemed to add the final touch to her misery. She buried her face in the front of his coat and howled. Perhaps he was put in mind of his youngest sister Marguerite's childhood griefs, though this girl was years older. He patted her head tenderly, at all events. Her dark hair was greasy, and she smelt strongly of the kitchen, even in the open air.

He looked regretfully down at the front of his coat, now damp with tears and mucus. "They see me coming. Shall I try and mend matters here, girl? Who's been beating you? I think you said, 'She' so I cannot beat her in turn. What is your name?"

"Katarina. I won't go back, Sir!" She bawled desperately, while he searched about in his pockets for a handkerchief. She looked startled, but used it to wipe her face and nose before handing it back.

"Where do you come from, girl?"

"Transylvania, Sir. Now I must go."

Émile cast a thoughtful glance at the house, a handsome, red bricked building, solid after the style of Queen Anne, yet exuding a dismal atmosphere. It seemed to decide him. "Then I will take you to *Madame ma Tante's,* for you will surely perish in the snow. Do not fear, I am with two ladies, and you will be safe enough. Kenrick may go to the Devil. Come with me girl, to the sleigh."

When Émile came back, holding the servant girl by the hand, the others stared. "I cannot leave her here; she is ill treated and would run away." He picked her up and put her on the sleigh.

Sophie exclaimed, "Ah, you poor thing, how you shiver. Come under these rugs with me." She busied herself giving the scrawny girl most of her rugs. Glancing up, she saw *Monsieur* Émile watching her. His expression had unfrozen by perhaps a quarter. He looked as though he were deciding she could be bearable sometimes.

The Count pulled at his moustache. "Surely we should take the matter up with Kenrick?"

"No. I will pay them compensation if they want."

"Honestly, Émile, whatever will you do next?" Morwenna moved away from the greasy kitchen maid. "No doubt this will cause many problems. Oh, who cares. Let us away."

Agnes, who by her breath had shared a few Christmas drinks with Georges, was voluble and emotional as she dressed Sophie for dinner.

"Well, Miss, we is all at sixes and sevens with *Monsieur* Émile bringing in this new girl.

"Madame Blanch,' he says to the Housekeeper – he must have tipped her well – '*I know I can rely upon you to treat this little wench, my new maid, kindly. Give her as much Christmas Dinner as she can eat, and some warm clothing and maybe a handerkerchief or so –* ' looking down at his coat, for it did look as though she had blown her nose upon it – '*And give her a bed somewhere warm, and we will talk again about training for her after the holiday. She said she had been beaten. If the bruises are bad, let me know and we will get the apothecary to treat them tomorrow.'*"

"*The dirty little thing needs a bath.' Madame* Blanch wrinkles her nose. Éloise – the parlour maid, you know, Miss – puts herself forward, all batting eyelashes and bosom. '*I will help. Her English is good, but she speaks French better, just like you and I, Monsieur. Tee-hee-hee.'*

"*Poor thing, not being able to speak Cymraeg like a civilised person. I will learn her.'* I say. *Madame* Blanch looks hoighty-toighty and *Monsieur* laughs. He says something comforting, like, in French to the little girl and turns to me. '*Do you and Éloise look after her, Agnes.'*

''Then *Monsieur* goes off, and Georges gabbles away with her in French. He says she is terrified of Kenrick, fearing he will come in and get her. That does make Georges laugh. '*Let him try and Monsieur Gilles and I will give him something to remember us by. Take heart, girl, he's well enough to work for, is Monsieur Gilles.'*

'She's from a place with the outlandish name – Transylvania, that is it. Her father died early, and her mother worked for Kenrick's first wife as folks say was so nice. Kenrick changed after she died, and started doing strange experiments and Katarina believes he is one of them human bat things, but for sure that is nonsense, Miss. Anyway, her mother brought her here but then died herself. Kenrick only kept Katarina on because of a promise to his late wife. It was good in *Monsieur*, Miss Sophie, to take her away from them nasty people."

"It was, Agnes!" Sophie's eyes sparkled. His Quixotic act had rekindled all her old admiration for *Monsieur*, though John and Harriet would see it as sure evidence he was deranged.

"All them lot working there either can't get other work or is touched. Is terrible things that they are starting to say hereabouts of Kenrick and his experiments, though the place was haunted before, *Nain* said. Don't ever go there by yourself, Miss."

Sophie shivered. "I think I shall manage to keep away without any sense of loss, dear." She glanced in the mirror. "I wish I had long black eyelashes."

"But Miss, you are blonde, and you cannot have everything. I do know a way of darkening them and making them look longer, if you wish me to try it."

"Goodness, is it paint? But I should like them so."

While Agnes began working on Sophie's hair, still chattering and sentimental, Sophie braced herself for the dismal task of warning her against becoming too fond of Georges, being – as Agnes' mistress – responsible for what Harriet would term her 'Moral Welfare'.

She realised she was as anxious not to offend Agnes as she would be with any friend. She was glad she had given the girl generous cash present she could little afford on St Nicholas' Day. She envied *Monsieur* Émile, who was so rich – despite the depredations of the French Revolution upon his family's fortune – that he could take on little Katarina and pay for her future without thought.

Envy him? She reminded herself – as she had several times when feeling indignant at his treatment of her – how poor *Monsieur* had lost his whole family.

Far from doing something to comfort him, as she wanted, she was somehow in a grotesquely false position of having distressed him further.

After breakfast, the Dowager Countess gave Sophie and Miss Morwenna the expensive boxes of sweetmeats brought by her nephew 'for the ladies'. Sophie knew the Dowager Countess had given him the slippers embroidered for him by Sophie, and she wondered if he'd put them on to aim some more kicks at the fire.

69

"There's lovely, these back curls have come up perfect…Was Georges asking of you, isn't it, thinking himself discreet, *'Did Mademoiselle Sophie always stay in England before coming here?'*

'So far as I know, I say, *'Why do you ask?'* He looks all conspiratorial, if that is the word. *'Gilles Long Legs is sure they met in Paris when he was – Ahem! – in disguise as a rogue of sorts, shall we say? They got lovey-dovey at a party."*

"Oh, dear!" Sophie felt her face burn as Agnes related *Monsieur Émile's* story. Agnes was saying, "I told him, *'I don't know how this misunderstanding comes about, but Miss Sophie is the sweetest mistress I could wish, so honest she does not know how honest she is.'*

'He says, 'It is a puzzle. I see that maid Éloise is eager to try and console Monsieur. A good thing, for he is in a foul temper.'"

Sophie felt nettled. She guessed this disapproval had nothing to do with maidenly modesty. She shot a sharp glance at Agnes bland face.

She drew as deep a breath as she could as Agnes put on her stays. "Agnes, forgive my curiosity, but I regard you as a friend, you know –"

Agnes broke off to plant a tipsy kiss on Sophie's cheek. "And me you, *cariad*!"

"But I am anxious about you becoming so – friendly – with Georges. He does seem a rogue, dear. What you said about the way he and *Monsieur Émile* lived in Paris – I do not want to be judgemental, he may well have come to regret it, but –" Her voice trailed off.

"The cards said they were rogues, isn't it?" Agnes' eyes sparkled. "Though you do not need to worry, Miss Sophie. I will tell you a secret. I would not take him seriously as a prospect for the long term, as I have a child to think of."

"Why, Agnes! Boy or girl?"

"Girl, Miss Sophie. She's two and named Eiluned. They don't know hereabouts how she is mine, for I went down to my sister as married a sailor a world away in Swansea to have her. Now my *Mam* takes care of her after I heard as the Dowager was looking for a new maid."

Sophie knew most respectable people would say she should be shocked. She wasn't. She could never regret a baby's coming into the world. "Had you told me before, I would have given you more free time to spend with her."

Agnes planted another kiss on her head. "Now that is you all over, Miss Sophie. Who wouldn't love you?"

Sophie was seized by the self-pitying thought that – happy as she was at Plas Uchaf – had Harriet and John loved her more, they wouldn't have packed her off here at all. She put it aside. Harriet would be the first to point out it was Sophie's own fault if she still faced the prospects of a poor relative; in her confusion, hadn't she overlooked *Monsieur* Émile's glittering offer?

Sophie regretted that bitterly. She hadn't objected to *Monsieur* Émile as a man, after all, having admired him from afar for years, while his touch when he had kissed her hand in greeting had set her a-tingle as no other man's. It was only when he had started to make insane passionate declarations that she had frozen with alarm.

As for Dubois Court, Sophie had heard how wonderful it was there. He owned a magnificent town house, too. It was all too bad.

To Sophie's relief, Georges wasn't called on either to serve or to stand and wait at dinner. Perhaps he was too drunk, if Agnes' condition before dinner was anything to go by.

They were lively over the magnificent Christmas dinner, though *Monsieur* Émile took no more notice of Sophie than civility required and a couple of covert glances at her in her low peacock blue dress. Of course, if she had taken a long time over her appearance today it was because she wanted to look nice for Christmas.

The Dowager Countess was displeased by Émile's removing Katarina from the Kenrick's. Still, as it was the first Christmas dinner they had shared in years, she merely clicked her tongue. "You demonstrated the rashness that characterises you, Nephew. The Kenrick's must be offended at so high-handed an action."

"I could not leave the little girl so, *Madame,* or she would run off into the snow, and might perish. However, I realise I have created an awkward situation for you and I will call upon Kenrick tomorrow and offer reparation."

Morwenna turned her arch smile on him. "Émile never could stay out of trouble for five minutes together. Well, Ma'am, Kenrick said

Mistress Kenrick would soon remedy his staff problems, so she must hire another kitchen wench, too. Kenrick himself has altered much since he used to live here! Recollect you working with him in the Late Count's laboratory over those summers, Ynyr and Émile?"

Lord Ynyr smiled. "It was work upon blood. Kenrick was different then, quite a cheerful fellow indeed. When Émile came over for the holidays, eager for riding and sword play, he found me immersed in natural philosophy. Recollect you, Cousin? You jeered me about it firstly, but were soon drawn in yourself."

Morwenna gave a pretty shiver. "There is a disturbing atmosphere in the hallway at Plas Cyfeillgar. Legend has it you may see something horrible there."

Monsieur Émile suggested lazily, "Possibly the man who roared up the stairs."

"Was not that absurd? I could scarce keep my countenance." Miss Morwenna giggled from *Monsieur* to the Count and back again.

Sophie, silently but smilingly following the conversation (as became a poor relative) started as she caught *Monsieur* Émile's eyes on her.

Miss Morwenna went on, "The ghosts there sound much more impressive than our own Grey Lady, who has not yet honoured me. Should she so, I shall offer her my best pink slippers, which might cheer her and render her name inappropriate."

The Dowager Countess said solemnly, "*Alors*, I myself have lived here nigh on two and thirty years without seeing The Grey Lady."

Morwenna wheedled, "Pray indulge us, Ma'am, as Christmas is the time of year for ghost stories. Ynyr must tell us one when the gentlemen deign to come up from their port."

They had another sort of ghost story. While the wind howled about the roofs and chuckled down the drawing room chimney, *Monsieur* Émile read to them the novel 'Of Terror' Morwenna brought out. "Everyone in Town talks of *Madoc the Magnificent or the Vampyre's Curse*. For my own part, I found it absurd."

It was. Sophie, putting to rights the Dowager Countess' sewing, found herself laughing outright as *Monsieur* Émile read to them – eyebrows raised – of the prosing speeches of the hero Eugene and the faintings of the heroine Lucasta, while Madoc's appearances were always greeted with cries of, '*Fie, you foul fiend!*' No wonder he was so unpleasant.

She found *Monsieur* Émile's voice melodious. Watching him, she was more than ever puzzled; he seemed so sane about everything save this insistence on their supposed meeting.

The oddity of an aristocrat admitting to living amongst ruffians in Paris did make her wonder about the workings of his mind, even given the desperate situation in which he found himself. She had been too astonished to think much about Agnes' and his own remarks about his criminal lifestyle (and that of his valet Georges). Now having leisure to think about it all, it seemed incredible. She couldn't help taking covert glances at him, so astounding was everything about him.

He caught her doing so and gave her a chilling look in return.

Meanwhile, the Dowager Countess did her embroidery with calm confidence and Lord Ynyr was holding his own with Miss Morwenna at chess.

Whatever would they make of their relative's history, did they know of it? Whatever would Miss Morwenna make of *Monsieur* Émile's proposal of yesterday?

———⊙⌒⊙ℰℐℛℐ⊙⌒⊙———

Lord Ynyr and Émile stood at the front entrance of Plas Cyfeillgar. The wind blew icily in their faces, and they knew it wouldn't be much warmer in the house.

"No birdsong, as usual." Émile poked at the boot scraper with one toe. "Did you remark that, Ynyr? No doubt they mislike the jolly atmosphere too."

"If he berates you, will you be as eager to challenge him* as you were yesterday?"

Émile laughed. "I liked not his attitude towards the ladies. A shame Mistress Kenrick is not arrived. I cannot believe she can be as lovely as rumour has it."

"Did you never meet her in London? She is beautiful indeed, yet I fear I like her not. Émile, I suppose we must obey Morwenna and look for something terrible in the hall."

A flash, as of distant lightening, made them turn. Kenrick stood behind them, though they hadn't heard him approach. His smile was knowing. "Gentlemen, this is opportune. I was having coffee in the morning room."

Émile bowed solemnly. "*Merci, Monsieur.*"

"That is kind." Lord Ynyr hoped they wouldn't be long in the miserable place almost as much as he hoped there wouldn't be some unseemly brawl. With Émile's hot temper, you never knew.

Kenrick took them through a side door. They wouldn't be able to report back to Morwenna about the shifting shadows in the main hall. He led them down flagged passage that had no shadows at all.

"One of these days you may care to look over the books in my study there, gentlemen. Then, there is my little laboratory." He gestured to the next door, giggling, and turned into one opposite.

This room was luxuriously furnished yet fireless. The cold was such that even Lord Ynyr, brought up used to the winter chill of Plas Uchaf, was glad there had been no servant to take their coats.

Kenrick rushed out and down a corridor leading off to shout down the well of the stairs to the basement. The Count wondered if there would be a repeat of the events of last time.

When Kenrick returned, Émile addressed him suavely. "*Monsieur,* I have come to admit to increasing your staff problems by stealing the little kitchen maid Katarina. I am willing to pay you back any wages, or whatever you deem necessary. She was weeping, just beaten by one of the women, and about to run away, which late in the day in such weather is not to be recommended, so I took her home with us."

Kenrick moved closer as Émile spoke. To Lord Ynyr's amazement, he sniffed the air with a series of quick twitches of his nostrils, like a dog, only to jump back, paling, looking repelled. Perhaps the garlic to which Kenrick was allergic lingered from last night's dinner on Émile's breath.

Kenrick seemed to need to recover before saying flatly, "I think the cook complained the wretched skivvy was run away. I know how it is with young bucks, and I would not fall out with one who might be so useful to me over a scullion. But sure the girl is very young?"

Émile's eyes flashed, but he replied evenly, "Katarina is a child of perhaps twelve and accordingly safe from my advances, *Monsieur*. In

Paris, my friends and I served men who took advantage of children entirely as they deserved."

Lord Ynyr noted his smile of savage delight at the memory. There were times when his cousin, scion of the Dubois, made him think of nothing so much as a pirate. No wonder he got on so well with his appalling valet.

Kenrick spread his hands. "I did not know she was so young. You speak of compensation, but I would rather have your assistance in my scientific endeavours. The girl was of little use. My Dear Wife persuaded me to keep her out of kindness."

The Count felt a stab of sorrow for Kenrick; something about Kenrick's tone made it plain the 'Dear Wife' wasn't the present one.

"Scientific' endeavours, *Monsieur?*" Émile raised his eyebrows.

Kenrick turned a challenging look on him. "Yes; I am interested in the nature of time, of access to the past, and of travel through time. I am sure you gentlemen know there can be no possibility within the current constraints of knowledge in effecting physical travel through time. However, there is another branch of knowledge which I believe may prove fruitful. I concede the methods I use are called 'magic' by the vulgar, yet in applying mathematical principles to the same I hope to bring precision to their use."

Émile regarded him inscrutably. Kenrick paced about. "I have finally been able to acquire a treatise written earlier this century by one who knew of what he spoke. I believe, gentlemen, through bringing this mathematical understanding to the use of thought forms set out therein, I may be able to bridge the gap between natural philosophy and magic and affect a form of travel through time."

He wheeled about to see them both repress a smile, and his own mouth tightened over his long eyeteeth. "You doubt me, gentlemen?"

"Forgive me, *Monsieur.*" Émile still smiled. "I have a sceptical disposition and am the worst person in whom to confide your unusual ambitions. *Alors*, regarding the more established spiritual convictions, it is all I can do to attend church sufficiently often not to become a social outcast."

Anger glittered in Kenrick's glassy eyes, but his tone was soft. "Indeed, *Monsieur* Dubois, you would be foolish to underestimate the power of natural forces used by mankind throughout the ages to influence material events. They all rely, one way or another, upon the use of thought forms."

Émile raised his eyebrows again. Lord Ynyr spoke soothingly. "Possibly, Sir. Truly, everyone must make his own choice concerning such issues; speaking for myself, I must see such mysteries as best left unexplored."

"Does not Your Lordship find such an orthodox approach confining?" Kenrick stood looking from one to the other, his ruddy cheeks crimson.

Émile – completely indifferent to his outrage – began to speak, but Kenrick darted over to the door. "Our refreshments are come at last!"

He flung open the door to shout down the corridor, "You have been long enough about it!" Back in the room, he stood before the empty hearth, arms sullenly folded.

A stout middle aged serving man brought in a laden tray. He wore a livery so ill fitting – the top half so tight it seemed in danger of splitting, the bottom half so loose, it looked about to fall down – Lord Ynyr stared. Émile's lips twitched. The man thumped the tray down on a side table with a look of triumph which turned to one of hatred as he turned to his master.

"We will help ourselves." Kenrick waved the manservant away irritably. The man trudged out, banging the door. Kenrick whipped about in outrage, but said nothing, going over to busy himself with the coffee things. He held a cup out to Lord Ynyr, and as the Count stepped over to take it, Kenrick's glassy gaze met his.

Those eyes appeared to grow; Lord Ynyr found his mind drifting. It seemed to him as he looked into them that hidden in their depths was a secret of massive importance.

He wrenched his gaze from Kenrick's. His mind cleared gradually to hear Kenrick saying, "…Utilise your admirable mathematical ability, *Monsieur,* as it seems this wretched mathematician will renege on his agreement to assist me. I am no flatterer, yet I have heard from those qualified to understand how your talent is outstanding, particularly in one whose university education was tragically foreshortened."

He cleared his throat, and his tone became oily again, though his eyes remained cold. "Yes, *Monsieur,* you can hardly have been immune yourself from an urge to reverse time."

At Kenrick's words Émile's eyes sparked angrily. Kenrick seemed oblivious as he went back to pacing about. "I know your gifts would be invaluable to me, for as I have told you, my own understanding of mathematics is limited." He gave a brief smile of expectation.

Émile didn't return it. "I thank you for the compliment, *Monsieur.* No doubt you are correct in asserting there is presently no means of harnessing sufficient energy to affect physical travel through time. However, speaking from my own, possibly uninformed, point of view, I see it as no reason to retreat into areas of superstition and unreason."

Kenrick's angry eyes still sought Émile's, but Émile was looking at his ill-tied neck cloth. "I confess myself disappointed to find both Your Lordship" – he bowed quickly in the Count's direction – "And you, *Monsieur*, adopt a hidebound attitude. I think that prating fool of a Vicar would be satisfied by the orthodoxy of your views. I have found a method of access to the past already." He suddenly let out a shriek of laughter. "The dead past, where our crimes lie buried, eh, *Monsieur* Dubois? I have often thought on how many of us are more fitted for dangling from a noose at Tyburn than enjoying the comforts of a drawing room. Are you then certain you wish to decline my offer, for I will not approach you again?"

Émile rose. "Your notions are intriguing, *Monsieur*, but I am too much of the sceptic to be of assistance to you." He lounged over to the coffee table to return his cup. "Thank you for the coffee. We will no doubt speak again. Presently, Lord Ynyr has matters requiring his attention. Regarding the compensation I must owe you for taking away little Katarina?"

Kenrick glowered. "No, *Monsieur*, the child was a burden. I require no payment unless it might be a few songs from that little chit who is companion to Her Ladyship – what is her name – Miss Sophie? She has a lovely voice. It would soothe the most savage breast, eh, *Monsieur*? "

Lord Ynyr saw Émile start to speak, seemingly provoked into meeting Kenrick's gaze, then instead pull his eyes away, shaking his head angrily as if stung by an wasp.

The Count addressed Kenrick coolly, "Miss Sophie came to us as my mother's companion, Sir, but she is become a valued family member; her delightful singing is but one of her accomplishments. Now we must detain you no longer. Please do convey our greetings to Mistress Kenrick when she joins you."

"Yes, *Monsieur*, we look forward to calling upon *Madame*."

Kenrick darted forward so quickly they braced themselves for an attack even as he put out his hand.

As Émile and Kenrick savagely wrung each other's hand, Lord Ynyr supposed his rakish cousin already schemed to cuckold Kenrick. He wondered if one day a primarily male substance in the human body would be identified as the cause of brawls, philandering and wars – though also, possibly, of energetic ambition. He was glad that, if it did exist, he seemed not to have an excess supply of it himself, being generally able to control his aggression.

But then he remembered how on his last trip up to Town, he had overheard the drawling Lord Dale repeat the rumour: '*That Scoundrel Émile Dubois and his Insolent Valet are Highwaymen, as Sure as Fire.*' Lord Ynyr had demanded he either retract or named his friends.* Fortunately, a granite eyed retired Colonel had smoothed things over.

Now, as they came out through the side door, Lord Ynyr and Émile smiled at each other, stretching in relief in the open air.

As they walked towards the stables, Émile laughed. "The man is a clearly deranged in some ways, Ynyr, though sane enough in others. I am not surprised this mathematician avoids working with him. A nasty piece of work, *bien sûr*. It was all I could do to keep my hands off him."

"I did notice, Cousin."

The dismal groom appeared. Émile dug in his pockets. "Here, boy. Nobody beats you, I trust? Ynyr, there are often posts open at Plas Uchaf for grooms."

"We cannot denude Kenrick of his staff quite, Émile."

"*Pourquoi pas?* It is no more than he deserves."

Chapter Six

ÉMILE WAS HELPING LORD YNYR in his laboratory. He handed the Count a bowlful of garlic he had crushed and lounged over to the row of windows to gaze down at the view. A bitter wind was driving flurries of sleet across the foothills.

"You know, Ynyr, Kenrick has some singular party tricks. When his fishy eyes met mine in his nice friendly house, Devil take me if I didn't feel I must pull mine away or be the worse for it. That is the first time I have had a nervous fancy. Morwenna's tales must be getting to me, eh?"

Lord Ynyr looked up from beating powders with a pestle. "Me too, Cousin. It was bizarre indeed, and no doubt something Kenrick has come upon through his grotesque investigations. What with his wild talk about dabbling in magic and the dismal atmosphere in the house, I will defer making another call there long."

Émile smiled round at him. "That is leaving aside the absence of a fire." Sleet pattered against the windows, and he stared out again for some moments before saying musingly, "Yet he has set me thinking."

"How so, Émile?"

The Count expected a joke, but Émile, his back still turned, spoke with unusual seriousness. "Time being one of the greatest mysteries, I am not surprised Kenrick is become obsessed by the notion of access to the past, though I am sure his claim to have it already is bravado."

The Count sighed. "I have been wondering since if that obsession, which by his own account is leading him into dangerous folly, isn't connected with the loss of his wife? Perhaps he wishes at least to set eyes on her again, even if he cannot communicate with her –" he broke off in dismay.

He hadn't yet felt able to raise the subject of Émile's own losses; what he had just said came close to infringing on that.

The eyes Émile turned on him were unreadable save for quickened awareness. "Then, Ynyr, it was poor taste on my part to jeer Kenrick about his bizarre ideas, however much I dislike him. I knew he lost his wife some years back, but didn't realise he still so mourned her, particularly as he's remarried this beauty. There is something about him makes it hard to credit him with such human feelings –" He broke off suddenly himself, gazing fixedly down at the gardens below.

Lord Ynyr saw Miss Sophie, muffled in the fur-lined cloak ordered for her by the Dowager Countess, but recognisable by the blonde hair escaping from the hood, hurrying along the path to the hothouses, carrying a small basket.

"Ah, Miss Sophie." Lord Ynyr was aware how his cousin, who allowed his social inferiors familiarities, treated the pretty Miss Sophie with reserve. No doubt Émile, knowing his own rakish tendencies, was ensuring he wasn't tempted into familiarity with his aunt's innocent dependant. That was typical of Émile; he was so much better than people generally thought him.

"She so charming a girl;" the Count said, "I confess I have to keep a hold on myself at times."

Émile's shoulders tightened, yet his tone was casual. "How so, Ynyr?"

"I own if her worldly position was nearer to ours, I might be tempted to think in terms of making her an offer."

Émile didn't turn round. He spoke after a few moments: "But as she is your mother's companion, Ynyr?"

Lord Ynyr sighed. "I know it must be out of the question."

The Count was surprised to hear Émile sigh too. They watched the flurries of sleet for some moments in silence. Then Émile turned about abruptly. "Now, Ynyr, what next with these herbs?"

The group at Plas Uchaf went to several Christmas festivities over the next few days.

Sophie went on taking great care over her clothes and appearance, whether they were out or at home. She even let Agnes tint her eyelashes darker and was delighted with the result.

She hoped she wasn't motivated in her wish to look at her best through some previously unsuspected streak of cruelty, for when she entered a room and *Monsieur's* eyes widened even as he tried to appear unaffected, she felt a tingle of delight even as she dropped her gaze.

During the outings, *Monsieur* avoided talking to Sophie as he did at Plas Uchaf. With other girls he was more forthcoming. Sophie told herself if she felt put out when *Monsieur* Émile smiled on a young lady while she kept her eyes on him as though trying to mesmerise him, it was because the girl played the coquette clumsily. Sophie prided herself on her own discreet flirting.

No, I am jealous, and must take care. It's demeaning and in view of his mad proposal, sadly ironic.

Monsieur Émile wasn't expected to take much note of his poor relation, and his coolness towards Sophie puzzled nobody.

Often, though, Sophie felt his resentful gaze upon her, noting her actions, no doubt thinking hateful thoughts. It made her nervous; sometimes she broke off in a conversation or stammered.

Monsieur watched her particularly when she was speaking to Lord Ynyr. Fate seemed to arrange things so that whenever the Count smiled at her warmly, or she laughed in a way that seemed encouraging, *Monsieur* Émile would glance across at them. No doubt, his belief she was 'after the title' was confirmed again and again, when within a couple of days of meeting with *Monsieur* it somehow seemed far less of a prize to her.

Sophie knew he had been as good as his word, saying nothing to Lord Ynyr about her supposed appearance in Paris. She liked him for it: despite his coldness towards her, she found herself liking him generally, if only for his liveliness and sense of fun.

Monsieur Émile flirted with Miss Morwenna, of course; she matched him in spirits. Sophie watched in turn as they joked together. She wondered if *Monsieur* was thinking of Miss Morwenna as a future wife. As Lord Ynyr's cousin with a small fortune in her own right, she was infinitely more eligible than Sophie. Of course, anyone in society was more eligible than Sophie.

Sophie told herself in Harriet's voice her bereft feeling was ridiculous. After all, someone attractive enough to take her mind off this oddity in whom she had come to feel a possessive interest could well come along soon.

Young Mr Lewis did just that, his pimples flaming with passion. "M– Miss Sophie, are you going to play? C–capital, nobody sings like you."

When Sophie was called on to sing to the company, *Monsieur* Émile generally rose to pace about.

He did so now.

Her Ladyship snapped, "Do sit down, Émile! You have just caused me to make a mistake in my embroidery!"

He bowed solemnly. "I beg pardon, *Madame.* That will never do."

Sophie, playing the interlude of the song, only just stopped herself from giggling outright.

Sophie felt like sending him a note (if only it was acceptable to correspond with a man).

'Dear Monsieur Dubois or Gilles Long Legs (whichever you are at the moment)

I am sorry I have bruised your feelings and your pride. It was unintentional. You have beaten me down so I am ready to agree there must be something in your belief we met in Paris, if you will only renew your proposals, because I have been taken with you these twelve years and more.

Your Poor Relative
Sophie de Courcy.'

Sophie sang in the music room with only her kitten for an audience, playing the lament from Handel's opera *'Rinaldo, 'Lascia ch'io pianga'** ('Let Me Weep my Unhappy Fate'). Sleet whirled outside, melting the snow in the winter bleak fields on the foothills while the wind buffeted the bare trees.

The kitten gambolled on the rug in front of the blazing fire. The Dowager Countess had given him, born in the autumn to the kitchen cat, to Sophie, who adored him. He was black and white, with a white tip to his tail as though dipped in a paint pot. She often took him with her to the music room.

She felt she needed practice. Lately, Miss Morwenna had taken over Sophie's music lessons. Sophie realised Her Ladyship's companion was lucky to have music lessons at all; still, it was disappointing.

The door opened. *Monsieur* Émile stood there. She paused.

She had longed him to come and renew their talk, horrible as it was. Now he was here she wished he would go away. Still, she was glad she was wearing her new peach coloured day gown which suited her well.

He signalled to her to go on singing, and so she went on to the end. Meanwhile he gave the kitten a smile and paced over to the window to stand staring out across the fields, arms folded across his chest. Of course his presence made her as nervous as on that first evening. Somehow, as then, she managed to sing her song better than she had yet. Certainly, a song about mourning an unhappy fate was appropriate.

At the end he turned to applaud. "Miss Sophie, your voice could melt anyone's heart. How is that for a *cliché?*" He looked singularly bitter.

"Thank you, Sir." She waited nervously.

He came and leaned on the instrument. "I have come further to demean myself. You should find that droll, *Mademoiselle* Sophie. I cannot put you out of my mind. I do love you; I cannot pretend otherwise. You may congratulate yourself, when I have known women enough and none of them have had such an effect upon me since I was a boy."

Sophie glowed with pleasure and trembled with apprehension. "No, Sir, please believe you do me an injustice."

"Do I?" He breathed rapidly.

She jumped up. "You do indeed do me great injustice, Sir. I am sure that you are telling the truth. You are convinced I lie."

Only ladylike inhibitions prevented her from saying, '*I wish I could say I remembered. I would love to have shared a kiss with you. I wish we could begin all over again. I don't want you to forget about me with help from Éloise, either.*'

"Please, *Mademoiselle* Sophie, do not keep on with this pretence! Only tell me you are alarmed by my villainous self, and I will court you more slowly, trying to reassure you that you have nothing to fear, though I am by nature impatient. But we must be honest with each other; I detest hypocrisy. Tell me, *ma petite*, what you were doing in such an area of Paris? I have wondered so long?"

She looked down at the floor, feeling her face red. A romantic novelist would write how she was 'as red as any rose'. She thought probably she looked as florid as a cook on Christmas Day. "*Monsieur* Émile, I would be happy indeed for you to pay court to me. I do not like hypocrisy either, and when you say you love me, I think I could easily return those feelings –" Sophie broke off, as unable to carry on as any of the heroines whose burbling modesty she had scorned as the candle guttered by her bed at Chester.

He was by her instantly, cupping her face in his hands. "Ah, my lovely girl, I knew I could not be so far mistaken about you! I was obliged to live on my wits too long not to be able to judge people quickly. So you give up this pretence?"

She sighed; his caress was delightful. The criminal history of which he had spoken – his being possibly somewhat mad – none of that seemed to matter when he touched her. She looked down at her shoes again. "*Monsieur* Émile, I am not pretending. This is so dreadful! What did happen? It must have been someone else."

His eyes hardened while he dropped his hands as though the skin of her face burnt them. "Then you cannot give me an explanation and I have been a fool."

"I am telling the truth merely, *Monsieur* Émile...Oh!"

He looked at her almost pityingly. "As you cannot explain how you came to be in Revolutionary Paris, *Mademoiselle* Sophie, I must come to a clichéd conclusion about your past adventures. You played the *ingénue* well to take in a cynic such as myself. *Alors,* I repeat you need have no fear I will tell *Madame la Comtesse*. Thank you for not enlightening her about my own discreditable past." He brooded for a few moments, looking at her speculatively.

She stared back at him, resentful under his gaze. Finally he made a dismissive shaking movement and pinched her cheek as though he had a right to touch her. "Now, Sophie, can we understand each other? You know how things are with me. Be kind enough to put me out of my misery. May I be ungallant enough to suggest we discuss the terms of the future relations to which I hope you will agree, before your charms drive me insane quite, and I am led off to Bedlam burbling of them?"

"I don't understand you, Sir." This wasn't supposed to happen to nicely brought up young ladies.

"You have the voice of an angel, which must suffice. Gilles Long Legs has effrontery indeed to reproach you over moral issues, *après tout.* You must forgive my ungallant abuse; every dissolute scoundrel, *ma chère,* cherishes the hope of some innocent girl coming to rescue him from himself. Disillusionment is bitter."

Sophie knew that she should scream or faint. Instead she felt like bandying angry words with him. In a trice he had demoted her from being worthy of being his wife – despite her *déclassé* status as his aunt's companion – into being only good enough to be his mistress. She was so disappointed she felt like bursting into tears. Before she gave in to these tears, however, she was going to give him the tongue lashing he deserved.

"You insult me, *Monsieur* Émile! You insist I was in Paris while I maintain I was not. From this you assume I must have been there due to some disreputable connection and you reason that accordingly, I am unworthy of an honest proposal. How can you speak to your Aunt's dependant so? You should be ashamed to stoop to such ungentlemanly behaviour, even were my past such as you appear to imagine.

'I can make no comment upon how true your recollections concerning your own disreputable past may be; you are however, mistaken about mine. You speak of hypocrisy, *Monsieur* Émile! Were I what you no doubt term a 'fallen women' then I would be no worse than a male rake, however much the world may choose to apply one standard to women whilst winking at immorality in men." She stopped through lack of breath.

During her outburst, his expression changed to one of astonishment. He drew back as if stung, blinking. Evidently, no other women had told him such home truths before. In her passion of disappointment, Sophie was glad to have been the first.

He laughed. "*Mon Dieu, Mademoiselle* Sophie, you are an actress indeed! Rubbish, my girl. It doesn't do, *ma chère,* to pretend to me. You are even more adorable when you are angry. We will get on perfectly, if you give up these insane pretences. Tell me what terms you wish, for at the risk of sounding like a stage rake, I must have you. Should you like to live in Dubois Court in Buckinghamshire? I will make over to you an independent income; if my treatment of you ever drops below the standard which you no doubt require, then you may turn your back upon me betimes."

She winced, too furious to reply. He infuriated her further by running his eyes hungrily over her, much as the Reverend Smythe Jones had gloated over his chops. "Come now, Sophie. Shall I give you a kiss so we can become reacquainted, and to remind you how you do not find me repulsive?"

Her insides quivered. As she paused, lips apart, he began to kiss her at once.

For a moment she responded, overcome with warm pleasure. Coming to herself, she pulled away, trying to recover the situation. He tried to pull her back but she slapped angrily at his hand. He let go and stood breathing heavily and staring at her. He evidently didn't go in for the use of force, which was the only good thing she could think of to say about him at the moment.

"I don't accept your terms, *Monsieur* Émile. It seems to me you should tread the boards also, as a caddish seducer. How many maids have you ruined?"

The moment she spoke, she bitterly regretted the taunt to her old hero. He answered calmly. "None. I have never been the first with any girl."

"You insist I am an adventuress? My family will confirm I was in England at the time you say we met, having never been abroad in my life."

He pinched her cheek again, looking pitying. "*Ma petite!* What else could they say, wishing you to remain in the confidence of *Madame la Comtesse?* Look…" He reached in his pocket and handed her a necklace.

She was speechless. It was identical to the one which had gone missing from her locked jewellery box some time last May. Unaccountably, a chill of fear ran through her.

Finally, she stammered, "But – how came you by this?"

"You know you gave it me, Sophie."

"That is impossible – Oh!" She threw her hands up in despair, and made for the door. He bounded across and caught her hands, necklace and all.

"I want an answer, you tiresome girl. I am becoming fit to be taken to the madhouse, burbling of your wonderful bosom and your irresistible *derrière*. Why are you so difficult?"

"This is awful. You might spare me your coarse remarks. You already have my answer."

"Surely you are not really aiming for my Cousin's title?" He did more eye flashing.

She glared back. "No, *Monsieur* Émile, I am aiming for the door. Please to let me pass." She pulled her hands away.

"You encourage my Cousin, who, being human is not indifferent to your wiles. I think you too ambitious, *Mademoiselle*. Perhaps it was rash in you to dismiss my own foolish offer, which you do not need to flatter yourself I will repeat."

Sophie, her hand on the door, felt if she didn't answer this then she would be angry for the rest of her life. Her words, however, struck her as being ludicrously self-pitying and melodramatic. "No, *Monsieur* Émile, I do not expect an offer from His Lordship. I was delighted at your own, for I had admired your exploits for years. All the time when you lived in danger, I prayed for you every night. But how can I say I remember what I do not, even though this necklace is mine, and you had it? I still will pray for you every night, but it will be as one who uses me ill."

She realised this worthy of Samuel Richardson's *Pamela**, but it was how she felt. She let out a sob, snatching at the doorknob, tears blurring her eyes, aware of him starting towards her again.

The kitten, which had slept on the rug throughout their angry exchanges, sprang to its feet, hissing wildly. It was suddenly icy and still in the room. The flames in the fire and on the candles on the pianoforte died down as though invisibly extinguished. *Monsieur* Émile's eyes dilated. "What the Devil?!"

They turned at a sudden tapping at the window. Sophie gasped as they saw a huge bat bumping against the darkening windows. It was five times bigger than any bat she had seen; worse, its horribly aware, beady red eyes appeared to be watching them. The kitten yowled with anger and fear.

Monsieur Émile flung himself out of the door opening onto the terrace, slamming it shut behind him, and loped down the flight of stone stairs leading to the gardens. She snatched up the kitten and ran over to the window to watch her grand relative down below in the darkening herb garden, searching about in the sleet.

After a couple of minutes he ran back up the stairs, and she realised that the fire and the candles were now burning normally. The room was warmer, despite the draft from the door, but Sophie was shivering uncontrollably as he strode back in, smiling at her. "That was an enormous specimen but harmless, Sophie, I am sure. We must ask Ynyr about it."

"Oh, it was horrible!" she was ashamed to be in tears from the shock.

"Why, you are terrified!" He came over and took her in his arms, kitten and all. Despite being damp from the sleet, he was warmer than she was. "I should not be doing so, eh, *ma petite? Monsieur* Gilles won't take advantage of you in such a state. Come closer to the fire while I mend it."

He drew her over to the fire as before in the library. It was burning brightly again, but he picked up a log and threw it on. Searching about for a poker and not finding one, he kicked the fire into more life. It reminded Sophie of his attack on the fire in the library on Christmas Eve. He must have damaged his boots, for she smelt singeing leather. Given his fondness for clothes, it was nice of him.

She shivered as she sat, still holding the kitten and the necklace. He looked concerned. "It was only a bat, Sophie, not Madoc the Magnificent or any of his relatives. I know you ladies don't like 'em, but they are harmless and have no interest in tangling in ladies hair."

"The c – candles went down."

"An unlucky coincidence, *chérie,* some draught. They would have done so had a mouse looked in. A trick of the light gave the creature those glowing eyes. I know what you need. Wait here." He went out and roared in French down the staircase to the basement. After some moments, she heard Georges' voice yelling back. *Monsieur* Émile bawled some instructions and then came back to her.

"Are you warmer, Sophie?" He came over and taking the kitten from her, put it on the floor, where it shook itself and rushed off. *Monsieur*

Émile laughed and placing the necklace on Sophie's lap, chaffed her hands. "Are you so scared, *ma chére?* Surely you do not believe *ma petite* Katarina's absurd tales of Kenrick and his wife?"

"What does she say?" Sophie guessed even as she asked.

"She insists he and his wife are Half Vampires, having been bitten yet lived to tell the tale, warning me Ynyr and I endanger ourselves in calling there, though happy I am fond of garlic. She has fashioned a wooden cross for each of us. My breath did disgust Kenrick, which no doubt *ma pauvre petite* would take as confirmation that he is indeed a monster bat. *Bien sûr*, it will be no loss for me not to call on him as I cannot endure him.

'He insists he will bridge the gap between superstition and natural philosophy by bringing to it the discipline of mathematics, for which purpose he tried to recruit me. I had to say him nay.

'Katarina has patrolled about this house, armed with garlic, to seal it against him, insisting having been invited in once, he is free to come and go as he chooses.

'Sophie, I am trying to make you laugh and you shudder even more, yet I must not take you in my arms again. We know where that will lead with a rogue like me and you will not have to do with me." He chaffed her hands some more. She burst out, "*Monsieur* Émile, indeed you should not go there! Once I thought I saw him appear by my bed –" she broke off, appalled at what she had said.

He laughed. "I am overcome with envy of the fellow, *ma petite*, and wish you would dream so of me. Ah, and rather more…But I must control myself. That you did so of him does make me dislike him the more."

At a tapping on the door he got up to sneak a quick kiss on the top of her hair before Georges strutted in with a familiar leer and a tray with a little bottle and a cup of hot milk.

"Have you called Agnes, Georges? *Mademoiselle* Sophie had a fright."

As he set the tray down on the side table by the *chaise longue*, Georges said something sneeringly in unintelligible French. *Monsieur* Émile laughed. "Georges thinks the sight of my face was sufficient to cause your state, but I suppose you are become used to its imperfections."

Georges left. *Monsieur* Émile poured what she was sure was brandy into the hot milk. He made her drink it and stood watching her, chatting of trivial things. Just before Agnes bustled in, Sophie said – the brandy having loosened her tongue – "I am much better now. I am ashamed, for I have been behaving like Lucasta in '*Madoc the Magnificent.*' Thank you for being so kind."

"Kind? That is not what you were saying a short time since. It seems to be my fate to treat you for shock, eh, Sophie? But you will not remember the other time when I did so, and you subdued me quite, you infuriating minx." He took the necklace from her, and fastened it about her neck, while his fingertips sent thrills down her spine.

He sighed and she joined in. "Here is Agnes. Agnes, *Mademoiselle* Sophie has seen something unpleasant – do not glare at me so, it was no part of me – and I leave her to your care." He kissed Sophie's hand quickly and his endless legs took him away.

"What was it, Miss Sophie?"

"A giant bat."

Agnes' jaw dropped almost ludicrously. "Oh, Miss! That is what they say all about the villages. "

Chapter Seven

THE LEWIS'S ANNUAL TWELFTH NIGHT ball was due. Agnes worked long making Sophie look as beautiful as possible; she washed her hair in a special mixture of juice from the hothouse lemons and camomile, bringing out the golden lights; she tinted Sophie's eyelashes again with the strange dark mixture which she applied with a thin stick, making them looked twice as long; she polished her teeth with salt until they gleamed.

Then, Agnes brought out the pale blue and silver ball gown which she had been working on for weeks. As she put it over Sophie's head, and it fell in rustling, silken folds to her matching blue dancing slippers, Sophie gasped. "Oh, it looks wonderful!" She had never had a dress half as lovely. "Agnes, you have done a perfect job." She kissed the girl on impulse.

Agnes giggled. "You are looking so lovely that maybe he will go back to proposing tonight, Miss Sophie."

Sophie felt her face go hot. Agnes had stopped troubling to call 'him' by name to Sophie, having divined – without needing her Tarot – there to be only one 'him' for Sophie now.

Despite her flushed face Sophie tried to sound indifferent. "If you mean *Monsieur* Émile, Agnes – that is unlikely. He has been avoiding me since the Quarrel in the Music Room. He has been polite, but distant." She had been unable to resist telling Agnes all the details of her confrontation with *Monsieur*, including his producing a necklace identical to her lost one.

Absurdly, though wondering how the rascal came by it sent an unaccountable shiver down her spine, since he had fastened it about her throat, Sophie was unable to bring herself to take it off. She was even going to wear it – along with a gold locket she had inherited from her mother – to the ball.

"His having your necklace points to something odd indeed, Miss Sophie. Georges says he has never known *Monsieur* Émile in so sour a temper, save when his poor younger brother and sister was killed. When Miss Charlotte died, Georges just said he hardly spoke for a week, isn't it?"

Sophie sighed. "There is no need to remind me how much he has endured, Agnes, or how brave he was in trying to save his family. It does not, however, excuse treating his aunt's dependant so."

Agnes looked at her, eyes sparkling, lips up at the corners. Sophie laughed. "Oh, dear! It is no laughing matter he should make such shocking advances. You look so pretty yourself it is no wonder about Georges..." She looked down to fiddle with her dancing slippers.

"Keep still, Miss! Is a tricky bit with these top curls."

"Agnes, what did Georges say about *Monsieur's* bad temper?"

"It isn't staying awake of nights, because *Monsieur* don't sleep well anyway, but he paces about looking like he is going to a funeral and he shouts about things, which is unlike him. Georges has told him straight he will not endure it and next time it must come to a fight between them. There, Miss, you do look perfect. You must keep on blushing like that."

"Truly, I am not looking forward to seeing Kenrick at the ball."

Agnes nodded. "I don't care what *Monsieur* Gilles says nor Georges neither, what happened in the music room – I mean with the bat, not *Monsieur* – cannot be natural, nor what goes on at Plas Cyfeillgar. Maybe what Katarina says is true. She is making more wooden crosses, and I am going to wear mine just in case, and I want you to wear one too, Miss Sophie, though I suppose you will be wanting one more grand."

"Oh, Agnes! But could a Beneficent Deity allow such things as vampires?"

"I don't see why not, Miss Sophie, seeing as there's them nasty mosquitoes in the world who don't seem so different only smaller. *Nain* did always say isn't it, Miss Sophie, suffering and wickedness is part of the Lessons we Must Learn Down Here...Now, then! No making water in there!" This last was addressed to the kitten, which was sneaking into the dressing room with a tilt to its tail.

When Sophie came shyly down the stairs, the Count and *Monsieur* Émile were already waiting in the Great Hall, standing by the fire with the dogs which forever surrounded it. Sophie thought them both so magnificent and negligently aristocratic she could scarcely credit that she, the *déclassé* Sophie de Courcy, was to be of their party. As they glanced up, *Monsieur* Émile's eyes dilated and even the calmer Lord Ynyr looked impressed.

They bowed greetings (which of course as her social superiors they need not). Meanwhile, *Monsieur* Émile looked on her as Kenrick had on that trifle and Sophie could hardly keep her face straight. For sure, this ball gown was shockingly low, and his protests about her bosom and his sanity came back to her.

Lord Ynyr said, "Miss Sophie, forgive my familiarity, but you do resemble a fairy princess tonight."

A short time ago, Sophie would have been delighted. For all her indignation over *Monsieur* Émile's taunts about her aspiring to Lord Ynyr's title, until these last few days she had allowed herself to dream about it sometimes.

Now the only attention that counted came from a lanky rogue who admitted to a criminal past, who suffered from delusions, who believed she deserved to receive improper advances and who had called her a name she couldn't find in the French dictionary.

"My Cousin is in the right, *Mademoiselle*." The rogue smiled at her.

Perhaps he wanted a truce. Despite his coolness towards her, when last night the Count asked Sophie to put him down for one of the dances, *Monsieur* requested one too. This made Miss Morwenna turn about, looking startled, as she always did when anyone noticed Sophie. Then she had smiled her congratulations to the companion.

Now, at *Monsieur's* words, the world was suddenly brighter. Sophie lectured herself: *Do stop being a fool; this is going to end badly for you. You must not let yourself fall for him like a ton of coals being delivered, never mind Agnes' nonsense.*

Lord Ynyr gaped, and Sophie saw Miss Morwenna coming downstairs, tall and elegant in oyster coloured silk with pearls gleaming in her glossy dark brown hair and at her throat.

Sophie thought she looked magnificent, and she glanced at *Monsieur* Émile, expecting him to be equally struck. To her surprise, his look was only one of mild admiration. He complimented Morwenna with the tinge of familiarity to which he was entitled as a relative, while Lord Ynyr recovered. Morwenna smiled at both the men before turning on Sophie a glance of assessment. "What a sweet frock, Miss Sophie. I expect you are looking forward to this jaunt?"

"I am indeed, Miss Morwenna." Sophie had been to few enough balls to find them wildly exciting.

The Dowager Countess came down the stairs in turn, wearing a magnificent lilac dress and her party face, though she disliked balls. Sophie could see how once you thought yourself too old to dance, balls must lose most of their appeal.

Her Ladyship looked them all over. She seemed satisfied. "You young people are a credit to me. Morwenna and Sophie, *mes chères,* you look delightful both."

Later, Sophie was to remember the stages of this evening as a series of pictures.

Footmen were handing in rugs to the carriage; then followed the jolting trip down the inky lanes to Llandyrnog*, with *Monsieur* Émile telling them about his first ball.

He had imagined he would cut a dash, but through a series of accidents, he managed within five minutes to tear his hostess's ball gown, knock over a candlestick, setting fire to the curtains, and to twist one ankle.

There was chaos outside the Lewis' house in Llandyrnog; the whole front was lit in a blaze of welcome, with carriages drawing up and footmen running about with torches.

Then the Lewis's were greeting them, the butler announcing them; finally they were in the ballroom with the smell of hot wax and music and Sophie's first partner was coming up to claim her.

Here the magic stopped, for this was callow and spotty Mr Lewis. Since he'd started coming out with his mother and older sisters, his infatuation with Sophie increased daily.

Sophie tried to put him at his ease, if only to make him dance better, for he soon began to wander upon her feet and on the hem of her gown. It was a wonder he hadn't emulated *Monsieur* Émile's younger self and knocked over a candlestick and twisted one ankle.

She saw *Monsieur* dancing with smiling Miss Morwenna. She refused to think about whether she felt jealous.

Soon, Lord Ynyr was coming up to claim her. She heard a stout matron sitting by ask her neighbours, "Who may be the young lady dancing with Lord Ynyr?"

"Her Ladyship's companion, a member of a cadet branch of the family. She is quite musical, I hear. It is kind of His Lordship to distinguish her."

"She is rather pretty." The matron spoke as though that was not allowed for poor relatives. "And who is the handsome naval officer with Mr Kenrick?"

"That is Captain Mackenzie, who has lately distinguished himself in a couple of naval engagements. The gentlemen are all agog to hear details, and the young ladies are all of a flutter about his looks, but he seems to have no interest in talking to anyone but Mistress Kenrick. Ahem!"

They exchanged a glance.

Sophie had noticed Captain Mackenzie; this not admiringly, despite his looks. His eyes fixed on her with a sort of gloating interest, but not a warm one. She was reminded of a spider moving towards a juicy fly.

Just then Lord Ynyr danced her past the arch dividing the ballroom, and she saw Mr Kenrick, leaning against a pillar close by and talking with the Captain, who looked like the hero of a book in his officer's uniform, with his sparkling dark eyes, curling dark hair and flashing white teeth.

Kenrick was impeccably dressed tonight (even Georges wouldn't have found fault with his cravat) but with his pudgy face more florid than ever in the heat and his lank hair, he made a dismal contrast to Mackenzie. He stood with his arms behind his back, looking as if everything was beneath his notice. His marble eyes, however, constantly roved over the crowd.

Sophie saw him fix his gaze on the oldest Miss Lewis, plump in white, her hair a profusion of ringlets. His lips twitched, showing his teeth, almost as if he was thinking of taking a bite out of her.

Even here in the crowd in the brilliant light Sophie shivered, remembering how his saliva ran onto her hand and her vision of him by her bed.

He's a vampire!

This ridiculous idea came as a sudden conviction.

Lord Ynyr and Kenrick acknowledged each other, while Sophie made a quick curtsy. As they danced away the Count looked perturbed. "Captain Mackenzie is a dashing fellow."

"Yes, Sir. Is he long with the Kenrick's?"

"I think he has business in your home town, Chester…What think you, Miss Sophie, of the new *décor* of this room? Our own ballroom needs refurbishing, and I was thinking of something similar."

Then *Monsieur* Émile was coming over to claim her. She was shy and looking at her shoes because of the dreadful tingling. At least, she knew that he was tormented likewise.

"You do not need to watch my feet, *Mademoiselle* Sophie, your gown and my ankles are safe enough."

She had to laugh. "That was so droll a story!"

"I saw your youthful admirer dancing upon your toes just now, though you were kind and smiled between wincing." He broke off from laughing to sigh. She saw he looked at the necklace.

She sighed too, to let him know she was as unhappy with the impasse between them. Neither of them said anything for a minute.

Suddenly he said, "I am going to be impertinent and say how beautiful you look tonight, *Mademoiselle*. I haven't had such a lovely partner in years."

She glowed. "Thank you, *Monsieur* Émile. That is a compliment indeed, for you must have danced with many beautiful ladies at the London Assemblies?"

"I have passed many dull evenings there. Should you like to live in Town?"

"For part of the year it would be exciting, but I do love the countryside." She blushed, wondering if he was thinking of his London town house. However, he was being as circumspect tonight as he had since the Scene in the Music Room. Perhaps following her rejection then he was abandoning his pursuit?

She didn't want him to give up his pursuit.

"I prefer the countryside too. The years I spent in Paris wearied me of cities. By the by, I trust you have got the better of the fright that outsize bat gave you? Ynyr was puzzled, suggesting it might be some exotic specimen escaped into the wild."

"But Sir, Agnes said several of the people in the villages claim to have seen such a bat. Surely it cannot be the same one?"

"Come, now, Miss Sophie, I hope you are not going to join with Katarina and the redoubtable Agnes in crediting these superstitions?"

"I think, Sir, Plas Cyfeillgar is a terrible house."

He laughed. "You must not start at shadows. Still, I have found little enough there to tempt me to become an *habitué*."

It was time for them to go in for the refreshments. As *Monsieur* Émile took her in, Sophie wished he could do so always. As he drew out a seat for her, she saw that they were near the Kenrick table.

Sitting there was a great incentive for *Monsieur* Émile to become an *habitué* at Plas Cyfeillgar after all. Mrs Ceridwen Kenrick was ten times more beautiful in her plum coloured gown than Sophie had imagined. Katarina's saying she was a monster seemed both absurd and possible at once, so inhuman was her perfection.

Sophie could only gawp at her incredible, voluptuous figure, her luxuriant black hair, her eyes, dark, flashing and slanting, her sensual lips, always in a pout, her skin as soft and warm as a ripe fruit. She had only one thing to say of such beauty: *Why can't I look like that?*

Monsieur Émile was gazing in open admiration, too – he wouldn't be a man if he didn't. Sophie's heart ached, for as he made his bow, she saw how Ceridwen Kenrick smiled encouragingly, so that Captain Mackenzie's eyes flashed.

The Dowager Countess and Lord Ynyr came up, making cold bows to the Kenrick party. Morwenna came in with an admirer who took supper with them. Sophie realised why she felt she had met Captain Mackenzie before. She had, in the shadows of the hall at Plas Cyfeillgar. Surely, though, he could not have lurked there?

She was too upset at the glances she saw *Monsieur* Émile and Ceridwen

Kenrick exchanging to give it much thought. She could hardly eat any of the refreshments, though she remembered to put some by for Agnes. The Dowager Countess was concerned at her lack of appetite. Sophie reassured her it was the heat and excitement.

Then, the miserable series of pictures began, which her brain ran through over and again in bed.

Monsieur Émile went over to the Kenrick table. He took Ceridwen Kenrick off to dance. Captain Mackenzie glared after them. Kenrick hardly seemed to notice; his eyes roved the room, looking for women over whom to salivate.

Sophie tried not to watch *Monsieur* Émile and Ceridwen Kenrick talking and laughing as they danced, so skilful they need not give thought to their movements. She sat talking to Lord Ynyr.

Morwenna came back from dancing, fanning herself violently and full of bright talk, and Lord Ynyr took her to dance too.

Then Mr Lewis was whining for another dance before Sophie could think of an excuse to avoid one. She trudged miserably about the dance floor with him. He trod on her feet and she didn't feel it. He stepped on the hem of her beautiful new dress and there was a tearing noise and she didn't care. She saw *Monsieur* Émile and Ceridwen Kenrick dance by, both laughing. The youth was asking her something and she had to swallow a great lump in her throat to reply.

Just then, a disturbance broke out at the near end of the ballroom, which opened onto a small annexe. There was a scream; the youngest Miss Lewis ran out, hand to mouth, to collapse into the arms of a dandified man nearby.

He looked astonished but gratified at rising to the occasion in catching her. She screamed again: "Lydia is dead!"

The musicians, ready to start on another tune, paused at this drama, holding onto their instruments. Lydia's mother was nearby, sitting with the other stout dowagers. She leapt to her feet to rush through the crowd, which parted before her. She had perhaps not shown such energy since Lydia herself was conceived.

Émile, Lord Ynyr, and other young men surged forward, as did Morwenna. Sophie feared to get in the way, and stayed where she was. She saw Ceridwen Kenrick exchanging a smile of contempt with Captain

Mackenzie as he sauntered up to her.

Rumours flew through the ballroom. Lydia was dead; she wasn't dead, but soon would be, for she had suffered a fatal injury from a dinner knife; she'd taken too much wine, and lay unconscious on the floor. The less polite guests crowded to try and peer through the half open door.

When Miss Lydia – the girl with the heavy ringlets whom Sophie had seen Kenrick eying earlier – was supported out by her mother and Morwenna, Sophie saw the blood dripping from her throat upon the bodice of her white dress.

The next morning, there was no chance of Sophie hiding her pink, swollen eyes from Agnes, who bathed them in a special lotion. 'There, there, Miss. It will all work out in the end, isn't it?' The eye bath made Sophie's eyes only a little less red and swollen.

"Oh, Agnes!" she sniffed, realising that she was bleating like one of the sheep on the mountain. "I have a terrible feeling."

Fortunately, at breakfast, the others were too distracted to take in Sophie's distress. The Dowager Countess was holding up part of the tapestry to the light and clicking her tongue over it when Sophie came into the sunlit breakfast room. Perhaps she had discovered a Sad Tangle in it. Lord Ynyr was concerned by his watch.

Morwenna was sleepy. Her sharp eyes took in Sophie's swollen ones, but she merely lifted her brows. She was going to travel to a friend's – accompanied by footman and maid, of course – to stay overnight. "I shall be a sluggard today. I wish I had arranged things otherwise, but I wished for diversion the day after a ball, when one is always dull. I suppose you gentlemen go for a gallop over the fields? "

"I think I will take a walk instead." *Monsieur* Émile, who was avoiding looking at Sophie, smiled at Morwenna. Fond of riding though he was, he had the eccentric habit of going about by foot at times. "That is, if my taskmaster can spare the apothecary's assistant this morning?"

Lord Ynyr glanced up smiling from his watch. "I will allow you a holiday, Émile...I fear my watch is stopped."

Monsieur Émile grinned. "Let us hope it hasn't been affected by

Kenrick's experiments with time travel, eh, Ynyr?"

The Dowager Countess looked outraged. "Could Kenrick's Mischievous Experiments do as much? It was a present to Ynyr from the Dear Late Count!"

Morwenna's lips twitched as *Monsieur* assured his aunt, "Your pardon, *Madame,* I jest merely. I am sure that Kenrick's mumbled incantations are ineffectual regarding his own person, let alone anything a mile hence."

Suddenly, Sophie felt at once breathless and disassociated from her surroundings as she saw herself.

She held a new born blond baby, while Monsieur Émile asked her, 'What shall we call him, Sophie?'

As she shook her head, trying to clear it, the odd sensations vanished. Her mind must be playing her tricks through lack of sleep, or she was picking up Agnes' ideas. She blushed, mortified.

"*Vraiment, Madame,* your pardon for making you anxious." *Monsieur* Émile glanced at the great clock on the wall. "Speaking of time, I have an appointment. Do excuse me, *Madame,* Morwenna, *Mademoiselle* Sophie, Ynyr." He walked out swiftly.

Sophie only paused to mutter some excuse before pursuing him as eagerly as he had chased after her that first evening.

He was already some way up the corridor but she scampered after him. "*Monsieur* Émile!"

He stopped, and she saw the tension in his shoulders as he wheeled about, eyebrows raised. "*Mademoiselle* Sophie?"

She felt her eyes wet and her lips twitching as she approached him. "*Monsieur* Émile, please don't go to Plas Cyfeillgar. You may laugh, but I believe Katarina is right in her fears about – about Kenrick, and – and his wife..." she trailed off.

He crossed his arms across his chest. "Why, are you concerned for me, *Mademoiselle*? I am flattered."

"Of course I am! I –"

He gave her his speculative look. "Do you have anything to tell me?"

"Only how I fear for you and I beg you to believe me that I have never lied to you and –"

He shook his head. "Ah, you stubborn minx. *Au revoir.*" He kissed her hand swiftly and bounded off to his doom.

Chapter Eight

THE MANSERVANT WHO ANSWERED THE door at Plas Cyfeillgar made a contrast to the one who had served coffee on Émile's visit with Lord Ynyr. He was tall and if his livery was tight across his shoulders, it was because they were unusually muscular. He was good looking in a florid way, his hair between fair and red. His savage blue eyes met Émile's with hostility.

"I believe *Madame* expects me." Émile handed over his card, which the man took with the tips of his fingers.

They turned at a flicker of light in the passageway opposite. Ceridwen Kenrick was there, smiling and holding out her hands. She was so beautiful in a purple dress that Émile's eyes widened. The man made a bow rivalling Georges' in insolence, span on his heel and marched away.

Ceridwen glanced after him, lips twitching.

"*Madame.* I am delighted to find you at home." Émile kissed her hand lingeringly, moving his lips up her wrist.

"You call upon me betimes, *Monsieur.* I fear Kenrick is out. Would you care for some refreshment? Come to the morning room." Her voice, with its slight Welsh accent, was caressing. "I note you have heeded my wish in keeping from that detestable garlic." She smiled suggestively, and he returned her smile. She turned and went up the icy hallway, while shadows shifted at the sides like a threatening mist.

Émile had eyes only for Ceridwen Kenrick's back view, of her full, round, wonderful hips and *derrière*. Unruly strands of her glossy black hair coiled down the nape of her neck like shiny snakes. It seemed he thought of another full *derrière* he had lately watched, of another, very different nape with strands of fair hair curling innocently, for he paused, looking wretched. Then he swore in an undertone and went on.

She led Émile to the room where Kenrick previously entertained him and Lord Ynyr. A fire burnt there now, but it was scarcely less cold. "Would you care for some refreshment now, *Monsieur?* Red wine, perhaps?" She fixed eyes glowing with mischief on his, and laughed outright, almost as if she knew how as Gilles Long Legs he took a swig of red wine before his dismal breakfast every morning to prime himself for another hateful day.

He pulled his eyes from hers, perturbation flickering in their depths. "Do not trouble, *Madame,* for I know you have some problems with your staff, which I have further depleted in taking Katarina from you."

She came closer. "Yes. So gallant of you! Were the girl not a scrawny child, I might envy her that quixotic rescue at your hands. Speaking of jealousy, how jealous that little girl who is companion to Her Ladyship your Aunt was of me, last night. She was almost in tears. Did you not remark it?" She laughed, her black eyes hard, her voice oddly soft.

He flinched and muttered.

"Does the prissy little thing know you are a ruffian, smuggler and highwayman, *Monsieur* Gilles Long Legs?"

He met her eyes, startled. "*Monsieur* Gilles Long Legs?"

He was lost then, for her eyes locked with his and trapped them. She giggled as she watched his jaw drop and his breathing quicken as he struggled to wrench his dilated eyes from hers.

His eyes glazed over and he stopped struggling.

She said in between delighted laughter, "You are a complete scoundrel, are you not? How shocked Society would be, did they know of one half of the things you have done. But I do not mind. I like it. Come and kiss me, you bloodthirsty ruffian."

Despite her insulting words, maybe he would have obeyed that invitation from such a beautiful woman even if she hadn't put him in a trance. Yet perhaps, too, one part of his bemused mind remembered Sophie, for his expression was partly anguished as he went to kiss her. Then as he began to caress her body, she pulled her lips away.

"*Viens ici, salaud.* Hearken to me, highwayman. When you hear those words, '*Viens ici, salaud*' remember well, you must do as you are commanded.

'Kenrick would have you use his methods – the animation of matter through the use of thought forms – in time travel projects. Such is magic indeed, as you and your milksop Cousin perceived. You are fools to despise such forces.

'I order you to begin investigations therein, for I have an interest in them too. Kenrick will let me amuse myself with you readily enough, if I use my power to subdue your will. He is not so good at inducing a trance as I, is it not so?"

She gave orders to Émile for some time longer, while he stood impassive, listening. Then she passed him a small old book. "Keep it safe and study it." She smiled then, as mischievously as a spirited young girl. "Now you must pleasure me. Come."

She lead him through a door, across a lobby and out through another door, up a narrow staircase. He followed with blank obedience, staring at her, breathing in gasps.

When she came up to a landing – icy, as was the entire house – and lit by fitful sunshine, she paused. "You are an arrogant young buck, Émile Dubois, are you not? I am going to bring you down." She laughed shrilly, like slivers of glass.

He made no demur. His eyes ran over her body with unthinking lust. She opened a door to a room. Inside – incredibly for this house – it was warm. "Come; undress."

He tore off his clothing by the ornate bed, from which the canopy was missing. She looked on him gloatingly. "You are in good condition indeed from all that fighting. I shall enjoy you." She took up a great leather bound book and propped it upon a side table behind the bed, on which she had already placed candles in front of a mirror angled to reflect the ceiling. She took a taper to the fire and lit the candles.

She laughed again. "Kenrick entertained me with your past deeds before. Now, I shall enjoy them once more."

She let down her mane of black hair and it made a heavy cloak to her hips. She flung aside her clothes. Her body was perfect, her breasts big but high and round, her waist small, her belly gently curving, and her hips as full as a semi circle. At the sight, he rushed to seize her, but she pushed him away. "You must wait. Go to the bed."

She strutted to the mirror and taking up a little instrument like a magnifying glass, ran it over the pages of the book. A flickering appeared on the ceiling and gradually resolved itself into a series of three-dimensional images.

She approached the bed. "You will not like looking at that. Keep your eyes on me. We must adopt the conventional position. You can think only of my body. Now, Gilles Long Legs." she drew him down with her onto the bed.

She looked up throughout. At first, she sighed. Then she sank her nails into his back and scratched, while she laughed until the tears ran down her blooming cheeks. "Ah, what a rascal you are! Such brutality! How sweet!"

As they came apart after that first coupling, perhaps the smart of his back – which was now bleeding – recalled Émile partly to himself. He glanced over his shoulder towards the flickering and his eyes dilated in horror.

Moving images below the ceiling played out *Les Messieurs'* brutal deeds in Paris. There was Marcel Sly Boots, there Felix the Professor, there the others, and there was Gilles Long Legs, dictating the action, leading the raids.

Ceridwen Kenrick didn't see the direction of his gaze, for she was lying back on the pillows, mauve lids closed, her fringe of eyelashes curling absurdly long and thick.

Her sculpted features gave nobility to her look; it seemed there could be no connection between her satisfaction and the images flickering above. Her eyes snapped open and she saw he stared at her now with a sort of wild dismay.

"I hope you are not coming to yourself, my adorable highwayman, for I want to enjoy you a good deal more yet. Pleasure me again. You can only think of my body."

The film came over his eyes once more. He pleasured her again. Meanwhile overhead the scenes moved on to Boulogne, and then, Hounslow Heath.

Georges was teaching Agnes to play poker. "The expression, *chérie,* is important. That is why they do say a poker face. Some more brandy?"

"I must not go tipsy to dress my young lady. She has already let me have half the day off to visit Eiluned."

They were alone in the servants' sitting room across from the kitchen. Georges stooped to toss another log onto the fire, and stretched luxuriously. The earlier wintry sunshine had given way to wild, driving winds, howling and buffeting round the manor. Then, over the sound they heard the back door crash open and unsteady footsteps crossing the hall.

"There's someone well in his cups by the sound of it – what the Devil?!"

Émile stood in the doorway, wild eyed. He was dirty and dishevelled, his shirt torn and gaping open to show a throat encrusted with dried blood, his hair in wild disorder and stained with blood too, his hands and arms dirty and covered in cuts, his fingernails broken and filthy.

He staggered over to a chair and leaned on it. "Georges – don't let anyone else go there! It was a wild beast tearing at me."

Georges jumped up. "*De quel idiot,* have you got yourself bitten by a mad animal? Agnes, stoke the kitchen fire and put on the kettle!"

Agnes rushed to do so. Meanwhile Georges sat Émile down in the chair, trying to find out what had happened. Émile denied he had been bitten by an animal, though he said again that Ceridwen Kenrick wasn't human. Georges saw tiny pieces of glass in his hair.

Whatever had happened, he was in a fever and making no sense. Georges and Agnes treated his wounds as they would had he been bitten by a rabid creature.

By a fluke, all the kitchen staff was away. The cooks and the kitchen maid were using the slack time of day for a trip to the village; the scullery maid was ill with the malaise which had been going about since before Christmas; the laundry maid was kissing the stable boy in the tack room.

Agnes cleaned the wound on Émile's neck. Her voice shook. "Georges, this wound is strange. It's as though it was made by two prongs."

Émile shifted under the scalding heat of the hot compresses. "It was That Jade, the disgusting –" He broke off, retching.

Georges jumped back, but not in time. "*Merde!* All over my best boots."

Katarina, alerted by some instinct, stood alarmed in the kitchen doorway. "What ails *Monsieur*?"

Georges – mopping his boots with his handkerchief – spoke heartily, "It is probably only the sickness going about, Katarina, but he seems to have cut himself nicely, so we thought it best to take care of those. Mop the floor, girl. Gilles, you could have avoided my boots. Agnes, we must put him to bed."

Katarina rushed up to Émile as he sat, still heaving. "Oh, *Monsieur*, you are very ill!" She dug in her pocket for the handkerchief he had given her and handed it to him. "Did you go to Plas Cyfeillgar?"

Émile slurred, "I am sorry, *ma petite*, to make such a disgusting mess." He staggered to his feet and swaying, rummaged in his pockets to hand her a tip which would cover her old wages for half a year.

Georges and Agnes took an arm each and helped him from the room. Katarina began to blubber as she went for a mop.

The wind howled about the roofs as Sophie practised in the music room. She had brought Jem the kitten with her, hoping his antics might divert her from this agony of jealousy and anxiety hounding her through the day. Her tears after *Monsieur* bounded off to Plas Cyfeillgar hadn't relieved her; more pricked behind her eyes continually, threatening to fall.

At one point Jem climbed half way up the priceless brocade curtains. She broke off from an aria from Mozart's '*Don Giovanni*' '*Il me Tradhita*' ('I Still Pity Him') to catch him.

She was laughing for the first time that day as Agnes came in. "Agnes, you shiver; come and warm yourself by the fire, there is a bitter East wind – What ails you?!"

But she knew; she sensed it as surely as she had sensed last night that Mr Kenrick was a vampire.

"Miss, we thought you might like to know. *Monsieur* Émile is come back from Plas Cyfeillgar in a terrible state." As Sophie stared wordlessly, Agnes went on, "He is in a fever, making no sense and he spewed all over

Georges' boots." Her lips twitched even in her concern. "Georges and I just put him to bed. A fight we had of it, too."

Sophie felt a surge of relief. "It may well be only the affliction of the stomach has been about."

"But Miss, he has funny punctures in his throat, and is cut too and says she is a wild creature – Mistress Kenrick, he means."

Sophie tried to speak calmly. "I will come and see what is to be done." *How absurd! As if there is anything I can do to help him now!*

Georges looked solemn as he opened the door. "They are ruined!"

"Oh, do be quiet about those wretched boots, Georges!" Agnes pushed him.

Sophie expected *Monsieur* Émile to look dishevelled and feverish, but the sight of him with his hair in wild, blood spattered tangles – in which some specks of glass still glittered – his face flushed, his eyes over bright, his hands and arms covered in cuts, alarmed her. She stole closer. Her heart lurched as she saw the puncture marks on his neck. She had prayed Agnes might be somehow mistaken.

She expected a hostile reception, but he smiled and muttered, "*Ma chére,* you choose to come to me now. You must give me time to get the better of this."

Georges turned to hide his smile. Sophie felt herself doing an imitation of a radish. "I have come to see if I can do something for you, *Monsieur* Émile, hearing you are ill." She put a hand on his forehead, which was hot enough to alarm her. "We must sponge him down, Agnes." This would be improper, of course, but she didn't care.

Agnes looked uneasy. "Georges and I did so half an hour since, Miss Sophie, with him cursing us throughout."

"Then we must do so again."

Agnes went to put a saucepan of water on the fire to warm to tepid. Georges wandered off to the dressing room, muttering bitterly. "A *Comte* sent his man over to enquire where I came by those boots…I heard they started a fashion at St James*…"

Sophie was shy of sponging down *Monsieur* Émile, but in fact, what with the sickness and the dried blood in his hair, he smelt unpleasant enough for there to be nothing erotic about touching his bare flesh, despite his spare and muscular body.

When they persuaded him to turn about, and they saw the long, inflamed scratches on his back, she was astounded. She found herself wondering for a moment if an animal could have done that to him after all.

Then, meeting Agnes' eyes, she realised Ceridwen Kenrick had made those cuts in a sexual encounter.

The world seemed to spin. Looking down at *Monsieur* Émile again, she felt like running away from this horror he had brought upon himself in his sexual abandon with such a monster. No wonder he called Ceridwen Kenrick a wild animal! From nowhere the memory came to Sophie of Kenrick nipping at her hand with his sharp white teeth, like some playful, unattractive puppy.

Agnes said, "Is proper rude *Monsieur* Émile was to the Count earlier, isn't it? His Lordship came offering his herbal remedy, and *Monsieur* told His Lordship to go to take his damned weeds to the Devil. Poor Lord Ynyr drew back all hoighty-toighty. '*I will overlook your rudeness, Cousin, for you are not yourself.*'"

Sophie stood struggling with herself. As if she sensed this, Agnes waited.

The villain shifted slightly, muttering, helpless in his delirium. Sophie knew then that she loved him too much to turn away from him whatever he had done. After they sponged him down, she stood and sighed. She was not looking forward to nursing a delirious and spewing *Monsieur* Émile after his treatment of her, but she couldn't bear to let anyone else take care of him either. She was thankful Miss Morwenna would be away until tomorrow.

When she and Agnes had to leave for Sophie to get ready for dinner, Éloise came up to take over, full of sympathy for '*Pauvre Monsieur*'. Sophie felt a further stab of possessiveness. Would Éloise be so eager to look after him if she knew he had probably been made into a – Sophie might as admit it – Man Vampire? She wondered that she wasn't more frightened of him, herself. Yet, surely the transformation couldn't happen in hours? How unbelievably terrible it all was. She must ask Katarina.

"*Zut alors,* Sophie, my nephew is come back ill from his walk and somehow cut himself. I cannot imagine what he has been about."

The Dowager Countess actually allowed herself to pace across the sitting room in her agitation. "*Après tout,* he is never ill, yet he has this sickness worse than any of the footmen and is delirious. We will have Dr Powell tomorrow. It is too bad dear Morwenna is absent; she would have it all in hand directly. I do not know how we shall manage about nursing him. I am not able for it myself, I cannot impose on my maid Mrs Brown, and our housekeeper *Madame* Blanch is ailing herself, though she promises to look in."

Sophie wasn't surprised the Dowager Countess couldn't impose on Mrs Brown to nurse *Monsieur.* Agnes said Mrs Brown detested him and Georges too, trusting they would both eventually meet with hellfire.

"I would be happy to look after *Monsieur* Émile, Your Ladyship." Sophie was anxious in case the Dowager Countess might forbid this as improper. "I am sure Agnes, Éloise and Katarina will be happy to help, and if *Madame* Blanch or the under housekeeper does look in now and then, we shall easily manage."

The under-housekeeper was much bribed by *Monsieur* Émile regarding Katarina's training, but unlikely to exert herself for anyone. Sophie hoped the Dowager Countess would find *Monsieur's* care by unmarried girls respectable with two matrons nominally involved.

"Sophie, this is kind in you. It is unfortunate my nephew should be ill when my silks need matching, but *après tout,* his health must come first."

———⁂———

Sophie got back to *Monsieur* Émile's rooms to find Katarina, clutching a jar of dried herbs and arguing with Éloise at the door. "I work for him, you don't!" They broke off to curtsey to Sophie.

"How now, Éloise?"

"*Monsieur* doesn't want any of those nasty herbs, *Mademoiselle.* He told the Count before you came." The girl must have rushed her bright chestnut hair, long eyelashes and other charms along to *Monsieur's* rooms as soon as she heard of his illness.

"I believe *Monsieur* would take the medicine were he in his full senses. Come then, Katarina."

Monsieur Émile was either asleep or in a stupor. Éloise sat by him while Sophie drew Katarina away where they could talk in whispers.

The girl said tearfully, "I saw his neck when he came in, Miss Sophie. We have to give him these to stop the poison or he must be a monster too."

Sophie's knees went weak at her terrors being put into words. "But – do you really believe these will prevent – such a thing – from happening?"

"There is a fair chance, but we will not know for some while."

Sophie sniffed anxiously at the herbs, which smelt strongly of garlic. "What are they?"

"Rosemary, sage, thyme, mint and garlic. He must have at least ten doses over two days..." Sophie's head whirled with horror, so she couldn't take in the rest of Katarina's information.

There was nothing to lose if they could persuade the awkward patient to drink the herb tea. Sophie and Katarina quickly made it.

They took the drink over to *Monsieur* Émile and gently roused him from his torpor.

"Marguerite, *ma petite*, have you something to show me?"

Sophie supposed he mistook Katarina for his youngest sister. Then, she saw that he was looking eagerly at a point to the left of Katarina, where some odd reflection from the candles and the fire was producing a flickering trick of the light in mid air.

Katarina eyed it too. Éloise, pouting disapproval as she poked the fire, didn't notice.

Sophie felt mean as she said duplicitously, "She wants you to have this drink she made, Sir."

He took it and sipped some, then grimaced. "*Tres bien*. I will save the rest for later – What?" He looked back at the shifting glow. "If you insist." He gloomily went back to sipping it. "No, stay! Tell me what you have been about today – "

The flickering was gone. He stared at the point where it had been, then with a sigh subsided back against the pillow, eyes closed, dropping the cup before Sophie or Katarina could catch it, spilling the remainder of the herbal brew on the floor.

Éloise smiled to herself.

Sophie followed Katarina to the dressing room to ask, "How came you by these herbs, Katarina? Are they the Count's?"

"Oh, no, Miss Sophie, I had them hidden in my box at Plas Cyfeillgar. After *Monsieur* took me from there, he had my things sent for and the herbs were still there." Katarina turned an adoring glance back at her rescuer.

"Find a cloth, dear, we must try again later."

Madame Blanch, the housekeeper, did look in for one minute. "How is the patient, *Mademoiselle* Sophie? So unfortunate I have the malady myself, and must dose myself with brandy. *Monsieur* would go out without an overcoat, which has probably caused the mischief."

Monsieur Émile wakened only to vomit. Then Sophie and Katarina had to examine the bowl's contents to see how much of the herbs were in it. They thought about half, which meant he had only retained a quarter dose so far. Sophie wrinkled her nose and Katarina went to make some more of the tea.

"Are you sure it is helping him and not making him worse, Miss Sophie?" Éloise demanded.

"It helped the others."

When they brought *Monsieur* Émile some more of the tea, he looked outraged. "Take that damned stuff away! It's you, Sophie?"

"Of course I am here. Please drink some of this. It will help you, please believe me."

Katarina whispered, "*Monsieur*, you must drink it, if you are not to become One of Them."

Whether he remembered Ceridwen Kenrick drinking his blood, Sophie didn't know. He seemed to be thirsty and swallowed some of it before looking at her resentfully. "Anyway, you have forgotten me."

Éloise was listening avidly. Sophie reddened. "I could never do so, Sir."

Horror lurked at the back of his eyes. "Everything is ruined; why is that?"

Sophie sat down on the bed without thinking. "This will help." He swallowed some more but then began to doze, leaning against her as on Christmas Day in church. She would like to put her arms about him, but instead she settled him back on the pillows.

Agnes and Georges came in. Éloise, needed downstairs, had to leave, promising to be back in the morning.

"*Ça va, Gilles?*" Georges looked down at his accomplice with reluctant tenderness. "Never could stay out of trouble for more than five minutes, could you?" He led Agnes off to the dressing room, where he often spent the night.

Sophie preferred not to think about what they might be doing. Weeks ago, she would not have credited a nice girl like Agnes behaving so, especially with such a rascal. Lately, her ideas had been shaken through her own infatuation with just such another rascal. She glanced anxiously at Katarina, but the girl appeared either oblivious or indifferent to the goings-on in the dressing room. Sophie settled her on a chaise lounge near the fire with a blanket.

Those words from Miss Morwenna and the Dowager Countess on Sophie's first evening came back to her, '... *There is a book of old vampire lore on the shelves here...Someone presented it to the Dear Late Count, knowing of his interest in myth...*'

Sophie must read it, and ask Katarina more besides. She sat down by the bed in a stupor of horror. *Monsieur* Émile dozed or rambled in French or English. Sometimes he swore in both languages. Once he urged her, "That Jade – keep away from the place, Sophie."

A couple of times he said, "*Viens ici, salaud.*"

Gradually, the household wound down for the night. The sounds of footsteps and distant voices died away. The tickings and creakings of a night house took over.

Sophie roused. The candles were guttering and a chill silence fell on the room. She knew what was coming before she heard the tapping at the window. She looked about wildly, wondering if she dared go and knock at the dressing room door. Her inhibitions outweighed her terror, and she didn't.

Suddenly, she knew she must see what was outside the window. She tottered on jelly legs to wrench back the curtain, her fingers as stiff and awkward as if she had sat on them an hour.

A giant bat hovered outside, staring at her with malevolent red eyes.

She fell away from the window, dropping the curtain. She found herself back by *Monsieur* Émile's bed – he was in no state to protect anyone this time – and dropping to her knees, she began to pray desperately.

"Oh Lord, protect us. Please let him not become a vampire. Let there be a cure."

Katarina had joined her. Then she became aware of *Monsieur* Émile, propped up on one elbow. He looked outraged and said hoarsely, *"Taisez-vous!"*

She hoped this was annoyance at being disturbed and his general irreligiousness rather than a sign that he was turning into a monster.

She squeezed Katarina's hand and coaxed *Monsieur* to lie down. Now the candles were burning steadily and the fire had flared up one more. She put a hand on his brow. "Katarina, we must sponge him down again."

While Katarina warmed the water, she stood by the bed stroking his forehead. He made no objection, seemingly soothed by it. It soothed her too.

Agnes and Georges came out of the dressing room, Agnes flushed and happy, Georges looking more conceited than ever. "How does *Monsieur?*"

"Very ill. We must have Dr Powell look at him as soon as may be." *To prescribe a cure for vampirism? How absurd. Certainly, no blood letting will be required; Monsieur has had more than enough of that.*

"Off to bed with you, Katarina." Agnes said briskly. "We will take good care of your precious master. There is no need to refuse to leave his side like a faithful dog."

"He needs the cure."

They argued in whispers. Georges jeered at the girls' terrors. "Vampires? Your Tarot nonsense was bad enough before, Agnes, but this! Are you saying Kenrick sleeps in a coffin like them things is said to do – with such a wife? Still, I do not want to say too much before you, Katarina, *ma petite.*"

"No, he doesn't need to avoid daylight, for he is not a full vampire, nor she. But they are dangerous monsters, nevertheless. *Monsieur* will be as they are, if he does not take a cure."

"*Quel idiocy!* There is a big bat been kept as a pet escaped and Gilles Long Legs has the illness the others had merely."

Agnes demanded, "What think you of the bites on his neck, Georges?"

"Done falling over in them mountain bushes as he staggered home."

Yet Georges made no objection to their using the herbs; his own mother in Provence had used herbal medicines. "*Alors*, it will make *Monsieur* laugh when he gets the better of this. Fear not, I'll keep your wild ideas to myself. Little wonder you wish them to be secret…There he is, spewing again. I will leave him to your care, *Mademoiselles.*"

Sophie kept telling herself she would go to bed shortly. She woke at about six, with her face buried in the covers of the bed. Agnes slept in another chair next to her, her cap disarranged, while Katarina dozed on the *chaise longue*, and Sophie thought they looked adorable.

In the icy drawing room at Plas Cyfeillgar, *Kenrick* was complaining about the cost of replacing the window Émile had broken in escaping.

Ceridwen Kenrick distracted herself by looking across the room at her reflection, thankful as a half human she had one. She liked to reassure herself by looking at her beauty; this shocking pink dress, cut off the shoulder, brought out the warm tones in her skin, setting off her inky hair.

A detached part of her mind spoke, as it did sometimes, try not to think as she would: *Your beauty is all you have left in life. Your emotions are no warmer than those of that monster sitting opposite you, complaining of domestic trivia.*

"I am minded to send the ruffian the bill. Firstly he sees fit to steal one of our skivvies, now this. To be sure in his past there are enough of those scenes of blood and gore with which you entertain your sweet self, my dear. Did he see your display, to react with such violence he could overcome Arthur? Usually our conquests are torpid."

Ceridwen played with her rings. "I regret he may have seen it. He seemed to object to my taking his blood, too. It is strange how humans resent that particular intimacy. He was in a trance when I left to deal with one of our domestic crises. I returned to see *Monsieur's* exit. I have not enjoyed such entertainment since I saw that play on Robin Hood.

'Arthur loves a fight and picked up the nearest weapon from the hall, but Gilles Long Legs had a cutlass. I was entertained by a fight worthy of Robin Hood escaping from Nottingham Castle. *Monsieur* managed to wound poor Arthur – one of us though he is – then kicked out the glass of the window and hurled himself through."

Kenrick scowled. "Women pretend to detest violence, yet they thrill to a fight. Such hypocrisy! Scarce wonder Captain Mackenzie is such a success with the ladies. He is worse than Dubois, which is saying much. The man is like a Marquis of whom I heard lives in Dubois' part of France – what is his name, *Comte* de Sade?* Still, what woman have I known who is not a Jade masquerading as a domestic goddess? Do I see a blush, Madam? No, it would be too maidenly. I digress.

'Regarding that ruffian Dubois, he is a criminal, and we must remember how their brains aren't those of the normal human. As he came so early to himself, I hope that he will respond to the orders you put in his warped mind?"

"I am sure of it, you need have no fear."

"Good. Both he and that ineffectual Lord avoided my gaze, but I knew I could rely on my little wife." He reached over to chuck her under the chin and she jerked her head away.

He rose and went to drop a kiss on her shoulder, while she shuddered. He laughed outright. "Good night, my dear. Stay not awake for me."

She didn't smile. "There is little chance of that."

"Are you ready to leave for Chester tomorrow? I collect Alick Mackenzie will meet us betimes? Arthur comes too if he is sufficiently recovered. Dear one, you are spoilt for choice quite."

He was gone.

She went over to the cabinet and took out the heavy book, mirror, candles and little glass. She hurried up to her bedroom, sighing with relief as she shut the door behind her, though of course, no door could keep out Kenrick.

She set up the book, and worked some time on the flickering lights and the shadows plunging on the ceiling. She swore, while beads of sweat and faint lines showed on her brow.

At last, she was rewarded. A solid Georgian house appeared above her, and she honed in ever closer until she had a bright nursery where stood a family group. A dark and lovely girl, her face so soft she was hardly recognisable as Ceridwen herself, held up a baby for the admiration of the man, handsome, blond and dandified, who smiled on them. She put the baby down on the rug, where she crawled and chuckled while they watched her.

115

Ceridwen spared no glances for the man, her eyes fixed on the baby. She let out a sob, but no tears came. She breathed hard, clutching her hands spasmodically: "Marcie!" She jumped up and flung open her arms.

While the baby seemed always about to crawl down from the ceiling, she never did.

Ceridwen stared in torment, her face distorted, while the visions above ran on. Once she gave a violent jolt, seemingly pulled slightly upwards. She shrieked, "Yes!" but the movement ceased. She covered her face, and groping, slammed the book to, cutting off the pictures and the gurgling.

Monsieur Émile continued in a delirium the next morning. The Dowager Countess sent for Dr Powell.

Sophie was snatching a couple of hours' sleep in her own bed when the doctor arrived, but Éloise told Agnes how Georges and Dr Powell had to restrain *Monsieur* Émile while he cursed the Doctor for a sneaking Bow Street Runner. Why he should object so to a visit from one puzzled Éloise. Sophie could imagine Georges' inscrutable look.

At breakfast, the Dowager Countess said mournfully, "It is good of you to take so much of the burden of nursing my nephew upon yourself, *ma chère.* It is too bad he should need your care now, when many of the staff are sick too, there are people ill in the village, another baby is due, the flowers are wilting in the dining room though we have the Bishop to dinner tonight and my sewing is somehow all of a tangle. "

"All this, dear *Madame*," smiled Lord Ynyr, "Only serves to show how invaluable Miss Sophie is become to us."

"Thank you Your Lordship, you are too kind." A couple of weeks back, Sophie would have batted her eyelashes at him. Now if her lids drooped it was through fatigue.

The Count went on, "Dr Powell says Émile will be better directly. The others are recovering and the doctor is quite won over to plant cures. I am happy you have prevailed on our awkward patient to take the herbs I left with him, Miss Sophie."

Sophie forced a smile before sipping her coffee. She usually drank tea, but wanted something stronger this morning. Over this elegant breakfast table it was impossible to credit how Her Ladyship had far more cause to worry than she knew. Gazing through the great window at the lightening sky, Sophie was glad that from this side of the house the roofs of Plas Cyfeillgar weren't visible.

Katarina told Sophie the sooner the cure was begun, the more effective it would be. Now, however, Éloise was with *Monsieur,* probably disobeying Sophie's orders to give him only the herb tea.

What an annoying girl she is, with her heaving bosom and sparkling eyes. Admit you fear your scoundrel of an admirer might transfer his interest to her, Mistress Kenrick having proved to be so savage a mistress.

Sophie had thought of telling Éloise the truth, but Agnes jeered: *"As well tell the town crier. Before we knew it that hen gast (old bitch) Mrs Brown would be trotting to the Dowager Countess and is most likely we would all be locked in our rooms as lunatics."*

Sophie thought over confiding in Lord Ynyr. Surely, he would dismiss her stories as lightly as Georges, though certainly with more punctilio.

Yet as they left the breakfast room, she found herself asking, "What think you, Sir, of the wounds on *Monsieur* Émile's neck?"

He gave her his kind smile. "Do not trouble yourself. Dr Powell is sure it is not the bite of a mad animal. Émile himself will tell us how he came by them when he is recovered and knowing him, jesting the while."

The Dowager Countess turned back. "*Alors,* Miss Morwenna will be back this afternoon to organise us all."

------ ⌾⌾⌾⌾⌾⌾⌾⌾⌾ ------

Miss Morwenna swished her russet dress into the sickroom shortly after two. As Sophie rose from her seat by the bed, she frowned on the Poor Relative accusingly. "Whatever has happened to *Monsieur* Émile?"

Sophie found herself stammering guiltily. "*Monsieur* Émile returned ill from his walk."

"He was well in the morning. But he is cut, too! Émile, is there anything I can fetch you?"

Émile opened his eyes. "Morwenna, I need my knife. Where's Georges? He must come with me."

"Why, you poor thing, you are wandering in your wits. Éloise, go for the cordial *Monsieur* likes sometimes. What is this dismal looking potion? Ynyr's herbs, for sure, ugh, and garlic, too. Very well, but I do swear by the cordial."

She dismissed Katarina and Sophie. "There are too many people here; anyone would think it was an assembly. I will see *Monsieur* Émile takes Ynyr's precious herbs…Please don't argue further, Miss Sophie!"

Biting her lip, Sophie went to the library. As she opened the door she remembered the scene with *Monsieur* Émile here. Fighting back a sob, she began to search the shelves.

The book on vampire lore wasn't on any of the lower shelves, though there seemed to be books about everything else. She couldn't find the catalogue, so looking for a section on myths, she scanned memoirs, maps, collections of sermons, scientific volumes and medical books. There were few on plant cures, for Lord Ynyr kept these in his laboratory.

Sophie pulled across the short ladder, hoisted her skirts carelessly and scaled it.

Finally, she came upon the selection on the top shelf over by the statues. She pulled out fully a hundred books, sneezing in the dust she dislodged, but found nothing on vampires. She turned impatiently at a knock at the door.

Agnes came in, giggling. "Oh, dear, Miss Sophie, is funny, though poor *Monsieur* Émile! You are wanted in the sickroom."

"By Miss Morwenna?"

"Miss Morwenna is too squeamish to watch *Monsieur* spewing up like a fountain, and is run away saying she has an idea for the dinner table tonight."

Over the next couple of days, Sophie became so tired that later she could never remember what happened sequentially. *Monsieur* Émile remained in a fever. She, Katarina and Agnes dosed him with the herbs, he brought most of them up again, and Sophie pulled her hair in frustration.

Agnes spent the earlier part of each evening with Georges in *Monsieur* Émile's dressing room. The rest she spent with Sophie, sitting up by him, while Katarina slept in snatches on the *chaise longue*. The sultry Éloise came as often as she could.

Miss Morwenna looked in to lay a tender hand on *Monsieur's* brow and then left quickly. *Madame* Blanch, the under housekeeper, Lord Ynyr and Her Ladyship looked in at the sick chamber, but never stayed long. Not calling in during the night, they never surprised Sophie sleeping with her head on the bed.

Sophie went on failing to find a book on vampire legends in the library.

Finally she caught Lord Ynyr alone. She thought she must seem furtive as she tried to conceal her desperation. "Your Lordship – you might consider this morbid, but I am interested in the book on vampire lore Her Ladyship once mentioned."

The Count's eyebrows shot up. "My dear Miss Sophie! I hope you are not joining Miss Morwenna in a fascination with the supernatural?"

"No, Sir, but I am interested to learn how people reconcile such beliefs with Christianity."

The Count smiled. "I doubt they trouble their heads about the finer points of theology. I think you will find a book in the library written by a believer who credits such nonsense. You know our librarian was obliged to take several weeks of absence, leaving a pile of books in that antechamber across from the library where he does his cataloguing. It might be among those. Do you know, Miss Sophie, these last few weeks absurd rumours have started in the villages? The Vicar is outraged. Perhaps it was these roused your curiosity?"

Tired though Sophie was, she sang after dinner each day. Morwenna said teasingly as they exchanged places at the piano, "Miss Sophie, I am more anxious than you over *Monsieur* Émile – having known him since the nursery – but you have lost your colour sadly, whereas I am determined to keep mine."

On the third evening, the Lewis family came to an informal dinner.

Sophie wore her peacock blue dress. When she sang after dinner, the younger Mr Lewis stood by the instrument, turning the pages of her music and looking intense. Morwenna gave them quizzing glances. Sophie was confident the youth would soon get over his infatuation. Hers with *Monsieur* was a different matter.

Soon, she left the company (young Mr Lewis's face fell absurdly) and went up to the sick chamber, first changing into her ordinary grey dress.

Agnes told her *Monsieur* Émile's fever was lifting before going with Georges to the dressing room. Katarina agreed to go to bed at last. Yawning, she explained how now the fever was abating, after one last dose tomorrow, the cure must be stopped. Meanwhile, it would be impossible to tell if it was working, as either way, *Monsieur* must develop 'Symptoms' over the next few weeks.

"Tell me what those might be?" Sophie tried to steady her voice.

Katarina's voice shook too. "In the Half Vampire, the teeth and nails sharpen, the monster side comes to the fore and the thirst for blood."

Despite herself, Sophie shivered. She put on a bright tone. "We shall not worry about that for now. You have been wonderful, dear." She kissed the girl, but then couldn't stop herself from asking, "Are there other cures?"

"Yes, Miss, but they cannot work yet..."

Sophie was left alone with *Monsieur*. She sat by the bed righting the Dowager Countess' embroidery and then her crochet work.

He kept his eyes closed and seemed to be asleep. She knew he wasn't. When she got up to do chores, she felt his gaze on her. Once, turning quickly, she even saw the glint of his eyes before he could close them.

Finally, tossing aside the crochet work, she moved her chair closer to the bed, and began to stroke his forehead. He allowed this intimacy, she supposed for the last time. Suddenly, he opened his eyes and looked full at her, his gaze going to her throat.

For a horrible moment, she feared he was thinking of biting her, but he muttered, "That necklace."

She said, "I swear I know not how you came by it, but you see I have worn it since you put it about my throat."

He was about to speak when there was a flickering. Sophie glanced about, saw it was coming from somewhere about the ceiling, and gasped in terror as pictures formed and spread down, so they were all about the canopy of the bed.

Monsieur Émile was clutching her to him, his eyes dilated as he pulled her head down onto his shoulder, hiding her face. "Not those accursed scenes from that Jade!"

But far worse – ludicrously too – they were both drawn up towards the moving shapes, which had solidified into crowded buildings, a squalid street. They were still clinging on to each other, and floating, as if in a dream. It was incredible; it was impossible, but it was happening. They struggled against being drawn into those living images, but the pull was inexorable.

"It's Paris. Keep with me, Sophie!" Despite being weakened by illness, he held Sophie so tightly he hurt her – and she clung to him with all her strength – but they were wrenched apart. She landed in Revolutionary Paris by herself.

Chapter Nine

Paris
May 1794

S OPHIE CAME DOWN GENTLY ON some cobbles in the middle of a narrow street. There was a strong smell of urine and rotting vegetables. *Monsieur* Émile was nowhere in sight.

Before she could think, a cart clattered past, the owner turning to shout at her as it clattered away.

Sobbing, she staggered to her feet, dizzy, her heart hammering so that she could scarcely breathe. She stared about desperately. The street was dark and narrow with rubbish littered at both sides. She noted a couple of primitive looking shops. It was warm, thankfully, and from the light that filtered down even into this narrow, dark alley, she guessed it must be some time in the afternoon.

A hulking, seedy looking young man was hurrying over to her, speaking in French. He was acting out concern, pretending to help her to her feet, but she could tell he felt none. He groped her breast with one hand and tried to get to her pocket with the other.

"Ugh!" She slapped at him furiously.

Laughing nastily, he felt at her bodice again while another man came up, eyeing her intently. On top of everything else, her assailant smelt of old sweats and dribbled urine. His teeth as he leered at her were rotten.

Disgusted, she slapped at him again. His accomplice was laughing delightedly. At this second blow the man became angry. Swearing, he slapped her back, catching her on the side of the face. She shrieked and an approaching man shouted. The lout snatched at her pocket, and a large woman ran towards them, yelling. The accomplice turned and ran, and Sophie's assailant took one look at the woman and ran fast too.

Sophie let out another hysterical sob. The middle-aged man was pressing enquiries. Her head whirled and she felt in a nightmare, unable to answer even in English. Meanwhile a young workman joined in the chase.

Everything was confused. "*Anglaise?*" another woman was asking. A group was assembling as Sophie tried to gather her wits.

The situation was desperate. *Monsieur* Émile had said the images were of Paris. She was in France, a country at war with her own, without money and with only a rough knowledge of the language. She knew no-one except her missing relative, who was somewhere here, half naked and ill. What could she do to help them both?

Then, she remembered his insistence on their having met in Paris.

"*S'il vous plaît, quelle date sommes-nous aujourd'hui?*" She knew the phrase well from her governess.

The man stared; certainly, she had spoken breathlessly, and her accent wasn't good. She repeated herself. He said something about '*mai.*'.

Of course! She had fallen asleep unaccountably on her bed last May.

The large woman came panting back, swearing. The louts and the workman in pursuit must have outrun her. Sophie asked hopelessly, "Gilles Long Legs?"

"Gilles Long Legs?" The woman looked Sophie up and down in surprise. She fired off questions which Sophie couldn't follow, then said something about 'Adeline's'. "*Viens.*" She took Sophie's arm. She smelled sweaty, too, though nothing like as bad as the youth. She led Sophie down the narrow, dirty street, away from the crowd, talking meanwhile.

Sophie's legs felt wobbly and her cheek hurt from that slap. The woman held her arm, and Sophie found her support helpful. The woman was so strapping Sophie was sure she was never troubled by assaults from seedy youths.

Ridiculously, Sophie brushed at her dress and fretted her hair had been disarranged in the fight. She realised her dress was the grey one that had seemed to mean so much to *Monsieur*.

The woman took her across a road scarcely wider than the narrow passage, avoiding another cart laden with produce. A group of small boys stampeded past. They passed a man selling vegetables, shouting so loudly Sophie wondered he didn't injure himself. He wore the red hat that for her was an object of terror.

The woman led Sophie down some roughly fashioned steps littered with rubbish to another lane. Facing them was an eating house with a couple of tables wedged into the narrow space outside.

A long lanky man in a scruffy brown breeches and waistcoat, shirt sleeves rolled up like a workman, lounged by the doorway, talking with two other men. Absurdly, seeing him in that outfit, which could have been cleaner, Sophie didn't recognise him a moment. Then she saw the slanty green eyes, high cheekbones and the freckles across the bridge of his nose. The others looked as wild as pirates, although the thin one with dark shadows under his eyes had a thoughtful air.

The woman claimed Gilles Long Legs' attention. He turned away from his associates, his look one of someone recalled to duty. As he gazed at Sophie, she felt ridiculous surprise to see their speculative, penetrating look unchanged. She saw mild pleasure in them as he looked at her, though, of course, no recognition.

The woman spoke volubly and accusingly. His eyes began to flash while the piratical looking men growled.

Gilles Long Legs held out a chair for her at one of the tables, asking if she was hurt.

"He slapped my face." Knowing how fluent he was in English, it seemed absurd to keep trying to speak in French.

"Ah, shall we speak in English? Hit you, eh? Did they take your money?"

"No, I had none…It is such a long story."

He was regarding her with indignant sympathy and concern, but showed no sign of falling in love with her at first sight. That was a disappointment. It even made her wonder if this could possibly be the same place in time and space where Gilles Long Legs had fallen so violently in love with her displaced self. Also, she was anxious that another of him staggered about bemused nearby.

The strapping woman was saying she would know the men again. *Monsieur* Émile/Gilles Long Legs addressed her by some familiar name Sophie was later to find out translated – incredibly – as 'Ma SlapEm.' He gave some order to the other men, part of which Sophie understood. "You look after her, Felix."

He was making off with the others when Felix shouted after him, stopping him in his tracks to make some point before beginning to cough. Gilles Long Legs gave a disappointed snort, reminding Sophie of his snorting

when outraged by her not remembering this meeting. He came back to her side.

Felix ran off, still coughing, with the piratical looking man and 'Ma SlapEm'. Sophie thought he looked in no state to be getting into a fight. Gilles Long Legs shouted some order after them. Still running, the dark fellow grinned over his shoulder in complicity before speeding away.

Sophie's grand relative turned back to her solicitously. He wore his dismal clothes with the same air of relaxed negligence as he did his finery. Sophie supposed that came of being an aristocrat; it gave you such self-confidence.

"Permit me get you a drink to – put you to rights." He looked triumphant at bringing the phrase out, and she had to smile. "I am sorry such a thing should happen to you here."

He bent and took a closer look at her face, even touching it softly with his long fingers. "He bruised your face, *ma pauvre petite.* Ma tells me they – they had their hands on you, *aussi.* If we can find them we will serve them so they will never do that again." He went into the squalid café, and was soon back with some wine.

"Take this. Then we shall have some coffee. *Alors,* more than that. Take a – a big swallow."

His eyes are not quite the same; there is something in them that is missing now; what is it? Of course, it is comparative hopefulness. He has only lost half his family at this time. One sister and his parents remain to him.

"You are very kind –" she paused; she must be careful not to say '*Monsieur* Émile' – he might think her some sort of spy. She was about to say, '*Monsieur* Gilles', but, remembering the title '*Monsieur*' was frowned on by the revolutionary government, and not wanting to risk getting him into trouble, she said, "Mr Gilles."

He didn't show any surprise that she knew about him; he must assume that Ma SlapEm had suggested they go to him.

"Do not be absurd. To me, it is a pleasure. What is your name?"

"Sophie de Courcy." She realised, too, admitting to the 'de' wasn't exactly discreet.* A true irony, in light of her family's *déclassé* status. He nodded, assessing her with the sharp glances of someone who had to live on his wits.

He showed no sign of associating her with the cadet branch of his family, though presumably he knew Mistress de Courcy was taking care of his sister Charlotte in England.

"You do not live – near?" Only his occasional pause as he searched for a word showed he hadn't spoken English in years.

"No, I – I found myself in this area by a mistake." The surge of energy which had carried her through the attack and its aftermath suddenly vanished. She began to shiver, though it was a warm evening. She felt herself begin to snivel and groped for her handkerchief.

He searched in his own handkerchief, but it was so grubby he gave it a shocked look and quickly put it away again. He took her hands and chaffed them. "Do not think we are all like to those swine in these rough parts."

A dishevelled women, her mob cap stained, came out with the coffee.

Gilles Long Legs made Sophie finish her wine.

"Will they find those men?" From the looks of Felix and the others, let alone the redoubtable – if less agile – Ma SlapEm, Sophie feared atrocities would be done. Detestable though the louts had been, she didn't want to be the cause of their murder.

Gilles Long Legs smiled savagely. "Should they, I shall be happy to get my hands on them myself. If the Professor hadn't recalled me I would have gone with them, forgetting I was to meet with a fellow here. Don't look like he is going to come." He went on rubbing her hands and beaming at her.

She would hate to think what the meeting was about or what violence these solicitous hands had done. For all that, his warm concern made such a delightful contrast to those two weeks just passed – eight months in the future – that she had to like him.

You rather more than like him, you idiot. You managed to fall in love with him during those two weeks of his icy resentment.

"What time is it, please?"

He reluctantly let go her hands and pulled out a timepiece. "It – how do you say? – wants ten minutes of four o'clock."

She rubbed her face ruefully. "Is my face swollen?" She patted her hair. "My hair is half down, oh dear. What a slattern I must look." She tried to pin some of her hair back into place without a mirror.

He bent over to touch her face again. "Your cheek is – is – *un peu d'enflée.*" His eyes flashed with violent thoughts for a moment before he went back to beaming upon her. "As you must realise I am hardly a gentleman, I don't suppose you will blame me if I am – how is it – insolent – and tell you outright it doesn't make you any less beautiful."

She tingled all over with delight. She was sure she must look awful but, as he somehow didn't see it, she suddenly felt glowing and beautiful. As she gazed at him the corners of her lips turned up by themselves.

She sensed with great relief there wasn't another Émile Dubois going about ill and in a state of undress in Paris, only this one. It was as if two of him had merged into one. But how? He seemed to have no memory of what was now the future. Surely this must be the day when she herself had unaccountably had fallen asleep? Here must be the explanation.

She smiled, feeling her eyes sparkle wickedly. "I think you are a gentleman in all the ways that are of any consequence." After all, what was a little villainy between friends?

He laughed. "You are an unusual well bred young lady. I do find that delightful." He stretched luxuriously and smiled upon her some more. "This idiot isn't coming. Good. I wouldn't have been in the mood to have a stupid, solemn discussion about – certain things – of which you wish to know nothing. How do you feel now?"

"Much better, I thank you." Sophie did some eyelash batting quite naturally. Despite the small matter of being lost and without any money in this rough part of a foreign city back in the past, she felt absurdly happy at the way that he looked at her. Now, she knew they were in the same point in time and space he had remembered after all.

"Now, may I be insolent again and ask what a young *Anglaise* is doing here?"

She sighed. They were at the moment she had been dreading. "You would not believe me if I told you, Mr Gilles, but I owe you an explanation."

He was looking at her intently, leaning on arms crossed on the table, "I think I would believe you, Mistress Sophie."

She blushed, remembering his taunts of the future. "I hope you will believe me when I say it was not through doing anything of which I should be ashamed." She saw the irony of feeling the need to defend her moral conduct to a man leading such a ruffianly existence; certainly, the world was hard on women.

She began, then: "I am here by accident. I came here because –" even as she spoke, the words seemed to echo in her ears and her tongue hardly to move. She felt she was in yet another reality or trapped between two. Overcome with dizziness, she gave up speaking, shaking her head.

He was bending over her in concern. "Why, you are faint still! Do not talk any more." He took hold of her hands again to chaff them (he seemed to have taken to that, and she liked it too) .Would you care for some soup? The food is good here. I forgot to eat today since my *petite déjeuner*." She suspected he often did.

"Would you forgive me if I do not explain until later? I would love some soup, but I left my money at home, along with my outdoor things."

"Don't be absurd. Of course I shall pay." Gilles Long Legs picked up the coffee cups and bounded off into the shabby little eating house to order.

He came out with a glass of wine for each of them. They were sipping these and smiling at each other when a passer by with a red face paused to stare at Sophie. With a look of wry appreciation, he muttered something to Gilles Long Legs Sophie could only partially translate. "High class company."

Dishevelled as she was, Sophie thought she looked anything but 'high class.'

"Not with you about us. Don't embarrass the young lady, idiot."

The man held out a hand, which felt she had to take. He kissed it passionately. Even before she could react Gilles Long Legs was snatching her hand away: "*Assez!*"

It had been much less disgusting than Kenrick's attack on her hand.

"Get away with you, or I will become annoyed, you're drunk." Gilles Long Legs spoke in rapid, slangy French, but Sophie guessed his words, for the man drew himself up outrage. He appealed to Sophie in a burst of eloquence out of which she could only translate, "*Mademoiselle...I have never in my life...*" Dismissing Gilles Long Legs' stupidity with a laugh, he tottered away.

Sophie and Gilles Long Legs took one glance at each other, and then burst out laughing. Perhaps it was a hysterical reaction to all her recent alarms, but she found herself giggling until the tears ran down her cheeks. Then they smiled on each other until the woman slopped out with the soup and more wine.

The onion soup tasted nicer to Sophie than anything she had ever eaten, despite their squalid surroundings. Still, they didn't pay much attention to eating, talking of slight matters suddenly delightful to discuss.

Once Gilles Long Legs gave his head a shake and looked confused a moment, but then smiled at her quite normally. "The others are long. *Alors*, I am not sorry. I will – escort you home – of course, but I am happy we must wait." His face brightened. "We are holding *une petite soirée* in our lane tonight. Felix plays a funny little whistle and Marcel plays the – fiddle. Would you come with me? No, *bien sûr,* you are too delicately raised."

"But I would love to come! Firstly, I must give you this..." She began to undo her sapphire necklace. "I would like to give you it as – as a type of surety."

He waved aside the idea. She found herself saying, "I want you to keep it anyway, as thanks and because – well, I want you to keep it anyway, and believe me honest –" The odd, disconnected feeling came back and she broke off while he looked at her in concern.

The catch was awkward, and as she fiddled with shaking fingers, two clumps of her hair came down. "Gracious, how annoying!"

"I will keep this only so you do not disappear quite." He put the piece in his pocket and she winced. This was awful; it was as though he had a premonition of what must happen.

Could she change this past and so alter the future by making him an explanation in time so that when they met again he wouldn't hate her for not remembering?

Besides, then he wouldn't go off to his doom with Ceridwen Kenrick. Sophie was realist enough to see how to a rake Ceridwen Kenrick must be a great temptation; still, from the way he had looked at her in the hall at Plas Uchaf, she knew he would have stayed away from her if only Sophie herself had said what he longed to hear.

"That would not be through any choice of mine." She struggled to speak, and once more was lost in a strange state almost outside time.

He asked anxiously, "What ails you, Mistress Sophie? You are not faint again?"

"I – I try and tell you and each time it happens, my head swims…"

He looked concerned rather than suspicious and went back to the hand chaffing. "Then we must wait, eh? I think you to be so sweet a young lady – forgive me my familiarity, for the reasons I gave you before – that I scarce need explanations for your delightful presence. It is strange, I had such a sensation myself an hour or so back, and not through excess. I will tell you of that later. Would you let down all of your hair? It is such lovely hair. Why before did I admire the brunette?"

Sophie knew her heavy, waving fair hair to be one of her best features. "Like to a schoolroom miss? Well, why not?" She unpinned the rest, and it tumbled about her shoulders and back, curling from the grips.

His eyes glowed appreciation. "You look as beautiful as a mermaid."

"We are a long way from the sea, here in Paris. No wonder I am lost."

"How can you be lost with me to look after you?" She delighted in his sentimentality. "As I wish to, if you allow me." He took her hand and squeezed it.

She said on impulse, "If the others bring back those louts, please do not beat them too badly." Again, she only just stopped herself form saying, '*Monsieur* Émile', which might make him think her some sort of spy.

"*Alors, ma petite* Sophie – if the Sly Boots and Felix have caught them then they will have already beaten them half senseless. I am glad of it. *Après tout*, we must make an example of them." He stood up. "Do not run away whilst I pay the bill."

She sat, waiting in a happy stupor. He was soon back, the woman bustling after him. She tried some English. This Sophie found hard to follow, partly because the woman didn't have many teeth, so Sophie nodded at everything she said.

Then she realised in horror the woman was suggesting, with gestures, how as Gilles had such long legs, no doubt another part of his anatomy was equally impressive.

Sophie felt her face burn. Gilles Long Legs looked abashed. "*Tais toi*, Adeline! She is a nice young lady."

The woman gave Sophie's arm a squeeze. Sophie congratulated her on the soup, while Gilles Long Legs gazed on her as if basking in the warmth of his glowing pride in her.

Then he took her arm, and they began to walk through the mild sunshine of the spring evening along narrow streets lined with miserable buildings.

If it all was squalid and foetid then Sophie's mood invested it all with a tint of glamour. People they went by turned to stare, and she thought if she hadn't been with who she was they might well shout after a woman they instinctively recognised as not only a *bourgeoise*, but *Anglaise*. Perhaps some of the small boys who struggled together might even have given chase, hooting.

The costermonger broke off from his stentorian roaring to address them quietly and hoarsely, "*Ça va*, Gilles? *Cityones, tu aussi.*" Gilles Long Legs told him to call in at the party. Sordid looking though he was, Sophie beamed on him.

Gilles Long Legs slowed down his long stride to suit her, smiling on her now and again. "I will be so proud to have you as a partner."

"I am so glad, Mr Gilles..."

"'Come, try, 'Gilles'...*Ecoute*, there's Marcel's fiddle."

"Gilles, then."

How could she explain what she must? She couldn't guess what had happened herself. She only remembered his exclaiming that the scenes on the ceiling into which they were pulled came 'From that Jade'. He had told her himself that Kenrick was experimenting with time travel.

Why, whenever she tried to speak of it to him, did she feel as if she was drowning in air?

They came to a ragged woman sitting on a sort of crate, suckling a threadbare bundle. Even as her companion halted, Sophie yearned for her purse. Gilles Long Legs was excusing himself and releasing Sophie's arm to grope for his money.

He spoke quietly and rapidly to the woman, but Sophie was able to pick up some words; he was insisting he owed the woman money for something. The woman stared apathetically over her baby's head as he forced the money on her. Sophie sent up a prayer for the baby as her rascally admirer took her arm again.

Then they were in a small square, a comparatively open space full of people for the most part ill dressed, with some of them, including women, wearing the notorious red headgear. These Sophie had been told were badges of iniquity, and yet their owners seemed to arouse no hostility in Gilles Long Legs. Of course, he was used to meeting people wearing them.

The ubiquitous rubbish had been cleared away here, and barefoot girls danced. The ill-looking man whom Gilles Long Legs called, 'The Professor' was standing on a strange little wooden hut to one side of the square and tootling away on a small tin whistle as if his life depended on it.

Sophie wondered how he could, for his cough worried her. His fellow rascal from earlier, who had dark curly hair and only differed from a stage pirate in that he had no earring or knife in his teeth, was playing a violin, eyes closed and a half empty bottle of wine by his feet.

A bright eyed girl with a smile ornamenting her worn dress came up. Gilles Long Legs greeted her as 'Françoise'. "This is Sophie. She is an *Anglaise*."

"*Bonsoir*." Then Françoise produced some English proudly. "Gilles nice."

"I think so too." Sophie smiled.

Meanwhile, the man whom Gilles called 'Sly Boots' climbed down to speak at length. He brought an air of violence to speech, his jaw tensed as though he chewed his words and would like to take a bite out of somebody, yet for sure he was no vampire.

Gilles' eyes did more flashing while his hand tightened on Sophie's arm. He caressed it softly while he spoke in a bitter tone. Marcel Sly Boots smiled savage agreement.

Gilles Long Legs turned to Sophie. "They searched but could not find those *salauds*. They met one of Southern Georges' people (Sophie could guess 'Southern Georges'' identity), and he said they'd put out word about them. I am angry such cowards escape the – the beating they deserve. But I would – be enraged, because it was you. I do like to avoid killing even such as they."

"I am sure you joke merely." Later, Sophie was to wonder.

Then a group of girls took Françoise off and Gilles Long Legs said, "Marcel said we were so taken up in our talk they left us to it and came straight here. It is not like me not to notice what is going on, but," he laughed and squeezed her hands, looking down at her meaningfully, "Everything is different today."

"Ah, it is." She looked back up at him adoringly. Then she thought she must hurry in making her explanation. There might be no need. He never had said how long she spent with him on 'that evening'. Still, she mustn't leave it too late. She sensed they would be back in the sickroom all too soon. Would he remember? "Do you believe that strange things can happen with time?"

He laughed. "*Bien sûr,* for since I met you has seemed as five minutes. Besides, I keep having a feeling of *déjà vu,* though I have never yet overset myself on so little wine. Minutes before you came, I had – what is your English? a 'funny turn'. I remember nothing save rushing to the door gabbling nonsense. The others came after me, thinking trouble afoot. Then we met."

"It was not the wine; it is part of what I want to say –"

Her words were lost in a shout of laughter from a group nearby; the strange sensation came again.

As she struggled against it she caught Gilles Long Legs in glancing admiringly down at her bosom. He pulled his eyes away. "Come and dance." He saw her pause, and urged her, "Do not be shy."

He led her swiftly into the middle of the group of dancers. They danced a lively sort of jig which made it impossible to say more than few words. Sophie saw her dress was causing a stir, though to her it was such an everyday garment. Some of the wilder looking girls wore their hair hanging down, too, so her own loose hair didn't trouble her.

The Professor was signalling to Gilles Long Legs from the top of the roof of the box like structure, so he led Sophie up to it. "We must speak in English, Professor."

The Professor smiled. "I English speak gooder than Gilles. Like you Paris?"

"I do indeed." Paris might be a dangerous, unpredictable place now, but she would love anywhere where she could be with *Monsieur* Émile like this.

"You make Gilles a man good."

Her rascally companion laughed, looking down at her, "I will be good, Sophie. To you, anyway."

Someone was calling over to the Professor, asking him to play something or other. Even as he agreed, he was taken over by another fit of coughing.

"His cough is bad." Sophie said in concern as Gilles Long Legs led her off. He flinched. "We are trying to get him to go away for a stay by the sea. He says he ain't heard of holidays."

"You must. But, Gilles –"

But he was pulling her close. "Come and dance again. I dread you will say to me that you must go home. Of course, I will take you, though I must dismay your friends, who must be respectable. Still, how I wish I could keep you here with me."

"And me too. I love being with you here."

They began to dance to the slow tune Marcel and Felix were playing. Gilles Long Legs squeezed her waist. "I must not be too amorous. Those louts earlier must have terrified you." Tingles of pleasure ran through her at his touch. It didn't seem to matter about the horrible brief groping from the robber.

She began again, "You see, I was saying about time –"

"*Je regrette,* but I must – what word? – ah, 'interrupt' to say you are the sweetest girl ever I met." He tipped her chin up. "I regret I must kiss you." He began to kiss her, and she found herself kissing him back. Then, realising that she was kissing a man in the street like a hussy, she went red, pulled her lips away and stared at her shoes.

He laughed, giving her a condescending chuck her under the chin. "You are adorable, Sophie."

"But Gilles – I want to tell you now how I come to be here."

"I can tell from your kiss whatever has happened, you are an innocent. Give me another kiss and I will tell you something I am sure you guess already. I am astonished, for I thought it could never happen to me."

"Oh, but it is in the street." She did kiss him, anyway.

"*Je t'adore*, I love you, Sophie."

She shivered all over with happiness. "*Je t'adore aussi*, Gilles."

Falling in love with *Monsieur* Émile back at Plas Uchaf had been like falling over a precipice. It had felt as if she clawed at a stone, a blade of grass, anything in her desperate struggles to hold back from her fate ('*You will fall for him like a ton of coals being delivered*'); yet inexorably she tumbled down the slope down towards the gaping abyss. She only realised she had tipped over the edge and was falling down the chasm on the night of the ball.

Here it was as if she reached the bottom of the chasm – dreading the impact – only to find it was not a hard surface, but in his arms.

Yet, he was so undeniable a scoundrel it was still shocking.

He evidently agreed with her about his character, "Sophie, can you really love a villain such as myself?"

"I do already."

His eyes glowed, and they kissed again. When they pulled apart he said, "I can hear singing."

So could she. It was herself, singing, *Ombra Mai Fú*. Only, she was not accompanying herself on an instrument, and she sounded sad.

She knew then her time was running out. "Gilles, please listen to me. When we meet again you mustn't hate me when I say that –" Then the disembodied feeling took her over again. She fought to speak, but made no sound. Everything was beginning to dissolve. A drunken man fell like a log at their feet and Gilles Long Legs whisked her out of the way. She felt the world spin and she hung on to him but was wrenched away.

––––––⁊⁊⁊⁊⁊⁊⁊⁊––––––

They were back on the bed, still holding each other. They gazed into each other's eyes, and Sophie saw in his all the tenderness of one moment or eight months ago. She could feel her own eyes glowing. "Do you believe me now?"

His voice, so vigorous moments before, was hoarse and weakened but just as caressing. "Ah, Sophie, I lived that twice, and you were telling the truth all along. I could not believe myself so far mistaken in you. I have done you great injustice. Can you forgive me?"

"Very easily."

"When I found myself in Adeline's cafe, for some moments I remembered everything. I leapt up, struggling to speak, while people thought that I was choking and tried to slap me on the back. Then it was gone. Now I realise you were trying to tell me what would happen but could not."

"I was trying so hard to tell you, but every time I lost all speech."

He kissed her. His breath was flavoured by the herbs from the cure, though a kiss from him would still have been exquisite even had it been sour.

As they drew apart, miserable recollection came back into his eyes. "And now it is too late. Even if you do not hate me for going to That Jade, now through my own pathetic philandering I must become a monster."

She stroked his face. "Do I seem to hate you? You mustn't despair about That Woman biting you. That is why Katarina and I have been tormenting you by giving you only the herbs to drink. Are you thirsty?" she added automatically.

"*Alors*, not for blood yet." Seeing her wince, he caressed her hair, smiling. She automatically glanced at his teeth, as so often during these past three days. She saw no difference, though they might be changing imperceptibly.

He made to sit up while she moved back to give him room. "What day is it? My mind seems to have been wandering a long time, though I know that you have been tending to me far more kindly than I deserve."

She handed him the cordial, and told him the day. "What can have happened? Has it to do with Kenrick's Mischievous Experiments?"

She glanced at the clock, wondering if time passed here when they were away. She had last looked at it minutes before she began stroking his forehead, and it was ten o' clock. Now it read five past three; it was so dark, it must be morning.

Perhaps Agnes had called in to find them missing? Perhaps not, for when Sophie had pleaded with her to sleep through and not get up till five at the earliest, Agnes smiled knowingly how she might.

Sophie wondered if their bodies had remained here, not vanished, as hers had disappeared at Chester. Otherwise, their bodies would have been in two different times and places at once. Then there was the fact that Émile would have been in France anyway, whereas she wouldn't.

Was that why the two of him merged into one? Such puzzles were beyond her.

He took her hand and stroked it, his eyes clouding. "That Woman did something with a book that made reflections of my life in Paris on the ceiling." He shuddered, looking horrified and going slightly green, so that Sophie selfishly hoped that he wouldn't be sick again. But he got the better of it, saying after a few moments, "Of course, I will not tell you about that."

He caressed her face just as he had in Paris. "I think I am dangerous to be about, *ma chère*. A ruffian and a monster haunted by impromptu trips through time. Surely you deserve better? I must not be selfish and endanger you, but how can I endure to let you go?"

She said, "We had just told each other something back in Paris when we were rudely interrupted."

"I love you, Sophie. That was true even when I took myself off to that cursed house to bring this horror on myself."

"I love you, too, *Monsieur* Émile, as with *Monsieur* Gilles Long Legs. You mustn't believe that a horrible fate is inevitable. Child though she is, Katarina knows more of this then we, and she is hopeful. She seems to see a – a non fatal vampire bite as a sort of illness, which can be cured."

He kissed her again. "We will talk more, my lovely girl." His lids began to droop, and he said, "But no forgetting me, Sophie. There is no excuse, this time."

"Do not joke about that! I am so sorry for it all! There is no way that I could have known, but I must have seemed such a contemptible liar. I hope you didn't hate me?"

"No, but it was like your answering me with a slap in the face. *Après tout,* I jeered at Kenrick's talk of time travel, *ma chère*, yet such a peculiar explanation might have come to my stupid head. Tell me, did you have any unaccountable happenings back last May?"

"Why yes, I was on the bed in a strange sleep one day, and Harriet said I had gone out, and I couldn't deny that there was dust on my clothes."

He nodded, but his eyelids began to droop. She kissed the freckles across the bridge of his nose – as she had so longed to for days – and he muttered something, fingering her necklace.

"I'm sorry, I caught not your words."

"This necklace was transported entire, like you from Chester. After you vanished, I still kept it in my pocket, as you know."

She drew his head down on her shoulder. With a luxurious sigh as he drew in the scent of her skin, he fell asleep.

Chapter Ten

"THIS DOES BEAT EVERYTHING, *MONSIEUR* Gilles! You are becoming as bad as the girls. Next you will be screaming at the sight of a bat." Georges hurled a log on the fire and sparks shot up the chimney.

Émile, resplendent in his crimson dressing gown if pale and thin, stretched out his legs to the blaze. "No, Georges. Next I will be turning into one. I may yet take a bite out of your horrible neck."

"*Merde*! The fever has disordered your brain, Gilles Long Legs. That and reading too many books and working out too many sums. I always said no good comes of overtaxing your brain, and now you have done yourself a mischief, it is clear. Here is Éloise with your *petit-déjeuner*."

Émile wrinkled his nose. "Thank you, Éloise, but I don't want that."

"*Monsieur* should try to start eating again." Éloise did some eyelash batting as she put down the loaded tray.

"Éloise, you have been most kind to me and I do want to thank you, but hark you, Georges, how I am tyrannised over by women. Never allow yourself to become ill."

Georges said, "The girls were wearing themselves out caring for you while you were sick, so the least you can do now is eat up your food like a good boy."

"I jest merely. Éloise, I know that I owe you all a debt of gratitude." Grimacing, Émile began on the food. "Find my pocket book, Georges."

"Do you suppose for a second you can reimburse me for those boots in which I cut such a dash respectable women used to pursue me in the street?"

"No, and I ain't going to try. I have only had my senses back a few hours, and already I weary of hearing of those boots."

Éloise fussed about, arranging things and pouring Émile's coffee, pausing to smile at him now and then. When Georges came back with the pocket book, Émile took out some notes. "*Ma petite,* I know that money cannot repay kindness, but it is better than no thanks at all."

"*Monsieur,* I could not take such a big present. What would people say?"

"Don't tell 'em."

"*Monsieur* is so kind that were I was less shy I would kiss him." Éloise made a show of putting the notes in her bosom. Georges shifted, muttering. Émile's gaze intensified. "Best that you do not, Éloise, for I may not have turned into a eunuch quite."

Madame Blanch called, "Éloise!"

Éloise pulled a face, curtseyed, and swayed towards the door, pausing to smile over her shoulder as she went out.

Émile laughed. Georges pretended to wipe sweat from his brow. "What she sees in you, I cannot imagine, and sweet *Mademoiselle* Sophie, too. By the by, I gather from the way *Mademoiselle* grinned from ear to ear this morning you have mended matters between you."

Émile put down his knife. "What happened was so odd that I could not believe it."

"Doubt me not."

"I don't mean anything like that, you dirty minded rascal. I suppose this next will appeal to you: it still sickens me to think of it, though, so let us not go into details, but you remember I said earlier That Jade pleasured herself by showing pictures of things I did in Paris on her ceiling? The canopy of the bed had been removed, I do recollect me."

"Ten to one you were in a fever already."

"It was part of the nightmare that led to her sucking my blood. I ain't going to whine about that, I brought it on myself, the girls warned me. Those pictures appeared last night, pulling Sophie and I into my exemplary life back then."

"You are raving again." Georges put his hand on Émile's forehead.

"Quite cool, ain't it? Besides, Miss Sophie ain't been in a fever. We relived that evening, or I did. I had a feeling of *déjà vu* at times. It was all new for *ma pauvre petite*. She was telling the truth throughout, and I was too stupid to connect it with Kenrick's talk about thought forms and travel through time."

Georges shot an uneasy look at the ceiling. "*Merde!* Kenrick should be locked away."

"Unlike you and I, Georges? Yes, I only hope that was the last of those living pictures and *Madame's* torture. More of that anon. I am besotted with Miss Sophie, Georges. Even before, I could not but love her. It has been torment. I want to marry her at once, but how can I, save she keeps me as a pet flapping about in the attics somewhere? I don't suppose *ma pauvre petite* wants to spend her wedding night in a coffin."

Georges laughed. "You will get the better of this foolishness once she has accepted you. *Alors*, I won't speak of some folk's odd tastes for coffins. Gilles Long Legs, when I allowed myself to run on so about Agnes you said, 'Spare me these sentimental effusions'."

"I was a bitter man then. Now, I am a lovesick bat."

"*Merde!* Eat the rest of that *petit déjeuner*. You will need your strength back for the wedding night, and not in a coffin, neither." Georges wandered over to the bureau just inside the open dressing room door, and picked up an old book.

Émile's head turned quickly. His tone was sharp. "Give me that, Georges!"

Georges smiled teasingly, glancing down at the title. "*Pourquoi*, is it something forbidden? '*On the Use of Imitative Representation.*' What the Devil is that? When me and Agnes was struggling to undress you we found it on you and put it there – Eh! What ails you?" Émile was up, snatching the book from him.

Émile looked startled himself. "That book don't concern you, Georges."

Sophie wore the grey dress to meet Émile in the music room. In the alleys of Paris, it became soiled about the hem; somehow, that dirt was gone. She fussed more than ever over her appearance and her hair. Still, with her eyes and cheeks glowing, she looked far better than she might, given her lack of sleep.

"Is glowing you look this morning." Agnes sent her on her way with a pat on the bottom. "See if my cards don't prove right."

"Agnes, you must take this afternoon as a holiday to go and see your daughter."

As Sophie made her breathless way to the music room, she thought she showed a pathetic lack of guile in being five minutes early, but *Monsieur* Émile was there already.

Her heart lurched as he came to take her hands. She was surprised at how quickly he moved, having been so ill hours only before. He looked paler – the freckles across the bridge of his nose standing out – and much thinner, his already prominent cheekbones jutting. He was newly bathed, his hair washed and styled and dressed once again magnificently yet negligently.

"You still look too ill to be up, *Monsieur* Émile."

He stroked her cheek. "Do not fuss, Sophie. All nurses are by nature bossy, and as such an excellent one you must be also. You know why I am here. I want to thank you, firstly, for looking after me so kindly and so undeservedly when I was ill and spewing disgustingly, too. Katarina has told me all about the cure that you were trying to get me to retain, and a thankless task you had of it." He shuddered. "Faugh! Those rank weeds."

Sophie had found them fragrant. "It was a pleasure, *Monsieur* Émile."

He kissed her hands as passionately as on that first evening, but then sighed and let them go. He went to stare out of the window.

Outside, the outlook was as dismal as on the day when he had come to her to make offers as disreputable as the ones she hoped he was about to make would be reputable. Gusts of icy wind buffeted the stark trees, flinging hail against the window panes. The sky was leaden.

"I can't look at you when I say this. Sophie, you must forget me. I have ruined my own miserable existence nicely, and I deserve no sympathy, neither. You and *petite* Katarina warned me enough. I must be unselfish for once and urge you to forget me, love you as you know I do. I may come to be a danger to those close to me. You don't want to marry a monster. I must take myself off somewhere."

Sophie came up behind him, and reached up to put her hands on his shoulders. "When you asked for me the first time, I was somewhat at a disadvantage; you said you would never ask for me again, but that was when you thought I was lying."

He muttered, "I was very insulting to you. I hope you will forgive me?"

"Do you know, I think I can…and I would be so happy to give you my own answer to a certain question, if you were to ask again?"

He turned about, eyes alight. "*Alors*, you deserve to be asked with all due punctilio, though I think I see some splinters on the floor, which I will avoid, as my springing up with a yell would detract from the gravity of the occasion." He went down on one knee and took her hand. "*Mademoiselle* Sophie, will you marry me?"

"Yes, *Monsieur* Émile. How can you doubt it? You must know how I love you!"

His eyes glowed. Leaping up, he seized both her hands. "Ah, Sophie, you know how I love you." She met his kiss. When they broke off he exclaimed, "Your *ingénue's* kiss! When I kissed you in this room before, it felt as in Paris. To think that I feared you must be an adventuress making a fool of me for her own entertainment, though how this squared with your being *ma Tante's* companion puzzled me quite. Will you really take the risk with me? Ah, my lovely girl, can I put you through this? You deserve much better."

He took a ring from his little finger, and put it on her ring finger. "*Voila*. That is much too big for you, but must do as a pledge until I buy you one that fits. I want you to have my sister Charlotte's necklace and rings, too."

She could almost purr like Jem the kitten. "I must wear this ring on a chain about my neck, I think; I don't want to lose it. I would be so honoured to have *Mademoiselle* Charlotte's jewellery, *Monsieur* Émile. I met her but once and she was so amiable. Oh, I am so happy I do not know what to say!"

"Some people might question your sanity, as I was bad enough before That Woman attacked me, and not just in France, neither. Do you want to hear about my crimes, because you should know who you are accepting? I have done terrible things. Of course, you must suspect it, having met me as Gilles Long Legs.

'That first winter in Paris, I saw a dead cat lying with its entrails frozen to the road; so was how I felt, for a long time after what happened at the *Château*. That made it easy for me to lead so brutal an existence. And yet, I flattered myself that in robbing purely from those who could afford it, I was better than those of my class who for centuries have sheltered behind the law to rob from the peasants, who cannot.

'Then I met you and you melted the ice about my heart quite, but when you vanished, it made things worse. Then, when it was finally over with *mes parents*, Georges and I escaped only to find Charlotte dying.

'Thus, I continued to live as a scoundrel in England for some months, which in light of my *émigré* position, was ungracious, to say the least – though you may be surprised to hear that I am an Englishman born – at Oxford. My excuse was my financial affairs were in a legal tangle, I did not want to sponge upon others and again I only targeted the wealthy.

'But truly, being a villain was become a habit with me; I combined society life and roguery at that time. I will open my heart to you as to no-one else, Sophie *moi,* and tell you how I longed for somebody to do both myself and the world a good turn and rid it of my worthless carcase." He stood, stroking her hands, and staring down into her eyes.

She squeezed his hands in return. "Don't say that! No, Gilles Long Legs, no more. It would not stop me loving you and only make me sad. But I do hope that you did not keep any money you made so and that – well, I sound as sententious as a character from Richardson – that you are sorry?"

"When you call me Gilles Long Legs, Sophie, it takes all the sting away. I gave the money away, *ma petite*. But I fear that I am a scoundrel by nature. Then there is the slight problem of the chances of my taking to flapping about and asking for a bite of your neck. I am glad that you wear a cross, *ma chère,* for who knows but you may have need of it, incredible though that seems to me now?

'I was talking to Katarina earlier. She has faith in those herbs; Cousin Ynyr would be delighted. Besides, she assures me that even should they fail, she has other tortures for me at her disposal. It seems even untreated I will never be a fully fledged, coffin sleeping vampire because *Madame* did not see fit to kill me outright. She was obliging enough only to poison me by leaving her teeth in too long. Katarina believes that at worst I must only be a Man Vampire, though that sounds bad enough. She tells me that we will not know for a month how far the cure has worked."

"That is what I gathered." Sophie went on tiptoe to take his face in her hands and kiss him softly on the cheek.

That led to them kissing more passionately. After a time he pulled away, laughing. "And I was worried that I was like to become a eunuch after – never mind! – Sophie, even apart from the fact that I don't know how long it will be before I start flapping about and squeaking at you, I want to marry you as soon as may be. Do you insist upon a grand wedding?"

She glowed. "No, I would be happy to marry you as quickly as you wish, *Monsieur* Émile."

"Who? Sophie, that terrible habit of calling me '*Monsieur* Émile' and even worse, 'Sir' must stop *immediatment*. You can call me 'Gilles Long Legs' now and then should I show signs of forgetting what a rascal I am. *Alors*, my lovely girl, I will write to your brother John at once, and I must ask permission of *Madame ma Tante* too. I must see about a special licence, and I will have to find a suitable house for us, mine all being let."

"I will give you the Chester address directly. I am sure that John will wish to give me away. But, I would like to ask you one thing."

"What, *chérie*? You look serious."

"When we had that quarrel, before – The Bat – came, you believed I must have a Guilty Secret. You will think me foolish, but I do want to know; had that been true, would you have despised me?"

He chucked her chin with that condescending gesture, but so tenderly that she didn't mind. Besides, he knew so much more of life than she that she thought that he was entitled to it.

"Somehow, that is typical of your sweetness, Sophie. When I was living as Gilles Long Legs, I knew many women who lived with men outside marriage who had babies too, and I had more respect for them than for many so-called respectable women, the Mistress Pamela's who barter their virtue in exchange for a good offer.

'No, it was because I thought you lied and acted a part that I was so furious. Do you know, I think that you could have twisted me round your little finger and got a proposal soon enough, for all my ranting, even had you accepted my terms. Still, I find it delightful that you are such an *ingénue*."

Remembering his insistence he had never debauched a virgin, she supposed that it was a novelty for him. As they went back to kissing, she could hardly wait for their wedding night herself. After a while, she forced herself to think of spiritual matters. She pulled away in turn. "Émile, will you do something for me?"

"Almost certainly; what is it?"

"Will you let me pray for us both? Now and at other times? I suspect that you are irreligious, so maybe I will seem priggish to you, but it would be a great comfort to me."

He gazed down at her for a moment with combined cynicism and tenderness. "You are foolishly devout, and I take the whole. Therefore, *allez-y*, my lovely girl."

He went to stand staring out of the window again – looking, she thought, towards the roofs of Plas Cyfeillgar. He drew from his pocket a knife – a very sharp, savage looking instrument – with which he pared his nails as he looked over the view.

Feeling foolish, she dropped down to her knees. While she murmured a prayer, his face was as unmoved as if she were reciting the details of a laundry list.

She finished. He turned about, as though coming back from a reverie, and came over to raise her to her feet. "Now, my lovely girl, I want that address. I shall write to your brother directly and then I must to *Madame ma Tante* as an act of courtesy. Ynyr is inclined towards you himself – as who could not be? – and I suppose he will be put about at the news, but nothing serious, I trust."

"Fancy you accusing me of rejecting your offer because I was angling for Lord Ynyr! I can confess now that I have been besotted with you since we met at that wedding when I was eight."

"I remember you as the sweetest little thing, too. I made that accusation through jealousy, of course, Sophie. I would not wish jealousy on anyone after my brief experience of it, least of all my Cousin Ynyr."

Sophie thought of Morwenna, but kept a discreet silence.

The Dowager Countess had just settled down in her sitting room with a new sentimental novel and a cup of chocolate when Émile tapped urgently.

Sighing, she hid the novel. "*Entrez*!"

She started to her feet as Émile rushed in, alarmingly haggard and excitable. "Émile! What do you out of bed?"

"*Madame*, I have come to ask you something. Do not worry, I am well enough."

"You look far from well to me. You should be in your room. Dear me! Sit down, *ma cher*. Why didn't you send a servant?"

"I want to marry Miss Sophie as soon as may be."

"What?!" The Dowager Countess forgot her romantic mood and hurried to test his forehead.

He jerked his head impatiently. "It seems, *Madame,* that I will be thought still raving for some time to come. Someone else did that this morning. *Alors*, the fever is gone. It is scarce a compliment to *ma pauvre petite* that you think I must be delirious because I wish to marry her. "

The Dowager never expected to see such spectacular proof of the cliché that a woman who cared for a man when he was ill could win his heart. "Really, Émile! How long has this been coming on?"

"From within minutes of our meeting."

"But you have been so distant towards her, Émile – though generally you permit such shocking familiarity from inferiors – that I intended to remonstrate with you."

Émile waved this aside. "That was due to a misapprehension, *Madame,* but we now understand each other and I want to marry her as soon as may be. I was thinking of applying for a special licence."

"*Mon Dieu!* I cannot understand how anyone could quarrel with Sophie, and when you had only just met her, too…Have you spoken to the girl?"

"Yes, and she is happy with whatever I chose."

The Dowager Countess suspected if Sophie wasn't careful, Émile would be saying that obliviously for the rest of their lives together.

He jumped up. "Do I have your permission to marry her, *Madame*? I do adore her; you need have no concerns regarding that."

The Dowager Countess thought how tiresome she had always found the passions of Southern men. Émile, seemingly detached and cynical, must have that side to his nature, too.

It seemed to her that lately he used all his energy to cause trouble. If he wasn't falling out with disagreeable neighbours by stealing kitchen maids, he was coming home violently ill or threatening to marry her companion. She was puzzled as to how he had grown up to be so impossible when Poor Dear Armand had him whipped regularly as a boy.

She felt a twinge of indigestion and gave up hope of drinking the hot chocolate. "Would you care for this drink, *ma cher*, as I have not touched it, and you look thin? No? I think Sophie should have some choice in her wedding arrangements, Émile. Surely she wishes to have her brother at least give her away? I do not wish to upset you when you have been so lately ill, but truly, I am far from sure you are in a suitable state of mind to marry an innocent young girl like Sophie. This is all much too sudden, dear me!"

He began to pace about. "As to that, *Madame,* I know I will never be good enough for her, but as she is happy to have me –"

"Émile, do not exhaust yourself, rushing about so! Regrettably I must remind you that Sophie is not a kitten, to be given to you on a whim."

He shot a resentful glance over his shoulder and came back to the desk to speak evenly. "I do not think of her in so insulting a light, *Madame.* I hoped that you would be happy to give your permission, but have to confess that I have already written to John de Courcy, requesting his consent and inviting him to give his sister away."

The Dowager Countess looked as though she had been sucking a lemon. "You know that John de Courcy will be so delighted at a Dubois making his portionless sister an offer that he will dash off his consent by return of post."

A quarrel seemed unavoidable.

Émile suddenly smiled. "*Madame,* the last thing I wish to do is quarrel with you, when you have been so kind to me. I know this is sudden, and I understand why you have misgivings in handing over Miss Sophie to me so quickly. I know you are become most fond of her and I am doing you no favour in depriving you of her. Would you like to speak to her? She is nearby."

When Sophie came in, transformed by joy, her eyes and cheeks glowing as she turned a worshipful glance at her roguish admirer, the Dowager Countess felt herself giving way. Impossible as Émile could be, her companion would never again receive such an offer as this. Had she herself treasured Sophie less, she would have thought of it as a misalliance.

As it was, the Dowager Countess saw that Émile – having already entertained society with his rakish adventures – could now give it an episode to delight romantics.

Lord Ynyr whistled as he worked on his cures. When Émile hurried in, the Count was as shocked at his appearance as the Dowager Countess. "Émile! Should you be up already?"

Émile smiled. "This becomes repetitive, Ynyr. I wanted to be the one to tell you my news. I have been in love with Miss Sophie since we met and today she accepted me –"

Lord Ynyr spilt a good deal of his precious stock of dried sage and St John's wort on the laboratory floor. "What? Émile, this is beyond anything!"

"Thus, as you confessed to me, Cousin, to a certain softness for her yourself, I do hope you are not too distressed by this news?"

Lord Ynyr was still staring. "But Émile! I am all astonishment!"

Émile took him by the arms, looking into his face anxiously. "Never mind your astonishment. I want to know if you are distressed, Ynyr, because I do not want you to hate me, and for sure had you won her I would find it hard not to hate you for it."

Lord Ynyr didn't know what he felt apart from amazement and a sense of grievance. "I scarce know what I feel, Émile. Why did you not tell me when we spoke before? Besides, you have been so distant to her."

"I was trying to control my feelings, Ynyr. I wish I could have confided in you."

"So do I, Émile. Well, I must congratulate you." As he gazed on his cousin's concerned look he managed a smile. "I must be delighted for you, Émile, though I cannot help but feel some envy, as frankly, while the world may say you have married an inferior, anyone who knows Miss Sophie realises otherwise."

Émile tightened his arms about him and Lord Ynyr noted with surprise how much strength he still had. "But you are thin, Émile! Should you even be up?" Then he remembered Émile's rudeness over his herbal remedies, and felt less sympathy. "However, it is the part of your *fiancée* to fuss over your health."

"Ynyr, I will help you to collect these herbs." Émile went down on his knees. Then, as he put out his hands, he suddenly froze, and watched Ynyr gather them up instead. "This is the second time today that I have been grovelling on the floor."

For all Lord Ynyr's smile and amiable manner, his heart lurched with disappointment and envy of Émile for knowing his own mind where he himself had dithered for weeks, unsure whether he cared enough for Sophie to set aside family tradition, unable to choose between the rival charms of Sophie and Morwenna.

Now Sophie was suddenly unobtainable, her allure was so bright that he felt her loss as keenly as though he had never debated which girl he should choose.

"So, mate," Georges jeered as he finished work on Émile's hair, "Have you forgotten about this Bat Nonsense now you have mended matters with *Mademoiselle* Sophie?"

Émile sighed. "Instead of asking *Mademoiselle* Sophie to marry me, I should take myself away from civilisation, before I become the menace to the neighbourhood the Kenrick *ménage* already are. You must hear more of the local talk about them than I do." He held out his hand and showed Georges his nails. "Like you my talons? They grow apace, for all I cut them this morning. I have just bribed the cook to stop putting garlic and herbs in my food."

"There is nothing in that, when you were ill for days."

"So, if you will not join with an honest half bat in acting against the Kenrick *ménage* then I must act alone and soon, too."

Georges was at the mirror, rubbing his special solution into his curly black hair. "You ain't in any state to fight anyone at the moment."

Katarina brought in a large steaming cup of the cure.

Émile groaned. "Believe me, I wish that it was a part of my delirium,

Georges, and when I smell this repellent brew, I wish it still more. Must I drink this, *ma petite?*"

She nodded solemnly. "It is the last *Monsieur* must have for a while."

Georges laughed. "You both are deluded. I have to be on my way, *Monsieur* Bat, for I am going to the village of Llandyrnog with Agnes and she is going to sneak out her baby for me to meet. I am in danger of becoming domesticated, too. It is sad. What became of the pair of careless rogues as we were?"

Émile shuddered as he began to sip the drink. "They were beaten into submission by women and children, Georges. What can be in this, Katarina? It tastes more disgusting than ever."

Katarina frowned. "It is the same mixture of herbs, *Monsieur*, save that now we must have nettle added."

Émile groaned and shuddered as he downed the herbal drink while Katarina stood over him, arms crossed. Chortling, Georges went to the mirror to make a smug couple of alternations to his outfit. "I leave you to enjoy that brew." He went out to the dressing room, whistling.

Émile broke out into a sweat as he finished the drink and shook himself all over like an animal. Katarina watched him narrowly as he drew out a handkerchief and mopped his face.

"Katarina, we will move house. I am going to wed Miss Sophie and you must be parlour maid proper. But I want you to work only part of the time, because I think you to be a clever girl who should have some learning, and I will arrange it. Agnes comes too. Shall you like that?"

She leaped up and down on the spot. "Above anything, *Monsieur!* I love Miss Sophie!"

"You are not the only one…But tell me, Katarina, something of Kenrick's routine. It is well that I should know these things."

"Why, *Monsieur* Émile? Besides, they are away now, I know."

"Because I do, my girl! Stop being obdurate and tell Émile."

She bit her lip. "No, *Monsieur* Émile, for I think that as soon as they return, you will try and destroy him, but I fear instead they will destroy you. You haven't back your strength. Kenrick is as strong as three men, having been a Man Vampire for years. Mistress Kenrick is as strong as any human male, though she looks so much a woman, and she has special knowledge of trances. Such comes with the vampire state, but most can put their victim in the trance for a little while only. All of us servants feared her gaze more than his. Then there is Arthur Williams, the footman, who was kind to me when he was a man, but now he is become one of them too; Captain Mackenzie is often there besides; she lately made him into a Man Vampire and he is enslaved by her, as is Arthur –" She broke off, gulping.

"Trances –" Émile shook his head suddenly. "Now, Katarina, do not weep, for what is one rogue more or less? But it will not come to that, I promise you. Why is it, girl, you never have a handkerchief? Take mine."

She wiped her eyes, blew her nose and defended herself "I do! I gave you one of mine when you spewed upon the floor."

"So you did, I remember me now." He gave her a quick pat on the top of the head. "Stop that weeping now, and tell me what I want to know, for I must go, with or without your help – Georges, forgot you something?"

Georges was glowering in the doorway. "You ain't doing anything without me, Gilles Long Legs."

Émile grinned. "Would I attempt such a thing? Yet I think I must, Georges, for I cannot let you risk your silly neck, comprehending not the dangers."

Georges' dark eyes glittered. "I suppose I must humour your madness, Gilles Long Legs. I will do what you say. I want to help you teach some civility to this lunatic and his toadies."

Émile smiled. "Good. Now, hold your peace, Georges, while we rave. Keep that handkerchief, Katarina…I gather, then, they – or it may be, we – who aren't Undead, sleep in beds, eat, and act quite normally compared to the full vampire?"

"Do not joke, *Monsieur*. The first Mistress Kenrick – she was so nice, and he was different then – laughed at Kenrick at first. He caused her death, though she was the only one he ever loved."

"He killed her?"

Katarina nodded. "We thought it an accident. She must have been running away."

Georges said solemnly, "A man as kills a woman is no better than a dog."

"Truly, Georges…How many of us happy walking dinners become Man or Woman vampires?"

Katarina flinched. "I heard if the vampire took more than a few mouthfuls then without the cure, it is certain."

Georges stirred uneasily, while Émile rolled his eyes. "This seems not happy, *ma petite*. How many does the cure save from joining the Noble Order of Bats?"

She fiddled with her apron strings. "Perhaps one in two –" She rushed over to take his hands. "But *Monsieur* must remember the other cures we shall use later!"

———— ✦✦✦ ————

When Katarina and Georges had gone, Émile put on his greatcoat and went through the grounds to the carpenter's workshop, the bitter wind buffeting him. When the carpenter opened the door of the workroom, the heat from the small fire made a startling contrast to the cold outside.

The man's young son was planing down a piece of wood.

Émile chatted amiably with them a while. The man took a low view of all foreigners save the Dowager Countess, and was surprised at Émile's friendly interest in woodwork.

Émile showed him a sketch. "I will need these – stakes."

"Do you wish the ends to be very sharp?" The man, having heard of Émile's fearlessness, was startled to see him flinch and pale before saying after a seeming internal struggle, "As sharp as you can make 'em."

"Now, *bachgen*, what wood would be best to make these stakes for the gentleman? Sir, are you ill?"

"It is nothing; I am still getting the better of that wearisome fever."

"I heard of your illness, Sir. My boy too, he missed the Christmas party, poor lad, though Miss Sophie brought him over his present and some treats." The carpenter chattered on, discussing with his son the best way to fashion the stakes. Meanwhile Émile shifted as uncomfortably as he had when tormented by Sophie's singing.

Finally, the matter was sorted out to their satisfaction. Émile tipped them extravagantly and went back out into the piercing wind with a cheerful wave.

"You don't think he wants to cut anyone's head off with those things, do you, *Tad*? After all, he is a *Ffrancwr*."

"No, *bachgen*, is his *Mam* and *Tad* had their heads cut off by rabble too fierce to wear breeches*. Always well dressed is Mr Émile."

At the sight of Sophie's radiant face, Agnes' put by her fears. "Didn't I always say, Miss? My Tarot cards said the fair man from overseas would ask for you."

They fell into each other's arms and danced in a circle. "You did, Agnes, and I wouldn't believe you! Oh, I am so happy! Her Ladyship says if you wish you may come with me. Agnes, I hope you do? Do you want Eiluned to live with us?"

At Eiluned's name, Agnes' face became as inscrutable as ever was Émile's. She hugged Sophie again. "Ah, Miss Sophie! Not at present. Recollect you people hereabouts are not supposed to know her mine, though there has always been talk."

"Oh dear, perhaps too, you are reluctant to move her to a house where *Monsieur* Émile is in danger of becoming –" Sophie couldn't say the words.

"We do not know that yet, Miss Sophie, and vampire or no, I am sure he would not bite a baby, but there are other reasons why it is best not. – I wonder what Lord Ynyr and Miss Morwenna will make of this? She had her eye on both, and didn't want to let either go. This will make her mind up for her. "

Sophie had to smile. "Agnes, you are wicked! Lord Ynyr is perfect for her, being so good natured. Now, the weather is so foul you must take my fur lined cloak for your trip to your mother's with Georges. For myself, I must search again for that book on vampire lore. It is infuriating! I have been through the library and half of the books in that ante room. "

After another hour's fruitless search amongst the books, it was time for Sophie to put aside her worries and make herself look as pretty as she could in her favourite blue dress for dinner.

She hoped it improved her charms. Anyway, Émile's eyes dilated at the sight of her as she shyly entered the room, while at the sight of him, magnificently turned out if much leaner, she glowed.

Meanwhile, Lord Ynyr came with his normal easy manners to wish her joy. She stole glances at his face now and then in between studying the pattern of the carpet. She was glad that her efforts to do what

Harriet called 'Drawing Him In' had failed, so now, instead of falling to his knees with a howl of anguish, he smiled congratulations.

Miss Morwenna, magnificent in rose pink with gold about her throat and ears, came over in perfumed glory to take her hands. Her smile appeared so friendly that Sophie could almost believe she imagined the resentment lurking at the back of her eyes. "*Félicitations*, Miss Sophie! I have just been berating *Monsieur* for being so secretive. It is too bad of him, but we cannot be hard on him when he is convalescent, though on top of all else he insists on a marriage within days."

"Thank you, Miss Morwenna. I hope that you will do us the honour of being bridesmaid?"

"I would be delighted." Sophie's fears that Miss Morwenna might have a Disappointed Heart disappeared as those sharp hazel eyes turned inwards to calculate how long it would take to have a gown made up.

The Dowager Countess roused herself to kiss Sophie warmly, meanwhile casting admonitory glances at her embroidery, as though daring it to put itself into another Sad Tangle.

"With this happy news, I clean forgot!" the Count said brightly, just before they went in to dinner. "Here is that foolish book the future *Madame* Dubois wished to see. I found it on the shelves in the morning room. '*The Legend of the Vampyre.*' I trust for all your rational beliefs you will make no objection to my lending it to your betrothed, Cousin?"

"By no means, Ynyr. I will attempt not to be too controlling."*
Émile's smile was so normal Sophie was sure in his case she must have been mistaken about that momentary flicker of hostility at the back of the eyes.

Chapter Eleven

Chester

HARRIET DE COURCY WAS PUZZLING over breakfast how to cut down on the use of candles in the servants' rooms while John de Courcy opened the post. Suddenly, he exclaimed with joy.

"This is a piece of news! Harriet, my dear, guess who is asking for our little sister Sophie?"

"The local curate?"

"No, he is a married man. Take another guess; scruple not about aiming too high."

His wife clapped her hands. "Surely not Count Ruthin?"

"Near as good. None other than *Monsieur* Émile Dubois!" he smiled. "He writes to invite me to give the bride away, saying that though he is sure His Lordship the Count of Ruthin will be happy to have us guests, he hopes to take his own house in the area this week. We must about arranging for our trip, as the wedding will take place by special licence during the time of our proposed visit. This has all fallen out most conveniently!"

"Excellent, John! Yet, the man is such a scoundrel. He has a dreadful reputation. If one quarter of the things spoken of him are true, then he will make an appalling husband for the poor little girl."

"Why, they may even pull well together. If not, then they can live separately after she has given him a couple of heirs."

"But how did she ever draw him in?"

"Yes, Harriet, she has done well. She is pretty, of course, but not outstanding, so I never expected her to make such a brilliant match. I was hoping that she would make something of her connection with our great relatives. I had written reminding her of her duty, but I never expected such news."

He went back to the letter. "I must write at once giving my consent. What a thing, Harriet, eh? Well, the sooner the villain marries her the better, before he changes his mind. He is probably suffering from a fit of conscience brought on by his excesses. These rakes tend to have such now and then, I collect. Perhaps he wants to ensure an heir, too, having lost his family. Dear, there will be no occasion for me to mention that it took some years for our mother to present me to the world."

"For sure not, dear, and it is lucky that his parents being dead, will raise no objection to the match."

He frowned. She poured him a cup of tea.

"The de Courcy's are as well bred as any Llewelyn or Dubois, Harriet. We have merely fallen upon temporary misfortune. Still, the future is bright! When this revolutionary nonsense is over in France, my future Dubois nieces and nephews will be able to take their places at *Versailles...*"

Plas Uchaf
Famau Mountain

Émile and Sophie were in the open top of the tower-like folly, his secret hide-out at Plas Uchaf as a boy. The day was bright, an icy east wind buffeting about. Sophie was warm in her fur lined cloak as she sat on the bench watching him carve on the wall with his fearsome knife, '*Émile Gilles Gaston Dubois loves Sophie Marie Louise de Courcy for always.*'

"Can I hold you to that, Émile, though I become stout and tell tedious stories?"

He grinned. "I would rather you resisted such urges, but I think I must love you anyway."

She dimpled, having just asked him to resist an urge himself two minutes before. They had been having one of their kissing sessions; caressing her large bottom that he so admired, he murmured, "Such a lovely *derrière* as you have! What a pity it is we must wait for this foolish ceremony, which means nothing to me, for as you have sworn yourself to me, I regard you as my wife already." He kissed her some more. "I don't suppose, *ma chère?*"

"Really, Émile!"

So, he'd gone over to carve his promise.

High up as they were here, the view down over the foothills to the Clwyd Valley stretched out beneath was even more magnificent than the usual ones from Plas Uchaf. Sophie kept her head turned away from the roofs of Plas Cyfeillgar and noted a farm cart trundling along the level track leading from there past the home farm.

Such an ordinary sight made the more grotesque the threat hanging over them so luridly recounted in '*The Legend of the Vampyre*', by 'A Traveller'.

Sophie had opened it in her room, hands shaking so she could hardly take in the words as she turned over pages brown with age.

> *'The tragedy of the Vampire proper is to be Undead until released by the One who Loves Him Sufficiently to expedite the Terrible Ritual of Driving the Stake through the Heart and Severance of the Head... The greatest care of the Loved Ones of those who have survived the Vampyre Bite must be to prevent the Victim from becoming another Predator, the Demi, the Man or Woman Vampyre, who on Death must become a Full Vampyre in turn unless these Gruesome Rituals are perpetrated upon the Corpse.*

> *'This apparently Human Creature has an Inhuman Nature, though he Respireth, Sleepeth of a Night and Dineth at table...*

> *"The most inhuman characteristic of the Condition, the Thirst for Blood develops typically within a month, the Passionate Man succumbing more readily than the Continent...*

> *'There is Unease in the presence of Religious Rituals or Artefacts. The Transformations of Shape followeth, although Transformations to Bat and Wolf cometh later...*

'Cure is Traditionally Attempted Through the use of Healing Plants, and should these Fail, the Cure of the Charged Wine. These I shall expound in greater detail subsequently...' Sophie's trembling fingers tore a page as she rushed to: *'...Equal portions of Rosemary, Sage, Fennel, Thyme and Mint to which must be added one twentieth of chopped Garlic, given for Three Days, to which the Nettle is subsequently added. For those Poisoned by Prolonged Exposure to the Fangs, this must be taken some couple of hours to prove efficacious...a Harrowing Wait obtaineth, while the Victim Inevitably, whether or not the cure is Proving, Demonstrates the above Symptoms... If these have not abated within some Couple of Weeks, then arrangements must be made to commence the Cure of the Blessed Wine..."*

Appropriately, the candle had guttered.

Shuddering, Sophie then skimmed over the details of this bathing of the patient in wine left in a church overnight. She was sure with the sceptical Émile, any form of healing by faith could only fail.

Now she jumped up and stooped to kiss the top of his hair, carefully, for she knew he disliked it disarranged. "*Monsieur* – I mean – Émile, I shall always think of this your promise still here, as the seasons turn into years. After this, I hate to speak of something so miserable as our fears, though I think we must."

He turned with eyes as near solemn as she had seen. He drew her up with him. He did some chin-chucking. "You are in the right, Sophie."

Her voice wobbled. "Katarina says this herbal remedy has an equal chance of success or failure. If the worst comes about, Émile, and you do develop a – longing for blood – Heavens, this is grotesque – I wonder if I should let you take a little at a time for me, to satisfy your thirst?"

"You are a brave girl to speak of it. I cannot judge yet, but I fear that restraint with you would be no easier for me in that than it is with the other sort of desire...Katarina tells me that if they escape being dispatched, the Man Vampire ages so laggardly that he may go on for two hundred and fifty years. *Bien sûr*, I would not like to live so long without you, but I will hazard that if our fears are realised, my devout girl would never agree to join me through religious scruple."

"Oh, my dear." She squeezed his hands. "I should think it over before giving you my answer, yet I think you guess truly, Émile."

The clock tower chimed one. He sighed. "*Alors,* my lovely girl, we will talk on this dismal topic again. I am determined that should I turn to a monster, you must be in a position to live apart from me. Accordingly, I have instructed my lawyer to settle such monies on you as shall make you independent and comfortable."

"Ah, Émile, it is so good in you, but don't speak of that." She sighed too, and they kissed some more.

Soon it became passionate. "Come, Sophie, we must to lunch or I will be back to suggesting we anticipate our marriage vows."

Émile and the Dowager Countess finally compromised about the timing of the wedding – Émile was to marry Sophie by special licence, but not for ten days, rather than within the week. Émile, having rushed to get the licence, hurried to set about renting a house called Plas Planwydden (Plane Tree Mansion)* outside Llandyrnog on the Denbigh Road, which the owners had only left days since.

He took Sophie to see it, along with their full staff so far, Agnes, Georges and Katarina.

Sophie knew Émile had written to a man in London whom he wanted to be butler and his wife to be housekeeper. The second chef at Plas Uchaf would condescend to be cook. Sophie felt so timid at the idea of running her own house that she was glad that Émile was taking care of much of that side of things.

Katarina ran to look over the gardens. Georges and Agnes went to look over the servants' quarters. As Sophie and Émile walked through the reception rooms, she exclaiming in delight at it all, Émile looked dubious.

"Believe it or not, this is one of the largest houses in the area after Plas Uchaf. But we shall be cosy enough here, and will tuck your redoubtable maid and my companion in wickedness up somewhere together. Do you like it?"

Sophie supposed someone who brought up in the Château des Oliviers might think this mansion cramped. "I love it! It is perfect, and so light!"

"I suppose it is a comfortable enough place. Can you endure remaining in this area a while, *ma chère?* I know the proximity of that Monster Bat household is repellent to you, as it is to me, but I think we must stay. I feel I should –" he paused before going on effortfully, "Try and destroy him, thought it seems disgusting to kill him for being the monster that I – I am sorry to dwell on this – may become myself. Besides, if I were careless, which hopefully I am not, it could lead to my going to the gallows. For some reason, that might distress you."

Sophie seized him to kiss him. "Oh, don't!" Then, she remembered Kenrick's own shuddering pause when he was about to speak of the destruction of vampires.

"Gilles Long Legs is suffering from moral scruples, my angel. Can this be the affect of your sweetness upon me? Yet my qualms become irrelevant when we think what a menace Kenrick must be to people hereabouts. *Alors*, we know the Vampire couple are away at present."

She thrust these horrors aside. "I love the house, Émile! It is perfect. Not at all too small! I am so lucky!"

He raised his eyebrows. "Some might contend that. Let us see the stables. You wish for a couple of donkeys, Sophie; they are stupid, stubborn creatures, but if you want them then you shall have them."

Sophie accompanied him out to the stables. While he strolled critically about, she hoped that he wouldn't decide against Plas Planwydden due to inadequate stabling. She was already in love with the place. To her relief, he decided they would take it until Dubois Court became free.

He said he would use the billiards room as his study. This was a shadowy room not far from the servant's quarters. Sophie wondered at his taste. "But my dear one, it is not at all one of the better rooms. Why not take the delightful bright one with the parquet flooring at the front?"

"No, this is just what I am looking for. It's quiet, and out of the way."

Something about his look made her ask as they went into the dining room, "Émile, I so hope you have no further strange experiences with time?"

He did some cheek pinching. "I think that it was a lingering influence which with luck will not happen again. Here is the dining room. We will have us a butler rather less stiff than Roberts, eh?"

Sophie laughed, gloating at the thought of the two of them dining alone together. Then she forced herself say, "Émile, for all you say, I feel so guilty about keeping what has happened a secret from Lord Ynyr and Her Ladyship, when they have been so kind."

Émile looked at a stained glass window, which dropped splashes of red, blue and yellow on the floor in the winter sunshine. It depicted a knight kneeling in apparent subjection to a dark, arrogant looking woman who put Sophie in mind of Ceridwen Kenrick.

"Why burden them with a horrible secret about which they could do nothing? Besides, even supposing we could convince them, would *Madame ma Tante* be likely to agree to your marrying a potential Man Vampire? Do you suggest I confide in the Vicar, perhaps at one of his Good Dinners? *'My dear Monsieur Dubois, I would not contradict you, though these beliefs of yours clearly border on the heretical, but please do recollect you how you have lately suffered a high fever.'*"

Sophie sighed. She was having made up for everyone at Plas Uchaf a tiny steel cross and chain as a leaving present. It used up most of her savings, but it salved her conscience a little about not warning people of what she knew. Agnes had gone about saying these were powerful good luck charms. The Dowager Countess thought it eccentric; Mrs Brown said it was Papist.

Sophie burst into admiration at the view of the Famau Mountain from the bow windows in the front rooms. "There are window seats, too, Émile!"

He laughed. "I see keeping you happy will scarce take much effort." He leaned on the window seat, gazing over at the mountains, purple in this light, and then looked at her, a slight flickering at the back of his eyes. "Ynyr admitted to a certain tenderness for you, *ma chère*. I do not blame him, but I am happy to have got you first."

Sophie had to smile. He made it sound as if there had been a stampede of admirers jostling each other to be first to cast themselves at her feet. It would have been gratifying to her pride if it had been so, though of course she would have rejected them all for him.

Upstairs, they came to the nursery apartments. Sophie was eager to see them, though too shy to suggest it. Émile was shockingly direct as he opened the doors, "We may with luck have a small resident for these before we leave."

Sophie, as a Proper Young Bride, cast down her eyes. Inside, she thrilled with eagerness. He went in for some more condescending chin chucking at her primness.

Then, a terrible thought struck her. What if none of the cures worked? Did Man Vampires father partially Vampire babies? Yet she could not mention it to Émile, cheerfully oblivious to such a dread as he was. It might make him delay the wedding while he investigated further; then, should there be any doubt over the matter, it might make him resolve that the best thing that he could do for them all would be to 'take himself off somewhere' as he had threatened.

She decided to do some research of her own and place her faith in the cures.

Katarina hurled herself up the stairs to join them. "*Monsieur* Émile, it is wonderful here! You must take it! There is a sunken garden with steps down and a sundial, stained glass in the dining room and an aviary!"

"*Certainment* that must settle the matter, *ma petite*. An aviary, eh? Sophie, I hope you do not want a flock of parrots and a monkey besides the donkeys, kittens and, of course, your tame bat."

"Georges will do for the monkey." Agnes said, joining them and noting Sophie's horrified look.

You will not be a bat! You must not be!

Sophie refused to believe Émile could ever turn into a blood sucking being. The idea seemed as ridiculous as it was horrible. He was surely as human as ever, though perhaps his nails did look a little sharp, and he no longer liked herbs and avoided garlic. She tried to believe that was all part of the cure. Hadn't Katarina more or less said as much?

———⌖———

"Agnes, it doesn't mention babies at all." Sophie thought her maidenly blush was ridiculous in the circumstances as she put down '*The Legend of the Vampyre*'.

Agnes' bright eyes were solicitous. "You look so pretty all pink that is no wonder *Monsieur* Émile falling head over ears for you…Is plain silly of that writer to miss out what matters. Well, Katarina doesn't remember any Half Vampire babies in her village, but is worrying for you that you don't know for sure."

Sophie got up to pace about, fondling the family ring Émile had given her which she kept on a chain about her neck. "I may be being selfish in taking such a risk should we have children; still, I fear I love him too much to let such a dread deter me."

Agnes went over to poke the fire, and then turned. "Is annoyed I am, about my Tarot pack refusing to give sensible answers to me this last while about all this. I have never known it act so. *Nain* used to say that happens sometimes."

Sophie, who'd been secretly hoping for some reassurance from the wicked Tarot pack, felt a stab of disappointment. "Yet perhaps *Monsieur* Émile will be long free of this by the time – there is need for concern. To be sure, my mother waited three years before John arrived."

Despite the menace hanging over them, Sophie went about singing. She might be living in a fool's paradise, but she couldn't stop herself. She sang for most of the day that Émile slipped on her finger a beautiful sapphire and garnet ring and she gave him back his other ring.

Nobody objected to Émile's reading to them '*The Lost Treasure of Count Boldino*' instead of '*Madoc the Magnificent or the Vampyre's Curse*'. It rivalled the other in histrionics, and as it wasn't about the supernatural, the Dowager Countess preferred it.

On that day, too, John's letter of consent arrived.

Honoured Sir,

It is with tears of Joy in my eyes, My Dear Sir, I take up my pen to accede to Your Request. A Marriage between your most Distinguished Self and my sweetest Sister is a Blessing that must Crown every other Hope...I cannot express my Delight at the idea of giving my Most Treasured Sister away at the Ceremony that will Join Your Souls as you have already joined Your Hearts. Being Privy to my Sister's Hopes as ever I was, I do know it is with you that she trusts her Worldly Happiness resides. I am entirely confident, Honoured Sir, to Give her to you with my Devout Blessing... I would further like to give you my Assurance that the Females of my family being all of them Excellent Breeders, I send her to be Your Wife confident that she will present you with a Son and Heir most speedily..."

The Count wrote to John (not even through his secretary) inviting him to bring Harriet to stay at Plas Uchaf as long as they wished. Sophie could imagine how that letter had been passed about John's whist club and Harriet's sewing circle.

To Sophie's disappointment, John and Harriet didn't bring the children, but they brought presents and so much affection that Sophie could almost believe she had been wrong in feeling that at Chester they saw her as a burden.

In awe of Émile at first, they were overwhelmed by his easy manners. If he repressed a smile at times at what they said, he was so affable to them that Sophie fell on him to cover his face with kisses of thanks whenever she was alone with him.

Perhaps a fulsome streak is after all a family characteristic.

Agnes made mouths about Harriet. "I am Glad that I do not work for That One."

Harriet advised: "Do not let That Forward Girl Take Advantage. That little girl *Monsieur* Émile has adopted is near as bad, while that valet of his is beyond anything! I caught him eyeing me as though I were a servant myself. He is a handsome wretch, to be sure. Sophie, you must put your foot down."

Far from it, Sophie wanted to make everyone happy.

Agnes said to her, "That Éloise wants to come to *Plas Planwydden,* but for sure you don't want such a flirty baggage making mischief."

Basking as she was in Émile's adoration, Sophie felt no threat from the girl. Besides, she couldn't credit that Éloise was debauched enough to have aimed to be Émile's mistress. Overwhelmed by a superstitious fancy that if she was kind to her former rivals, Émile wouldn't turn into a vampire, she said, "Oh, I've no objection."

Agnes raised her eyebrows. "I would not advise it, *cariad,* I mean, Miss Sophie."

Georges swaggered up and made his mocking bow. "*Mademoseilles.*" Agnes frowned. Sophie went away, singing.

"*Jolie* Agnes..." He gave her nose a gentle pinch, but she jerked her head away. "Don't, Georges! I'm too busy to talk. I will never get this gown finished in time."

"It makes no matter, she can wear something else." He caressed her waist.

She pulled away. "Stop it!"

He crossed his arms. "*Alors,* tell me what I have done? Please do not mutter 'Nothing'. Treat me to the torrent of accusations *immediatment.*"

"Ow!" she sucked her pricked finger. "Look what you have made me do! Go away, Georges, I am in no mood for your nonsense."

His eyebrows were mingling with the wavy black hair he wore tumbling over his forehead. "Never before have I endured a women speaking to me so and returned for more. But I will endure it and more from you, *chérie,* and put it down to Good Enough Reasons." He swung his muscular shoulders as he swaggered away.

"Humph!" Agnes went back to her sewing.

"I will be nervous at this dinner, Agnes. Everyone will be looking at me, trying to ascertain what *Monsieur* mile finds so special about his Aunt's companion."

"There's so lovely you look, Miss Sophie unless they need spectacles, they must see at once!" As she spoke, Agnes' brown eyes sparkled almost as much as ever.

Sophie pulled her thoughts from her own concerns. "Agnes, is anything the matter?"

"It will pass soon enough, Miss. I am become much too fond of Georges; it is not what I planned. It was ill advised in me to let him meet Eiluned. He is too much of a rascal, and I must think of her."

Agnes was looking too sweet for it to occur to Sophie to be moralistic. Instead, she felt a stab of sorrow for Georges, whom Émile said was truly in love with Agnes. She realised how she liked him. "I cannot deny he and his master have been rascals both. But Agnes, for all he is so rakish, I know his feelings for you to be sincere."

"He will get the better of it directly. There's a big difference between marrying a rich rascal and marrying a poor one, Miss."

However shy Sophie might be at the dinner, she saw that John and Harriet, seated in their places of honour, looked – for the first time that she remembered – content with their lot.

Sophie tried not to gaze gloatingly for more than half the time at Émile, so magnificent in the blue coat she liked best. He was still so thin his cheekbones jutted, but as lively as ever.

Dr Powell rubbed his hands. "Miss Sophie, you never thought where your stay at Plas Uchaf would lead you."

Lord Ynyr smiled brightly; John agreed vehemently, "Indeed not, Sir!" Morwenna looked as though she reserved her own opinion about any plans the *déclassé* de Courcy's may have had in sending Sophie to Plas Uchaf.

Seeing Mr Lewis down the table, looking like a rejected spaniel, Sophie fell to wondering how to help him transfer his passion to someone else.

The Reverend Smythe-Jones smiled from Sophie to Émile. "Apart from my pleasure at such a happy event involving–" he gave a sort of sitting bow to Émile, "Two such delightful new members to our little community, a wedding will distract attention from the ridiculous – almost Gothic – tales that are being put about."

In his distress, he needed to take a sip of claret and sign for another helping of the pie before continuing. "The shocking thing concerning it is, that they do not just come from ignorant farm workers, but from respectable people who should know better. The other day a shopkeeper actually asked me if I believed in vampires. You can imagine my response. I blame the circulating libraries, myself."

Morwenna put a handkerchief to her lips to hide her smile; Sophie looked at her plate. The others murmured polite agreement.

"I can well imagine, Sir." Émile's eyes were twinkling. He was squeezing Sophie's knee under the table, and it sent such delightful shivers down her spine she could hardly sit still. If there was an element of Otherness in him now which added to those shivers, she preferred not to dwell on why that was.

Chapter Twelve

"*MERDE*!" ÉMILE – NAKED AND dozing off – opened his eyes to stare at the flickering about the canopy of his bed at Plas Planwydden. .

He jumped up. "Is this a wedding present from That Jade or has it attached itself to me?"

The images began to solidify, to expand, showing a wind swept heath, an overcast sky and a group of men in masks sitting about by their horses.

Georges came through from the dressing room. "The coat you want for tomorrow – what in the Devil's name –-!" He glared up in outrage rather than alarm.

"Keep away, Georges, you don't want to join in the fun. I may be drawn in. I could try running away, but it might come after me –"

"Get away from it!" As Émile didn't move, Georges dragged him away from the bed. He swore as the swirling images followed them and Émile yelled, "Leave go of me, Georges!"

The next moment, they were pulled up into the pictures and landed on Hounslow Heath on a late summer afternoon.

———✦———

Émile and Georges both stumbled. Their accomplice Tom cursed. When the nerves are strained, any unexpected sound or movement infuriates.

It was an overcast warm afternoon, the air on the heath sweet. A distant curlew took flight, its sleepy cooing retreating.

Georges saw his own horror reflected in Émile's eyes, and even as he fought to speak, he saw Émile struggling too. He felt himself fainting and gasping as he fought to bring out the words.

Still struggling to speak, Émile caught at Tom, who seeing the horror in his eyes, stared, speechless at what he took to be *Monsieur* Gilles in a funk. Émile stammered out, "Beware–" Then he choked. Georges snatched at Tom's arm, but Tom flung it off, swearing.

Then there came the sound of horses' hooves and rattling wheels. Tom shouted and leapt on his horse, eyes wild, rummaging for his pistols, while Émile and Georges did likewise.

As the coach drew in sight, they fired overhead to intimidate. Tom roared, "Stand and deliver!"

Having heard somewhere that is what highwaymen said, he said it. Likewise, seeing *Messieurs* Gilles and Georges being gallant to the ladies, he played that part too.

There was a chaos of whinnying, plunging horses, the driver swearing, a woman screaming repeatedly, "I told you!" A male voice shouted querulously: "Why don't you do something, you lubbard? Did I pay you for nothing?"

Georges' mind swam, the clarity of his foreknowledge fading, though he still remembered enough to know he and Émile had been here before, and that something horrible would happen. The details came to him in sudden flashes, only to disappear the next moment.

Automatically he was joining Émile in reassuring the women, "Please do not fear for your safety, *Mesdames*. Permit us hand you down…"

Tom was asking if any of them wished to dance. Some order was restored. *Monsieur* Gilles helped a stout matron down and Georges was all attentiveness to a younger, while Tom did a few turns with the third.

A shouted order cut through the air, followed by shots.

The passengers cried out and the horses panicked once more.

Georges usually loved an escape on horseback, the wind in his hair, the mud splashing up underneath the horses beating hooves, the sound of the pursuit dying away.

This one began with disaster. As Tom jumped into the saddle, a shot caught him in the back. The horse reared and neighed. He jerked, fell sideways, and screamed as it bolted, dragging him by a foot caught on the stirrup through bushes and over stones, turned from a bold highwayman to an embodiment of pain. The women, crouched now by the carriage, mingled their shrieks with his.

Georges' first pistol jammed. He saw a soldier aim for him, a lanky fellow similar in build to Émile, who fired on him. The man fell with a shout, clutching his shoulder. Tom's screams from the thicket behind were still loud as the horse dragged him away.

Émile tried to calm his own plunging horse, while Georges, freeing the blockage in his weapon, fired on the stout sergeant he thought had shot Tom. He cursed as he missed, and gaining his horse, turned to fire on him with his second pistol, hating the man's red, excited face, crimson in contrast to the scarlet of his jacket.

Émile turned to shoot behind him with his second pistol, aiming for him too. The man seemed to have a charmed life, for he ducked and the shot sang over his head.

A couple more shots missed them as Émile leaped on his mount and she reared again. Then he and Georges were galloping into the thicket after Tom, the soldiers chasing and firing.

They came on Tom soon. He lay still, having come apart from the horse when in its panic it ran up against a sapling. He was torn and bleeding all over. Georges noted the blood trickling from his ears, which satisfied him Tom was dead or near enough to make no difference.

Émile reined in and threw himself down to retrieve the broken remnants of the most arrogant Gentleman of the Road.

"Do you think you are Sir Lancelot?" Georges cursed as Émile managed to drape the inert body over the front of his saddle while another shot from their pursuers winged overhead. Another hit the trunk of a sapling in a shower of bark while a bird shot upwards, squawking. Georges took aim with his second pistol at a glimpse of red and smiled nastily as he heard a cry and confused shouts.

Then they were off again, with Émile urging Georges to go ahead; his own overburdened horse couldn't make good speed. Georges knew – though he would never have admitted it – he would have stopped for Émile should there be the slightest chance one spark of life remained in him, but he cursed Émile for insisting on rescuing the remains of Tom.

How they escaped, Georges never knew, for there was little enough cover; perhaps the soldiers were stupid; perhaps Georges' last shot had killed the sergeant; Georges hoped so.

Again and again he sensed this having happened before, how they should not be here at all; something about Émile told him he felt it too. Meanwhile, somehow they eluded pursuit, hiding behind the largest bushes, taking a convoluted route across open country. Tom still breathed raggedly when they arrived at Mr and Mrs Kit's.

———⁓⁓⁓⁓⁓———

They watched Tom dying in the bed, still mercifully unconscious. Georges finally brought out, "This has happened before. I don't mean one of us being shot, I mean everything –" He stopped speaking as the drowning feeling overcame him.

Émile spoke with an effort, "I feel so too…" His eyes told Georges the rest.

Mrs Kit had helped undress Tom without comment beyond wincing at his injuries. She folded ancient, holey blankets underneath him. His breath now came with the rattling Georges and Émile knew well. They shared a bottle of brandy and waited.

"I should have guessed from that miserable publican *salaud's* sneaky eyes."

Émile roused from where he sat, head supported on one hand, eyes resting on the figure in the bed. "Of course, Georges, we cannot expect everyone to share our own moral uprightness."

"Informers is different, and you know it…Poor sod was cut to ribbons, eh?"

The flickering on the ceiling came and their eyes met. "Again–" Émile choked.

———⁓⁓⁓⁓⁓———

They were back at Plas Planwydden, dropped softly on the rug, gasping with relief to be away from Tom's rattling breath.

Émile staggered to his feet, naked once more, and shaking himself. "I would have given something not to have relived that one, Georges. I only knew what must be in those first moments, when I could see you trying to warn the poor bastard even as did I." He pulled on his robe and paced about in the dim light.

It was still dark outside. The fire had died down to glowing embers and the room smelt strongly of wax, two of the candles having just guttered.

Georges went up to him and placed a hand on his arm. "*Mon pauvre ami,* I thought you deluded. I assumed *petite Mademoiselle* Sophie was submitting to your madness. Now I believe you." He gave the arm a squeeze. "It must have been a torment for you."

Émile smiled, and putting his hand on Georges', briefly returned the pressure. "I am not used to soft words from you, Georges. Tom's agony was too strong a meat even for That Jade. I remember now she got up to turn the page on the book by the bed before it began. "

"Think you this is some enchantment?"

"I don't know. It may be Kenrick through her uses me for experiments, much as some use rabbits. I cannot see *Madame* troubling to focus on my meeting with Sophie, neither. It may be she skipped past that, too, and that somehow made it come to me. She liked the brawls and the raids.

'Sophie told me how she remained aware of how things were throughout her time with me in Paris. She tried to tell me, but couldn't speak. It was so with me, when I dropped down into the cafe, but my awareness lasted but moments, leaving me with the feeling tantalised us at Hounslow Heath, yet not so strong. At times during this last trip, my memory near returned."

He paced about. "What goes on, Georges? For sure our current bodies were not there, for we had the clothes and pistols we wore last summer. I'd have looked silly enough, eh, trying to hold up a coach stark naked, without a pistol to speak of? But Sophie was wearing that grey dress, both by my bed and in Paris. She gave me her necklace and I was able to keep it, which is strange indeed.

'I have read something that suggests that we have many bodies, the outward one being the most corporal. I believe that whilst Sophie's material body travelled so from England last May, when we were drawn back together we left our physical bodies behind, having them in that time and space already."

Georges stared. "You talk in riddles, *Monsieur* Gilles, yet it does sound like to what Kenrick rambled on heretofore." He glanced over at the bedside cabinet. "There's the funny little book you had on you when you came back that day. '*On the Use of Imitative Representation*'. Eh, did Kenrick give it you?"

Émile's look struck him as evasive. "Why think you that, Georges? I believe I picked it up on Ynyr's shelves. Georges, with this hanging over me, how can I marry Sophie and risk her so apart from the menace to her and everyone I may become as a monster bat?"

Georges glanced at the clock. "It approaches seven. Too late and as a gentleman, you cannot call it off besides."

Émile ran his hands through his hair. "Time has gone askew, Georges. We weren't up late for all we drank well. Some hours have vanished. On the last occasion, I was too confused to make much of it. How long were we back there? Four hours at most, even counting the endless ride. This thing has always happened when I am half asleep. *Mon Dieu*, Georges, how can I risk my angel being caught in anything like that?"

"*Alors*, there will be no danger of it happening tonight, for you won't be doing much sleeping for sure."

———⟨∘⟩⟨∘⟩⟨∘⟩———

Sophie sang as Agnes dressed her in the wedding gown – an altered cream ball gown she had only finished in time with help from Éloise and Katarina. "Agnes, it is perfect! You are the cleverest girl!"

A smile kept spreading across Sophie's face. She knew there was no dignity in her behaviour.

Harriet and Éloise were helping too. If Éloise felt resentment, she hid it well.

When Katarina looked in, Harriet sent her on an errand.

Sophie protested, "But I want Katarina back soon because I asked her to help with my bouquet."

Katarina was too happy at going to live at *Plas Planwydden* with her four favourite people to trouble about Sophie's sister-in-law. Besides, she, Agnes and Georges were already invited to the wedding.

She had already done an Exclusion Ritual to keep vampires out of Plas Planwydden (this didn't keep out those who were already part of the household). Last night, she had gone about Plas Uchaf carrying out a final protection rite. She feared the Count and Dowager Countess might invite Mr and Mistress Kenrick over in the future, but there was nothing she could do about that.

Harriet was secretly too impressed with Sophie's cleverness in catching her rakish grand relative to scold her for long about staff discipline. Besides, having seen the familiarities Émile allowed, she supposed Sophie was changing to suit him.

"It's lovely Miss Sophie looks!" Agnes kept exclaiming, as she finished Sophie's hair.

Sophie thought how the One Thing nobody mentioned on the wedding day was surely the one foremost in everybody's mind, unless hers was particularly improper.

The Dowager Countess had appeared in Sophie's room two nights ago, looking as though she'd swallowed a poker and actually clearing her throat: "I assume, Sophie, that your late Mama or your sister Harriet* have told you of the Duties of the Marriage Bed?"

"Yes, Madam." Sophie needed to fight down an urge to giggle, though the snatches of talk she had overheard might have made her cry instead.

"Yes, well, as you are so clearly in love, it does make it easier…"

Sophie looked forward to the Duties of the Marriage Bed as she stood with her party at the front steps.

John took out his watch – the tower clock was in sight, but he only trusted his own timepiece – and smiled. "We won't set off for five minutes. We must make the young devil sweat it out. Recollect you how Harriet kept me waiting?"

When her party arrived at the church, Sophie suppressed another giggle at the look of relief the magnificent Émile shot over his shoulder. Had he dreaded she might vanish again? As she began the leisurely walk up the aisle on John's arm, despite the eyes on her, she couldn't stop that gleeful smile from coming.

Émile – who normally avoided churchgoing if possible – had attended twice in the last week to make sure that, 'I do not suddenly fall down at the entrance, clutching my throat with a horrible gargling, though it might provide some entertainment and Mrs Brown would be delighted.'

As Émile slipped the wedding ring on her finger, Sophie repressed a start. She knew how often he needed to trim his nails these past few days, sometimes, when nobody else was by, taking out his dreadful knife to do so. Now she saw why.

The nails didn't only look sharp; they were taking on the hooked, inhuman appearance of talons.

The reality of marrying a man who might become a monster came to her as a sudden shock. She raised her eyes to his.

Those slanty green eyes showed purely human adoration as he said, "With this ring I thee wed."

Her heart felt as if it was expanding. She let her breath out, telling herself it was one of the symptoms brought on by the cure, as predicted by Katarina.

The Reverend Smythe-Jones said, "I now pronounce you man and wife. You may kiss the bride."

Sophie's insides lurched as Émile's lips met hers and her only thought about those nails was a vague hope he would trim them before bed.

She looked forward to that night throughout the wedding breakfast at Plas Uchaf while Lord Ynyr made the toasts with his usual ease.

John made an embarrassing speech. It began, "It is with the Deepest and Most Humble Joy that I raise my glass in Honour…" and finished, "To my Dearest Sister, now Rejoicing under the name of *Madame Dubois!*" Sophie blushed throughout, but that was appropriate for a bride. She was again grateful to Émile for keeping his face solemn and his response amiable.

While Harriet, Agnes and Éloise dressed her again to leave for Plas Planwydden Sophie couldn't help singing: *'Ombra Mai Fú.'*

"I always said to John that that angel's voice of yours would finally get you well settled." Harriet fussed over her sash. "We are well pleased with you, dear."

Harriet and John were to go home themselves the next day, and Harriet couldn't wait to call in triumph on everyone she knew. Meanwhile John intended to write a book: *'A Short History of the Families Llewelyn and Dubois'.*

At Plas Planwydden, the staff was lined up to greet the bride. Sophie did yet more blushing as she smiled on them.

Agnes looked thoughtfully at the new butler. He was a fat man of perhaps thirty who greeted Sophie with as low a bow as he could manage. "*Madame* Dubois." The width of his smile astonished Sophie.

That wicked grin betrayed him; she knew at once he would be at home in the company of Marcel Sly Boots and the others. She could recognise a scoundrel now, and guessed him to be a prize specimen.

She shot a glance at Émile. He was all unconsciousness, smiling acknowledgements to everyone (there seemed to be no difference in the appearance of his teeth).

Sophie greeted the housekeeper standing next to the butler. Mrs Kit was tall, stout herself, though nothing like as fat as her husband, and older than he. Her pale and oddly inexpressive face was long and plump. Under her smartly starched cap her dark hair was lank.

As her calculating dark eyes ran over Sophie, Sophie wondered how she and Agnes would get along. Émile had offered Agnes herself the job of housekeeper, but she had refused, saying she preferred to remain Sophie's maid.

Agnes had told Sophie how Émile wanted to reward her for caring for him during his illness. She had turned up her short nose at his offers of money: '*I told him: 'I did it because I happen to like you, Sir. But should you ever start treating Miss ill, then it is she as shall have my loyalty.'*

'*So he says, "Agnes, I'll even forgive you for suggesting I would ever ill treat her. Loyalty is my favourite virtue, ma petite. Will you take a rise in wages instead?"*'

Now, Émile looked at Sophie wryly. "Come and see the stables. There are a couple there whom you will like." (So he guessed her opinion of the couple she had just met.) He took her arm and they went round the side of the house. "Mr Kit is a good fellow, and has done me favours; Dolly near saved my life. They have had foul luck. I am sure My Angel would not have me turn my back upon them."

"No indeed, *Monsieur* Émile."

He whistled and came to a stop. "We are back to that; you are put out indeed."

Sophie forced a smile. "No. If they have been good to you then I must like them."

"By the by, regarding my continued good behaviour, I thought you might like to know that I received this letter from my solicitor today. Perhaps it will make up for my taking on poor old Kit and Dolly."

Sophie glanced at the letter, which was written in legal jargon and concerned his settling on her a sum of ten thousand pounds. "Émile! I could rant about your goodness like to the newly married *Pamela* herself."

He smiled. "I put Morwenna's copy down long ere I came to that."

A furious braying made them turn, laughing. Sophie rushed over to admire the brown male donkey who was bawling his disapproval of the world. Meanwhile the grey jenny munched at a pile of hay. "Émile, you got them for me! I wish I had a carrot. What are their names?"

"Jean and Jenny. Shall we see if we can find a treat for them?"

A weedy boy came up to them. "I have something, Mistress, er, *Madame* Dee – Doo –" he gave up on the name.

Émile smiled on him. "The head groom should be with us betimes. Meanwhile, are you both managing?"

She hoped this groom wouldn't be another disreputable connection of Émile's.

To be to be fair to Émile, he had offered to tell her his whole criminal history when he proposed. For sure, when she asked him not to, he hadn't pressed her further. Well, it was too late to worry about such matters now.

It was a mild day for late January and they spent some time with the donkeys and horses. The Count's wedding presents to them were in the stables, too. Émile's was his two favourite mounts from the Plas Uchaf stables. These were head flinging, tall creatures he had to fight to ride and which Sophie found alarming. The Count had given her the placid mare who had so often taken her down the lanes to the villages.

They loitered a while in the grounds. Sophie thought these perfect, with the rose and winter gardens, thickets, terraces and formal, yew fringed walks. Émile caressed her arm and once he assaulted her waist. He had cut his nails, but suddenly, the approaching Duties of the Marriage Bed loomed alarmingly. She slipped out of his clutches to admire the sunken garden. From his wry look as he joined her, she could see he wasn't fooled.

The sun was setting as they went back to the house. Sophie suddenly dreaded one of the vampire bats would appear, but none did. She knew while Katarina had worked to safeguard the grounds against them this protection was limited. Now, Sophie felt more than ever how they should warn people. There was no sense in spoiling the day by raising the matter with Émile; he would reiterate it would be senseless while they could prove nothing.

"*Certainment*, you are eager for one of your English cups of tea." He took her arm again and they went through the house, now shadowy, to the drawing room. It was fragrant with hothouse flowers – as was the whole of the house – and she rushed over to the new piano with delight. "Oh, thank you!" She saw the ornamental boxes of sweetmeats all over the room. "Thank you for all these, too, *Mon* – er – Émile." Apart from these, there was the whole *trousseau* he had insisted she order.

"Give you me a kiss in thanks."

She gave him the kiss, but so reluctantly he sighed and releasing her, went to fetch a taper to light the candles on the piano. "You can thank me by singing that song, what is it called? '*Ombra Mai Fù*'."

She sang and played his favourite pieces for some time. She feared more assaults on her waist, but he didn't make any. Instead, he leaned on the piano, intent.

Wandering over to the bookshelves, he entertained her with some of the titles: "'*Eighty Eventful Years in Athrington.*' Where is Athrington, *ma chère?*

'*A History of the Dowling Family of Croydon.*' Three volumes of that, too. The excitement overwhelms me."

As Sophie failed to eat her dinner – a pity, for there was roast chicken and trifle, her favourites – she thought how ridiculous it was for her to behave like Richardson's Pamela on her wedding eve. Still, she suddenly wondered why people were so sorry for old maids? They never had to go through this.

Émile meanwhile told her funny stories. These included one so absurd Sophie wondered if he was making it up to test her credulity. She always remembered it; it was about a madman he had known who insisted on feeding his horses hot chocolate.

She forced a laugh, shifting in her seat.

"Hmm." Émile looked at her quizzically. He turned to the first footman (Thankfully, the jovial butler was not in the room). "We will serve ourselves, thank you."

The footmen left with bows. Sophie stared after them anxiously, though she realised Émile was unlikely to demand his marital rights at the dinner table. "Have another glass of wine, *ma chère*."

"No, really."

"Only a little, then. Let us toast Absent Friends."

He came round the table, and insisted they toast absent friends several times. She remained rigid as he pinched her cheek. "Sophie, you are looking terrified. Sure it is ironical that I once suspected you of being an adventuress! We will give up on this dinner and I will drink my port. Then I will come and teach you (she started in horror) – *Zut alors*, Sophie! – to beat me at chess."

He spent some time on this hopeless task. She had no talent for chess normally, and now she was worse.

Émile laughed at her puzzlement. "Let me show you a good trap – known as the fork, I believe – which Morwenna used on me. I was writhing so as I first heard you sing that song by Handel I didn't even see it and she took my Queen."

A rapid voice in Sophie's head spoke in slangy French. Somehow, she got the sense of it, as one does in dreams: *Marcel Sly Boots has a trick called the knife!*

Momentarily, the breathless sensation which overcame her when she had the vision of the blond baby and whenever she had been trying to explain things to Émile in Paris came back.

Recovering, she said to Émile, remembering that first evening, "Was it so?"

"Of course, my sweet one! You have no idea how you made me suffer."

She rose to kiss him, but a knock came at the door. It was Georges, who held a muttered talk with Émile in unintelligible French.

"Sophie," Émile came back to stroke her cheek, "A tedious matter claims my attention. I will be back as soon as I can, but it may be two hours. I am sorry I must go off so on our wedding night. Perhaps you should like to have Agnes for company in the meantime? I am sure you wish for some time to face up to the Terrible Ordeal, though I promise that I shall do my best to make it as unlike one as I can."

Sophie could think of nothing more reassuring than to have some time with Agnes. She said on impulse, "Émile, I do hope your errand is not dangerous."

He laughed; his eyes were veiled, but that wasn't unusual. "When, *chérie,* do I ever do anything dangerous?"

Agnes jollied Sophie along, playing cards with her. At a quarter to ten, she brought up – no doubt on Émile's instructions – one of the brandy-in-hot milk drinks he favoured as a curative for nervousness. "Honestly, Miss, there is nothing to worry about with the right man, and you love him, don't you? Well, then. *Monsieur* Émile did ask me to leave your hair down."

Perhaps he wanted to do some fearsome, unguessed at sexual act involving her hair? Sophie shuddered.

Émile shifted, glancing at the clock that hung above the blazing fire that was one of the main attractions of the inn. "Of all nights for the boy to be late!"

"You have my sympathies, *mon ami.* But as I had the good luck to run into him and Katarina says you must needs have special permission to enter *chez* Kenrick, I thought it best to meet with him as soon as may be. The poor brat seemed nervous enough to change his mind without a good bribe and some encouragement."

Émile grumbled.

Georges said suddenly, "I recollect me your rage when we came here first, and you told me *Madame* ignored your proposal. Now, I understand your humiliation."

Émile stared. "Do not tell me Agnes has done as much?"

"I never thought to see the day when I would propose, leave alone be rejected by some country wench burdened with a baby outside wedlock. Agnes has been distant of late, and would not tell me why. I thought that – though I am skilful – we had been caught out, and she feared I'd given her a belly. I said if so I would be happy to marry her, and she laughed at me!" His nearly black eyes blazed.

Émile's lips twitched. He took a quick drink of porter before saying solemnly, "That was insulting enough, *bien sûr.*"

"She said, 'No, *you have taken care of that side of things well enough…* Georges, I am sorry, but we must part. You are too much of a rascal, and I have a child to think of'."

Émile swore in his sympathy. A weedy boy who looked too young for a tavern approached, his eyes searching the room as though he feared that he might see one of the Kenrick's hanging from the ceiling.

"Sir." He bowed awkwardly to Émile.

"Come and have a drink, boy."

A group of farmers smoking pipes by the fire were staring openly at an aristocrat eccentric enough to drink amongst them. Émile indicated the back room, visible through the bar, fireless and deserted. "We may be better yonder." He ordered drinks from the bar and waved amiably to the group as they went through to the icy room.

The boy gazed at Émile, eyes wide. "She Changed you."

Émile was impassive. "Then I must put my faith in *ma petite'* Katarina's weeds."

"I am glad you took Katarina away, Sir."

"So, *Mon Dieu*, am I! Mind, boy, you don't need to go back, after you have aided us. Know you anything of Kenrick's goings on?"

"I keep away from it, Sir. But we all know them to be blood suckers – Mistress Kenrick has made the Captain and Arthur Williams into bloodsuckers too. Master Kenrick does wicked things with time. When the house was let, the front hall was always a terror to us, but now, strange things are everywhere. I know the shade of Captain Mackenzie walks there, yet he is alive –"

He broke off as the Landlord came through with the drinks, looking anxious himself. "Sir, beware for your servants. That recruiting sergeant is back, and looking for trouble."

"Thank you, *Monsieur*." Émile turned back to the boy, who was gulping his porter. "I wish for ease of access to the house and Georges tells me you will ask us in." He took out his pocket book, and the boy, who had bent away from him at his words, moved closer. "Here is an advance."

The boy had no sooner taken the money, than the door crashed open. Strapping and jovial, his face flushed with success, the recruiting sergeant leaned in it with two of his men smirking behind him. The boy made a nervous movement towards the table, perhaps thinking of climbing underneath.

"So you are Frenchies, eh? I hate all Frenchman. But you can't be them *Jacobins*, they wouldn't allow it." The Sergeant swore, turning to Georges. "Why don't you come and fight the bastards like a man?"

"I'd like to fight." Georges jumped up eagerly as the boy cowered back. "But *bien sûr, Monsieur* cannot join the common ranks and the boy is too young."

The Sergeant swore some more in denial. "Too young? You can't be too young to fight them lot! You come have a drink with us, fellow. What's your name?" He draped an arm about Georges, urging him towards the still open door.

Émile drew another man confidentially to one side. "My friend is impulsive. What a nice little *massue,* may I have it?" He plucked the weapon from the man's pocket. "Run, boy!" he called to the boy, who was already skirting his way round the group to the door.

"Give me that!" The heavily built man lunged at Émile, who picked him up with one arm and tossed him over the bar. The man landed upside down, feet waving. The other man charged. Émile dodged aside and the man sprawled across a table, looking astonished.

Émile and Georges hoisted the hefty Sergeant and ran him out across the yard to plant him head first into the half empty rain barrel with a splash like that of a diving walrus. The boy had gone, and the Landlord and the other customers watched and chuckled.

Émile and Georges were still laughing as they rode through the starlit night out of Llandyrnog. Georges broke off. "There's a woman out late."

A woman, who by her brisk walk ey guessed to be young, was in the dark lane ahead of them. She turned about, throwing back her shawl.

"You should not be out at this hour alone, *ma petite*. Where do you live?" Émile asked.

She answered slowly, her Welsh accent strong. "I went for porter for my *Nain*, Sir. She is ailing. Is but five minutes."

"For all that you should not be alone, like Red Riding Hood. *Alors,* Gilles, you are desperate to go to Mistress Sophie, I will see after *Mademoiselle*."

"Then behave yourself, Georges, with an innocent."

"You ain't the only one knows how to be gallant. *Au revoir*…Will you trust me enough to come up on my horse, girl? We must take care with *Nain's* porter. You see, I speak some Welsh already? Until yesterday I courted a Welsh girl."

"Remember what I said about behaving, Georges!" Émile rode off.

"Ain't you afraid to bring a strange man here, *ma petite* Mair?" Georges asked as the girl set the jug of porter down on the earthen floor of the barn. It was icy cold even amongst the hay.

She merely smiled. He saw her teeth – so often in poor condition amongst working girls – were white and healthy, if a little too long; strangely, one beyond the canines was half grown. Then her hazel eyes had locked his, and they held a secret so important that nothing else mattered.

As she kissed and sucked his neck lasciviously before sinking in her teeth, he was only displeased because it distracted him from understanding this secret.

Chapter Thirteen

SOPHIE LAY WRIGGLING HER TOES in fear on top of the bed, shuddering in her new nightdress despite the blazing fire Agnes had made up. She was remembering snippets of confidential talk between Harriet and her friends: '*She cried and he slapped her face...*'

When The Enemy finally came into view, it was a relief, as in some old soldier's story.

Émile invaded via their adjoining dressing rooms, candlestick in hand, wearing his crimson robe. He set the candlestick down on the mantelpiece, and came to sit on the bed and smile at her. "*Viens ici –*" he paused, as though confused, and then he went on smiling, "Sophie, you look as lovely with your hair down as you did in Paris. And your sweet feet! I have never seen your toes before and I fall in love with them at once."

She had sat up to greet him with open arms, but now she lost her nerve and scuttled under the bedclothes. She peeped out as he pulled off his robe.

So that is how a man looks when he is aroused! It is both alarming and a little ridiculous. He does have nice muscles; I will explore those when I am less shy.

He got into the bed and reached for her (his nails were still blunt). "There is no need to hide like a squirrel, my lovely girl. I do love you and we are made for each other."

"I love you too, Émile, but..."

"You are nervous. *Alors*, so am I, because you are a virgin and I do not want to shock or hurt you."

That made it easier. They kissed and then he guided her hand down. It put her in mind of an awful book she once came across in the housekeeper's bedroom in Chester which told how 'Z' put the hand of 'X' on his penis and she '*Stimulated his organ to a purple, swelling passion*'.

Now, Sophie put that information to good use.

In that pornography, X then went on to use her lips, at which point Sophie had dropped the book. Did people do such things? Surely not the married couples she knew, who as often as not called each other 'Madam' and 'Sir' over the breakfast table? Now, she resolved she would do that shocking thing herself soon. She was too shy tonight.

He managed to remove her nightdress, murmuring to her the while as to a frightened animal, which she supposed she was. He kissed and fondled her and she began at last to melt and to caress him in turn. Even in the dim light of the candles, she could see the scars on his back, still not completely healed. She thought she felt them too.

"You have the most beautiful *derrière* imaginable. I must kiss it, and perhaps, another part of you, if *Madame* will permit such appalling freedoms."

When he came to enter her, it did hurt. She whimpered. Instead of slapping her face, he paused. "Does it hurt you too much? Shall I stop?"

He was being so nice she resolved to be stoic. "It doesn't hurt too much; don't stop." She chewed her fingers a little.

Then it stopped hurting and became pleasurable, in fact, perfect; shivers of pleasure started to run through her, then gradually her insides began to contract and to spasm and she began to squeal ridiculously, like a demented mouse, which might have been embarrassing had he not been groaning himself.

Then it was over and they were lying tangled together, their breath rasping as she realised that all her fears had been absurd.

"But that was so nice!" She realised 'nice' was a weak word for what she had felt.

He opened his own eyes. "You are so natural, so perfect. You see it was not so terrible after all. Earlier, *ma pauvre petite*, you looked as though you feared I might take a bite out of you. I assure you, I have no such urges so far."

She wished he hadn't made that joke about biting, but she put it out of mind to tell him how she had been in love with his freckles across the bridge of his nose since she they first met a dozen years since.

"Lucky enough for me; I hate the ugly things."

She thought those freckles seemed lighter as she gazed on them now, but perhaps it was the flickering candlelight.

They were still tangled together when they fell asleep, hours later.

It was light when Sophie wakened to distant but furious blowing and snorting sounds. "Whatever is that?!"

Émile, holding her and gazing down into her face with a look of delight, laughed. "One of your idiotic donkeys, *bien sûr*." He kissed her nose. "So you are finally mine! I can scarce credit I could be so lucky. I have been gloating over you these fifteen minutes, and kissing your face gently enough not to waken you, but that creature is less considerate. You look so beautiful in the morning with your hair about your shoulders like a mermaid that I can scarce believe you real."

Sophie glowed at his words and kissed his nose in turn. She sat up, pushing her hair back, and smiling at her fears of last night about *Monsieur's* wanting her to leave it loose. "My love, it was so sweet in you to give me the donkeys, the piano and all those other presents…I wonder what time it is?"

"*Alors*, Agnes has tact enough not to bring your chocolate this morning until you ring. Sophie, my sweet girl, regarding time, I have something to confess to you…"

She knew at once what it must be. She stared at the canopy of the bed, as if looking for the swirling lights that came before the living pictures.

"Thus, I was hauled back to an episode, the pretty details of which there is no reason for you to know. Georges tried to pull me away, and was drawn in so."

"Oh, Émile!" she heard her voice whine. "Were you *Monsieur* Gilles?"

He smiled and pinched her cheek, amused. "Ain't I always?"

She seized him about the neck. "You were in danger!"

He was looking inscrutable. "Nothing worth speaking of, *ma chère*. But I fear for your safety, Sophie. I begin to suspect this will be a regular thing with me, that when you took on the great prize of the ruffianly Gilles Long Legs, you also got as part of the bargain impromptu trips to that rogue's lawless past. I would not have you involved in those episodes for a kingdom. I should have sent you a message advising you to leave me at the alter, if you saw fit, but as Georges and I did not return until the morning, there was some difficulty."

She held him tighter. "Émile, as if this would deter me. After all, the Other Danger did not."

"Yet of nights I think I must leave your bed betimes like some illicit lover rather than *ton mari,* for it seems to happen when I am half asleep."

"I would only follow you, Émile, and you cannot stop me short of locking your chamber door against me."

"*Certainment*, that would be a sad irony in view of my desperate attempt upon your virtue not so long ago. Recollect you my speech? '*I must have you, before I am led off to the madhouse, burbling of your wonderful bosom and derrière.*' I hadn't then become acquainted with these delectable plump knees and adorable toes." He did some tickling.

Sophie wriggled. "Oh, stop! It is too bad of you to make me laugh, Émile. If you locked me out I would steal the key." "And if I had the locks changed?"

"Then I would bawl loudly and bring humiliation on us both." He laughed and held her tightly. "*Alors*, if I see the flickering, I will put you out of bed. You are a foolish girl, Sophie, and I would not change you, though I do not deserve you."

And I certainly do not deserve you!

Sophie ignored this detached internal voice that sometimes made cynical remarks, even while the rest of her was carried away by sentimental excess. Wasn't she married to the dauntless *Monsieur* Émile whom she had admired from afar for so many years?

She stared at him adoringly. It was as well you didn't wear people's faces out by gazing, as she knew she would be doing it constantly. He stared back equally adoringly. They began to kiss. His nails were sharpening, but it didn't seem to matter.

Some time later she came out of a doze to say, "She must be acting to some purpose?"

Émile kept his eyes closed and didn't answer for some moments, so she thought him asleep. Then he said, "I am not sure if it is That Jade. If so, she may be trying to break my spirit, for while I would not for the world tell you how she used me, I think she hates me."

"Hates you?" Sophie thought of Mistress Kenrick at the ball, laughing and joking with Émile. If she hated him then, she concealed it well. "But why?"

"You do not understand hating or evil, *ma petite,* but I saw them in her eyes. I don't care about her motives, neither. We won't sour our first morning together by speaking of her any more, but I will keep you safe, whatever happens. I am not going to endure this tamely, though I must wait on events for now. You will be delighted to hear they will be away for some time, so presently I can do little. Georges and I laid our plans; now for certain reasons with which I shall not trouble you, I begin to think we must alter these. Meanwhile I must think over what best to do. You must not worry."

"Ah, my poor Émile!" Sophie showered more kisses on his face. She knew it would be as much a waste of time trying to persuade him not to confront Kenrick as it would to urge him to change the colour of his eyes. She ordered herself not to agonise over it until the time came.

He gave her some kisses in return. "Now I am sure you want your hot chocolate, and you must reassure Agnes how I used you as gently as may be." He jumped up to put on his robe. She kept her lashes lowered – she was still shy – as she admired his muscular body in the light of day.

Sophie felt her cheeks go hot as Agnes bustled in, eyes twinkling. "*Bore da* (Good morning) Miss Sophie – I mean – *Madame* Dubois. You do look so pink and contented, my lovely."

Sophie blushed some more, so happy she took several sips of the hot chocolate before she detected a bitter taste. "Why, Agnes, this tastes odd."

"It is the same recipe…Now, what does *Madame* care to wear from her *trousseau* this morning?"

Chester

"I would do anything to have you mine. You have the name of an enchantress and you are one indeed." Captain Alick Mackenzie and Ceridwen Kenrick were in bed together. With the combined dusky good looks of each, they looked like an erotic painting commissioned by some debauched patron of the arts.

It was dawn. Kenrick was asleep in another suite of rooms, a sated bat. Somewhere up in the servant's quarters, Arthur Williams slept too, his thirst quenched. But neither was happy, now or ever.

Alick Mackenzie's penetrating dark eyes were intense; Ceridwen was looking bored. She glanced at the ceiling, thinking longingly of Kenrick's book.

Mackenzie had sometimes stood and witnessed crew members getting the cat o' nine tails*. A couple of times Ceridwen stole Kenrick's precious book to enjoy looking at these punishments. Some of the sailors were swaggering, arrogant young men when brought up to the deck, and Ceridwen enjoyed seeing how long it took for their spirit to break – for them to scream with every lash as their back became a stream of blood – until finally they sank into unconsciousness.

Mackenzie realised that she wasn't listening and his dark eyes flashed. He was used to women fluttering about him. It was part of her appeal to him that she treated him with such coolness, even after they became lovers. "Do you hear?"

She turned her own eyes, almost black and beautifully slanted, upon him. "What? Oh, yes! You will be going off to fight the French soon. Well, they will have some work of it killing you!" She laughed outright.

"It is not that of what I was thinking." He caressed her face, but she ducked her head impatiently.

"I never imagined the day would come when I would say this to a woman who I cannot even rely upon to be faithful to me." He seemed about to grind his sharp teeth. She sniggered.

He was unable to keep himself from going on. "I know that Filthy Frenchman has been your lover."

She laughed. "Faithful to you? Anyone would think you were my husband, not my Dear Kenrick. If you mean Dubois, as a matter of fact, when we were dancing, he told me by a fluke he was born in this country. In Oxford, I believe, like Richard *Coeur de Lion*. Therefore, he is not strictly either a Frenchman or an *émigré*. Filthy, perhaps. Was he my lover?"

He gazed at her. "Come away with me. Everything will be different.

I care not how it affects my promotion. Leave that dismal Kenrick creature. "

"Be quiet. You become tiresome."

At this final humiliation, he jumped out of bed. She tittered again. "Is the hero on his way? It is impossible to make a dignified exit stark naked."

He made no reply and began to pull on his clothes, stony faced. She closed her eyes and seemed to have dozed off. In his Captain's uniform, he was as striking and handsome as any hero in a book. Over by the dressing table, he ran her comb through his wavy dark hair and bitterly put on his hat. He paused at the door to stare back.

She was wearing a white silk nightdress, unpinned, her creamy throat and a large part of her full, high bosom revealed. Her closed eyelids were a delicate mauve, her lashes like fur. Her jetty hair spilt over the pillow and down the side of the mattress.

Gulping, he wrenched open the door and slammed it to behind him. As he stalked down the corridor, an early maidservant stared in awe and admiration.

She was fortunate he was too angry to notice her. He went on his way instead, heading instinctively to the harbour to make his breakfast of some unlucky women who wouldn't believe her luck in having attracted so handsome an officer.

Plas Uchaf
Famau Mountain

"I hope you will oblige me with a song, Morwenna?"

Morwenna couldn't refuse the Count's diffidence. Yet she murmured, despite herself, "Of course, Ynyr, though I make no claims to have as angelic a voice as the former Miss Sophie."

Lord Ynyr's eyebrows went up. "Yours is a lovely voice, Morwenna."

It had been an effort over the past few days to hide his gloom. While he realised it wouldn't have been sensible to marry Sophie himself, he couldn't stop feeling unhappy that Émile had come along and done so. He realised that to be mean-spirited, which upset him more than anything.

Of course, Morwenna duly noted the mournful air of another victim of the now *Madame* Dubois' wiles.

They were in the second sitting room, which also had an instrument. By tacit agreement, they had come here to escape the Dowager Countess. She was out of sorts for different reasons. She was put out at Émile's depriving her of both her companion and his own cheerful company; she had indigestion and her crocheting was already in a twist. Besides, her maid Mrs Brown was annoying her by dwelling on the talk of sightings of giant bats.

The Dowager Countess had fidgeted and complained of the babies who insisted on being born and the depleted Poor Box. Sophie may have left two beautiful shawls, some bonnets, frocks and bootees in readiness, but the Dowager fretted these couldn't last long.

"What shall I sing, Ynyr?" Morwenna asked him now.

"Let us have some Welsh songs."

She played, 'Men of Harlech'. Then she broke off to rise from the piano and approach where he stood, staring into the fire. "Lud, Ynyr, this will not do. I will set the proprieties aside, and say that I think we are both feeling a little hurt and foolish."

He smiled ruefully. "Morwenna, that is so like you! I do feel a little deceived, yet I have no reason."

"I think their secrecy was extraordinary. You and Émile have ever been such good friends you are bound to feel let down by it. I confess I do myself. There was something constrained in his attitude towards the girl, but that was all. I could tell she admired him."

"And I must admire Émile for his setting the opinion of the world at nought, Morwenna."

"Certainly, that is always commendable." Morwenna caught sight of the *Louis Quatorze* clock. "My goodness, Ynyr! I must up to dress for dinner at once!"

Lord Ynyr hurried over to open the door to bow her out. "Morwenna?" As she turned about, he added – scarcely knowing what he meant – "I am glad you are still here."

Morwenna suddenly felt a rush of warmth. He had twice the looks of Émile, if only one quarter of the dash.

Émile was the talk of her friends for his adventures and gallantry in France in smuggling out Charlotte while staying himself to try and save his parents (particularly as he never willingly spoke of those times).

She had been proud of him, while wishing to subdue the rascal into becoming a fervent admirer. His falling in love with their Poor Relation instead was mortifying.

Still, often finding Émile wearing, she had decided some time before his startling news that if she could bring him to make an offer, it would only be to turn him down gently. He needed a wife who would listen to him in quiet admiration. In that, he had been sensible to marry Miss Sophie, who would be happy to gaze wonderingly upon him indefinitely.

"I am glad I am still here, too, Ynyr." Morwenna was dimpling as she went out.

The Count had meant to say he valued her company; how she was more dear to him than the now *Madame* Dubois. That, however, was only part of what he wanted to convey; he wished to say too he feared for Sophie without knowing why.

It had something to do with the strange look flaring in the back of Émile's eyes now and then since his illness.

Lord Ynyr wandered over to one of the windows and pulling back the curtain, stared out a while through the darkness towards the roofs of Plas Cyfeillgar. He frowned and once he muttered, "Nonsense!"

Part Two

Chapter Fourteen

Plas Planwydden
February 1795

É MILE AND SOPHIE WERE PLAYING chess in the library. A minor blizzard raged outside, so Émile was teaching her chess rather than riding.

This was a much smaller and warmer room than the library at Plas Uchaf. Sometimes Émile read to her here in the evenings, while owls hooted outside and she did her work for the Poor Box, wriggling her toes by the crackling fire.

"You must needs trick me and lure my pieces to their doom. Think in terms of Machiavelli, Sophie."

Sophie didn't like to admit to not having heard of Machiavelli. "But it is so difficult. I would rather you won, anyway. Or better still, both of us."

"*Alors,* this is a game of wits, *chérie.* You must cultivate some competitive spirit for it. Now see, I have placed my Bishop and Castle so I have your Queen trapped in a pincer movement."

Sophie looked about the board. "Couldn't I tempt you away with my Knight?"

"Of course not. They are not valuable enough to distract me from your prize piece."

Katarina played on the rug with Jem the kitten. Sophie had insisted she not work this morning (Katarina usually worked in the morning and took lessons in the afternoon) having the symptoms of a cold. Sophie then settled her by a roaring fire in the sitting room and her books, but she invaded the library and they hadn't the heart to send her back.

Sophie stretched luxuriously and wriggled her toes. The doom hanging over them seemed remote. The wind might howl eerily down the chimney, but the room was cosy. She roused at a bawling from the stables. "I do hope the horses and donkeys are warm enough."

"*Bien sûr,* I told the stable boy to increase their hay…Sophie, taking into account where my Knights are, do you really want to do that with your Queen?…Now, there are some urgent matters I must be about. Meanwhile, see if you can find a means of rescuing your Queen. I have left some pieces vulnerable." He kissed her hand.

Sophie laughed. "No doubt you can see how to save her, but I fear with me she is doomed." Troubled suddenly by what Agnes would call a 'Bad Feeling' she added, "Émile, I'll hazard you intend to go out into the snow. Do take a greatcoat and take care too."

As Émile bounded up the stairs, Mrs Kit, who was standing further up adjusting a picture, slipped, overbalanced and plunged towards him with a cry.

He caught her easily with one arm, and half carried her down to a nearby chair. "*Mon Dieu,* Dolly, I thought that it was me who was liable to take flight."

She sat gasping while he rearranged her cap. "Sit you down, you have had a shock. I will fetch you some wine to settle your nerves."

"No, indeed! You must learn to act the grand gentleman again, else folks will be guessing how you lived before."

"They would never have the imagination, Dolly. *Alors,* here is Éloise, and I leave you with her."

Mrs Kit's puzzled gaze followed Émile as he loped up the stairs once more. Then she rounded on Éloise. "Less of those flirty looks, girl! A young girl like you ought to be ashamed. You'll keep away from Georges, too, if you Know What's Good for You. As for Guto, I warned him yesterday a fair face don't mean a good heart."

"Yes, Ma'am!" Éloise impassively fixed her sparkling eyes on Mrs Kit's own face. She knew her position to be secure, having gained *Monsieur*'s lasting friendship through nursing him.

When Émile opened the stable door, letting in an icy blast, his greatcoat speckled with snow, Georges was watching the groom finish saddling the horses. "Put up the thick blankets, boy."

The bitter wind covered them with snow as they rode to the Famau Mountain. As the lane opened up onto the foothills Émile brushed snowflakes from his eyes yet again. "Pretty weather for this jaunt, eh? Let us hope for no more foiled attempts due to carpenters."

"When first I saw snow, I found the stuff magical." Georges looked haggard in the harsh light, although the wind whipping their faces brought colour to his former pallor.

"A magical landscape is appropriate... *Arrête,* you have had oats enough!" Émile tapped his mount as it tried to poke at the hedgerow, though there was no foraging to be had in the snow covered landscape.

"Georges, you are unwontedly quiet. I know that fear has no part in you, so it must be *jolie* Agnes, *n'est pas?*"

Georges snorted. "She gives herself airs so that I almost hate her."

"I know too well. But for her former care of me and more importantly, her loyalty to *ma petite,* I must love her, so try you to endure it gallantly, Georges. When *Madame* and I drove past yesterday, did I not spy you with the red-headed chit we met after that comedy with the *brigadier?* I trust you behave yourself with so young a creature?"

They were on the long, flat track which led round the side of the mountain to Plas Cyfeillgar. Georges said, "Mair Jones. She begrudges me a kiss."

"Jones, Jones. Why does everyone hereabouts have the same name?"

They stopped talking as the snow smothered roofs of Plas Cyfeillgar came into view. Smoke rose from a couple of chimneys at the back of the house.

The snow muffled beat of their horses' hooves seemed loud in the silence. They tethered and blanketed their mounts outside the gates. Émile brought out his watch.

"We are early. I want you to take no chances, Georges. It is different for me, but as I take it you want to stay human, make sure you have the – the poisonous stuff to hand. I wonder I have not smelt it upon you."

Georges sneered. Émile stared at him. "What have you been about, *mon ami,* you look ill?"

Georges sniggered. "Your face has ever looked ill to me, Gilles Long Legs."

"There is something to be said for turning into a monster, besides inhuman strength and seeing in the dark, namely the disappearance of my ridiculous freckles."

They walked through the bitter gusts of whirling snowflakes by way of a shrubbery to the courtyard at the side of the house. They felt eyes on them as they tried an unpretentious side door. It was not locked, and opened easily. They gazed suspiciously about the flagged, bright passageway.

Émile made to go in, and then froze on the threshold. He shook his head, avoiding Georges' eyes.

Georges spoke softly. " Is it so bad a fate, *mon ami,* to lose the threat of the worm and the grave?"

The weedy boy from the pub came down the passage, his eyes darting nervously about. "Come in, Sir." He beckoned, hand shaking.

"Thank you, boy. Now get you gone." The boy rushed past them out of the house.

Georges followed Émile into a passageway scarcely warmer than outside.

The water from the snowflakes melting on their heads ran down their faces as they moved up the corridor, coming out into the main hallway. Émile pointed with his drawn knife to a passage leading off opposite. As they moved towards it, the shadowy figure of a man in naval uniform lunged at them, cutlass drawn. They jumped to confront it but it vanished, leaving them staring about, wide eyed.

"The Captain himself, as the boy said." Émile muttered.

Georges swore under his breath. They went towards the door which Kenrick had indicated was his study. It too was invitingly unlocked. Émile flung it open and stood with his back to it, scanning the room for the enemy, while Georges sprang in.

The room seemed deserted. All was icy and orderly. There were book lined walls, locked chests, bureaux, and a great mahogany desk. The blind was half open, swaying in the draught from the wind howling in the bleak shrubbery outside.

A leather book was open on the desk, and on it laid a sealed envelope weighted with a small magnifying glass. A great mirror was propped against the desk, so as to show the ceiling, and two candles stood ready. Between them was a letter, addressed to, '*Monsieur* Dubois or Gilles'.

Shutting the door, they went over to the desk. Émile sliced through the letter's seal with his blade.

'*Monsieur,*

I expect an Unceremonious Call from a Ruffian such as yourself. I make no complaints of your Conduct; for sure you are in no position to make any. However, I think it probable you will set out to destroy me, and would be reluctant to do the same by you in Self-Defence when much could be gained through our Collaboration. Cast aside Human Prejudices must become irrelevant to you; credulous peasants place their faith in weeds and religious artefacts; you are not so deficient. You are fated to become as I and My Little Wife.

I refer you to the contents of this Book. While I hazard you were not compos mentis when she made sport with it, yet I think the Procedure will be Familiar to you. Light the candles, use the glass, and wait upon events.

I shall be away a while, Conferring with a Fellow Inventor, but expect the man to prove a Charlatan, though possessed of some insights. On my return, we must speak again.

Mistress Kenrick calls, thus I sign off. She will be the Belle of every assembly, as she was of the Lewis' delightful Twelfth Night Ball which we both so enjoyed.

I remain Monsieur, Yours Faithfully,
Goronwy Kenrick.'

Georges gave up trying to read the note over Émile's shoulder. "What does he mean by it? Seems plain he needs teaching manners more than I thought."

Émile was staring down at the book's thick, cloth like pages, upon which were the blurred outlines of half visible pictures. "He recommends me to try this. Shall I do so here and now, Georges? I wouldn't do anything that might endanger Sophie and the others at home."

Georges frowned. "If that book has to do with this time travelling, it may be a trap to suck you away for good."

"True enough and all the better for *ma pauvre* Sophie. I need to light the candles. I note the fire has been laid." He took up the flints by the grate and set to work.

The fire was soon burning brightly. Émile's soaked greatcoat steamed as he came over with a taper and lit the candles on the desk. "Stand you over by the window, *mon ami,* and do not interfere as you have ere this."

Georges lounged over to stand by the long windows against which the wind hurled gusts of snow. Despite that, it seemed safer and warmer outside, though inside the fire crackled and sparked.

The door swung open. They rushed over to it, but heard only a sighing of the wind somewhere higher up in the building.

Émile shut the door and lit the candles with a taper. He moved the glass over the barely visible outlines of the pictures. "Keep away, Georges." The room seemed to darken in contrast to the swirling light illuminating the ceiling. The shapes were playing over the ceiling, moving down.

The Château des Oliviers appeared. Lord Ynyr sat rolling marbles in the sunny courtyard. Émile opposite distracted him with jokes, Bernard squatting between. The bright Provencal sun played over them.

The picture changed. Émile and Georges heard sounds of crackling even before the swirling forms coalesced, showing the night of the fire. Through the smoke they made out the blurred forms of Georges leading Charlotte, hunched with coughing, along the corridor. Bernard stumbled ahead. Émile appeared, dragging along the stout nurse and carrying Marguerite, while the ancient tapestries caught and fell in lashing flames.

The vision disappeared. The ceiling was blank, the room lit only by the candles burning on the desk and the fitful light from outside. Georges and Émile were holding each other, wild eyed and panting.

For a minute, neither of them spoke. Then Georges muttered, "The bastard!"

Émile said softly, "Remind me to kill him for that, Georges."

———— ⚬⁓⚬⊂⁓⊃⚬⁓⚬ ————

"Émile, to ride out in such weather!" Sophie rushed at Émile as he and Georges came snow-covered into the hallway. She began helping him off with his greatcoat, so that Guto stood back. "You too, Georges, soaked through!"

Émile smiled down at Sophie, gently restraining her from undoing his greatcoat. "Are we likely then to melt? Don't fuss, *chérie*. I think I will manage this myself." He pulled it off himself and handed it to Georges.

Sophie saw there was something conspiratorial about them as Georges smiled on her too. She knew Émile well enough now to sense something had disturbed him, for all his act of normality.

"Some mulled wine will put us to rights, Mistress Sophie. *Monsieur* takes his highly spiced." Georges went sloshing upstairs with the greatcoats.

"Guto, please see to it." Sophie said with dignity. She wondered if she would ever get used to having a whole staff at her command. At Plas Uchaf she had always felt that she only enjoyed their services by default; now she found it difficult not to do things for herself.

As they went upstairs she took Émile's hand, which was surprisingly warm to the touch, and squeezed it. His nails were sharp in her palm, but she was getting used to that. "I feared for you, Émile."

"This fussing would be absurd were a chill my greatest danger. I thought you became accustomed to my riding in all weathers at Plas Uchaf." On the bend of the stairs, he took her in his arms, wet as he was. "It is I must keep you safe, my lovely girl…Now, I think you guess how I would like to warm myself."

Through all the lovemaking that followed – while the snow pattered against the windows and the donkey bawled in the stable until Katarina ran out, cloak over head, to give him some carrots – Sophie sensed something changing in Émile had further altered.

His otherness was more marked. His touch was still caressing and gentle, yet his nails more resembled talons, and when shivers ran up and down her spine, they were not solely of pleasure.

And yet, this otherness, this element of fear, added to her excitement. Now he seemed to be particularly interested in kissing her throat. Once he even nipped it gently and then seemed to pull back. Even more alarming was the thrill of delight which shot through her.

If – though now it seemed more a 'when' – he did want to take her blood, then she was going to have to struggle against herself as well as him. She hadn't foreseen that.

Sophie thought she could use her lips like an expert already. He did what he called 'Paying My Respects to Your Most Wondrous Part" in turn, kissing it deeply and lingeringly. "How I adore this delightful blond tail." She sighed and wriggled.

But a memory flashed through her of their first night together, when after seeing her virginal blood, he had been solicitous, kissing the offended part tenderly. Yet he had kissed it lingeringly. It was so hard to say where his body lusting ended and his blood lusting began. Probably Émile himself didn't know. She wondered how he would react, when her monthly time came? This was a topic she certainly wouldn't find in any book, though the wives of Man Vampires must always have known.

Now the pleasure was too great to give any attention to that or anything else.

Afterwards, she wondered what happened to all the people who must have been bitten by vampires over the years. She had tried to question Katarina discreetly, but the girl retained only childish memories. Some of these people she recalled as human later, and immune from the vampire bite. But others she thought may have suddenly disappeared.

She turned to look at Émile. He was gazing bleakly at the ceiling. At her movement, he smiled on her. "I would like to stay here with you, but must make myself presentable for dinner. You missed your tea, my lovely girl. That will not do, we must have Agnes bring you some." Though his look was tender, she could see preoccupation at the back of his eyes.

She was almost as nervous about their first big dinner as she'd been about the ball which Émile held in her honour last week.

This had been as successful as she hoped. Émile asked her to wear the blue and silver dress she wore for the Lewis' Twelfth Night ball. She had never thought to be so happy in it.

When Agnes was undressing her after the Lewis' ball, as the dress rustled to her feet, Sophie had sniffed while Agnes patted her, saying, 'There, now, Miss Sophie, it will all work out.'

At their own ball, Émile had gazed on Sophie as though she was the belle, though she was sure everyone else awarded the prize to Morwenna, who glowed in gold. It was wonderful Émile should see things differently. Sophie had shivered with happiness as she stood receiving the guests with him, delighting in his dashing appearance and easy manners.

Now as then, she wanted to do credit to him so nobody could say: 'The Poor Relation Monsieur Dubois' has taken to wife is at a loss in society, my dear.' It would have been so much easier, though, to be relaxed and charming at social events without the terrors gnawing at the back of her mind.

She ran a hand down his chest to his belly. "I hope I have warmed you sufficiently, Sir."

"You have, *Madame,* poor Georges is welcome to his mulled wine." He kissed her nose and jumped up to pull on his robe.

"How does he take Agnes' rejection?"

"Ill, though he only grunts." Émile bent to throw a couple of logs on the fire. "I would blame the wench did I like her less, for I have never known him to brood over a girl who did not want him."

He rang for Agnes, and strode through into his dressing room.

There, Guto answered his next ring. "Georges is gone out again, *Monsieur* Émile."

"In such weather? Has he taken leave of his senses? Never mind, see to my bath like a good fellow. I must needs undergo the hardship of dressing myself."

Newly bathed and dressed for dinner, Émile was starting for Sophie's rooms again when he stopped short, staring at the great book from Kenrick's study that Georges had left on the bureau. He swore and groaned.

Picking it up, he went downstairs to his study, where a cheerful fire crackled. He locked the book in a drawer in his desk, and paced about. Then, he picked up the other book from Plas Cyfeillgar, *'On the Use of Imitative Representation'.* Snatching up his pen, he began to write down a series of figures. The wind moaned outside, chuckled down the chimney, and rattled at the windows. The light was poor at his desk, across the room from the fire, but he didn't light a candle.

Some time later, Émile was roused by tapping at the door. It was Guto, candle in hand. "His Lordship the Count of Ruthin, Sir."

Émile jumped up. "What? Is it so late? Show him in at once, Guto. Ynyr, forgive me, I was carried away in my reading."

Lord Ynyr seized Émile's hands. "Émile, you are hard at work on something for sure. However do you see, it is so dark in here?"

"I ever had fair night vision." Émile took a taper over to the fire, and lit a couple of candles. "Ynyr, it is good to see you. How are you all at the Manor? Does it snow again? Come and warm yourself." He began to stoke the fire, which was now low.

Lord Ynyr leaned against the desk, chatting. He picked up one of the books on the desk. "Forgive my curiosity, Cousin. We always nosed in each other's books. *'On the Use of Imitative Representation'?* Whatever may that be?"

"That, Ynyr, is something that I couldn't tell you as yet." Émile's expression was veiled. As the Count glanced through the book, Émile stirred and asked him about the horses Lord Ynyr had given him.

Lord Ynyr answered absently. "Whatever you think best, Émile, you are more the expert." He went on leafing through the book.

"Come Ynyr, let me show you about the house, there was no time when you dined here before."

"I will enjoy that, Émile. This is a bizarre work indeed. How did you come by it?"

"I don't recollect." Émile moved about restlessly.

"It says something here about 'Thought Forms', on which point it might find agreement from our friend Kenrick." Lord Ynyr stopped laughing as he caught his cousin's gaze. "Surely this cannot be the matter on which you worked so eagerly you forget to ring for lights?"

Émile's tone was casual, though his eyes were fixed on the book. "I believe we were precipitate in dismissing such notions."

Lord Ynyr froze. "It would seem to amount to a form of magic."

"Say rather the control of certain inexplicable forces."

"Émile, you perturb me. You sound almost like to Kenrick. Do not tell me that you are gone over to his notions?"

Émile came over to squeeze the Count's shoulders while Lord Ynyr flinched at his steely grip. "*Bien sûr,* Ynyr, we should not allow our dislike of the fellow to prevent our objective assessment of his ideas." He almost snatched the book from Lord Ynyr's slackened grasp, putting it by, Lord Ynyr thought, with a look of relief. "Now, Cousin, trouble yourself no more about these matters, but let me show about the house as we had so little time when last you came."

Meanwhile, Sophie smiled as she put to rights some of the Dowager Countess' embroidery, while Her Ladyship apologised. "This is kind in you, *ma chère* Sophie, when you must be fully occupied already, but Mrs Brown is become clumsy with her needle."

Morwenna – who now treated Sophie warmly enough almost to convince her that she surely had been mistaken in thinking Morwenna's former attitude scornful – smiled at her. "Sadly, I am little better. Sophie, we are all delighted to see how you have tamed Émile."

—⦿⦿⦿⦿⦿—

"I love to see you in that pink dress now you are mine. That first time I saw you in it I suffered agonies, *ma chère.*" Émile murmured to Sophie in the passageway later. She was wearing the ruby necklace from Charlotte he had given her, and while he looked his approval, he said nothing.

She covered his face with kisses in her sympathy. Then, seeing Mrs Kit moving stolidly towards them, she hid behind him. He greeted Mrs Kit casually.

"When do these titled folk come? I ain't seen a Lord before, nor a Dowager Countess neither."

"They are here already, Doll. Recollect you, Guto showed them in?"

"What, that boyish fellow a Lord? But he ain't got any presence! My Kit's got two times his. But then, I was surprised when I heard as you were gentry yourself. I say, '*What, that long, freckled fellow, what can skin rabbits as well as any of us, a Lord's cousin? Never!*'"

Sophie spluttered, groping for her handkerchief. Émile grinned.

"Never mind, Dolly, perhaps the Dowager Countess will meet with your approval."

It was a successful dinner, with Émile now as lively as always. Lord Ynyr and Miss Morwenna were glowing, and Sophie, having seen them at her ball, knew why.

If Miss Lydia Lewis, the girl who fainted and cut her neck at the Lewis' ball, had turned down the invitation on the grounds of unspecified poor health, her younger brother entertained them by making it clear he was replacing his former hopeless passion for Sophie with a new one for Morwenna. He gazed on her awestruck, as though he had never seen her before.

Lord Ynyr kept on looking at Morwenna like that, too.

Nobody spoke of the Absurd Stories going about. There was some war talk, and a couple of the male guests looked covertly at Émile as they remarked how the Recruiting Sergeant and his team suddenly disappeared.

Lucien sent up excellent dishes, and there was enough pigeon pie even to satisfy the Reverend Smythe-Jones.

Morwenna told a story against herself in the manner of Émile. "I tried one of these centrepieces which are *Madame* Dubois speciality. I prided myself on how nicely balanced was the intricate middle. Imagine my mortification when halfway through dinner, some of the dried grasses toppled into the fowl."

Even the Dowager Countess laughed. Sophie felt as dull as an old shoe in comparison. Luckily, Émile didn't see it; his eyes kept straying over to gloat on her. Her lips turned up of their own accord, and as he smiled back, she saw his teeth were sharper. It was a slight difference, invisible to a stranger. As she clenched her hands, she noticed something else.

He had always liked rare meat, laughing at how the British burnt it, but tonight his beef was so rare she wondered he bothered to have it cooked at all. She made her invariable prayer: *Oh, let the cure work!*

In the drawing room Sophie invited Morwenna to play. While Mr Lewis listened spellbound, Sophie asked Lord Ynyr about the herbal cure he used for the girl bitten near *Seren* Farm.

She asked too – she must seem inquisitive – about his cure for Miss Lydia, who was rumoured to have strange symptoms of restlessness at night and a retraction of the gums.

As ever, the Count was eager to talk about his remedies. "I was using two mixtures of herb. One with primarily a combination of rosemary, sage, thyme, mint, fennel and garlic, afterwards one with a proportion of nettle and St John's wort added."

It seemed like enough to Katarina's cure.

"How often did you recommend she take it, Sir?"

"Call me Ynyr, please. Are we not more doubly related now? I thought it best for her to have it six times a day at first, reducing after the first four days."

Sophie went to take Morwenna to one side to offer her a present of a cross. "You may laugh, Miss Mor – Morwenna, but I believe it protects one from many unpleasant influences. I wear one myself."

Morwenna laughed. "You are not perchance going over to Rome, Sophie, as you did the same by all the staff before leaving us? Émile is shockingly irreligious, so this cannot be his influence. Sure it is a kind thought and I will wear it accordingly."

Émile came up behind them. He smiled on Morwenna while covertly caressing Sophie's back. No doubt in his rakish experience, he had done it often enough. Now he seemed accustomed to his talons and they scratched Sophie's flesh tenderly, a part of the caress.

Chapter Fifteen

T HE FAIR-HAIRED GIRL LOOKED THIN, *alarmingly so. But then, she was in a decline.*

In the manner of dreams, her lips didn't move. "Take care. Recollect you – Recollect you 'Viens ici, salaud'. " She said the words reluctantly. The last one meant nothing to Sophie.

"But you're –" Sophie began. Their eyes met.

Then Mademoiselle Charlotte was gone.

———— ❧✦❧✦❧✦❧ ————

Sophie woke with a start as the clock on the stairs window sill chimed three. For the first time, Émile was gone.

She leapt out of bed. With some remnant of modesty, she pulled on her nightdress. Not even pausing to pick up the guttering candle, she rushed through her own dressing room and the intervening door to Émile's.

The room was faintly lit, like hers, by the embers of the dying fire. He wasn't in there. Thankfully Georges wasn't either, having a far better room than the one under the attics allotted to him at Plas Uchaf.

She rushed through to Émile's bedroom and gasped with relief. He was sitting at a table, wearing his deep blue dressing gown, working on some papers. The room was lit only by the glowing embers in the fireplace. He turned with the look of one preoccupied. "Sophie, I hope my poor sleep is not infectious?"

"Oh, Émile, I thought–"

"That I had turned into a bat?" He may have meant to speak lightly, but his tone came out sour.

"I feared you were drawn into the past again."

"*Alors*, I would have woken you by pitching you out of the bed." He gave her a chuck under the chin. "Do not trouble. I often sleep ill, as I have told you. I am working on some formulas merely."

She glanced at the sequences of figures. She could only just make them out in the semi darkness (it was startling, even alarming, how he could see so well without more light) though they would have meant nothing to her even had she been able to see them clearly.

Someone once told her people with a talent for music often shone at mathematics; she didn't seem to have the mathematical ability. It was a mystery to her how Émile could make sense of such things. She gazed at him, wondering at the clever thoughts flitting about – no, not that word, too redolent of bats – taking place, rather – in his head.

Then, sensing something evasive about him, a suspicion took her. She put her hands on his shoulders, and spoke at once. "You have said Kenrick believed with the application of mathematics, he could introduce a precision to some form of – of magic."

His guarded expression destroyed her hope he would chuck her chin, laughing at her absurdity. "He did, Sophie. I never expected such dramatic proof that he wasn't raving."

"But Émile, surely you would not experiment with his awful ideas yourself? I know I am ignorant of such things, but does the Dowager Countess not have the right of it when she speaks of his 'Mischievous Experiments'?"

He smiled, eyes still veiled. "*Eh bien, Madame ma Tante* has ideas rigid and outdated in all things, *n'est pas*? To some extent, so does Ynyr. He gave me these arguments this afternoon. I have no choice, my poor girl. Kenrick has involved me in his experiments whether I would or no, and I must do what I can to understand what happens."

"Émile, would you really attempt time travel through these rituals, too?" She searched those inscrutable eyes for reassurance.

She found none.

He squeezed her hands. "I say I have no choice, Sophie! I did not begin this tussle with Kenrick, but he has taken liberties with me and I will see matters through to the end."

He was too masculine to react any other way, of course. She let her hands drop from his shoulders, and paced about in the dim room. "Kenrick wishes you to do precisely that, Émile!"

He looked irritated. "That hasn't escaped my attention, Sophie. You do not think I dance to his tune? Yet I must fight him on his own ground. I am amazed Kenrick has overcome these problems, incompetent mathematician as he is, to initiate travel to what we might call a past time stream. Perhaps he blundered upon some crucial factor. I was saying as much to Ynyr and he seemed absurdly concerned by Kenrick's methods."

"Émile, of course you did not enter into this combat willingly! It is all so complicated, for I know well it was travel through time brought us together. Yet though I am ignorant of these matters, I fear it to be pernicious, as surely all of Kenrick's magical rituals must be?"

Now, he melted enough to jump up and take her face in his hands. "Try not to worry. I will be careful."

She put her hands up to squeeze his shoulders lightly, revelling in those delightful muscles. As she stroked him, a vague memory of the dream made her speak again. "I do not know how to say what I must, Émile –"

"What, chérie?"

"Émile, do you have an interest in time travel because of your lost siblings?"

His face froze but she saw her answer in his eyes. She rushed on, "I understand what a temptation it must be now you know Kenrick has access to the past. I do not understand what is involved, but I fear something awful may happen. You know how when I came back in time you were able to see me and talk to me –"

His look of outrage faded. "And to kiss you." His eyes were tender now, but fearing distraction, she hurried on, "Do you wish to go back to the past as your present self to alter it? I could not, but –"

He looked surprised. "Clever girl."

She wasn't annoyed by his condescension, having been brought up to accept it as natural in men rather less clever than he. "Forgive me for mentioning this – I am sorry to have to speak of something so painful to you – but is it you wish not only to see your brother and sisters, but perhaps, to – to succeed in rescuing them?"

Now he looked agonised. "Sophie, I would not fail them twice. You cannot guess at how many times I have relived that night."

She hated having to go on. "Ah, Émile, I wish you could save them, and change everything! But – might it not somehow alter the present? I feel foolish in hazarding these ideas, when you know so much more of them than I, but I do wonder. What if we are apart, never having come together, as a result?"

He tightened his arms about her. "I promise to be careful, Sophie. Of course, I do not wish to change the present in so far as I have you. My visit to the Kenrick *ménage* that day brought us together, and yet what happened is fearful to you."

"Is it not still fearful to you?!" The words rushed out.

"That is in the main because I fear to lose you through it." He watched her closely.

She let that go for the moment. "Émile, of course you did your best for your brothers and sisters that terrible day."

His sigh was almost a groan. "It wasn't good enough, Sophie."

"Can you talk to me about it? It might help you." She wondered – but nobody ever spoke on such matters, so she had nothing to go by – if Émile's silence on the topic of his lost siblings and their horrible end might be preventing him from recovering from their loss.

He sat silent for fully two minutes. Then he stood up and with a bow that was slightly mocking, offered her the chair. She sat down in it and he sat himself, eccentrically enough, on the floor with his back to her. She put her hands on his shoulders again, and as he talked to her his muscles became rigid and his voice was hoarse, while she shuddered now and again.

'I would be a hypocrite if I said that I was fond of my parents. I hardly knew them, and mon Père would give a box round the ear for any infringement of his Versailles notions of etiquette while ma Mère was given to religion and melancholy. Sometimes, I think when mon Père was especially provoking, she prayed over us, wringing her hands. That was unpleasant

enough. She must have been happy once, but I never remember her so.

'Generally, though, we didn't see much of them. Our old Nurse was far closer to us. When we were over here, and I stayed for weeks with Ynyr's family, I envied Ynyr having a father in the late Count, who was approachable.

'Ynyr often came to stay. We would play marbles in the courtyard, with the sun on our backs.

'Later in Paris, I asked myself, is the cold or are my insides frozen? Recollect you my telling you of a dead cat squashed by a carriage on the frozen road out of Paris? Of how I felt like to it? It was that made me able to live so savage an existence. I sense you look at me in concern, ma chère; I am glad you know not what I mean.

'Charlotte was a year younger than I, always practical, yet with an other- worldly side to her nature. In some ways, your Agnes puts me in mind of her.

Bernard was younger than me by two years, a quarrelsome scamp; he looked much like Georges. We never got along; I never would have believed how I would yearn to hear his voice disputing something, anything, but once more.

Marguerite, ten years younger than I, was my favourite. Whenever I had been away, I would look for her first. I believe it was partly because something about Katarina reminded me of her that I could not leave her to the mercy of the Kenrick's.

One day out hunting I met Georges, whose mother had been a maid at the Château. Later, he condescended to be my page. He was closer to me than my brother, for we each recognised in the other a rascal.

'When the riots broke out across the country, I came back from the University to warn mon Père, pointing out how the people had suffered since the bad winter ruined the olive crop. He would not listen. Ma Mère clicked her tongue at the peasants forgetting their Christian resignation. They carried on with their engagements as ever.

'In this, mon Père displayed the same form of obduracy sustained him on the day of their execution, when he offered Madame ma Mère his arm, for all the world as if they were stepping out to their carriage for a social occasion rather than for a journey by open tumbrel to the guillotine. And so they went to their end, with him looking through the crowds as though they did not exist, which contempt led the rabble to hoot and hurl things, while

ma Mère was praying for God to forgive them.

'I feel you flinch, Sophie moi. I begged an oblivious universe ceaselessly for it to be over, for I felt I must stand in the crowd to see it all. My parents having sent me word not to dare to intervene, I had to respect their last wishes and stand by, clenching my fists. It was only afterwards I noticed the cuts where my nails went through the skin.

Yet, their end was not so unfair. After – what happened in Provence – mes parents had embroiled themselves in political intrigue in the north. Après tout, they had lived a large part of their lives acquiescing in the brutal treatment of the peasants. So many times mon Père ordered me whipped as a boy when I questioned that. Always, I vowed when I came to run the estate, things should be different. Bien sûr, they are different indeed!

Our parents were away overnight when things ignited.

'Georges and I for some nights slept in an anteroom, swords and pistols at the ready. When the locals attacked we were first shooting over their heads, but they came in waves, and soon we were cutting at them through those long windows while the sweet night air gushed in. We forced that wave back, but meanwhile some got in the other way and lit fires. The ancient tapestries were so dry they made a perfect fuel.

The Château was easily alight. Georges and I gave up trying to fight the rioters off; there were too many. We ran for the youngsters and the old Nurse.

I could not get Marguerite out of the nursery without her favourite doll, and all the while I could hear the crackling getting louder as the Nurse's face turned to a strange colour. As we came out into the gallery I met Georges, forcing Bernard up the corridor with threats and hauling along Charlotte. As we went spluttering up the long gallery, the tapestry was blazing up and coming down, and I was saying to Marguerite, 'Do not worry, Émile will not let a little thing like this absurd bonfire get in his way.'

'Then the Nurse fell in an apoplectic fit. I wondered how I was going to carry her as well as Marguerite, for she was stout – but one look at her staring eyes told me she was dead.

"It is only lately I have recalled how, as I struggled along, I thought I saw myself. I believed it the affect of strained nerves at the time. Now I wonder."

Sophie shivered again as she went on caressing his shoulders in silence and he continued.

'*We took them out through one of the windows to the terrace and the outhouse roofs. There were rioters all about the front and sides. We couldn't tell what they might do. We knew them all, but people madden in a riot, so we hid the youngsters in one of the outhouses. So many times, Sophie, have I cursed myself for choosing that particular building, yet it seemed the safest.*

'*Georges and I went for horses, leaving the others in Charlotte's charge. By some fluke, part of the Château roof fell and crushed the furthest outhouse roof.*

'*Georges and I were galloping the mounts back – we'd had to deal with a few rioters to get them – when we saw the roof collapse.*

'*We saw Charlotte's feet projecting from under a pile of beams. We thought her dead; her face was blackened, but later we found it was only soot and she was hardly hurt, though her hair was singed half off. But as for the others…*

'*I saw what was meant by the phrase 'death in her face' as we took her to a safe place. She never did get over it. I felt mad, but at a distance. It was only later, when she was safe out of the country I began to rant and rave. Georges had to jump on me and hold me down while I gabbled crazily of revenge. Whenever any man I could fight gave me excuse, I attacked him like a maniac. Georges – hardly given to moderation himself in that – thought I was become a little mad. He was right, certainment. Then and in my brutal life later, I hoped that someone would serve me a good turn and finish me. It was so in England, after Lotte died.*"

Sophie murmured, hugging his tight frame, "Ah, my dear, I am so sorry. Perhaps I should not have made you speak of them. I hoped that it might make things easier to talk of them, but…" She turned him about – he submitted with surprising docility – and drew his head down onto her shoulder.

After a couple of minutes, he looked up at her. "It is a relief to talk to you about it. I would not tell anyone else that story. The only person who I could endure to sympathize with me about it is you."

A little later she murmured, "Don't think this presumptuous in me, my love, for I know while I have lost a sister and my parents, it was in the course of nature, and so different; yet, might it not it be better – I can guess how hard this must be for you – to accept what has been – dreadful as it was?"

He muttered, lips against her skin: "Don't ask that of me, Sophie."

Chapter Sixteen

G EORGES, HAIR PERFECT, COLLAR AND necktie magnificent
if pasty in the face, strutted towards the door leading to
the outbuildings.

Agnes, coming down the stairs with a tray, stopped him. "You know
Mrs Kit's orders, Georges. Take your cross!"

Georges glowered. "I take orders from nobody."

"Hoighty toighty, it's a rule of the house. You are looking poorly.
Is it the drink or are you wearing yourself out getting excited about
some girl?"

His eyebrows shot up. "Do you care?"

Their eyes met for a moment before he dropped his. Putting the tray
down on a shelf, she fumbled in her pocket for a home made wooden
cross. "Wear one of these from Katarina, Georges."

He thrust it in his pocket. "Is she any better? Is *Monsieur* still reading
to her?"

"Yes, and breaking off to say, '*Zut alors*, what is this nonsense, Katarina?'"

Their eyes met again then he suddenly turned and banged out.
Agnes, shaking herself, marched off with the tray.

The footman Guto still looked so out of place in his livery as he stood
in Émile's study, gazing at him in enquiry, it seemed as though he was
about to discuss the whereabouts of some strayed cow. Instead, he said,

"Here are the stakes, Sir, cut up as you ordered."

"Good, Guto. Stoke up the fire with 'em…Burn the – the sharp ends firstly." Émile spoke through his teeth as he looked at the remains of the stakes brought with them on the move from Plas Uchaf.

Guto threw the sharp ended pieces onto the fireplace. "Forgive my forwardness, Sir, but I think you need a good blaze. You shudder."

"You speak true, boy. *Alors*, mind you come back betimes to mend the fire."

When Guto had gone, Émile glared at the burning stakes and swore. "That filthy bloodsucker will not escape me, though I become even as he."

Some time later, he sat at the desk, legs stretched out and looking endless as he lounged, watching the mirror hanging nearby, on either side of which were two sconces with candles burning.

The stakes having burned away, he had allowed the fire to die down, though a cutting north east wind buffeted about outside, and he was in his shirt sleeves. His green eyes were as fiery and savage as an animal's.

The mirror was clouding, shapes moving across the ceiling. Then they were gone.

"*Merde!*" Then he started and listened intently. "The rascal!" He jumped up, vanishing in a mass of specks which sparked as they dissolved.

Georges staggered a little as he tried to saunter up the passageway. He muttered and swore in French and looked bemused, his face still paler than earlier.

Émile was on him almost before Georges saw the faint flicker, seizing Georges' arms with fingers which felt like iron pincers. "*Mon ami,* you might have confided in me."

Georges' clouded eyes sparked. "What, *Monsieur* Gilles? Can't I go out without your chasing me with questions?"

"Come into my study, Georges." Émile soothed.

Georges was still bellicose. "Stop digging your fingers into me like to some officer of the law."

Émile laughed and relaxed his hold, urging Georges towards his study with a gentle push which sent him on his way by several steps. "Forgive me, Georges, I forget my new strength. An officer of the law is something to which I have never ere now been likened."

The study door was locked, and Émile momentarily looked bemused himself. "I forgot that, too. Wait, I don't think this will shock you." He vanished in another flicker and the next moment was ushering Georges in.

He drew Georges to a chair. "Georges, you look sick and your neck bleeds." He pulled down Georges' collar to look closer at the wound. The bleeding had been staunched, but the stains and the punctures were marked.

Georges drew back a little. "Keep your own horrible teeth out of my neck; I don't like the look in your eyes."

Though Émile's eyes were flashing inhumanly once more, his tone was steady. "Did They target you? Came They back by stealth? Can you remember anything? It is daylight, too, but so it was with me."

He went to take a decanter and brandy glasses from the cabinet and poured some for Georges. "Can you face this, or are you as sick as I was?"

"I only feel a little weak. *Ma petite* Mair has been luring me to her this past fortnight." Georges swallowed some brandy. "You know, the girl we met in the lane. Mair Jones. Lord Ynyr didn't succeed in curing her for sure."

"Of course, idiot I am! So she was the one bitten! I would clean the wound with brandy, Georges, but I sense you are partly one of us already, and we need fear no other infection. *Mes petites* would start you on their poisonous weeds, though they have had no more success with me than has Cousin Ynyr with this girl, and he used much the same as Katarina. "

Georges' eyes met Émile's. "I don't want to be treated. Now you ain't human, Gilles Long Legs, do you regret it save as it affects *petite Madame* Sophie? I do not have any such worry, Agnes having rejected me. Who would choose to be old? This way, we escape that fate. I see how you delight in your new powers, and I want them too. Éloise still chatters of how you caught Dolly with one hand, and she's weight enough to be an object of terror to most men should she tumble on them."

Émile's taloned fingers arranged Georges' collar and neck cloth to hide the wound. "*Alors,* we cannot have this girl killing you, Georges. You might find it difficult to persuade wenches back to share your coffin. You need some soup." He rang the bell. "We must keep her away from you, for you look less a Provencal than a ghost. Did she penetrate Katarina's barriers? I fear for our humans, if so. "

"She met me in the barn at her farm, it is another good thing about the change, you feel the cold but little. Whenever I came to myself, I had taken off the – That Thing from Katarina. I think my blood becomes not human, for this last time, she drew away almost at once. She is a sweet thing, she is always crying when I wake up, and has worked upon me slowly, unlike *Madame* Kenrick with you. About our humans, ain't Katarina said it's impossible to secure open places properly? You and I went uninvited into Kenrick's grounds. Houses seem different. You couldn't get in without the boy. I knew no more could I, though I couldn't speak."

"I should have guessed then. Here's Guto…Guto, can Dolly prepare for this rascal, who sickens for something, some of her marvellous soup as soon as may be without offending the cook?"

"For sure, Sir. Let me mend your fire."

When Guto had gone, Émile went over to the window and stared out at the shrubbery. "Georges, now I can confide in a fellow bat. I fear I cannot make do with bloody meat any longer. When I look on the sweet neck of Sophie *moi*, the urge seizes me. I should warn her and the others, yet I do not see now why it is so bad for *ma femme* at least to join me. It is these miserable religious scruples hold her back, this belief in the soul. Otherwise, *ma petite* would never let this come between us. Georges, you and I have seen much proof of the ethereal nature of the human spirit, *n'est pas?*"

"Don't speak to me of *les femmes'* prattle of Matters Spiritual; I endured enough of such with Agnes' Tarot cards. She chattered of foreseeing black magic and a clash between Good and Evil."

Émile grinned. "Are we now, Georges, on the Devil's side? Perhaps we ever were. *Eh bien*, it is well we gave Dolly orders everyone in my household must wear – those Religious Symbols. Must I send them off? They would be unhappy; hereabouts there can be little enough work giving better than starvation wages, and I cannot say I am willing to emulate Kenrick and live in discomfort with such drudges as have no choice but to endure living with a monster."

He shuddered. "Two hours since, I perforce had Guto burn those – sharp pointed things made up at Plas Uchaf. We cannot do to Kenrick as we planned before and I suspect him to be impervious to normal weapons."

Georges shuddered too. "We must do for him another way, then. About staff, you pay well, and they'd still be under threat from Them Others."

Émile threw open the window. Pulling a knife from his pocket, he hurled it so the blade slammed into the bark of a tree in the shrubbery across the way.

Georges pulled out his own knife, and cursing at his own weakness, threw it so that it thudded into the bark next to Émile's.

They exchanged grins. "Nice trick Marcel Sly Boots taught you, Gilles. You see I am near as proficient as you."

"We must practice further, Georges, for we may well have need of a precise aim." Émile moved his head, listening. "Now *ma pauvre petite* comes trustingly back from the village to the Wicked Brigand's Castle." He winced. "She sings so blithely, I cannot bring myself to tell her what has happened. Sure, if *ma pauvre* Katarina had not been confined to bed then she would have guessed your secret."

Georges listened too. "They have been to the village to see Agnes' infant lives with her sourpuss of a mother. The baby and I took to each other at once. I would even have been happy to be a father to her. Can you believe it of Southern Georges, Gilles? But then, who would ever think of you as marrying a little chit *sans le sou?*"

"You want the girl still even as I cannot endure to be apart from her mistress. We must court them gently, Georges, as with the other. *Après tout*, what sane woman would not choose to be young and pretty for one hundred and fifty years and more? You may yet win *jolie* Agnes back. We could be so happy a household, *n'est pas?*"

———⟨⟩———

Sophie hummed again as she came back from taking a last minute check on Katarina. "At least she takes liquids now. I hope we may tempt her with some of that syllabub tomorrow. Goodnight, Agnes, my dear. I so envy you Eiluned, she is delightful."

She ran her finger down Agnes' cheek. "Agnes, you look sad! You said there is a great difference between – well, you said 'a rascal' who is rich and one who is poor. If it is only a matter of money keeps you and Georges apart, I am sure *Monsieur* Émile would be happy to help –"

Agnes' lower lip jutted. "Is good of you, Mistress Sophie, but I believe that fickle Georges has a new girl already. Besides, he is too much a rogue. I must put Eiluned first."

Émile came through the dressing room door in his dark blue robe. He smiled on Agnes as she took up her candlestick. "Do not be hard on him, *ma petite,* I know he pines for you still. Remember I will make you both financially independent whenever you wish."

"You are a nice rich rascal, *Monsieur* Gilles." Agnes made her curtsy. "Though you have a bat's hearing."

Émile laughed as the door closed behind her and came to play with Sophie's hair as she stood by her dressing table, careful not to scrape her with his talons. "Such lovely hair as you have."

His otherness sent tingles of fear and excitement down her spine. His eyes, too, were altered, the flaring having now come to the front. Their gaze wandered below her chin, as they had repeatedly at dinner even as he told her absurd stories. She was tingling then.

"My lovely girl, I must be honest with you, though you will be alarmed. These last couple of days I change apace, and now when I look at your throat, I want to nip it, ever gently. I have fought this because I love you, and you want me human. Now I do not think I can fight it long. I should be heroic, and tell you to go. I cannot."

"Oh, Émile!" she tried to stop her lips from trembling. "Do try and struggle against it a little longer! The cure yet may work."

He caressed her face. "I think not, my poor girl. I know Katarina has told you a tale of the cure working best when seeming not to work at all, but that makes no sense. We have failed to keep me human. I remember you telling me as a child you were kind enough to draw me as Theseus and Achilles, semi-mortals indeed, eh? But you can be semi-immortal with me now. You must not let your religious scruples hold you back, Sophie; *bien sûr* I suspect them to be heterodox enough. Think, if there be vampires, then they must be part of the natural order of things, no more damnable than other blood sucking bats."

"Émile, there are other cures yet –"

She sniffed while he snorted. "*De quel absurdité!* I have seen that book of yours. *Vraiment, 'The Cure of the Charged Wine'*, I wonder they did not recommend use of the mummified bones of an ancient saint while they were about it. My poor girl, delude yourself no further about these superstitions in which *ma pauvre petite* Katarina places such faith."

Tears were coming now. "But crosses protect us, Émile, therefore –"

He took hers between thumb and forefinger. "As does that disgusting herb it sickens me even to think of, Sophie. That is not evidence of Divine protection, but of natural aversion. Besides, how far do the religious symbols protect you? This seems to have little affect on me. *Ma petite*, it is not just from me your pretty neck is in danger. The thought of Kenrick or Mackenzie getting their teeth into you makes me wild. It must be me who bites you. I will do all I can to keep you and the other humans safe from the Kenrick *ménage*, but –" He fumbled in his dressing gown pocket. "How is it none of you girls ever has a handkerchief? Monster or no, I cannot bear to see you weep." He dried her face.

She took the handkerchief to blow her nose. "Émile," she thought her voice wobbled grotesquely, "I wish I could join you with a clear conscience, but I am sure it would be wrong to despair of a cure. This may be a test for us. I believe you will be your old self again yet, and all will be well."

"Do you have that from Agnes' Tarot set? Ah, *vraiment,* I don't want to hurt or frighten you, Sophie. It is not just my desire for your sweet blood drives me; I still love you true, as I ever must, however much a creature of dread I may become to others. I want nothing to stand between us. Why, my lovely girl, would you be so cruel as to condemn me to live for perhaps a couple of centuries without you, as must happen do you insist on remaining human? Eight months without you was endless torment."

"Ah, Émile..." She gazed into his eyes tenderly, but in their sparkling depths she felt a strange pull on her senses, and she dropped her eyes.

He caressed her chin. "You believe in a Creator with a beneficent plan for mankind, including no doubt, even semi-demonic creatures such as myself. Surely such a Being would forgive you for joining me?"

"I make no doubt, yet that is no excuse for giving in to despair so soon, Émile."

He looked playful rather than desperate. He pinched her cheek, and she flinched back from his steely touch. "Do you remember your terrors at the beginning of our wedding night? You know now that you had no cause to fear me then. It is so with this, if you will just give yourself to me." He began kissing her. His thirst for her blood seemed to merge with his other desire.

She didn't kiss him back, but for all her fear and her distaste at his wanting to drink her blood, warmth shot through her. His lips went from hers down her jaw, heading for her throat.

She pulled away. "Émile, when you made me that offer in the music room, I couldn't with an easy conscience have given myself to you, though you have no idea how I wanted to. It is even more so, now."

"Forget your worries, my lovely girl, they make no sense;" he murmured, pressing her towards the bed. "Trust me. No more talk. It wasn't with words that I soothed you our first night together." He kissed her some more and caressed her breast. His fingers came into contact with the cross, and he moved them away. "This wretched thing becomes hot. How can you endure to wear it?"

She caressed his face. Suddenly the inhuman flaring in his eyes no longer frightened her, nor her sense of his otherness. "If I agreed to join you it would amount to despairing of God's mercy, and–"

"God's mercy? *Bien sûr,* I have seen much of that, my girl." He pulled himself away and made for the door. Unluckily, his exit was made ludicrous by his having to pause to free his erection from his dressing gown.

—⚬❧⚬❧❦⚬❧⚬—

Émile paced about his room, swearing. Then, snatching up a candle he went downstairs, his light making surging shadows on the walls as he stalked through the house. The fire was dying down in his study, but he didn't bother to stoke it. He placed his candle on a table nearby and sat down to work in the dim light at his desk. He scribbled formulas, then sat lost in thought. He took out the book '*On the Use of Imitative Representation*' and read it for a while.

He brought out from his desk a large memoranda book with blank pages, and putting it on the desk, stood gazing long on it. Then he went back to writing more figures.

Outside, owls hooted in the clear, frosty air. After a couple of hours, Émile's eyes began to droop. He jerked himself into alertness, and worked some more, but at last he began to doze, his head falling forward onto his arms.

Someone knocked at the door even as the tiny specks of flickering light began to play on the ceiling. Shaking himself, Émile started up to unlock the door.

Mr Kit stood outside.

"What?" Émile mumbled, still half asleep.

"I know you don't like to be disturbed in here, *Monsieur* Gilles, but Georges tells me and Dolly a fine tale –"

Émile whirled about as light on the ceiling intensified and moved downwards. "*Merde!* Get back!"

Mr Kit held his ground, eyes goggling, his meaty hands grasping Émile's shoulders. Above their heads opened a scene inside a rough café. Georges and Émile were sitting at one of the tables. The pictures ran towards them, almost wrenching Émile from Mr Kit's grasp, so Mr Kit staggered; still he hung on to Émile, who drooped against him. Émile seemed asleep, his breathing even. Groaning in horror, grasping the collapsed Émile, Mr Kit staggered backwards, staring up at the ceiling.

"I want a shave." Georges felt his chin with disgust, thinking longingly of the barber's shop they went by earlier. "We may be living like to vagabonds, but I detest looking like one. For sure you need one, too."

The dishevelled Émile – surely in little danger of being recognised as an aristocrat now – turned from gazing out of the window, and drank some of his coffee. "It's up the road, ain't it? I'll join you soon."

Georges supposed such matters still meant little to him and now he no longer had to put on a brave show for his remaining sister, he couldn't conceal it. He would have liked to squeeze Émile's shoulder, but couldn't under the looks of the other men in the café, scornful of a couple of foreigners from the South.

He glanced across at the man opposite, whose eyes he felt on them; the man averted his gaze. Satisfied, Georges strutted out to the street, pausing to salute two passing girls. Encouraged by their giggles, he lingered to talk.

Suddenly, Émile froze, eyes dilating, shaking his head and slopping coffee on the table as he nearly dropped his cup. He muttered aloud, "This has been before!"

The man opposite, having finished his bread and cheese paused in picking his dismal teeth to sneer. He was strongly made, with the shoulders of a navvy, and wore a long scar from cheekbone to jaw with pride.

Another labouring man, also heavily muscled and savage looking, dark with dried sweat, hair matted, came into the cafe. The first man beckoned to him and they muttered together. Then the man with the scar moved over to where Émile sat, eyes still distant, while the other laughed behind.

"One of them filthy Southerners, eh? I know what you do with your mothers and sisters!"

Émile's eyes snapped into focus. The other man pulled out his knife, chuckling happily.

Émile went for them at once, vaulting across the table as though on cue. Outside, Georges heard the commotion break out. He dashed back inside, pushing past other customers escaping.

The following fight was epic in savagery, though short. Mr Kit, standing frozen, the sleeping Émile draped across him, chortled out his approval at the other Émile's moves above their heads. Besides knives, the conflict involved head butting, kicks, leaps across furniture, dramatic falls, struggles and gouging as blood sprayed dramatically about. The owners took refuge in the kitchen while the customers went outside, one man dodging back in to snatch up his food.

It ended with Georges leaving the sweat stained man bleeding and unconscious on the floor, one arm clearly broken, while Émile dragged his semi-conscious opponent outside to bang his head up and down in a puddle of combined filth.

A dark man, wild eyed and flashily dressed, prowled up with the bouncing step of an athlete. He stood watching the entertainment with a gentle smile. Another quarrel had broken out. A couple of the spectators had placed bets; one of them, realising he had backed the losing side, now pretended otherwise. This dispute was however, limited to threats. Meanwhile, the others greeted the newcomer respectfully.

Nobody interfered with Émile until Georges tapped his shoulder. "Bon, ça suffit! No-one deserves to drown in piss and shit."

Émile whirled about, staring wildly. Gradually he released his grip on the man, threw him to one side, and stood up gasping, blood trickling down his face from a gash at his hairline, shaking his head.

The stranger smiled his understanding, as though Émile were only guilty of a lapse in taste. "They call me Marcel Sly Boots, by the by. Now, why do they do that?" He laughed as at a great joke. "What are your names?"

Émile hesitated only a second. "I'm Gilles."

"Georges."

"Marcel; I want to buy you a drink, mes amis, for a piece of work well done."

The scene was fading; Émile was stirring and muttering.

"Lumme!" said Mr Kit. He hadn't been able to follow any of the French. The sounds were anyway muted, though he caught a whiff of the urine in the puddle in which Émile had ducked the man's head.

Émile wrenched his own head from Mr Kit's grasp. Mr Kit realised how tightly he had been clasping him. "That was a nice little fight, Gilles."

"That is one way of putting it. It was confused to me, so mad with battle lust was I …Curse that Kenrick. I haven't had one of those jaunts in a while. I hoped I was free of them. Kit, am I mistaken in thinking my body remained here all along?"

"You did, and sleeping like a baby." Mr Kit glanced nervously at the ceiling. "What was it?"

"It was one of those little trips through time of which I warned you when I made you my irresistible offer. So, whatever part of me travelled through time, this body remained here. Yet Sophie's family found her missing from her bedroom when it happened to her. She retained a full awareness. I think her case different, as she was not there already. More of memory was left with me this time, yet I was too full of bloodlust to let it deter me."

He sighed. "Kit, I should never have been selfish enough to marry Sophie, though we were like to break our hearts over each other."

"It is done now."

Georges came briskly up the dark hallway, without a light. He looked in. "What ails you two?"

"I clean forgot, Georges has just come and told me he's gone and become one of these Man Vampires, too." Mr Kit told Émile. "Before I saw them pictures I doubted, but now it seems to me that anything could be true."

"Saw what?" Georges stared about suspiciously.

"Mr Kit saw a return of the little disagreement we had with those fools when we first arrived in Paris led to my joining Marcel Sly Boots and the Professor's band of outlaws, while you went in with the others."

"What we all need is a drink." Georges made the suggestion with a naïve freshness, as though he had never made it before.

Mrs Kit stirred the hot toddy. "I will tell you straight, Gilles Long Legs, when Kit told me as some woman sucked your blood –"

"*En flagrant délit*?" Émile suggested sourly from where he leaned against the fireplace.

"I don't know any of your foreign talk, but does that mean improper'? I said she must have been touched and you got wild ideas about vampires from her antics. As for being pulled into the past, for all I know one of these wicked people what meddles in the dark arts could do as much. It's not so different from Agnes telling the future with her Tarot. But I've seen you change, *Monsieur* Gilles, and now I believe you. I'm sure I don't know where it's going to end."

"I thought to tell you in the morning about Georges, there being something I wanted to talk over with *ma femme*, but Georges now having enlightened you, I suppose I should ask you if you still want to stay, Dolly? I don't know if you are fond enough of bats to wish to live in a household with an increasing population."

"We can't let a friend down, Doll." Mr Kit intoned.

Georges grinned at him. "I knew you would say as much."

Dolly straightened her mob cap and her front*. "You are in trouble, Gilles. These Kenrick's are nasty pieces of work for a surety."

"I've met worse, but they tended to be human; still *après tout*, in those days, so was I." Émile reached over to pat her arm.

Dolly looked down at his talons. "Georges was showing me his nails and all. Kit wouldn't forgive me did I drag him away from this.

Then there's silly young Mistress Sophie, marrying you despite all. We will stay. What with that wench going about biting folks and with you wicked young bucks, we must be extra careful about crosses, Kit.

'Look at Georges there, preening himself at turning into some sort of a bat! I never thought to meet with such goings on in the middle of nowhere. It's all this Kenrick's fault for bringing back this nasty stuff from the foreign place with the outlandish name – Tran –"

"Transylvania." said Georges. "That's where his wife died."

Chapter Seventeen

S OPHIE WOKE TO A SUDDEN chill. She must have sobbed herself to sleep.

Now Émile was in the room, and she opened her eyes to the candle guttering and the fire suddenly dying down.

She sat up, pushing back her hair. "You gave me a start, Émile." Even as she spoke, she realised how feeble that sounded in the circumstances. His otherness had intensified.

He still wore his robe. Instead of getting into bed with her, he knelt down by it. There seemed to be a horrible parody here of her own nightly devotions.

Now the fire and the candle burnt normally again.

"Sophie, forgive me for my temper outburst earlier. It is hard for me to accept you would condemn me to centuries without you, as I said then, when I think on how it was when I lost you before. I dread now you want to leave me. I hope I don't appear to you as abominable as the fiend Madoc the Magnificent? Please don't scream like the ladies in that novel, but I do so long for you to join me."

She took his hands, feeling the talons against her palms. "Émile, I would never leave you. I wish I could join you, as it would be a comfort to you, yet, as I said before, if I agreed to it –" She saw the trap too late. Debate with him must always hazardous, when her beliefs were based on intuition, and she had been educated to decorate a drawing room, not to dispute ideas.

"Exactly – Come here, Sophie!" He followed his verbal pouncing on her with a literal one. As she dodged back he caught hold of the sleeve of her nightdress. It gave a ripping sound and a ribbon burst open.

Émile breathed heavily as he stared at her shoulder and partly exposed bosom. "Look me in the eyes and tell me you don't really want to join me."

She looked down. He took her chin in his hand and began to force it up.

"It will not hurt, *ma chère*." It was like a parody of a seduction. His eyes met hers. They grew larger. She tried to shut hers, but the lids wouldn't move.

She began to struggle, but she knew she couldn't escape. His fingers had been strong as a human. Now, they were alarmingly so. Overcome with a horrible passion, he began to move his lips down her face, nibbling the flesh without sinking his teeth in, going down her throat.

At this attack, she was frozen, no warmth flooding through her.

He came into contact with the cross.

Again, he found touching it uncomfortable, although, unlike Madoc the Magnificent, he didn't yell or leap back. He gave his head an irritable jerk, then released her hands and began to try to undo the clasp. His fingers were shaking, and he fumbled. She snatched at his hands, grazing herself on one of his claw like nails. "Émile, No! Stop! Don't force me!"

There was a crash, and stumbling footsteps up the nearby stairs. "*Merde!*" Then there came a thud, as a body redounded off a nearby wall. It was Georges, going up to bed drunk.

"*Ce putain de mur!*"

Émile started. Even in the dim light, she could see the change in his eyes. He let go of her, and sank face downwards on the bed.

Through their ragged breathing, she listened to more thuds and bad language as Georges completed his journey up the middle stairs.

Sophie put a hand on Émile's shoulder. "It is not your fault."

He muttered something into the bed covers she didn't catch. She stroked her hand down his back. He twitched angrily. Touching him being disallowed, she said, "I love you anyway."

He didn't reply, as if she had done him a wrong and not the other way round. After a time he fell asleep.

Sleep was impossible for her. She knew this was merely the beginning, and as she had entered into it with her eyes open, she had no right to feel sorry for herself. For all that, she did. After a while, the cock on the home farm crowed and some jackdaws sounded the beginning of the dawn chorus.

She gently turned Émile over, and held him so his head was cradled in her arms. There were so many points of adoration to be wondered on during this inspection – this tour of love – her nightly ritual.

He had long dark eyelashes a girl would envy, unusual in someone fair. She could look forever at his profile, the long, firm sweep of the jaw and the lines of his nose and chin. In the candlelight she could make out the fading freckles on the bridge of his nose she so adored. She told him so, repeatedly.

People would think her mad, doting like this on a vampire. Nobody was as kind to Madoc the Magnificent. He was always greeted by cries of, 'Fie, you foul fiend!' No wonder he was so unpleasant.

"I am so glad I married you, whatever happens…I would never do the things I do with you with anyone else…"

Émile sighed and stretched out, the corners of his lips turned up. She wondered of what he dreamt.

—⸎⸎⸎⸎⸎—

He woke her kissing and caressing her. He was back to as nearly his normal self as he could now be. The wild flaring in his eyes was subdued compared to last night and he concentrated his attentions on parts of her other than her throat. She didn't know if he remembered what had happened, but was happy to surrender.

Half an hour later, she tried an oblique reference to it. "Georges was very drunk."

She knew from his guarded look he remembered. "*Eh bien.* Sophie, I will tell you at once; he is become a Man Vampire."

"But how? Surely you didn't –"

"No, I am not that way inclined, nor yet so thirsty." Sophie tried not to shudder. He went on, "My poor girl, this will upset you further. It was the farm girl who was bitten before Georges and I came here. She has been feeding on him this last week."

"Oh, goodness! I must get some of the herbs, though we mustn't worry Katarina."

He sighed with impatience. "Surely you do not cling to the hope of those miserable plants having any affect on him after such proof of their ineffectiveness on me? Anyway, he would not consent to it. Before *pauvre* Katarina was taken sick, he was avoiding her in case she should guess and pursue him with them. It seems he envied me my new state." He looked at her wistfully. "It is nice someone appreciates it."

"It is too bad of him. It is too bad of you to speak so."

Those new eyes regarded her as though she were being bigoted. "We are fast becoming rivals to the Kenrick *Ménage*, Sophie. Perhaps other households will begin to tempt away our staff in turn. It seems scarce fair not to warn them of the Bat Invasion, but –"

"Oh, Émile!" Sophie wailed.

"I am sorry, *chérie,* it is no joking matter for you, but you know my way. If I were to warn the household, it would be tantamount to standing in the square at Denbigh or Ruthin and making a public announcement through a trumpet, and would probably only cause Ynyr and *Madame ma Tante* to contact a London doctor to come *à la hate* for a discreet look at us both. From the human point of view that would be unfortunate, given Kenrick's activities." He took her chin between his finger and thumb. "I fear I behaved badly myself, my lovely girl. I am sorry I tried to force you. It was too like to rape for me to be anything but ashamed of it. It is happy Georges' clamour brought me to myself."

She noted he made no mention of how uncomfortable he had found the cross. She guessed too he would be apologising for an attempt on her neck often from now on. Worse, what if the time came when he saw no need?

She forced herself to speak. "Émile – recollect you my suggestion if you did become a Man Vampire then you might take only a little blood from me at a time? Surely I should let you do so now? I must not put my own convictions or safety above that of others."

Besides – on a less elevated note – she feared he would take blood from other women. Insanely, the idea made her jealous.

"I know for sure now, I could not trust myself to stop in time to keep you human. Believe your favourite monster when he tells you now, as he may not be able to say as much again."

"Agnes, I am so sorry. It is all so dreadful."

"Well, Mistress Sophie, it is just as well he's no longer my lover." Agnes' fingers were shaking as she worked on Sophie's hair. "I never did like bats, and for sure I could not endure the thought of one about me. I could tell he was up to mischief and I should have guessed what from his ghastly look."

"I only hope that Katarina has more cures, but we must keep this from her until she is better." Sophie glanced down at the book. "Here it only mentions the Charged Wine and later on, amulets."

She stirred uneasily under Agnes' fingers as she read. *'He who has been Transformed by numerous Small Attacks rather than one Weighty one will experience these changes the sooner.'* She put up her hand to squeeze Agnes'.

Jem the kitten was on the window sill, watching a robin singing in a tree outside.

The birds have not gone, anyway. Sophie tried to stop such thoughts but her mind raced on: *Is it the vampire presence or the magic that has driven them from* Plas Cyfeillgar? *Now, Émile begins to do such things here.*

"I don't know why I snivel!" Agnes pulled out her handerkerchief.

Sophie patted Agnes' hand. "Agnes, you must be worried constantly about baby Eiluned. I know Katarina has been over to protect the cottage, yet still you must be concerned."

"*Mam* takes care with their crosses. Is fortunate she learned enough through *Nain* to believe in things of mystery – Now, then! No piddling in there!" This last was addressed to Jem, now sniffing about in a corner.

"Georges, I should send Sophie away, but I can't bear to be parted from her." Émile and Georges were in the workroom leading off from the kitchens, sharpening their knives and swords on whetstones.

"She wouldn't go."

"Didn't she swear to the Creator in whom she places such trust to obey me not long since?" Émile paused in his slashing to regard him. "How do you feel now?"

"I become strong enough to take on two of them Mad Inventors at once. Was Kenrick always deranged, by the by?"

Émile smiled. "What is madness, Georges? Reliving that little frolic in the café, it seems to me I was not demonstrably sane then myself. Kenrick was ever a cold fish, his ideas more real to him than people, except it seems this lost wife. I understand his desperation to see her again, but the way he and That Jade have gone about things has put me out a trifle. *Eh bien,* everything could be happy enough yet, if only I can bring *ma petite* round."

They paused, hearing something. "It is Agnes." said Georges, "Going down to the wine cellar." He thrust his knife back into his pocket and made for the door.

Émile, filing his talons with the tip of his blade, said after him, "I take it you have not yet the biting urge? It is early, yet it comes of a sudden."

A couple of minutes later, the boy who had let Émile and Georges into Plas Cyfeillgar, now installed to clean the boots and knives and hide things from Mr Kit, came up the corridor, candle aloft. Taking in the open basement door, he dodged down the first few stairs to peep down at who was inside.

Seeing Georges and Agnes illuminated by her oil lamp, talking below, he darted back up the steps to lock the door.

"No, Katarina, you must keep to your bed until you are eating properly. Try to finish that nice soup and bread or Mrs Kit will scold and not allow you any of the syllabub we had at dinner."

Sophie spoke sternly, but Katarina – whom Émile allowed to empty the apple stores for the donkeys and climb on the furniture – said, "You could tell her."

"I go in fear of Mrs Kit, Katarina, and besides –" Sophie broke off as the fire began to die down and a chill wind swept through the room, bending the flames on the candles and casting whirling shadows on the walls.

Katarina was bolt upright in bed. They both stared at the windows as though trying to see through the drapes. "It is One of Them."

Sophie and Katarina clutched at each other, both screaming before they knew it. Mrs Kit appeared at the door. She must have guessed from the extinguishing fire and candles what it was, for she shrieked loudly enough to be heard in the village.

As a tumult broke out downstairs – doors flung open, voices raised in enquiry – Sophie heard the bounding steps of someone taking the stairs four at a time.

"Can it get in?" Mrs Kit gasped.

There was a flicker of light and another blast of icy air. A figure stood in the room, tall and athletic, with dark curling hair. His eyes were flashing as Émile's when predatory while his teeth gleamed in his sea-bronzed face as he grinned.

Captain Mackenzie made a snatch at Sophie and she leapt back, pushing Katarina behind her with one arm. "Come here, my lass!" he was trying to catch her gaze while she averted hers, backing away.

Mrs Kit rushed forward, pulling out the chain of her crucifix and thrusting the cross towards his face.

He didn't cower back like Madoc any more than had Émile, though also like Émile, he found it hot, for he jerked back his head back and put out a hand, hurling her backwards. Her fall shook the floorboards and she shrieked again.

Mackenzie lunged towards Sophie again even as she and Katarina pulled out their crosses in turn. As they brandished them at Mackenzie the dashing footsteps crossed the landing and Émile rushed past them to leap on Mackenzie.

The Captain nearly overbalanced with the force of the attack. They wrestled together, staggering over to the window and nearly going through. Émile had his knife out and was trying to get past Mackenzie's guard, but Mackenzie was far stronger, holding him off as he reached for his own cutlass. He even found time for some abuse. "Tail chasing French cut throat!"

As they swayed against the window panes again, Sophie rushed towards them only to hesitate, longing to burn Mackenzie by thrusting her cross into his face, but fearing she might catch Émile, not knowing if now it might burn him whether he was in a predatory mood or not.

Out of the corner of her eye she saw Mrs Kit stagger to her feet.

Katarina snatched something from a side table and darted forward to hover about the fighting Man Vampires like a fly before she lunged inwards, pressing something against the back of Mackenzie's head and leaping away.

He let out a roar. Émile hurled him backwards and they hit the window with a cracking retort. Their forms dissolved in a mass of sparkling and another blast of cold that nearly extinguished the candles, while the creeping flames in the fire turned green.

As Mrs Kit shrieked again, Sophie dashed over to the window and Mr Kit panted into the room.

Émile appeared in the dark below, as did a wolf. It leapt at him, howling a continuation of Mackenzie's savage roar. and he slashed at it.

Fists clenched, sobbing in frustration at not being able to help, Sophie and Katarina watched. Mr Kit flung open the casement, letting in another blast of icy air. He brandished a pistol, which he kept trying to aim at the wolf Mackenzie, but Émile and the creature were both changing position too quickly for there to be a chance of it.

Mr Kit swore; Sophie didn't blame him. She saw blood on the wolf's fur, and couldn't tell if it came from him or from Émile. Then the wolf was a grey blur vanishing into the pitch dark of the shrubbery with Émile rushing after it.

Sophie wrung her hands; Katarina wailed, "He will fight and the Captain is much the stronger!"

"Where is Georges?" Sophie swung round to Mrs Kit, who stood massaging her bottom and cursing Mackenzie.

They both rushed the door to shout his name down the stairs.

"Georges!"

Viens ici, salaud!

The phrase jumped suddenly into Sophie's mind even as she was seized with that feeling of suffocating disorientation she knew from before.

It was gone even as Mr Kit passed them in the ambling trot which was the fastest that he could run. "I'll shoot the bastard!"

"Be careful of Émile!" Sophie fought off the lingering feeling of drowning in air.

236

Émile ran through the shrubbery, never faltering or tripping over a tree root in the velvety blackness. He rushed through the wild garden and the woods, where he sensed the wolf had gone. Other creatures plunged in the thicket. Once he came upon a startled rabbit up on its hind legs, chewing bark from a tree.

Up by the small plantation of bamboos forming a barrier between the woods and the upper paddock, he dodged from tree to tree until he sighted Mackenzie. Here, in the space of some yards between the end of the trees and the bamboos, the Captain waited, cutlass held ready, as the breeze rustled the bamboos behind him.

"Dubois." His Northumberland accent seemed incongruous in a monster. "I forgot to congratulate you on your marriage to that little chit from your aunt's household. I nearly had my fangs in her, then. Just the thought makes you want to kill me, eh? Unlucky for you that I'm going to cut you up instead. We can fight here without your humans joining in.

'I wish I had killed you when you were yet human yourself. I can't shoot you, neither, not being changed long myself, but I can perhaps still maim you, as you are not fully changed. For sure we can cause each other some pain. We shall see. I have never tried this with another Man Vampire, though I would I could cut Kenrick into slices. You like an ungentlemanly knife fight, and so do I. I came up from the ranks, you know."

Émile didn't waste any breath on words; as in the café, he went in for the attack at once. Mackenzie laughed at the ferocity of the assault. He parried Émile's lunge with a whirling movement, followed by a slash which nearly caught Émile across the face.

They stalked each other, closing, struggling, lunging, slashing and parrying. Mackenzie was stronger, but Émile was so quick that he startled the Captain, who spoke again.

"Do you delude yourself that you can protect your little bride from me long? Only think of it, Dubois, my hands on her nice round bubbies, my teeth in her neck."

Mackenzie went on to make a series of obscene suggestions regarding Émile's relations with Katarina.

Émile showed no sign of hearing as he tried methodically to maim Mackenzie.

Mackenzie taunted him with ever more filthy and outrageous gibes. Then he remarked, "I admire your self control, *Monsieur* Gilles. Your talents are wasted in abusing this country's hospitality by terrorising the roads about Hounslow Heath. We need such bloodthirsty ruffians to fight the rebel scum in France."

Émile showed no interest in this suggestion.

A thrust of Mackenzie's got through his guard and as he jumped aside to avoid it he stumbled, and Mackenzie's knife gashed his chest.

As blood began to well through the front of Émile's shirt, Mackenzie's teeth flashed in a laugh. "Careless, *Monsieur!*" He aimed for Émile's groin and as Émile dodged back, he laughed again. "I will cut off that straying member of yours."

They went on assiduously trying to mutilate each other. Now they both had gashes on the arms and chest. Émile was breathing heavily and fought more defensively. He looked weary.

Mackenzie was wary, sensing this could be some ploy, yet there was something more mechanical and hopeless in the way that Émile fought now. The Captain risked moving in, making for Émile's stomach.

He was hit by a concussion and found himself on his back, fighting the waves of dark unconsciousness that swam across his vision and gagging at the violent pain in his head. He struggled to dislodge the wild eyed ruffian on his chest, arm flung back to deliver the finishing blow.

As he drew back his arm, Émile froze, seemingly unable to deliver that thrust to pierce Mackenzie's heart. His eyes slitted and he panted with the effort as he fought to bring his knife down.

Even as he paused, struggling, Mackenzie dissolved into a mass of glittering specks that drifted apart as they vanished.

Breathing hard and swearing, Émile dropped to the ground in front of the bamboos swishing in the icy wind. Then he heard the blundering sounds of a human hurrying through the dark.

Mr Kit came into view, dark lantern in one hand and a pistol in the other. Émile got to his feet, the gashes about the chest and arms bleeding freely. "Kit, is Sophie safe? You missed the fun."

"Don't fear for Mistress Sophie. Where's he gone?"

"Flapped away, as we bats say, to fight another day, *malheureusement.* It was the Captain admirer of that Jade's. Devil take me, I couldn't put the knife through his heart as I would were I still brimming over with humanity. Still, it would have led to awkwardness."

"Was he acting on Kenrick's orders? You bleed apace, Gilles. We'd better get them cuts bandaged up. "

"These silly little scratches are nothing. Quite like old times, eh, Kit?"

Sophie and Katarina stood trying to peer through the darkness, arms about each other and shivering. At first they could see or hear nothing outside but the repeated hooting of the owls and the distant barking of a dog fox. Then once they heard the distant, jeering voice of the Captain but nothing from Émile. This silence from him made them even more distraught.

"Can Half Vampires kill each other, Katarina?" Sophie forced herself to voice her terror.

"I don't think so, and for sure they can't shoot each other, but they can be badly hurt, as both of them are only recently Man Vampires." Katarina wrung the hem of her nightdress between her fingers.

Then they thought they caught Émile and Mr Kit's distant voices.

With trembling hands, Sophie put Katarina's robe about her and they went downstairs towards the commotion of raised voices. Agnes came hurrying upstairs, her cap disarranged.

"Is somebody locked me and that nasty Georges in the basement! Mr Kit's gone out after *Monsieur* and Georges is mad to be left, but I said we don't know if there are humans come too."

They passed Guto in the kitchen corridor, solemnly dosing Éloise with brandy. Georges came up, looking as outraged as though someone had jeered at the arrangement of his cravat. "*Madame* Sophie, *Monsieur* is wild to see with his own eyes there isn't so much as a scratch on either of you, but fears to alarm you with his own bloody appearance. He has cuts merely, nothing to fear."

In the kitchen Émile, stripped to the waist, was washing the blood from the gashes to his arms and chest.

Mrs Kit scolded and cleaned them too. "I tell you again they are quite untouched, *Monsieur* Gilles, though my fundament is sore bruised where the devil pushed me over, well padded though it may be. Going to them covered in gore ain't going to make them happy. If you ain't in a fever by tomorrow, I am Queen Charlotte. That across your chest will go nasty, as sure as fire."

"Dolly, you forget I am half a bat these days, and will be as good as new in no time. It is a sorry thing I wasn't able to dispatch him when I had the opportunity – Sophie! Mrs Kit assures me all the *salaud* accomplished was to leave her with a bruised *derrière,* but that he could do as much drives me wild."

Sophie and Katarina were wailing aloud at Émile's blood streaked appearance, and Sophie took over the job from Mrs Kit. Before he let her treat him he kissed her hands, murmuring to her, "This fussing in ridiculous, *ma chère*, they are superficial merely. Besides, given my own caddish attempt to spill your own blood, you should not be so sorry to see somebody has done the same by me."

Mrs Kit tactfully withdrew to the other side of the room, huffing.

"Émile, what happened?"

"I was anxious to slice him into pieces for his attempt on you, and he tried to do the same by me. I couldn't make an end of him, try as I would, though I didn't split his skull it was no fault of mine. *Ma chère*, we must accept if he could get in, someone invited him and we must discover who."

Katarina said, "I can do the ritual again, *Monsieur*, but it will not keep him out if someone asks him in."

Émile sighed. "I must needs bully my staff to find out the truth."

Mrs Kit huffed some more. "For sure Mr Kit will have it all out. He's calling them together now. "

"When I find out the *salaud* who locked us in that cellar!" Georges fumed. "I am mortified at having to stay and mind the women, Kit having gone after you while we still banged and roared!"

"I hope you don't do that disappearing trick often, Gilles Long Legs, I don't like it." Mrs Kit went to the fire for the kettle, which was now rivalling her in puffing. "Scalding hot water, I do swear by that. Excuse me, Ma'am." She poured the steaming water onto a cloth and applied it savagely to Émile's chest. That made him stop talking and Sophie and Katarina bite their lips.

Mr Kit appeared. "The boot boy has up and gone with his box. The wretch must have been the one, and has left in a panic. That saves us a deal of worry, never knowing who is the traitor among as and when one of them bat folk – begging your pardon, *Monsieur* Gilles – I mean *Monsieur* Émile – can get in."

It took a long time for the household to settle.

Émile gave the staff a lively speech of reassurance on how they were unlikely to have any more trouble from the mad Captain illicitly let in by the boot boy.

Georges brooded. Lucien, formerly the second cook at Plas Uchaf, looked cynical and fiddled with his moustache after the way of Lord Ynyr, while the footman Guto said he was glad to see the last of the cheeky brat.

Meanwhile Katarina became tearful. Sophie took her in her arms and led her back up to her room. "You poor little thing, you have seen too much of these horrors already!"

Agnes, following, glanced meaningfully at Sophie. "The panes in your windows is cracked, letting in the draught, and need mending."

"I did the ritual again." Katarina sniffed. "They cannot enter without being asked, were the windows open."

Sophie said, "Perhaps you should come into my room for tonight, but then I must tend to *Monsieur* Émile's cuts to try and stop them from festering."

"They shan't, Mistress Sophie, he has changed too much now." Katarina wept more at the thought.

Sophie winced, but Agnes was brisk. "Then that is the first good thing I have heard about being a Man Vampire, though Georges strutted in the wine cellar like to some cockerel, trying to impress me, and expecting me to admire his nasty growing claws and fangs. Don't look so sad, Mistress Sophie, there's these other cures. I went down there to fetch some wine for the Charged Wine. Meanwhile for sure *Monsieur* Émile wouldn't be happy with Katarina in your bed; I will go in with her." With her back to Katarina, she pulled a face that said, '*In the absence of better company.*'

Sophie fretted, "Whatever shall we do about the boot boy? He acted the ingrate sadly after Émile's kindness, but I fear what may become of him if he is run away in the cold just as Katarina was about to do back at Plas Cyfeillgar."

Agnes snorted. "Don't fear for the little sneak, he will be gone to his *nain's* past Denbigh, her as always spoiled him rotten as too good to be a servant. Éloise has the vapours about going to bed and that dolt Guto is offering to stand guard outside her door."

"My lovely girl, what have I brought you into? I must hate myself for it, though I hope you change your mind and permit me those caresses it turns me sick to think of Mackenzie imposing on you."

She spoke hastily. "These gashes must smart so, Émile, and Mrs Kit's treatment, too!"

"Sophie, I have suffered worse from a horse dispatching me into a blackberry bush." He took her in his arms. "Come now, and let us get some sleep in my bed."

"Surely the soreness will keep you awake? We can try. Use me as a pillow in the way you like."

They lay a long time, weary but not sleeping, he with his head resting in its favourite place on her bosom. This was comfortable for him, but not for her. She lay awake while the night went by with hooting of owls, song from a nightingale, sporadic bleating from the sheep in the field over the way and an outburst of braying from the male donkey.

She tried to empty her mind for sleep, but couldn't as the worries whirled about her mind and his head felt heavy on her bosom. Émile was awake too; often when she looked at him, his eyes were open, head turned towards the window. She supposed he was looking out for the wolf's return. Now, Sophie began to worry about everyone else in the area.

Émile caught her gaze as she looked at him again. "Go to sleep."

"Can you not sleep for the soreness?"

He raised his head from her bosom. "You know I rarely sleep well. The idea of Mackenzie or Kenrick at your bedside, slobbering to get his teeth into you! Kenrick tried as much himself, before I even came here. I will let them get to you or any of my humans over my dead body."

In the light of the guttering candle his eyes did some flashing. He took her chin gently between those inhumanly strong, taloned fingers. "Sophie, I don't want you, Katarina or Agnes or any of the others to go outside the grounds without Georges or myself or Mr Kit. From this time, I don't want any of you out in the grounds alone."

"But Émile, nobody who was wearing a cross has been bitten."

"Georges did wear – that – at least part of the time, and the minx had it off him. Do as I say like a good girl. As Mackenzie proved tonight, you, Katarina and Agnes are my vulnerable points which Those Others must target. When I think of what might have happened through my own stupidity in taking that sneaking boy into my household I scarce can keep still."

She felt herself hedged about, as in a chess game. "But Émile, I will be a prisoner quite!"

His mood changed then, and he laughed almost playfully. "Your brigand has you surrounded by his wicked retainers in his terrible castle, *ma chère.*" He settled his lips against her skin, sniffing it appreciatively. He murmured softy, "You smell so delightful, my little human. I can sense the sweet blood coursing through you –"

"Émile, what did you say?"

"What? My usual besotted ramblings merely. Go to sleep, pretty one." She lay awake, eyes closed, feeling entrapped.

Chapter Eighteen

É MILE PROVED DOLLY WRONG BY eating his breakfast ham, eggs and bread with appetite. Sophie, glad he wasn't eating bloody meat, noted that while stiff, he was in good spirits. "These foolish little cuts mend apace, *ma chère*. Do not fuss so. I have already been out when the man came about the glazing to the window in your room. Is your green dress new? You look lovely in it."

Sophie found herself glowing, and when she glanced at herself in the mirror she did look prettier than she expected, given the worry and sleeplessness. Émile himself was still reflected in the mirror; she supposed it was only full vampires who weren't. No doubt, Ceridwen Kenrick would have been put out if she couldn't admire herself every day.

She asked suddenly, "Émile, what means '*salaud*?'"

His eyebrows shot up, and he burst out laughing. "It is a swear word, and for sure it sounds ridiculous enough on your pretty lips. How did you come to hear it?"

"I think you said it, when you were in a fever."

"I clearly was a foul mouthed as well as troublesome patient, *ma chère*."

"Émile, I want to go and make sure Sian Jones wears a cross. I am worried for her, with her sister a vampire now; you really don't know. Katarina has long since sealed her house, but I feel I must."

He sighed. "If you insist, Sophie, I will take you."

"Are you sure the ride will not be too uncomfortable?"

"For sure not."

The weather being dry, Émile insisted Sophie use the trip to the village to put in some riding practice. As they made their way along the muddy lane, Émile was, as ever, all smiling encouragement, as he was when they played chess.

Sophie adored the sight of him in his blue coat, admiring how despite his stiffness, he sat easily on the strong, wilful horse. She loved her own lilac riding habit – part of her wedding trousseau – and felt bold in handling her own Myfanwy, who plodded as usual.

Sian Jones' belly was impressive already. She tried to curtsey to Sophie and Émile; they had to smile as they pleaded with her not to trouble. Meanwhile, she fixed her eyes on Émile with more than mere nervousness at a visit from the Lord of the Manor's cousin.

"There is no need to make yourself uncomfortable, *Madame* Sian. I will pass the time with those elders while you ladies talk." Émile lounged over to where a couple of red faced, elderly men sat shouting on a bench, seemingly oblivious to the bitter east wind blowing in their faces.

Sian didn't look surprised; Émile's eccentricities were already well known. Inside, Sophie handed over her basket of treats, remembering coming here with Lord Ynyr last summer and the girl's Grandmother telling them that the baby was dead.

Sian's English was fluent, though like most of the villagers, it was her second language. When Sophie made her discreet speech and offer of the cross, Sian's look was veiled. "It is kind in you, Mistress. Do you wear a cross yourself?"

Sophie was annoyed with herself for blushing. "Yes, and our staff, too. I think it wise at present. We should not let prejudices deter us from such a wonderful protection."

Sian frowned. "Begging your pardon, Ma'am, but *Mam* says we shouldn't."

"It would be such a relief to me were you to protect yourself by wearing it."

"You know it's true what they say, don't you, Mistress? About the vampires?"

Sophie swallowed and nodded.

Sian's eyes went to the window, looking over at the bench where Émile chatted with the old men, amiable Man Vampire that he was. She seemed to be working herself up to some question. Sophie knew what it would be; had she Maintained Correct Distance, Sian never would think of asking it. She had a wild vision of one of the maidservants confiding to Harriet that John was a vampire.

"Ma'am, they say that Sir Émile was bitten at the Kenrick house."

Sophie knew her look gave her away, for Sian's eyes dilated, alarming Sophie that these horrors might bring on premature labour. "Little Katarina has been giving him herbs from the first."

"My sister was bitten before him."

Sophie tried to sound confident. "You must not worry about it, Sian, though you must protect yourself with the cross, for the plant cure His Lordship left with her is the same as Katarina's. Please concentrate on looking after yourself. I am sure we will defeat this awful scourge in time."

That sounded like a one of the rallying speeches from Eugene, the ineffectual hero of 'Madoc the Magnificent or the Vampyre's Curse'. Sophie wasn't surprised Sian looked unconvinced. "But Ma'am, things is getting worse."

Sophie tried a bossy tone worthy of Harriet. "We must try to be patient. Meanwhile, you must to wear the cross whatever your *Mam* says and are not to fret. Do try some of this hothouse fruit…"

———— ⁕ ————

Agnes met her in the hallway, while Émile – less stiff already – strode off to his study.

Agnes drew her upstairs, and then spoke in a whisper. "Mistress Sophie, these orders *Monsieur* has given Mr Kit are too bad. We need to take the wine to church, but I cannot go out without Georges now and that won't serve."

Their eyes met as Agnes went on. "There was no keeping Katarina in bed and she guessed at once about Georges. Of course, when she tried to get him to take the remedy he laughed outright."

Sophie found herself whispering too. "The book didn't say if the other cures could work if the first hadn't been tried. It said little of the cures and so much about the horrors. I will go through it again. I so hate reading it!"

"Last night, when I was locked the wine cellar with Georges, for sure he was furious he couldn't get at that Captain – for Their hearing is so sharp he could follow everything people said. Still, he found time to laugh nastily and gloat at me, '*Aren't you scared to be trapped with a monster? I am tempted to Make You Mine!*' and suchlike. Is horrible he is become already, though mortified he was he couldn't yet escape by changing form."

Sophie winced. "Agnes, you are brave. But I do not like to work behind *Monsieur's* back."

"Yet we must, Mistress Sophie, for Katarina says the cure of the Charged Wine is painful, and by that stage, none will agree to it. They have to be surprised into taking it. In the meantime, she is working on amulets. They may help."

"Oh, dear! Well, I shall take you and Katarina to Llangynhafal Church tomorrow, for the church in Llandyrnog is being repaired this week." Even in her anxiety, Sophie felt a stir of pride at her pronunciation of the Welsh names; Agnes was a good teacher. Then she wondered if Émile or even Georges could still enter a church. She was sure neither of them thought to try since the wedding. She had gone as usual with Agnes and wished that she had taken the wine then. "We must hide it there and come back for it."

"In Llangynhafal Church the Lord of Ruthin's own pew is full of hollows under the carving, and will make it easier to hide away the – " they turned at a movement in the hallway below.

A dark, tall man, swathed in a greatcoat with many cloaks, was striding in high boots towards the passageway leading to Émile's laboratory. Sophie only glimpsed his profile for a moment, but she thought he wore a mask. Agnes clutched her arm.

Even as Sophie hoisted her skirts and dashed down the stairs, Agnes behind her, the figure vanished. As she reached the corridor opposite there was nothing to be seen. She ran to Émile's study and knocked loudly.

"Who is it?" He sounded irritable, and Sophie guessed at once he was at work on what the Dowager Countess would call 'Mischievous Experiments'.

"*Ma chère?*" Émile smiled wolfishly as he opened the door, perhaps thinking he looked genial.

"Émile, I saw a man in a greatcoat come up from the hallway, and then vanish–"

"What?! Stay here!" He was gone.

She and Agnes clutched each other. "Could that Captain have got in?"

They heard Émile and Georges' yelled instructions and running feet as the search began, with Dolly's voice raised in expostulation. Katarina came trotting to join them, holding a couple of leather bags, which Sophie supposed must be the amulets.

The doorway to Émile's study was still open. Candles burned in the sconces at either side of the mirror close to his desk. Sophie could see a large memoranda book open on the table nearby, and a closed leather bound one.

She could also see an old book with a faded gold title on the spine, 'On the Use of Imitative Representation.' She had heard Émile say that Kenrick talked of using something called 'Thought Forms' in his magical experiments with time. Was that 'Imitative Representation'?

She felt it wrong to spy about Émile's study, when he always discouraged her from knowing anything about this strange work with which he hoped to counter Kenrick's. She dreaded its nature, which he didn't deny was magical. Yet she felt drawn to the doorway, almost as if by a force stronger than her will. Agnes and Katarina followed fearfully.

Sophie looked down on the open memoranda book at the odd, faded pictures, which seemed to quiver, almost coming into focus. She was aware of the others behind her.

"Don't, Miss, it's dangerous!" Agnes forgot Sophie's married status in her alarm.

A large hand was placed on Sophie's arm. "That ain't something you want to look at, Mistress."

Sophie spun about. "Mr Kit!"

"Funny things happen in here." As he tried to insinuate his bulk between them and the desk, Sophie senses his anxiety to get them out.

She felt indignant. "Not only in here! Is the intruder found?"

"No, Mistress Sophie, but we are searching the house and grounds."

Sophie remembered something odd about the figure. She didn't know if it made her more frightened or less so, but she blurted it out.

"Agnes, when I saw the figure in the hall, I think I saw part of another floor behind him."

Katarina gave a squeal, though that peculiarity could hardly be worse than the things the girl once dreaded every day in the Kenrick house. Agnes took Katarina's hand, her eyes widening.

Émile was in the doorway, all smiling reassurance, though Sophie could see his resentment at their intrusion sparking at the back of his eyes. "*Mesdames*, we have found nothing so far, but whom better to protect you than Mr Kit? Tell me more of that figure and promise me should you see such another, you will keep well away from it. But trouble not yourselves greatly, for I believe it to be insubstantial, without full consciousness."

He came to take Sophie's hand; at that moment he seemed to her no longer half human; he felt purely inhuman.

———— ✦✦✦✦✦✦✦ ————

"No more after this, or I will be in my altitudes* and useless as a guardian for our humans."

Émile placed his bottle of wine down by the chair. He was in his study and the worse for drink. Used to putting it away, he had taken more than the amount on which even he could appear sober and was talking to himself.

He clicked his tongue. "Mischievous Experiments, eh? I cannot keep away from 'em. So Tom has turned up, and not through anything I did. What else can Kenrick do in the way of manifestations with time? I have need of something to distract myself from these worries. Why cannot those delectable women safeguard themselves from his bite at least by joining us? I dread finding he has sank his filthy teeth into one of them. There's always a danger another of the servants will take a bribe or he may hypnotise one of them." He stretched his hand down, searching for his glass without looking. "*Viens ici —*"

Saying this seemed to disturb him. He shuddered, shook his head violently and swore. He raised his glass. "*Salaud...* What ails me? *Salaut —*" At that, he dropped the glass and leaned back in the chair, eyes closed, and sweat breaking out on his face.

Muttering angrily and again shaking his head, he got to his feet, his stiffness gone. He stared at the illuminated mirror by the desk, breaking off to curse himself now and again. Finally, the image of the *Château,* stark against the night sky, appeared.

He was breathing as though he had been running. The images blurred, coalesced, and resolved into one of a corridor filling with smoke. Émile gazed at it, wild determination in his eyes. "I do not care for my own worthless carcase, and its loss might well do my lovely girl a good turn."

He opened the book and taking up a little magnifying glass, began to move it about on the open page. Part of the ceiling brightened and images of stumbling figures began to swirl. Loud crackling and snapping sounds came sharply and a faint smell of burning.

Émile stood gazing up for some moments, and then he lurched and sank to the floor. A blurred image of him appeared above, stumbling towards those other figures. His mouth opened, but no sound came out. He reached out his arms, and then seemed to struggle desperately against some force, his streaming eyes – half shut against the smoke – fixed.

The images vanished. Émile was stirring on the study floor, while out in the frosty air came the sound of crows calling loudly and repeatedly as though questioning.

He muttered, "I knew it! I was there outside my old self!"

He sat on the floor for some time, his head in his hands. Then he got up, shaking himself again, and went back to looking through a series of jotted formulas and figures.

Some time later, he raised his head at a distant sound, and went out, striding quickly through to the back of the house.

As Émile turned into the kitchen corridor, Georges marched towards him, face frozen; they both ducked down as a plate whirled towards their heads to smash against the wall behind them.

Émile grabbed Georges arm, bringing him to a halt. "How now, Agnes? I hoped we were friends."

"I'm sorry, *Monsieur* Émile, it wasn't meant for you, but is disgusting!"

Georges struggled and reddened, unable to break free from Émile's grasp. Émile grinned at Agnes. "What has this rascal been about?"

"You know full well, *Monsieur!*" Agnes met his eyes steadily. "And I hope you don't start doing the same by the Mistress neither. But as she don't look quite as content as she did, I wonder."

Émile wore his inscrutable look. He squeezed Georges' arm. "Come, Georges, I need some relaxation, and I want your company on a trip to the little town of Denbigh."

The barmaid in the Castle Inn wasn't surprised to see the young Frenchman back again, having told him of her nice room and how pretty the other barmaid was, should he care to bring a friend.

If anyone had dared to call Alys a floozy or say that the Landlord was a bully* then she would have slapped his or her face. If her gentleman admirers gave her presents, it was her affair; if she gave away part to keep the Landlord sweet that was between the two of them.

She had guessed these two foreigners were scoundrels, if only from the way they bought everyone in the inn a drink. She asked *Monsieur* Gilles what he did for a living. He wore clothes well made but old; cast-off finery, no doubt; typical of such a flashy rogue.

"Before Christmas, I worked helping my cousin, whom you might call an apothecary. I breed horses; at the moment I am resisting the urge to breed bats." He smiled on her, and she decided she liked him despite everything.

"Ugh! Why would anyone do so?"

Meanwhile, his friend had her friend on one knee, tickling her.

Upstairs, after a few kisses, she came to herself to find *Monsieur* Gilles bathing her neck. He forced on her a sum she thought ridiculous, though he had taken nothing for which she would have demanded payment. Perhaps he suffered from problems with virility?

Her friend wouldn't tell her the details of what had gone on with the other rascal, though Alys knew she received a huge present, too. The young men hurried off, looking sheepish, promising to return.

They did, soon enough. *Monsieur* Gilles undressed her to her corsets, and responded to that normally enough, but then she remembered nothing until she came to herself on the bed. This wasn't through a lamentable performance on his part, as he didn't even begin to enjoy her. She found the marks on her neck, too, while her friend went about in high necklines for a while.

Alys didn't mind; *Monsieur* gave her so much money she was able to marry and start up her own lodging house. Of course, she heard the talk about vampires, and laughed. You wouldn't catch her being daft enough to turn into a bat!

Sophie suspected Émile and Georges had gone out to sate their appetites for blood. She chewed her fingers in a torment of anxiety for Émile's chosen victim, and jealousy of her too.

Émile hadn't bothered to let her know he was leaving the house. No doubt he thought a man was under no obligation to do so. Naturally, it was different for her.

That he should leave them in Mr Kit's care so soon after the sinister figure's appearance made her suspect he was confident it had nothing to do with a vampire attack. Certainly, as she described its high boots and caped greatcoat, Émile, Georges and Mr Kit had looked conscious.

Mr Kit patrolled with a deliberate air. Sophie was sure he hid a pistol in his clothing. What use was a pistol against a vampire? Of course, Mr Kit's might have a silver bullet in it. Perhaps Émile had been able to order one to be made up before he started to change? There was no point in asking Mr Kit; his answer would be evasive.

Once Mr Kit opened the door of Sophie's sitting room where she sat sewing with Katarina. His conspiratorial air seemed to seep through the space, annoying her. "Mr Kit!"

His tone was suave. "I am just following orders, Mistress Dubois."

Katarina bit her thread with a loud snap. Sophie started. "Don't do that, dear, you might chip your teeth. Mr Kit, as *Monsieur* Émile doesn't wish us to go out unaccompanied; I want to take Katarina and Agnes to arrive early for morning service at Llangynhafal church tomorrow."

Mr Kit looked bland. "What hour, Mistress?" Naturally, he was shameless about having no idea about service times.

She told him, and he gave his peculiar bow, a sort of plunge of the head, and withdrew. He at least didn't have a bat's hearing.

Agnes knocked. "Excuse me, Mistress Sophie. Where do you wish to take tea?"

"Come in, Agnes. I don't think *Monsieur* Émile is back, so I may as well have it here. Mr Kit is to escort us to church tomorrow. I ought to hope he will come in with us, but matters being as they are, it will be easier if he stays smoking and whistling outside."

"Is not troubled by conscience he is, Mistress Sophie. I do believe the figure we saw was one of them –" she glanced at Katarina – "Old Associates of his."

"And Georges' and *Monsieur's*?" Katarina's eyes were sharp.

Sophie spoke brightly. "Most likely. Now tell us of the amulets you made, Katarina, for it touches not upon the subject in that book."

"They are near ready. The difficulty will be in hiding them in the victim's clothing."

Sophie's voice lost its briskness. "It is so disappointing the herbs have not proved effective."

Katarina shook her head. "It is difficult to know for sure yet, Mistress Sophie, with the symptoms being the same whether they work or no."

"You can imagine how *Monsieur* jeered at the notion of amulets."

"Amulets aren't to be scorned." Agnes said stoutly. "*Nain* did always say done properly they are powerful. It is them mountebanks* who have given them a sad reputation." She dimpled. "I will plant one upon Georges, if only to serve him out for being so nasty in the wine cellar."

———⊙୧⋙⊙⋐⊘⋒⊙⋙⊙୧⋙⊙———

Émile took Sophie in to a dinner table as luxurious and inviting as always. The candlelight set off the glow of the plate and illuminated Sophie's centrepiece, the spread of dishes and the stained glass window. As ever, Émile dismissed the servants so they could talk intimately.

He might pass as sober to a stranger. Sophie knew him well enough to sense how blunted his sensitivities were, though that might partly be his new inhuman nature. As he came over, as always, to help her to food, prickles ran down her spine. He now seemed to be as lithe as ever, and he exuded an air of being sated, horribly satisfied.

At least, he would have been scrupulous about only taking a little.

Meanwhile he smiled upon her in a way that put her in mind of the wolf trying to convince Red Riding Hood how it was harmless. She met his eyes only to pull hers away, trying to hide her shudder. "How are you now, Émile? I trust those cuts are not too painful?"

He looked startled. "I had quite forgot them, they mend apace. And what did My Lovely Girl this afternoon? I hope you were not too alarmed by our singular visitor, *ma chère*. At last I begin to understand how all this comes about. Keep your distance from such, but as I said, I do not think such incomplete visitations bring full strength or awareness with them. Still, I must be watchful." He chucked her under the chin, his talons tenderly grazing her skin.

She kept herself from flinching back. "I had sufficient novelty for the afternoon in that visit. I practiced my music, and then Katarina and I did some work for the Poor Box. And you?"

"My Good Girl and her Good Works…Does *Madame* want some of this fowl dish?" He helped her to it. "I cudgelled my brains in my study, after which Georges and I took some relaxation in Denbigh. I believe it is the county town, though *bien sûr* hardly more than a village. My girl, you look alarmed."

She mumbled something. He looked offended rather than hurt, and turned to glance in the mirror. "I don't look much worse than ever I did. It is so much the better those ridiculous freckles about which you are so sentimental have faded." He sat down and began to eat, but soon shot at her: "You guess, *chérie*, about the late Tom?"

"The late Tom?" Her voice came out as a whisper, but with his new hearing he had no trouble in understanding her.

"He was shot in an ambush at Hounslow Heath. It was a balmy summer's day with curlews making a sleepy sound until the shooting began. Georges and I enjoyed the fun once again, courtesy of Kenrick, the night before you swore yourself to me. It is nice to think in a way Tom survives. Of course, my little believer would never doubt his continued existence. By the by, where do you consider that rogues such as myself go when they die? You have never enlightened me."

She sighed aloud. "Of course, your rescuing Katarina says nothing about you, whereas if you were a regular churchgoer, never doing a charitable act, you could reasonably expect a place in Heaven. You will laugh, and I hope I don't sound sententious when I say I am sure we will all eventually meet and understand each other in the next world."

He showed his animal's teeth in an indulgent leer. "All of us? What a tender believer it is! Just think on it, your sweet self and Agnes and

Katarina too, myself, Georges, Tom, Mr Kit, Dolly, Kenrick and That Jade, Captain Mackenzie and Kenrick and his lackey Arthur Williams all united in a state of eternal bliss. *Eh bien,* I would not deprive you of such a hope, my sweet one. Just allow me to send Kenrick and the Gallant Captain ahead betimes, eh? " He laughed, and began to eat again heartily. Clearly, the blood hadn't interfered with his normal appetite.

This jovial remark made Sophie leave what remained on her plate. Now Émile became, for the first time since she known him, self-pitying. "What have I done to deserve such distrustful glances from *ma femme?*"

Sophie kept silence, torn between sentimental sympathy towards him and the desire to laugh at the absurdity of a maudlin vampire.

"You see me as a beast, complete with teeth and claws. You are horrified by Gilles Long Legs after all, particularly now he thirsts for your blood. Don't protest, I see it in your eyes. Ha! For all your talk of loving me forever, no doubt you agree with Lord Dale."

"But I must always love you–" she began, but he was still talking.

"When I relieved him of his valuables, outrage got the better of his fear as he croaked, '*You are That Scoundrel Émile Dubois! I know you by your eyes!*'

'I said in a London accent, '*What me, a foreigner?*'" I did enjoy distributing that part of his wealth to the women and children on the streets. But I realised it was as well to take up Ynyr's pressing invitations to come to Wales. Here I met the girl who made such a fool of me at a certain *soiree* back in Paris..." He rambled on in maudlin gloom.

"Émile, you are wrong, I –"

"Don't blather, my girl. You broke my heart then and are like to do so again with your rejections of me." He gave her a filthy look, and then got to his feet adroitly for one under the influence of drink. "Now I must patrol about and see if I have to fight off any more attempts on these miserable ingrates of humans under my care. Do not test me too far, *ma femme.* Yes, I know you have plans afoot. Don't believe for an instant you fool your tame wolf..." Still rambling, he left, swaying slightly.

Plas Cyfeillgar
Famau Mountain

Kenrick was putting up a long portrait back in its usual place in his study on the outer wall. He spoke to it, as he often did. When not communicating with it, he drew the heavy green velvet curtain over it.

"I could not endure to think of those low criminals near you when they called, staring, perhaps even defacing you." His jaw worked in fury at the thought.

Behind him, a flickering came on the ceiling and began to play downwards. Moving pictures formed and coalesced, turning three dimensional and running down the walls. He turned, stared, started towards them and subsided to the floor, breathing evenly.

The horses pulled the carriage up the track. All about, the mountainous, wild landscape of Transylvania was as dramatic as a stage backdrop.

As they came to the hill, the coachman jumped down, cursing the passenger for not joining him in sparing the horses.

Inside, Kenrick sprawled, gasping and staring, eyes wild. Finally, he choked out, "I must stop her --- she must not run and fall..." The carriage moved ever more slowly, finally coming to a halt. There was a rap at the door and the man's head, surmounted by a disordered thatch of hair, appeared in the window, insisting that Kenrick must get out. Kenrick stared, uncomprehending. The man became voluble.

Finally, Kenrick cursed him and climbed out. He looked about bemused, and then began to walk swiftly, urging the coachman on with gestures.

The coachman was as surly as any of those who served Kenrick seemed fated to become. As the horses plodded on, their flanks steaming, he muttered in his own language. Kenrick became angry and took a swipe at one of the horses with his cane. The man reproached him in a torrent of his own language and Kenrick turned on him, hissing and barring his long teeth. The man jumped back, eyes widening, and made the sign of the Evil Eye.

Kenrick moved past him, starting to run. The man made the sign again just as Kenrick stumbled. He called out in triumph as Kenrick seized his head and panted, eyes wild. Then with a spasmodic clutching movement, Kenrick was on the ground, wheezing. As the man came up to him, brandishing his cross, Kenrick's eyes showed no recognition as his breath came in gasps.

"Vampire!" the man cried, and Kenrick's eyes gradually cleared. He muttered, "Put that wretched thing away, you miserable superstitious fool!"

Kenrick lay on the floor of the study, still gasping. His look changed gradually from one of dazed astonishment to one of exultation.

He clenched his fists: "It can be done! I was joined to my old self. I remember, afterwards, finding myself on the ground and that fool's terror of me."

Ceridwen stood staring down at him. He looked almost with hatred at her lovely face and wonderful figure, those eyes as hard as lovely marbles.

Her tone was sharp. "What ails you? Are you in a fit?"

"I have been wrenched back in time and in space, across to Transylvania." He spoke coldly now, unwilling to show his emotion to her.

Ceridwen's eyes quickened. "I felt a strange sucking myself from those images."

"Now I have more than ever need of that Dubois' mathematical skill. I cannot afford to wait. This may not last. As well I thirst, my dear, and I called in at Plas Uchaf to leave my card only the other day."

Plas Uchaf
Famau Mountain

Morwenna wandered about her bedroom, singing.

She had dismissed her maid early, wanting to spend some time alone before she went to bed, gloating over the things Lord Ynyr had murmured that day. Now, whenever she thought of him, it was with a melting sensation. It was odd how before she'd never thought of the Count romantically, for all his good looks. True, she'd angled for him while always truly liking him too, but now, a spark had caught and flared between them.

Odd, that she should suddenly feel so cold outside, when her insides felt so warm. She shivered even as the candles started to gutter. She turned, astonished to see the fire burning low and Kenrick standing beside her, hands stretched out.

Even as she cried out in fear, she became fascinated by the secret in those cold eyes. To find it out mattered more than anything.

In the moment that Kenrick's teeth entered her neck, she had a glimpse of its nature.

It was a human secret, with a smiling woman. She was plain and insignificant, but with a tender understanding in her eyes that transcended intelligence as she held out her arms in welcome: 'We have been apart too long.'

Chapter Nineteen

É MILE'S EYES GLOWED IN THE dark. He sniffed the skin on Sophie's half revealed bosom appreciatively. He sniffed quickly, like an animal, and sighed. She was still fast asleep, seemingly trusting once more after their reconciliation, her arms still about his neck. He kissed her face, murmuring endearments. She made a small noise of satisfaction, holding him tighter before sinking back into sleep.

He began slowly and gently to disentangle himself, murmuring soothingly to her the while. Perhaps that reminded him of his murmured reassurance to her that first night together; anyway, he risked waking her by softly kissing her some more. She sighed as he placed her arm on the pillow, and he smiled on her for a moment before leaving.

Éloise was up early in the cold dark of the February morning to light the fires. The servants might be indulged at Plas Planwydden, but still must do such tasks. She hurried along the passages to the breakfast room, shivering so the shadows her candle cast on the wall lurched.

When a figure appeared down the passage, she started. Then she saw that it was only *Monsieur* lurking in the hallway.

Even in the light of the candle – for some reason he didn't have one – she noticed he was looking strangely bright-eyed, but was his usual self otherwise. She thought him magnificent in his rich dressing gown. His look of interest didn't surprise her, though she was flattered. She curtseyed, glancing up at him.

He smiled amiably. "You are up betimes, Éloise."

"I must light the fires. But you are up early yourself, *Monsieur* Émile." She fluttered her eyelashes. He started to look odd. She thought she knew the reason, despite the early hour. She giggled, and approached him, her lips pursed.

"I am going out for an early ride." His eyes suddenly fixed on hers, and he went on to mumble something about, "Nothing about your neck."

She thought that he was going to scold her for not wearing her cross. She'd taken it off to put on her necklace for town on her half day yesterday, and forgotten to put it on again. Remembering the tales going about the villages, she'd been relieved to meet no demonic bats on her way home in the cart with Guto.

He muttered again, "Run away, girl –"

"You wish me to go?" She knew he didn't, and stayed, fascinated.

He moved towards her, and began to stroke her glossy hair. She thought the flaring and animal green in his eyes mad and drew back. Then she lost interest in escape, because they had locked with hers and the most important thing in the world was discovering the secret hidden in their depths.

She saw it, too. It was a courtyard on a drowsy summer's day, and some boys playing marbles on warm flagstones. *Monsieur* Émile was carrying her to the chill of the breakfast room, lying her down on the *chaise longue* near the fireplace and biting her neck, but that was of no interest in comparison.

By a huge effort, Émile wrenched his lips away from her throat after three mouthfuls. They moved, trying to fasten on her neck again almost of their own accord. He took out his handkerchief to staunch her bleeding, while she slept on. His eyes were beginning to clear, and he shook his head and cursed himself as he worked to stop the flow. He had to use saliva to clean the wound, muttering to himself, "Let us hope my spittle is not as poisonous to *ma pauvre jeune fille* as That Jade's was to me."

She was shivering. He wrenched off his coat to cover her and hurried to light the fire with the equipment. When it was burning, he examined her neck again. The bleeding had stopped, helped no doubt by the chill in the great dim room, which was only slowly beginning to lift.

He whispered to her, "When I leave the room, you will wake up, believing you have just lit the fire, not remembering anything of this, nor wondering how you came by this money. You will hide the marks on your neck, though wondering not how you came by them." He put some coins in her pocket, pulled on his coat and disappeared.

———— ⌇⌇⌇⌇⌇ ————

"Church?" Émile, helping himself to ham and eggs, looked resentful at Sophie's request. "I have things to do, *cherie*. You have been praying enough of late to excuse you from regular attendance, *bien sûr*." He raised his eyebrows.

She thought of those times when, slipping out of his sleeping embrace, she knelt down by the bed, praying desperately. She should have taken into account his hearing was now that of a bat. She was nervous, too, as her peculiar sense that he had taken blood from another woman was back.

Guto scratched at the door and handed a note to Émile. "It's urgent, Sir, from Lord Ynyr."

"It must be, when we were due to dine with them tonight." Émile tore open the note and his eyes dilated, then blazed.

"Émile, what is it?"

"Morwenna is like to die."

———— ⌇⌇⌇⌇⌇ ————

"If I had only warned you." Émile whispered to Morwenna, squeezing her unresponsive hand, while she lay ghastly and comatose. "The others might have jeered me, but with your fascination with the macabre, you might not. I so hate myself for this. Forgive me, *ma petite*."

Lord Ynyr was by him, looking startled as well as distraught. "Émile, whatever are you saying? Surely, you do not blame yourself? Most likely this is not the same contagion you had weeks since."

Émile whipped about, guilt still in his eyes. "More of this later, Ynyr. For now, when comes the doctor again?"

"This afternoon." It was the first time the Count had ever known Dr Powell not be optimistic, save when the patient was already nearly dead.

Sophie came from talking to the Dowager Countess, who lay on her couch with her smelling salts and a miniature of her two late daughters. She had refused to hear of Sophie's helping to nurse Morwenna.

"*Vraiment*, Dr Powell seems unsure of the nature of this illness. It might be contagious, though he speaks of a startling depletion of the blood for which he can find no explanation. It seems far worse than the one through which you nursed Émile. I cannot prevent poor Ynyr from haunting the chamber with his potions, but I will not have you put yourself at risk, when you are lately married. We have sent for Morwenna's old nurse, and if anyone can rally our poor girl, it will be she...No, Sophie! Please respect my wishes."

Sophie sighed, feeling guilty. Desperately sorry for Morwenna, she was the more eager to help nurse her because she was ashamed of her own former lingering resentment about how Morwenna had treated her as The Poor Relative. She was ashamed too of her jealousy over Émile's anguish over her. Her only comfort was how much worse matters would be had she suspected Émile.

As they walked down the gallery, the long windows gave a view out over the mountainside and Émile glared across to the red rooftops of Plas Cyfeillgar.

Lord Ynyr looked down at Katarina, patrolling the formal garden. He sighed, thinking of how when Émile arrived at Plas Uchaf last Christmas, he had been the bereaved one, but now their positions were to some extent reversed. "Émile, there is the child you and Sophie are in a way to adopting. How your position has changed since you came to us! You are blessed indeed."

Émile blinked. "Blessed, eh?" he muttered, but was too preoccupied to make the answer that would normally come to him. Meanwhile, Sophie saw Mrs Brown glaring at him as though weighing him for the gallows.

The bitter wind blew flecks of snow in their faces as they rattled down the mountain paths in the pony and trap Émile had insisted on driving himself to save time on the mountain tracks. He brooded in silence. Sophie knew he would go to confront Kenrick.

They came to where the lane branched off to the more level path leading to Plas Cyfeillgar, down which the Count's party had ridden on the sleigh last Christmas. She sensed his longing to confront Kenrick at once.

She said, "Someone must have invited Kenrick inside, but poor Morwenna cannot have worn her cross."

Émile turned on her his inscrutable look. "You shiver, and Katarina having been ill, we must get you home betimes for hot soup." Then he tensed, listening, a wild longing in his look. "What is that?"

Sophie and Katarina could hear nothing, but a few moments later, they caught the thrilling cry of the wolf. Sophie tightened her arms about Katarina. The horses plunged and Émile had to get them under control before pulling out his pistol.

"It will be no use." Katarina's teeth chattered.

They heard no more. Émile urged on the nervous horses, glaring about them. Once Sophie thought she saw a flash of grey some hundreds of yards off.

As they left the mountains behind, coming down towards Llangynhafal and, Sophie supposed, relative safety, she clutched the basket with the bottle of wine concealed at the bottom. "Émile, I know you wish to have us home as soon as may be, but I know too Morwenna would wish for me to stop off at the church to pray for her."

Her conscience pricked her, though she was telling part of the truth.

Naturally, he looked indignant and harried, making a dismissive gesture. Then, muttering sullenly, he drew the trap to a stop and handed her down. "Be quick about it, Sophie."

He was too preoccupied to take notice of Katarina's own version of his Inscrutable Look as she jumped down too.

Sophie sighed with relief that he made no offer to accompany them. Certainly, there was nobody about to hold the horses, yet Sophie wondered if he could have come in had he wished.

———❧☙❧☙❧———

The household was in uproar. Émile loped about angrily trying to find his duelling pistols. He was obstructed by Katarina and Sophie pursuing him with tears. Georges stood by grinning savagely, while Agnes shook out the cloaks.

"Mr Kit!" Émile roared through the door leading to the kitchens. "Where is the rogue?" He turned to where the youngest footman was enjoying the drama. "Go and find him, boy. Katarina, let go my coat-tails, this becomes annoying!"

"I must speak with you, *Monsieur* Émile." Sophie sniffed.

"Who?! *Tres bien*, Sophie. Katarina, leave me be! Go for some soup or I shall become angry."

"Come then." Agnes led Katarina toward the kitchens. Émile took Sophie by the elbow – reminding her of their first meeting at Plas Uchaf – and opened the door to the little sitting room.

Sophie gasped, "I fear in your anger you will try and destroy Kenrick, and it will end by his destroying you. What point to take a pistol? That book says –"

He stalked about, seemingly once more tempted to take kicks at the fire. "A weapon may come in handy with the lately human footman, anyway. I have no choice but to go there, my girl, if only to protect your stubbornly human self. Kenrick meant this as a warning to me you will be next, and I cannot endure it. It was easier for him to enter my cousin's, that is all. Katarina may seal the house against them, but did not Mackenzie gain entrance?" He breathed hard.

'It only takes another member of staff accepting a bribe for either Mackenzie – not being human, ere now he will already have recovered his headache - or Kenrick or *Madame* to gain entrance. Katarina tells me the ritual makes it more difficult only. They can still enter after repeated invitation." He paused. "Either I go there, or I send you to *Madame* de Courcy's in Brighthelmstone, along with Agnes and Katarina."

"Oh, no, Émile! I would never leave you in the midst of all this. I do so feel for you and want to help you; you do not wish to be rid of me?" Sophie's tears began to stream and she groped for her handkerchief.

He came over to take her in his arms. "Of course not! Your monster still adores you, but there is no time for this now." He searched in his pockets and handed her his own handkerchief, then kissed her.

Sophie blew her nose. "But what might She not do?"

"You do not think I go there for the pleasure of That Jade's company? I can think of nothing sweeter than her serving me as she did before."

"She is so sinister." *And beautiful.* "Kenrick will have you join him in those dreadful experiments. You will not say what you have been about in your study, but for sure you are working on similar lines."

"It would be hard for me to explain to a non-mathematician. Besides, I think you happier not knowing, *ma chère*. The thought of Kenrick getting to you brings me out in a cold sweat. Which is it to be? Do you stay here or must I pack you off to safety elsewhere?"

"So, you are already become the husband and master rather than the lover and order me? I implore you not to go to that place."

He chucked her under the chin. "I am sorry to have to turn down any request of yours. Do not fret, *chérie*. From your fussing, anyone would think me still human."

She laid her hand on his arm. "About the remedies for Morwenna, Émile –"

He bit his lip. "The remedies for Morwenna, Sophie, will most likely be the – the –" he was unable to continue.

Sophie knew it was not just horror at the thought of a stake being driven through Morwenna's heart which stopped him.

He went on, "Surely even you accept now, *ma pauvre petite*, those miserable herbs are useless? Doubtless poor Ynyr will add to her misery by dosing her with them himself, poor girl. To think of her being taken by that slug Kenrick of all people! My spies have let me down, giving me no warning of his return. *Alors*, Kenrick shall not get at any of my other humans…Wherever is that rogue?"

Eyes wild, he dashed out.

Georges strolled up to Émile as he thrust his second duelling pistol into his belt. "Them weapons won't be any use, as you couldn't do for Mackenzie."

"If I can cut him up good it will be something."

"This ain't sensible, Gilles; there's two of 'em, and stronger than you, having been changed longer. Wait until we find Kit, and then I'll come too and we stand a chance. Not you alone."

"I'm not waiting. Stay and mind the humans. I expect more trouble in that quarter."

"As you like, Gilles, but Kit can't be far. If you ain't back by half after three, I come after you like to your nursemaid."

"Make sure and put on your bonnet, then, Georges."

As ever, no birds sounded or stirred in the grounds of Plas Cyfeillgar as Émile rode into the deserted courtyard. Snowflakes danced about as he tethered his horse, which rolled its eyes and stamped.

Émile kicked the front door, roaring, "Kenrick!" Flecks of paint fell to the doorstep. Émile kicked it and roared again.

There was the flicker as of distant lightening, and Kenrick stood by Émile, smiling gleefully and holding a savage knife. "Dubois, Gilles Long Legs or *Monsieur* Gilles: you wish for a sordid brawl rather than a proper duel? No pistols?" He was trying to catch Émile's gaze while Émile avoided his.

Émile fondled his cutlass. "Either."

Kenrick clicked his tongue, then began moving about Émile in a sort of dance of wariness, giggling. He did not have Émile's muscular development, yet he moved with the agility of a great cat.

'I take it this temper outburst is due to my having feasted on that haughty beauty Miss Llewelyn. *Monsieur*, has the little puss you married told you how once I came to her by night? Her breath unluckily reeked so of garlic, it made me ill. I trust she excludes it from her diet since your marriage? Did you pull up her skirts for a diversion in this out of the way place? Did Her Ladyship take a moral stance, and instead of casting her off, insist on your marrying her? Is there really to be a premature heir? Yet, I think the delightful tales that circulate overlook how short a time you stayed at Plas Uchaf." His eyes were calculating grey marbles as he assessed Émile.

During Kenrick's speech Émile changed colour several times over, his fingers tightening on the knife handle. "Come on!"

Kenrick giggled, staring into Émile's face. "You think to kill me, but cannot. You are no longer human enough to repeat what you did to Mackenzie in a vulgar brawl; we cannot fight at close quarters. I am too much the gentleman – something I am sure evades your understanding – to accept a challenge from you, knowing that I could drop you with an ordinary shot and remain unscathed myself, for you could not endure the vicinity of that miserable ore you would need for shot to finish me."

Émile's breath came quickly.

Kenrick sniggered again. 'I would enjoy killing you, were a disgraceful end at Tyburn not the deterrent to me it clearly is not to you. Besides, one would have the misfortune to survive many hanging attempts. Why, one would have to be beheaded or drawn* to put an end to ones' torment.

'I despise a rake and you are a criminal besides, unable to keep your hands off other men's wealth or their wives' privates. Gentleman of the Road? You and that man of yours were cut throats in the gutters of Paris. But I need you for my experiments."

"No more talk."

"Let me demonstrate, you fool!" Kenrick jumped forwards, slashing at Émile's face.

Even as he moved and Émile lunged to parry the thrust, they both came up against an invisible force. Émile struggled against it, while Kenrick turned and put away his knife. "Do you see now, Gilles Long Legs? Even days since, you couldn't kill Mackenzie, only injure him, and now you cannot even do that to me. When you came here to kill me, savage as you are, did it not occur to you what fate awaited your humans did you lose the fight?"

Émile thrust away his knife and patrolled about, looking fit to choke with rage. "I didn't intend to lose or to finish at Tyburn, but now you have me over a barrel. If I don't come in with you, you will batten on my other humans. Yes, I could send them away – but you might find them out."

Kenrick drew back. "I overlook your coarse manner of expressing yourself. As you lived long amongst ruffians, doubtless you have got out of the way of civilised manners. Say rather if you work with me, then I give you my word as a gentleman the remaining humans in your household will be safe from me and mine."

Émile looked unimpressed. "Does that include Mackenzie?"

"I cannot answer for that wild beast Mackenzie. I don't believe even the British Admiralty can control him. He is become a nuisance with his obsession with my wife. I would you had killed him in your little fracas. Could he, he would have killed me long ere this."

He sniggered again. "Miss Morwenna's blood was a fine claret on my tongue. You breathe heavily, *Monsieur* Gilles. Your fury over her is territorial instinct merely, when for sure you have begun to bite yourself. Undead, she will be more powerful than we, and what matter if humans do not approve the change?"

Émile stalked about some more. Then he stopped and spoke flatly. "If you can send me on these jaunts through time, why need you my help?"

Kenrick stared. "What? You have had that also?"

Émile looked back expressionlessly between his eyes.

Kenrick strode about himself in his excitement, rubbing his hands. "I did not send it you, *Monsieur*. There is a leak of power, some extraordinary warp. In my study last night, I was pulled back through time and space to when and where I have been trying to reach. This renders you the more necessary to me, as it may not last, and to exploit it so I can travel at will must entail tightening the mathematical approach. "

Émile stood prodding at the boot scraper with one toe. Finally, he looked up. "Let us get on with it. The weather is bitter. I must stable my horse."

Kenrick smiled; with his cold eyes and long teeth, he looked more savage than when angry or morose. He wrenched the bell rope by the door. For once, his call was answered speedily; a bitter looking elderly man trotted through the courtyard door.

"See to *Monsieur's* horse, fellow." Kenrick moved to the side door through which Émile and Georges had entered. "Come in. I must trouble you for your pistols and cut-throat's blade, to avoid accidents."

Émile walked away some paces. "I have no choice." He turned about. "Catch!" He tossed the knife to Kenrick.

Kenrick fumbled his snatch at the handle, grazing one finger so as to draw blood. He let the knife clatter to the ground, cursing. "That was foolish, *Monsieur* Gilles. I might have construed it as an attack and fired on you, for unlike myself, you will yet be vulnerable to gunshot wounds."

Émile watched Kenrick as he staunched the blood. Kenrick bared his teeth again. "Think you now how tempting this blood must be, were it only human?" He stooped to retrieve the knife and Émile handed him his pistols. Kenrick said, "Enter!" and they went into the icy corridor leading to the back of the house, Kenrick moving catlike ahead of Émile.

"I am in my laboratory today. Do not trouble about Williams; he is the confidential servant, like to your fellow ruffian. He entertains us with the latest news; it was he told us of your hasty marriage. I must needs have him stand guard should you be tempted to mischief."

The muscular, fair-haired Arthur opened the laboratory door, sneering. While Kenrick locked that heavy door, the footman went over to unlock a narrow one leading off, which led to a small storeroom. Here he put the knife on a shelf, retaining Émile's pistols. He came back, locking the door and stood aside watching them, one pistol trained on Émile. "I like these, Master Kenrick. I think I shall use them instead of mine."

Kenrick giggled. "Understand, *Monsieur* Gilles, gunshot remains deadly to a new Man Vampire for a while. Therefore, beware." He giggled again at Émile's look of suppressed rage. "I lock the door, for here I think you will find again a force keeps a novice Man Vampire like yourself from turning tail by dissolving."

The great room was gloomy, the blinds drawn. Émile's glanced at Arthur, at the shelves and benches of equipment, crowded with candles and candle holders, at the mirrors hanging or leaning against the walls, at the small fire smouldering in the grate that did so little to dispel the chill of the room, and the locked doors to the storeroom and the passage.

His gaze settled on a great, leather covered book at the desk in the middle of the room. The faded freckles on his nose stood out again as he blanched.

Kenrick watched him narrowly. "Recollect you this? You made use of the book I prepared for you the day of your informal visit. One of my lackeys must have requested you enter. Two of the wretches have scuttled away in our absence. Have any sought refuge in your vampire household?"

"As you have invited me in yourself, it don't make any difference." Émile said carelessly. "I wouldn't employ anyone I could bribe."

"No, Gilles Long Legs? I knew you wouldn't be able to resist my invitation to look into that book. Curiosity killed the bat!" Kenrick shouted with laughter. "Forgive me, *Monsieur*. I have a weakness for a joke, as do you yourself, though you are sullen company at present." He giggled some more at the outrage in Émile's eyes and took up the book.

"You hate me for what I showed you. Did I hear an echo in our hallway of your pathetic dream of killing me? Those scenes haunt you ever, coming between you and sleep. Yes, when we met again after so long, I saw in you what I know from myself, a terrible longing to alter the past, which was one reason why I knew we must work together. I am a cold philosopher in all but in this weakness for one human; I would change the past for my late wife."

Arthur watched Kenrick closely as he went on, "Yet, this *misalliance* of yours has come inopportunely. You are not long a Man Vampire; you may have some sentimental feelings towards this little chit on her promotion*. That might make you anxious not to change the past for fear of altering the present. For myself, no such considerations apply."

Arthur's gaze quickened. Émile stared back impassively. "That ain't a matter of concern for you, given it's your past you want to alter."

"Perhaps. But rather than a partly willing partner, it will render you my unwilling accomplice, co-operating through territorial possessiveness over your humans, especially that rosy little blonde. Arthur, pass me that book and those ensconced candles, keeping an eye on this excitable Gallic the meanwhile."

Arthur sniggered, and Émile regarded him with detached interest as Kenrick went on.

"We are far closer than I imagined in bringing about a pathway through which we can visit the past. I returned cursing from probing the ideas of the equivocal coward in Chester, yet my time was not wasted, for he had insights into levels of existence as may yet prove invaluable. I take it in your experiences, you relived the past, able to interact with those you met, as it was with me?"

Émile looked still more taciturn, perhaps disgusted by the thought of speaking of his meeting with Sophie to the cold being before him. He spoke flatly again. "I was, yet unaware of that after the first minute. I know my physical body didn't move."

"Mistress Kenrick assures me nor yet did mine. Those moments are evidence of a consciousness and one of our forms of body moving into another strand of time, *Monsieur*, which we shall work to extend. Yet I think it possible that in some circumstances, the physical body may travel also, but the difficulties arise when it already is located somewhere else, albeit in another time."

Kenrick picked up the heavy leather book with the pages of half visible pictures of past events. Émile watched stonily as he lit the candles, took up a magnifying glass, and three dimensional images began to flicker on the ceiling.

"*Diawl!*" Arthur shifted, eyes dilated, as a narrow street came into focus. There was Émile in his shabby clothes and shirtsleeves, joking with a costermonger, while the dark and voluptuous girl with him turned over the vegetables.

"Quite a beauty, eh? But that is the wrong page." Kenrick turned the page and the pictures ran across the ceiling and part down the wall. He turned to assess Émile, "Happy memories!"

Émile's face was impassive as a three dimensional vision of himself aged about fifteen appeared below the ceiling. He was riding up to the Château des Oliviers. Bernard came into view, eagerly spurring on his horse, followed by another older youth. As they trotted across the front courtyard, they passed near a group of small girls, including Marguerite. They had broken off from some game involving two wooden dolls and heaps of picked flowers to quarrel bitterly. One girl darted forwards to tug at another's hair and another pushed her away. The nurse, sitting some distance away in the shade, sewed on oblivious.

As the boys approached, Marguerite shrieked a greeting and the others joined in. Émile waved, as did the dark boy, but Bernard didn't deign to notice them.

Kenrick turned the page and smiled on Émile. "Gone forever, *Monsieur!*" The scene at the Château des Oliviers ran down the wall and disappeared as Kenrick snapped the book closed. "Now, have we an agreement?" He seemed to find collusion in the bitter look that Émile turned between his eyebrows, for his smile was oily. "To work."

They discussed the irregular appearances of the surges of power which created a gateway to the past and of possible explanations, speaking with icy politeness. Émile worked for some time on one set of calculations, while Kenrick tackled another.

Once, he turned to Émile. "While I may not have your gift for higher mathematics, should you try and play tricks upon me, *Monsieur*, I am not such a looby I will not suspect as much, and I will regard you as having broken the terms of our agreement." No doubt thinking of where that must lead, his mouth began to water, and he took out a handkerchief to dry his lips.

Émile didn't bother looking at him. "I am not such a looby as to try."

As the courtyard clock struck the hour, there came a knocking at the door.

"My little wife wishes you offer you some refreshment, *Monsieur* Gilles."

Émile stiffened, but said smoothly, "You must give *Madame* my regrets. I am previously engaged."

Kenrick shrugged and went over to unlock the door. Ceridwen Kenrick was there in a low plum coloured dress, her cheeks flushed, her slanting dark eyes shining, lips parted in the smile of a young girl looking forward to a party. As ever, there was something indefinably inhuman about her, even apart from the sharpness of her eyeteeth.

"Here is the dear little thing to receive your excuses, *Monsieur*." Kenrick stood by the open door, his sneering grin a caricature. Émile sullenly went into the corridor.

"I keep your weapons as surety, Monsieur Gilles." Kenrick slammed the door behind him.

Émile made his bow. "I cannot accept your invitation, *Madame.*"

"Oh, dear." She dimpled. "You are angry yet. I cannot blame you. I was careless enough to leave my teeth in you long enough to poison you, and to scratch savagely besides. Truly, I did not mean to be so wild. You must blame your attractions. Such a nice form as you have, rivalling the Captain's, even better than Arthur's. Then, I think you may have seen the images of your former life as a ruffian, and taken offence."

She was trying to catch his eyes, still dimpling.

"*Au revoir, Madame.*" He made his bow and turned away.

"*Viens ici, salaud.*" Her tone was soft. He stopped, and struggled, wild-eyed and swearing while she laughed at him. "I order you to stop. You cannot fight your urge for me. After we have lunched together, you will be overcome by bestial lust and pleasure me." She approached him warily, for he was still breathing hard and trying to escape.

She enjoyed watching the outrage in his eyes. "You arrogant creature, there is no point in fighting to go home yet to your insipid little wife. You are lost. I see you do have a conscience of sorts; I should have realised as much from how you remained in France for years, fighting to save your parents."

Chuckling happily, she stood watching him struggle against the blanket that came down between him and his faculties. Then, seeing his eyes glaze, she came and took his hand. "Come to the morning room."

In the morning room, a table was laid for two. Outside, a formal garden was desolate with winter, silent save for the buffetings of the chill wind. Here, even in the summer, bees sounded but none of the visiting birds sang.

Though a bright fire burned in the grate, the room was chill. "Sit down." She smiled. Émile sat wordlessly. Ceridwen went out into the corridor and screamed down a flight of stairs leading to the basement.

A sullen male voice yelled something back.

"Hurry up, *twpsin! (fool)* I am hungry!" She frowned, clearly hearing something else, and screamed again, "I understand what you say, take care! If you annoy me I might lose my temper and begin to bite, and who knows who? Bring the food at once!"

She returned smilingly to the table, where Émile sat staring blankly at nothing. As she approached he ran his eyes over her body with a dull sort of interest. She caressed his face, stroking the faded freckles about his nose so adored by Sophie, while he looked at her emotionlessly. "You are uncharacteristically quiet, Gilles Long Legs. Come a little bit to yourself, not enough to regain your willpower, but enough to speak, as I do not wish to lunch with an automaton."

His eyes were stirring. His tone was almost normal. "From the way you used me before, I suppose you hate men."

She smiled coldly. "No, I was merely enjoying you, after the fashion of we half humans. Hatred is a human emotion, like love. As regards my view of men, *Monsieur*, one man can ruin a woman's trust, if he works hard enough. I decided I wanted my husband dead and–" for a second human emotion showed on her face, "And something else – and I set into motion forces of which you begin to be aware. I realise I should have waited rather than taking the first means appearing in the form of Kenrick." She fiddled angrily with a knife. "Yet, his assurance of youth and beauty for so long was tempting indeed."

Oddly enough, here Émile spoke, showing his patriarchal prejudices.

"Put that down; I never like to see a woman with a knife."

"Humph!" she said. "Such a domineering male it is! Yet, I believe it must go with having a penis. How unfortunate such a strange organ is necessary to a woman's pleasure and fecundity."

Instead of spluttering into his wine, Émile said flatly, "*Vraiment, Madame.*"

With a bang, the manservant with the grotesquely ill fitting livery came through the door, staggering under the weight of a laden tray. As he approached, he nearly slipped, but with a backwards flapping heroically regained his balance. This triumph was reduced by the sound of his jacket tearing. He approached resentfully, while Ceridwen glared at him.

"Get out of my sight, idiot!"

The man breathed heavily as he left the room, a rip showing across the top half of his jacket. Ceridwen screamed after him, "Cease that infernal wheezing or I might feel the urge to change into a She Wolf!"

The man almost dived from the room.

"As yet, I feel no urge to change shape." Émile said tonelessly.

"Pour the wine." She lifted the lid of one of the dishes, revealing beef that had been cooked for perhaps a few seconds, lying in a pool of blood. "Help yourself, my adorable cut throat. You feel no urge to do what? I hope you are not referring to pleasuring me? Oh, to shape shift into a wolf or bat. No, but I see it in you already. "

"You came to Plas Uchaf as a bat."

"Yes, and I saw you this morning, when I was a wolf. You will make a nice wolf for your Little Red Riding Hood. Indeed, there was always something wolfish about you, with those green eyes."

They ate heartily, Émile's trance state having no effect on his appetite. On finishing, Ceridwen stretched and sighed. "That fool can cook well, if nothing else." She smiled at him. He watched her breasts swelling and lifting under the tight bodice of her dress. A vague apprehension showed in his eyes.

Seeing it, her inhuman smile became indulgent. "You look almost alarmed; so amusing in a rake! No doubt it is unfortunate I won't let you be faithful to that insipid creature you have married, but really, I am sure like my own scoundrel of a husband by the time she is big with your first child you will be unable to contain yourself any further." She got up, and wandered over to him to caress his face once more. "Do you love her?"

Even in his trance state, Émile seemed reluctant to answer.

"Come, I demand an answer!"

"I love her more than I have ever loved anyone, ever." This was said dully.

She blinked. "Once I felt so, for the wretch I married, later paid out so deservedly by Kenrick. If suppose if I remained much of the human, I might be jealous, as you are an appealing rogue; I might order you to stop loving her."

Alarm definitely moved in his eyes now, though he could do nothing, not even remove his gaze from her wonderful black eyes.

"Still, your mind would put up such a resistance it would be tedious work trying to overcome it. I cannot be bothered to attempt it. I only care for one, and she is dead.

'Kenrick wishes you to keep working with him on travel through time. You must do so. Yet beware, for I think he means mischief against you too, and I do enjoy you. Now, you can think of nothing but your lust for me. Come and pleasure me."

He jumped to his feet, breathing heavily and rushed to take her in his arms to kiss her, one hand going down to pull up her skirts and caress her full bottom. She pushed him away. "Come, you must wait at least until we get upstairs."

Chapter Twenty

"THERE NOW, *CARIAD*, DO NOT take on so. It is not in them nasty folks' interest to harm him." Agnes was hugging, stroking and patting Sophie, who was nearly bawling.

"Oh, I am being like the feeble Lucasta in that novel '*Madoc the Magnificent or the Vampyre's Curse*'. I laughed then, for all she ever did was faint and cry and plead with her *fiancé* Eugene not to tackle the vampire. Oh! Eugene never got bitten himself, of course. Ah!"

"*Monsieur* Émile will be safe enough. Georges said Kenrick wants him for them sums as he needs for this nasty magic with time."

"That is near as bad!" Sophie hiccoughed. "I know how he longs to undo what happened to his family. In the beginning he and Lord Ynyr laughed at Kenrick's odd ideas, but when he was drawn into this, it must have brought back the old torment. I think at the first too, he may have hoped to alter what happened the day That Woman changed him, but now he becomes happy to be a monster, Agnes!" She sobbed again outright.

Agnes put her arms about her again. "There, there…Georges is the same. Is too bad they are not only a pair of rascals, but vampires, too."

"Agnes, you do not whine, and I know you still care for the rascal."

"For sure I must put Eiluned first."

Sophie went on hysterically, "Yet, it was Émile's being bitten brought us together, and my ending up in Paris. I would not change that. It is all so complicated. I fear his meeting with That Woman, when they are the same now." She glanced anxiously in the mirror. "I look awful. I must stop crying, or I'll look even plainer in contrast to her."

"He don't like her, for sure. He'll be back betimes. I am going to make you some tea." Agnes gave Sophie a last squeeze, and got up to rummage in a drawer for another handkerchief.

From the kitchen, Agnes heard unsteady, heavy footsteps in the hall. Remembering Émile's dramatic return from Plas Cyfeillgar, even though he could hardly be turned into a Man Vampire twice, she rushed to open the door.

Mr Kit, his face covered in blood, swayed in the inner porch.

Georges patrolled on the terrace, which gave a view over the grounds and beyond to the mountains now whitened with snow and the lane which Émile must take on his way back from Plas Cyfeillgar. Georges was oblivious to the bitter North East wind buffeting him. Now and then he broke off from his angry puffing on one of Émile's cigars to swear.

He saw the distant, mounted figure. "Stupid bastard!" His form wavered and came back. On the second attempt he vanished with a flashy whirl of iridescence.

Émile rode into the stable yard, looking sour but healthy, as the stable clock struck three. He jumped down and handed the reins to the stable boy. "Georges, I return betimes. Here, boy, some oats in his fodder, he deserves it. For sure those stables are near as dismal as the house. Avoid those people at all costs, boy."

As he walked with Georges from the stable yard, Émile cursed. "I called to hear the news of Morwenna on my way home. There is no change. My head felt oddly muddled as I set out from Kenrick's accursed place...Georges, I cannot believe it!"

"Gilles, I warn you, you do stink of perfume. *Petite Madame* Sophie might be put out. How fares the skin of your back, this time?"

Émile disarranged his hair in his fury. "That Jade must needs be a witch, Georges! It is unaccountable otherwise."

"Is it, given her looks? There is no need to make excuses to me. I am jealous merely. She would have been welcome to cast a spell upon me, though with such a body she doesn't need such to tempt me."

Émile breathed heavily in his indignation. "I did want to be faithful to Sophie, you lout. That Jade reduced me to a beast, slobbering with lust, my head empty."

"Then you are not so in general with the ladies?" Georges sniggered. He went on laughing under Émile look of fury. "I'll run you a bath, before you get into disgrace with Mistress Sophie."

Émile shook his head. "*Alors, Madame* used a deeper version of the trance, merely." His look changed to become – ludicrously in an Eye Flashing Man Vampire – sheepish. "I cannot complain of That Jade acting so to gratify herself, when I did the same for a sup of blood. I hardly knew what I did, and I think it so with us when it comes upon us. We cannot stop ourselves. I only took a couple of mouthfuls from the barmaid Alys and from *ma petite* Éloise, so they will not join us. I don't want you biting Éloise, neither."

Georges whistled. "So you have taken from her?! She dangled after you from the first." He sneered. "Except for *La Belle* Lola, I never wished to go where you have been before; that applies to where you have had your teeth as much as your member."

"Hold your noise, Georges; I am in no mood for your puerile ramblings!" Émile vanished in a flash.

"Hoighty-Toighty, Gilles Long Legs. You will be still more angry when you hear about poor old Kit's beating." Georges achieved a spectacular display with his exit, with shades of silver and blue to add distinction to the effect. As a novice Man Vampire he was proud of this, though he breathed heavily as he arrived in Émile's dressing room.

Émile had recovered his temper. "I must to my bath, Georges, or Sophie will be turning me out of the house to hang upside down in a tree."

"What did that *cochon* do?"

Émile paced about. "You were right, I could not fight him; his man retained my pistols. He sniggered out his conditions. I must go along with them for now. I do not like what I learn from my calculations. There is a charge of power, as yet scattered and sporadic. Kenrick cannot realise the extent. It is why we have these excursions through time, and it seems he has been on one himself since his return. If it goes on, I may have to move the girls away."

Georges cut in. "You ain't going to like this, Gilles, so I didn't want to tell you at once. Mr Kit was set upon by a group of them villagers."

Émile came on Katarina in the passageway leading to Mr Kit's room. "*Monsieur* Émile, you gave me a start!"

"What? Ah, I appeared on a sudden. How is poor old Kit?"

"Sore beaten – I am so glad that you are safe home!"

"Yes, they were bound to make me a vampire all over again. No more tears, *ma petite*, or I shall increase your lessons. Dolly, how does Kit?"

Dolly came to the door, glaring at him. "Them nasty yokels may count themselves lucky there were four of them with clubs, else he would have served them as they deserved."

"How bad is it? Let me have a look at him. Is Dr Powell sent for?"

"Of course. This is all your fault, *Monsieur* Gilles, luring us up here with your promises when we would have been better off back home. You, child, go and see if there is any more of that tincture downstairs. Your precious master's back, long teeth and all, that's all you care for."

Katarina scampered off. Georges said, "Dolly, you ain't fair. Gilles told you of the problems here."

Dolly moved over to the bed. "Not about gangs of murderous bumpkins he didn't."

Émile winced as he ran his eyes over Mr Kit's swollen face, eyes already half closed, nose bloody, lips split and swollen. He was lying back on his pillows in a sort of daze. At Émile's query he stirred, grunted in pain, and muttered, "Lured me out, one of them did, Gilles, and the others sprang on me."

"Do you think they've broken anything?"

"Dolly says not."

"That settles the matter." Émile smiled at Dolly, who glowered back at him. "Would you know 'em again?"

Georges' eyes sparkled. His face fell as Mr Kit said, "They had their faces covered."

"Said they anything?"

Mr Kit was moved to smile. "They spoke Welsh mostly, and no-one to translate for me. I did hear Kenrick's name. As they left me on the ground they said in English, '*Tell your master we don't like that sort of thing round here.*'"

"What did they mean by that?" Georges was as indignant as if Émile's and his own behaviour had always been exemplary.

"What could they find amiss in a Frenchman turned vampire? Kit, what can I say? I'm sorry. This after all the favours you and Dolly have done me. Does my wife know of this?"

Georges said, "Agnes wouldn't have her troubled, she said the poor girl was upset enough already what with you going back to that place."

"I'll to her at once. Ask Dr Powell to talk with me after he's seen you." Émile went out with Georges.

When they were left alone, Dolly said, "Kit, the young bucks seem like they always were at present, but it comes in fits and starts. It's horrible seeing Gilles vanish into nothing, and looking at you with them funny eyes and now Georges acts so too. Now, on top of all else, them locals try and kill you. You and I are going home as soon as you can travel."

Kit mumbled something.

"What are you saying?"

"How about honour?"

"Honour? Don't you come that with me. Do you think yourself one of the Knights of the Round Table? There weren't any fat ones."

———◦✐◦☉◦✐◦☉◦✐◦———

Émile found Sophie, swollen eyed but composed and wearing a new apricot silk gown, in her sitting room. The kitten Jem watched her as she tried to beat herself at chess. At the sight of Émile, she dropped her piece as she started up and he rushed to kiss her.

The kitten was less enthusiastic in its greeting; it hissed and hid under the sofa. Émile didn't seem to notice, but even as she enjoyed his kisses Sophie wondered if its hostility was to do with further changes in Émile himself, or whether the atmosphere of Plas Cyfeillgar still hung about him.

Émile took her chin between finger and thumb, gazing into her face. "*Ma chère,* I forbade you to worry about me and you have defied me... I rode up to enquire after Morwenna on the way home, and she is neither better nor worse."

She squeezed her arms about his neck. "My dear, if only she rallies...

Émile, what happened with Kenrick?"

"He and I came to an agreement of sorts. There was no help for it, and do not think I enjoy the prospect of working with him. I must submit for now."

Sophie searched his inscrutable face. "Did you see – That Woman?" She was still worried her weeping had made the contrast in beauty between Ceridwen Kenrick and herself dismal. Somehow, the sharp-eyed Émile couldn't see it; those eyes delighted in her.

"She came to the laboratory. I gather *Madame* entertains herself with Arthur in the gallant Captain's absence. Previously, I thought her viciousness was the nature of a vampire, but now I become one myself, I know how little I have changed." He didn't notice Sophie flinch as he gave her a self-congratulatory smile, caressing her hands in savage tenderness.

"Kenrick stood giggled and triumphed over me. To safeguard my humans I have no choice but to endure such usage. I should spirit you away, but I will defer that as long as I can, as I dread the prospect of being apart from you." His eyes were momentarily more human. "I must feel a spark of sympathy – even for him – in his wish to undo the past."

"We could both leave the area, Émile!"

His drew back in outrage. "I am sorry you believe I would run away."

She sighed. "Of course you would not. I dread being apart from you full as much... My dear, I know what a temptation the thought of changing the past is for you. Yet it is such dangerous work, and I fear what may happen. Purely for myself, I fear to lose you, one way or another, but there may be terrible consequences generally – Ow!" He had squeezed her hands.

"Forgive my roughness, I must be careful of my strength. I must be careful also with these Mischievous Experiments, *chérie,* given you have poor taste enough to fear the loss of your wicked brigand. You must not worry; the last thing I want is to wake up at Plas Uchaf with things altered, so that following our Quarrel in the Music Room, dismay at my ungallant offer has led you to accept a proposal from some sneaking curate." He kissed her again.

She pulled her lips away. "Émile, I must know what is happening!"

He chucked her under the chin. "But how, *chérie?* As you are no mathematical blue-stocking,* for which I am thankful – imagine being married to such a one – how could you begin to comprehend what Kenrick is about?"

"What are you drawn into, Émile, by him and by That Woman too?"

"My girl, I said this morning, I must either go there or I send you away. You made your choice."

He smiled. Sophie realised his Man Vampire self managed to put his worries about Morwenna aside. He was even playful. "*Ma femme* shows signs of becoming a domestic tyrant already. I must forestall her, or else we shall fall to quarrelling. No more on this, Sophie. To add to our concerns, Mr Kit has suffered a misfortune at the hands of some locals." He told her of the ambush.

Guto's knock cut short her exclamations. "Dr Powell has made the examination, Sir." The kitten, fur erect, rushed out from under the sofa and dashed past him out of the room.

"Show him into the drawing room, then, Guto. For sure he deserves some hospitality for coming out so soon in this weather. My little captive looks dissatisfied."

"Émile, it is awful about Mr Kit! It must be particularly disturbing for you." Sophie broke off, thinking how this attack by the villagers must bring back memories of the riots for him. "I am sorry, yet I have to speak of this other trouble. Even though I cannot I understand the theoretical side of Kenrick's activities, surely you could tell me more. You try and protect me: you shouldn't."

She squealed as he snatched her up. He held her up above his head effortlessly. His strange laugh was alarming. "Still haranguing me? What shall I do with this domineering little human?"

"Stop!"

He walked about, holding her up high, shaking with wild laughter. "Shall I put her somewhere where she can't get down?"

Sophie gasped. He went on walking about with her, overcome by inhuman laughter. "Shall I kiss her? What a sweet neck, how am I supposed to resist it? And it is through my not resisting it I can best protect you, stubborn, church-going, adorable little fool as you are –"

"Stop it, Émile!"

He did some more Inhuman Chuckling as he put her down. "Now, we must stop this dallying, for I must to Dr Powell."

Anyone would think she was begging him to carry on with such treatment. Breathlessly, she stuck to her point. "Émile, I must oppose you over this!"

His eyes hardened, though his wolfish smile remained. "Any more and I shall become angry. *Après tout, ma petite ingrate*, you wish to remain here and remain human too, yet you berate me for doing my best to protect you."

She squealed again as he pinched her cheek hard enough to bruise. She couldn't tell from his glittering eyes if he had done it on purpose. "Yet it is such a sweet defiant human, she melts her demon lover's heart yet. Let us not quarrel, *ma chère*. I will be back as soon as may be to play some chess with you."

Sophie chewed her fingers as he vanished in a flash.

———— ⚬୨ଽ୧ଡ଼ C/୨ଡ଼ ୨୧ଡ଼୨ଽ୧ଡ଼ ————

"Dead as a doornail, as you English say." Éloise – her neck for once covered – was talking to Agnes as Sophie came upon them in the passage leading to her bedroom.

Agnes looked shocked, but couldn't let Éloise's mistake go. "I'm Welsh. When did this happen?"

"They say last night. Her sons found the body –" Éloise broke off to curtsy to Sophie, her eyes taking in the details of her tear ravaged face.

Sophie put on a cheerful tone. "Agnes, it is time for me to dress for dinner."

Agnes frowned at Éloise. "Éloise and me was just agreeing the upper shelves in the library needs dusting terrible, weren't we now, Éloise?"

"Do they? See to it sometime over the next couple of days, please, Éloise. Mrs Kit has troubles enough at the moment."

Safely in her dressing room, Sophie said, "Goodness, Agnes, we are spoilt for choice as to what to worry over! Who is dead?"

Agnes returned from the dressing room with Sophie's favourite blue dinner gown. "Is a woman on the Denbigh Road has been found dead and they do say there were marks on her neck."

"Horrible, Agnes!"

"I must find out more; you know how these stories get about. But is proper worried everyone is now about the goings on at Plas Cyfeillgar. They say a giant bat was seen there at that time, but…" She broke off.

Sophie smiled wanly. "*Monsieur* has just told me about poor Mr Kit. It must have to do with the people connecting us with Plas Cyfeillgar, I think, though *Monsieur* has only been back there for the first time today." She bit her lip.

Agnes paused in unfastening her dress to give her a quick pat, and Sophie sighed. "I think the story has got out about what happens here, with *Monsieur* and Georges acting strangely, *Monsieur* locked away doing odd experiments and so."

"Is disloyal."

"I cannot see it so. Though *Monsieur* may be generous, do any staff get riches enough for their masters to deserve unquestioning loyalty? But you and Georges are different, Agnes. I think of you as my friend though I rely on you to do my hair and my costumes. Now I must say something while I have the courage." She swallowed. "I knew from the beginning that we might not find a cure, though I trusted we should. I have made my bed and must lie on it – *Monsieur* Émile would probably make a grotesque joke about my making my coffin and lying in it – while little Katarina worships him so she would follow him to the gates of hell.

'Your case differs entirely; I shouldn't ask you to endure this, and things must become worse. I know he wants to reward you for your kindness to him when he was ill. Why not accept that present, Agnes, and leave while you can, particularly as now poor Georges is become a Man Vampire too? "

Agnes smiled. "You shan't persuade me to leave, Mistress Sophie, but is like you to try." She stroked Sophie's back hair. "These are such pretty back curls, I am sure *Monsieur* Émile loves them."

"I must be braver and fight harder."

"That's the spirit, Mistress Sophie!"

Sophie's clenched her fists. "He will go to that dreadful place, Agnes. I don't like to speak against him, but I believe it was that connection as much as anything made him so sinister and unfeeling only now. He thought I was enjoying his rough sport as he lifted me near to the ceiling! My kitten has turned against him, too. Luckily, the horses have not yet done so."

"It isn't speaking against him when we are trying to Save Him from Himself, and Georges, too. Well, as men can be insensitive, Man Vampires must be worse. Katarina should have the amulets ready tomorrow."

—◦◦◦◦◦◦◦◦◦◦◦—

Sophie dreaded more fearsome playfulness from Émile when they met in the drawing room, but he looked grim as he greeted her. "Dr Powell tells me Mr Kit will soon recover himself, but Dolly is resolved that they must leave, Sophie."

Sophie was astonished at the stab of regret she felt. "Oh, dear!" she realised that she had come to like them as she had become very fond of the wicked Georges.

His insensitivity continued. Looking over her chess game, he laughed outright. "For sure these opponents are well matched in foolhardiness, Sophie. Can you really not see the folly of your white bishop venturing there? These black pawns are taking pawn sacrifice to the point of absurdity."

"Then I am happy to give you a little diversion."

Over dinner Émile was largely silent. Sophie supposed him to be brooding over Morwenna.

She realised how torn his feelings must be. She knew he blamed himself for not warning his relatives at Plas Uchaf. She suspected the part of him which remained human must dread Morwenna's death the more for knowing a transformation to a full Vampire must happen and would be hideous for her relatives. He must feel he ought to advise them on the horrible tasks necessary to prevent that, yet knew too his nature would stop him. Throughout, and at the same time, she suspected his Man Vampire part thrilled at the thought of Morwenna's change.

She felt for him in this grotesque dilemma, trying to divert him with some light remarks. He responded politely but discouragingly.

During one of the long silences that fell over the long table, Sophie's eyes strayed to the garish stained glass window, now illuminated by light from the chandelier. For some reason, now she felt fascinated by its lurid depiction of a mediaeval knight kneeling to a woman standing dominant over him, their eyes locked. Her hard expression and her black hair often reminded Sophie of Ceridwen Kenrick; this evening it did so more than ever.

Sophie thought of how she tried not to detest That Woman for what she had done. After all, she couldn't help what was now her nature, any more than could Émile and Georges. She forced herself to pray for Mistress Kenrick every night along with all other vampires, yet towards her, her heart felt cold and unforgiving.

As she gazed, it came to her that since that first terrible visit to Plas Cyfeillgar, a glazed look sometimes came into Émile's eyes that differed from the inhuman flaring. The picture of Kenrick's cold grey eyes, trying to catch hers, stirred in her memory. There came to her mind a phrase from the book, *'The vampire possesseth strange powers of persuasion, connected, tradition has it, with the eyes.'*

Émile followed her gaze. "A terrible piece of artwork."

Another idea stabbed at her.

He implied today he saw little of Her. I don't believe him. He came to me newly bathed, though the workings with Kenrick are surely not malodorous; he might have felt polluted by his visit, of course, and longed to wash that away. Still, I fear Other Reasons for his taking time to bathe.

Émile lingered over his port, while she comforted herself with music in the drawing room.

When he joined her, he was unfeelingly playful again. "I have been listening to you, Sophie. I want you to sing the aria you played in the music room the time I made an attempt on your virtue – a sad song – sung by a captive. Now you are mine, I shall enjoy listening to that. Even now, you are not as fully mine as I would wish. You seem always to be resisting my wicked advances one way or another." He leered.

"*Lascia ch'io pianga (Let Me Weep My Unhappy Fate)?*" She spoke lightly, but as she began to sing, her voice wobbled and she missed a note.

Émile clicked his tongue as she stopped playing. "This will never do, my girl! Your tutor Mr Jenkins would be shocked. Start over."

Sophie felt inclined to snivel, but controlled herself. This time she kept her voice steady. At first, he smiled ironically, and seemed to revel in his own nastiness. "Isn't she just like a caged bird?"

Then, as she sang and played on, he began to stir uneasily. Finally, he went to lean on the fireplace, staring down into the fire. She felt as sorry for him as she did for herself.

She finished and as he remained there without turning round, she jumped up and came over to caress his shoulders. "I meant it when I said I always shall love you, Émile, no matter what."

He sighed, and turned round to caress her face, eyes anguished. "You will have your work cut out, my girl. I do adore you so I must have you with me no matter what, which is a torment to both of us."

She took his hands. "Émile, I know you are suffering too on Morwenna's account, and I can guess how difficult it is for you. If the worst comes about, I will take on the task of telling them what must be done –"

His eyes dilated, and he winced, his hold on her hands tightening, making her wince too. Softening his hold, he bent to kiss them, and spoke hoarsely. "Thank you, Sophie, you melt your monster quite by your underserved kindness. If it comes to that pass, I must tell them the beginning of story, though I cannot go on to the end. But firstly, I will try and spare you by trying to write it down…Play something cheerful now."

———— ❧✦❧✦❧✦❧ ————

Émile's tender mood lasted through the rest of the evening. He read to Sophie, and took her to bed early. As he removed his shirt and she admired his body she saw his gashes healed; even the scars were fading. She gasped.

Catching her eyeing him, he laughed. "You are become shameless, *ma chère femme*. If you are going to eye me so, then it is only fair for me to do the same by you."

She forgot her fears, and the feeling between them was nearly as it was on that first night. But afterwards, she thought he went back to looking as though he was tempted to bite her. She drew away in dismay.

He looked offended. "For all what you have sworn, I am become a monster to you."

She was sorry, for all this reproach was so unreasonable, and took him in her arms and Ooh'd and Aah'd over him for some time…

…Until she realised that he was trying to undo the clasps of her crosses, only his fingers fumbled as though it burnt him…

She squealed and jumped out of bed.

He cursed and seized her arm, speaking as though she were overreacting. "Calm down, my girl. Your religious artefact protects you from your thirsty bat."

She was wakened in the small hours by his fingers at her neck. Though his eyes were closed, and he seemed asleep, his hands were busily trying to undo her cross. She flinched away, and his clawed fingers pursued her, reaching for her neck again. His eyes opened a slit, showing a glare of inhuman green, and his lips were drawn slightly back, so that his eyeteeth showed.

She settled down far away from him. The hands wandered a while, and then gave up.

Plas Uchaf
Famau Mountain

"Wishes to see me?" Lord Ynyr, eyes heavy with lack of sleep, stared at Roberts.

"So he says, Your Lordship. I told him I doubted you could see him and he should see someone else and he said, '*Mais non!*'" Roberts looked contemptuous.

"Has my Cousin sent him?"

"He did not say so, Your Lordship."

"I suppose I can spare ten minutes; show him in, Roberts."

As Roberts tried to bow out, his back made such a cracking Lord Ynyr winced and forgot his fears for Morwenna for a moment. "Truly, Roberts, have I not told you to abandon ceremony when we are alone? It pains me to hear you."

As Roberts left, the Count spent a moment wondering how to persuade him to retire without hurting his pride before he went back to worrying about Morwenna. Then Roberts was back with the Count's former under chef Lucien.

The Count addressed the man in French, as always. "I trust all goes well at Plas Planwydden?"

"Your Lordship, forgive my intrusion. I have reason; I believe *Monsieur* Émile is become a vampire."

Lord Ynyr jumped up and went to stare out of the windows. After a minute he was able to speak. "Explain yourself, man!"

The man irritated the Count by ticking off points on his thick fingers. "He went to the Kenrick house, for reasons I prefer not to mention, for I know We Should Not Judge the Weaknesses of Others." He looked meaningfully at Lord Ynyr.

The Count stared back coolly. What the Dowager Countess called Émile's 'incontinence' (and Ceridwen Kenrick's too) were old stories, though he was outraged the fellow should mention them.

Lucien went on, "Your Lordship knows what everyone says about Kenrick and his wife. When he came back, *Monsieur* was ill. Then he sent down asking for no more garlic or herbs in his food. He has never taken them since, though before he liked his food seasoned like a civilised person. Before, again like civilised people, *Monsieur* Émile liked his meat rare, but now he takes it near raw. His teeth and nails are altered.

'Then he gave orders the staff is to wear crosses, only I have witnessed since he cannot say the word, and he wears not one himself, though *Madame* does. I am a good Catholic anyway, but some of the others objected. Mr Kit – and he is a strange man to be butler, as Your Lordship must know, but that is neither here nor there – tells us it is because of the Kenrick household. 'You cannot be too careful.' But now I have seen *Monsieur* vanish into thin air when he thinks nobody sees. I think he has bitten one of the maids. Either he, or *Monsieur's* ruffian of a valet, for I believe he is become a vampire too, for today his nails –"

Lord Ynyr burst out, "Silence! How dare you ramble this insolent nonsense to me of my Cousin?"

"I am not an ignorant peasant, Your Lordship. But I have seen enough. What they say is true."

"If you truly believe this catalogue of absurdities, then the happiest thing you can do is leave my Cousin's employ, and seek treatment from a doctor. I fail to see why you call upon me."

"Am I to remain silent as *Monsieur* Émile and his man spread this terror about? The girl Éloise wears a kerchief about her neck on a sudden, though she slapped my face when I asked to see her throat. Besides all this, *Monsieur* Émile – who is as pleasant a young master as I have met, so that his staff love him, as well Your Lordship knows – does fearful things in his study. I believe he is now in league with Kenrick."

"Not another word! You are overwrought, Lucien, and I would take a more serious view of these slanders were they less laughable."

Lucien stood up, squaring his shoulders. "Then I must look elsewhere for assistance. I have heard the illness which has struck down Miss Morwenna is like to that of the girl Mair Jones, who now has retracted gums and walks out at night–"

The Count's normally calm eyes flashed in a way worthy of a Man Vampire. "Get out, you are raving!"

Lucien turned away; then his sense of drama brought him up at the door. "May I remind Your Lordship the sweet former Miss Sophie is in the household, in danger from this horror, while *Monsieur's* most trusted staff are no better than a group of brigands."

Lord Ynyr winced. A voice sounded in his head: '*The Mysteries of Udolpho'!** He spoke calmly again. "Please do try and recollect we are not in a Gothic novel now, Lucien."

"That is hard to realise, Your Lordship, down at Plas Planwydden." The man looked triumphant as he bowed his leave.

Chapter Twenty-One

S OPHIE SAT UP FOR HER hot chocolate, pushing her hair out of her
eyes and realising, as often before, she had neglected to put her
nightdress back on. Émile exuded heat, there was nothing Undead
about him in that.

Agnes drew the curtains. "Katarina has the amulets ready,
Mistress Sophie."

"Thank goodness."

"Not before time. Georges is become a nuisance, and not just to me.
At breakfast he was fingering his teeth, all unaware, staring at Éloise.
Then followed me out he did, sniggering nastily, but that fool *Monsieur*
Lucien came after and so Georges must needs content himself with a
wild cackle before going to see about *Monsieur's* coffee."

"Oh, dear, Agnes! What news of Mr Kit?"

Émile had refused to allow Sophie to help nurse his ally: '*No, there
is help enough with the maids. I would not allow another man to enjoy the
kindness you showed to me when I was in a fever save he were in danger of
his life.*'

"He is still abed, badly beaten as he is, and Mrs Kit abusing us
Welsh so unfair."

"*Monsieur* says that they will leave, and it makes me sad, for all I
have felt – I hope wrongly – what with *Monsieur* not wishing us to go
out without Mr Kit and Georges as guards that I am hedged about,
almost as when *Monsieur* Émile surrounds me at chess."

Agnes met Sophie's eyes. "You were not wrong, Mistress Sophie."

Sophie saw that denial was foolish. "You are a brave girl, Agnes."

"No, I am stubborn. Now did you say last night you wanted a bath before breakfast?"

"Fetch out my cloths, Agnes, for my time is due." Sophie spoke cheerfully as she stepped into her bath, doing her best to hide her anxiety.

Agnes did some calculations. Unlike Sophie, she could do sums in her head rapidly. "Your time is overdue by seven days, Ma'am." She dimpled. "I was beginning to think it was past time, but what with one thing and another I lost count."

Sophie, startled, did the calculations herself, much more slowly. Agnes was right; for the first time ever, she was late, and her cycle was always exactly twenty-eight days. She blushed under her friend's thoughtful gaze. "Very likely it means nothing. I have had shocks enough to upset things, goodness knows!"

Agnes would have none of this. "My own came on the dot as always. Well, Georges was good at Being Careful, I will say that for him."

Sophie blushed even more, remembering a maid in Chester she'd overheard talking crudely about 'withdrawal'. "Goodness, Agnes! It cannot be. I have heard my sister Harriet say —" she was going to add, 'That you feel strange.' But she wasn't sure, now she came to think of it, that she didn't feel strange. With all the distractions, she hadn't spared much thought for her internal sensations.

"Has your bosom begun to tingle?" The uninhibited girl ran her eyes over Sophie's breasts, which were always a little swollen as her time of month came up. Sophie couldn't believe she had conceived already. This was a dreadful time in which to become pregnant! A semi vampire baby was an unbearable thought. Katarina's not remembering such babies provided little reassurance.

"Well, I shall see. It would be unfortunate now, Agnes." She winced. "That is a ludicrous understatement! I am tormented by the fear nothing may cure him and now I may have yet nearer cause to worry!"

Agnes brought the towel over as Sophie stood up, and wrapped her comfortingly in it and patted her reassuringly. "You mustn't worry, Mistress Sophie, I believe all will be well yet."

"Agnes, is that based on a reading of your Tarot cards?" Sophie tried to keep the eagerness out of her voice.

"No, they give me clouded readings still. Is annoying when we have need of guidance from them. No doubt it will pass." Agnes began combing out Sophie's damp hair. "Is lucky you are to be so fair."

Sophie, having silently longed for illicit reassurance from those usually intrusive Tarot cards of Agnes', bit her lip. Still, she refused to believe she could be pregnant so soon, anyway. She was almost sure that she could feel a slight cramping, as if her flow was soon to begin.

Katarina came in a little later with the amulets. "They must be as near to the skin as possible. If not, then under the pillow or in the clothing. I will try one in Georges' coat."

———— ⚬⁓⚬ ⚬⁓⚬ ————

Émile was already at the table when Sophie joined him. As he smiled at her and bowed with his usual punctilio, she felt he somehow knew what she had plotted; that he discounted it as a threat, even finding her hopeless struggles amusing.

Perhaps it was only her uneasy conscience that made her think so. For sure, she and her fellow conspirators were careful to speak only in whispers.

Émile's mood was distant again. He didn't dismiss the footmen. They breakfasted in grand, formal style, sitting opposite each other at the great table, surrounded by wooden faced attendants. Just so must his parents have taken their meals at the *Château* in Provence. Sophie had little appetite and some form of indigestion – a burning in her chest. She nibbled pound cake while he ate his ham, eggs and rolls with his usual appetite.

After the meal, he came to kiss her hand, murmuring, "I hope we will see each other over lunch. I have much to attend to. You must to your own tasks, one of which will be to dissuade Mrs Kit from leaving us. You ladies know how to do such things."

A confusion of feelings and thoughts churned in Sophie. Most prominent amongst these was pure indignation. Since her talk with Agnes, she had to admit that Émile – knowingly or otherwise – kept her virtually a prisoner, surrounded by his henchmen and not allowed outside the grounds.

Yet she knew that were she foolish enough to accuse him he would seem outraged. He would point out how, as she insisted on remaining human, he was protecting her in having her accompanied by men he knew he could trust.

He would also say – no doubt in a tone of strained patience at her feminine lack of logic – how only yesterday, he suggested that she go and stay elsewhere as an alternative to his going to Plas Cyfeillgar. How then could she accuse him of keeping her as a captive?

At that point, he would certainly laugh condescendingly, while his mocking eyes told the truth.

Of course, they both knew all along she would never leave him in such circumstances; he had been manipulating her throughout. But that was only something they both knew. He had logic on his side.

Now, she was supposed to try and persuade one of her guards not to leave. It was, as her brother John would say, 'slightly too rich'.

Yet, it was not simple either, for she still didn't know how far this altered Émile was aware of his own motives. As for Georges and Mr and Mrs Kit, she didn't suppose they went in for introspection. Mr and Mrs Kit were after all – as Agnes would say – 'Nice Rascals'. She had come to like them, coarseness and all, just as she now liked the impossible Georges.

She bit her lip, thinking of the wine in the church and the amulets. What if neither of those worked either? The idea was unbearable. "I will try, Émile."

"There's my good girl." He did some patronizing chin chucking.

"Émile, do take care what you are about, should you go again to Kenrick's."

"*Bien sûr, ma petite.*" He smiled approvingly at her docility and kissed her hand again before leaving the slow way – by the door.

That was considerate of him.

"You wanted me, Ma'am." Dolly sucked her underlip.

"Mrs Kit, I am so sorry for what has happened. I understand Mr Kit is a little better today? That dreadful attack must have been shocking for you." Sophie realised the absurdity of trying to Keep Up Appearances Before the Servants. "Some of *Monsieur's* actions must have aroused hostility amongst the locals."

Mrs Kit breathed heavily. "With good reason, Mistress Sophie. The nasty things, to set on my poor Kit so! He ain't one of these Man Vampire things. And Georges jumping out at Agnes! Speaking frankly, I don't know how you have escaped *Monsieur* Gilles' teeth so long. Them two was as nice a pair of Gentlemen of the Road* – beg pardon, I mean gentlemen – as you could meet ere this. Just now I came on them plotting something, laughing together, and the sound were fair bestial. It sent shivers down my spine. See as what's happened only through this house full of human bats and *Monsieur* getting funny notions into his head about time travel."

Sophie sighed. "I am sorry for it all. We must remember *Monsieur* Émile and Georges are not themselves, Mrs Kit. They show the symptoms of this terrible scourge."

She didn't expect her words to have any effect on Mrs Kit. She was merely going through the motions of asking her to stay so as to keep her promise to Émile. She was accordingly startled to see Mrs Kit's eyes soften. "Mistress Sophie, there is something in what you say. I will think on it." She made her curtsey, exuding magnanimity.

"Now, please tell me, Mrs Kit, if there anything more that we can do to make Mr Kit more comfortable."

—◦৶৻৹৻৴৻৲৻৶৻৹৻৶৶৹—

"Shocked, Appalled, Desecration of the Dead, Barbaric Rites Intolerable in a Christian Country..." The Reverend Smythe-Jones eyes were popping, his face suffused.

Émile, by contrast, was pale; he breathed hard. The Vicar became confidential. "I have not, of course, revealed the full details for what has been done to the corpse to my wife. Such things are unfit for the female ear."

"And mine." Émile muttered, and then shook himself. "For sure it is a sorry business. I must detain you no longer, *Monsieur*, as no doubt you are busy with your parish duties."

"By no means, *Monsieur* Dubois, else why would I have a Curate?" The Vicar, remembering that Miss Morwenna Llewelyn remained between life and death, hastened to offer some phrases of spiritual comfort to her relative.

Émile fidgeted. Suddenly, his horse, which the last couple of days was unusually restless, turned its head and tried to bite him. He struck it and had to fight it as it bucked and then reared. *"Au revoir*, Reverend! I must give him his head."

The Vicar had withdrawn his own head into his carriage. "My compliments to your wife!" This last was shouted as horse and rider galloped away up the lane to the Famau Mountain.

Fighting with his horse, laughing wildly now and again at the memory of the Reverend's face, Émile came to the stables of Plas Uchaf. Throwing the reins to the groom, he warned, "Careful, boy, he is skittish of late. Leave him go if need be."

The horse allowed the groom to lead him away, looking back over his shoulder at Émile and whinnying with apparent disgust.

"Monsieur Émile." Roberts even managed a smile for Émile as he came behind the footman who opened the door and waved the man away.

"Roberts, how does Miss Morwenna?"

"Things remain the same with poor Miss. There's His Lordship now."

Lord Ynyr was coming up too from the back of the great hall. "Cousin, come in."

Émile stepped in. "Ynyr, I won't trouble you long. I only called to enquire for Morwenna." He squeezed the Count's shoulders, while his cousin winced at the iron grip. "Would you permit me to see her a moment?"

"If it will ease you, Émile. You must take some refreshment, for it is a fair ride from Plas Planwydden. Roberts, please see to it."

Morwenna's old nurse barred the sickroom doorway, glaring at Émile.

Émile smiled on her. "Don't you remember me, Ynyr's Cousin Émile? I remember you well from when we were children and her parents alive."

She gave his teeth a second glance. "That French boy. A menace, but that is boys." She unbent a little. "You mustn't disturb her long."

Lord Ynyr drew her away by the elbow, talking about the draughts, to where Mrs Brown sat dozing in the chair in the dressing room.

Émile winced at Morwenna's ghastly pallor, as he had on his first visit. He bent over the bed, reaching for her hand, only to start back, wrinkling his nose. As he wheeled about, spluttering and choking, his streaming eyes met the dilated ones of Morwenna's nurse.

Lord Ynyr stared as Émile staggered over to the doorway, weak kneed and overcome. As the Count went over to him, he heard the nurse exclaim: "The poor young man! He is a fine fellow, too. A shame he has such pointed teeth."

As he mopped his eyes, Émile focused on the Dowager Countess who stood at the dressing room door, watching him. He made a shaky bow. "*Madame.* Sophie bid me ask you if there is aught that she can do to help and if you will not change your mind about letting her into the sickroom?"

The Dowager Countess looked sadder. "No, I forbid it. I am sure she prays for Morwenna."

"You may surely rely upon her to do that, *Madame.*" Émile let out a wild laugh.

Mrs Brown's eyes were as round as marbles, while his Aunt drew back, frowning. "*Alors,* Émile!"

Émile struggled to stop laughing. "Forgive me, *Madame,* Cousin. I believe I am out of sorts." Muttering apologies, he went backwards from the room, while his aunt and cousin moved after him anxiously.

"Émile, come and have that mulled wine." Lord Ynyr urged. "You have ridden out in bitter weather."

"I was passing this way."

Suddenly, Lord Ynyr guessed who Émile was calling upon and spoke coldly. "I heard Kenrick was back."

Émile only stayed to swallow the spiced wine. He squeezed his Aunt's hand as he took it to kiss it, and she squealed. With more apologies, and a last tormented glance at Lord Ynyr, he left.

"His nerves are disordered. He has bruised my hand. His nails did look so odd." The Dowager Countess rubbed her hand as they stood by the bow windows in the morning room, watching the lanky mounted figure battling his horse down the track towards the red roofs of Plas Cyfeillgar. "I believe he is going to Plas Cyfeillgar. I thought he detested Kenrick."

"It seems that he is doing odd experiments on the same lines." Lord Ynyr was tormenting his moustache.

"If he is engaging in such Mischievous Experiments then he has brought his nervous state upon himself."

Lord Ynyr scarcely heard her. He was battling himself against an opponent far stronger than Émile's horse. Nightmare ideas crashed up in surges against his reason, and he dreaded that they must soon topple it.

Sophie saw nothing of Émile until dinner. He was in his study for part of the morning. She fought the urge to go and knock so that she could spy in at the door vulgarly. Besides, there was no point; he would make sure that nothing important could be seen.

She knew he rode out somewhere later. He left word he would be out for lunch. Agnes told her Georges had gone out too.

"Is up to no good he is for sure, from the smug smile on his face. I have put that amulet under his pillow. Here's one for *Monsieur*, for while he spends most nights in your bed we must have one in his."

At dinner Sophie's throat closed at how Émile's meat spurted blood at the touch. She'd had little appetite all day, and felt out of sorts. As at breakfast, Émile didn't dismiss the servants and greeted her with his usual gallantry. As then, he was uncommunicative after telling her that Morwenna's state was unaltered. He was newly bathed. She sensed again, too, that he was somehow sated; but now he felt so alien to her that she wasn't sure.

His inscrutable look suddenly exasperated Sophie. "Called you at Plas Cyfeillgar, Émile?"

His glittering eyes met hers. "It is an excellent thing to be sociable."

"It is indeed, if one is permitted to go out to be so."

Far from looking annoyed, he seemed to like that, smiling wolfishly. "I regret that Mr Kit's misfortune has prevented my Good Girl from going abroad to do her Charitable Works."

"I am sure he regrets his misfortune yet more, Émile, and it didn't stop me from working upon the Poor Box. We begin to run short of thread; I think they stock it in the village shop. I suppose I must needs send Agnes with Georges as escort, but he is out."

His eyebrows shot up. "Then send a footman with a list of your requirements. We cannot have the Poor Box neglected, my pretty one."

Again, the light from the chandeliers illuminated the stained glass window opposite Sophie, throwing splashes of blue and red on the floor.

As Sophie turned her eyes from Émile to that picture of the dominant woman, she felt there was another thing that she must remember connected with this image, something that *Mademoiselle* Charlotte was urging her to recall in that dream she half remembered. She was suddenly certain it had been Charlotte, communicating from beyond the grave.

When she looked at Émile again, it was compassionately. "Shall you teach me more chess later, Émile?"

"*Bien sûr*, after dinner I shall show you more tactics."

"How, my dear one, shall I ever outwit you?"

----- ✺✺✺✺✺✺✺✺ -----

Sophie left Émile to drink his port in solitary state, or to invite Georges to join him. In the drawing room, she went to the instrument to play a couple of new songs from Mozart.

Suddenly, she was overcome by an urge to see what Émile was doing. He would be outraged, regarding her re-appearance as a sign of intolerable bossiness, even that she was becoming another Harriet. For once, she didn't care. She hurried back to the dining room.

When she opened the door, Georges had indeed joined Émile.

They had other company, too, in the shape of half formed, shadowy beings grouped about the table.

Émile was in his Vampire State, smiling wolfishly about him. "What do you mean, I don't want to go doing such things? I ain't to blame for this. But as they call upon us, it is only manners to make 'em welcome. *A votre santé*!" He raised his glass to the figures.

Georges looked drunk. His lengthening teeth flashed as he shook with laughter, and the glint in his eyes was more reckless than ever. "They can't even – they can't –" he was laughing too hard to continue.

Their sinister companions were a group of rough men with a nautical look. There was a low murmur in the background, as of some drinking house. They were sprawled about, lounging against the chairs, and a voice spoke in what Sophie recognised as French. The most dreadful thing was that they were communicating with Émile, or anyway, could see him, for she heard the name, "Gilles Long Legs."

"Oh, goodness!" she shrieked before she could stop herself.

The others turned about, and hostility flared in Émile's eyes before he got up with a forced smile. "*Le Diable, voici ma petite femme.*"

She clung to the door handle, her legs weak. "Oh, my God, Émile!" "*Vraiment*, you must not blame me, Sophie. I did not initiate this visit "

She turned and scurried away. Though she could hardly run from the situation, still she abandoned all dignity and ran anyway, fighting back sobs.

"Sophie!" She knew, even as she dashed off, that Émile could overtake her in moments, but she had to flee.

It seemed he chose not to pursue her, for as she rushed up the stairs she heard the door below close.

He came up half an hour later, as she sat trying to do something with her swollen eyes. On top of everything else, he appeared in a flash.

She squealed. "Don't do that, Émile!" It came out sounding testy, like any wife rebuking her husband for a trying habit.

"I am sorry, Sophie. I do it without thinking. Eager to come to you, I arrived precipitately. You mustn't be angry with me about that visitation, they came uninvited. You must have seen that unlike you and me in Paris, they were only partly here, as was Tom when he scared you in the hall. Neither were Georges and I pulled through ourselves, though to be sure there is a build up of power such as even Kenrick can see. This begins to make sense to me, but for sure it must terrify you."

For all his sympathetic tone, his eyes retained their inhuman glint, and she was wary of him. He came up behind her and squeezed her shoulders. She got up and he took her in his arms. She found no comfort in his embrace. Now he did not feel even partly like the Émile she loved, but a sinister replacement.

His hands were caressing her back, his touch alien, his breathing quickening as he began to kiss it. "I cannot resist this soft flesh of yours, and my longing serves our need to protect you from Kenrick's *ménage*. It must come to your joining me anyway, *ma chère*, as I cannot believe you would condemn me to centuries without you, as has to happen, should you stay human."

"Oh, not again, Émile!" Now she sounded like the same testy wife irritated by her husband's constant sexual advances. His terrible loss of humanity was becoming a series of wearisome marital tussles. She was unwilling to enter into another argument with him. She found such discussions difficult. Her conviction that it would be wrong to let him make her a vampire was based on intuition, not reason. This awful conflict was the more wearing for her because she felt – she must admit – strange.

She forced herself to speak softly, while he continued to caress her with his own fierce tenderness. "Émile, love you as I do, I cannot join you, though I have thought of how awful it will be if I become old and wrinkled while you stay young. But I have annoyed you before by saying that giving in would amount to despairing of God's mercy."

She thought she must sound smug and detestable. Probably he agreed as he snorted: "And I shocked you by saying I despaired of God's mercy a long time ago, that night in the *Château* and ever after."

She put her hands on his, though she was alarmed by the look of his nails, now only long and sharp, but hooked. "Émile, does not the power of these little crosses make you wonder?"

Hostility flared in his eyes. "Has your praying for me done the slightest good? Nonsense, my girl!" He gave a savage laugh – which he may well have meant to be an indulgent chuckle – and bent to take her face in his hands. She dropped her eyes and he hissed, "Look at me, Sophie."

She still looked down. "If only we knew you could stop yourself I would be happy enough to let you bite me and take some, but you said before that you do not believe that you could limit yourself with me." She was wondering again if and when her menstrual flow started what its effect would be on him. If it didn't, his thirsting after her blood must be the more dangerous.

He made a sudden lunge at the chain, moving with such speed that she had no sense of what he intended. Astonishingly, it held as she let out a squeal of pain as the metal jerked against her skin. Cursing, he dropped it as though it was hot.

She dodged backwards. The next moment they were playing out an absurd scene, with him pursuing her round the bed like a caricature of a lecher, saying meanwhile in a tone he probably thought was tender and persuasive – but which was in fact gloating and sinister – "Do not be so foolish, my lovely girl. Come here to Émile, *ma petite femme*! I do believe the superstitious artefact has cut you. Let me kiss it better." He even had his tongue ready to lap at her.

In his previous attempts to seduce her into letting him bite her, she'd felt a surge of warmth. Now, as with his other attempt to force her, her entrails seemed to freeze.

"Oh, horrible!" she wailed, as she rounded the bed a second time. "Émile, I will chew garlic for sure!"

"That would make me spew at once, and surely you had more than enough of watching me at that when I had that fever? I cannot believe you would be so unkind to me –" he dodged forward and would have caught her, but tripped over her slippers and fell flat on his face.

She dashed, still wailing, into the dressing room while he got up, swearing, his nose bleeding.

"Miss Sophie!" Agnes was at the dressing room door, her candle held aloft casting looming shadows, astonished enough to address Sophie by her unmarried name.

Sophie's fingers were trembling so that she could hardly lock the door, sobbing, "Oh, Agnes!"

Émile was at the other side, his voice sounding thick from his bleeding nose. Sophie found time to hope that it hurt him. "Sophie, open the door! You know I can come in anyway."

"Come in by all means, *Monsieur* Émile." To Sophie's horror Agnes did open the door with one hand, even as she fumbled in her pocket with the other. She smiled nastily, brandishing a clove of garlic.

Émile, who was mopping at his nose with a handkerchief, moved back while – like Madoc the Magnificent whenever anyone produced a crucifix – he 'paled visibly'. "Agnes," he muttered nauseously, "Get out of this and take that foul thing with you. What do you mean by interfering between me and my wife?"

"I suppose you would say as much was you about to murder her, and this ain't so different. You are becoming a nasty vampire apace and you should be ashamed!"

"Agnes, take that thing away or you can leave my house!"

Sophie let out a wail, but Agnes seemed unperturbed. "I will when you can eat it, as then is your proper self telling me so." Seeing him swallow some of his own blood and flinch with disgust, she gloated, "Is your own blood you are drinking now."

Émile's eyes flashed, which was less impressive with his nose bleeding. He turned away, still mopping at his nose, to stand with his back to them. His form wavered and came back again. Perhaps he was distracted by his bleeding nose. He had to try again before he vanished in an angry fizzling of sparks.

Sophie burst into tears. Agnes put her arms about her. "Is downright mean of him. I am becoming accustomed to this, for Georges jumped out at me from the pantry just now. I had my garlic in my pocket, and will get one for you. Silly in *Monsieur* Émile not to smell it if They are so sensitive to garlic. I suppose he would had he not that bleeding nose which I hope you gave him with a good clout in the face. "

"Ah! Where has he gone?"

"Doubtless to get Georges to join him in drinking more than they ought."

"What if he comes to prefer Ceridwen Kenrick? For surely, though he could not endure her before, as he changes, he must find he has more in common with Those People than with me. Oh, Agnes – and I did so love him the way he was." Sophie blew her nose in a way that would have horrified the Dowager Countess.

Agnes snapped her garlic in half. "Is you he loves, for all his acting the monster. I think you must carry this always."

Sophie stuffed it into her pocket. "Agnes, it's awful that Georges pursues you so. I am not speaking in obedience to *Monsieur* Émile when I say you must safeguard yourself by leaving."

Agnes' eyes sparked. "Leaving you here alone, Mistress *Sophie*, when I bet you have none of them cramps? No, I am not going, that is final. I never thought to see things like this happen here in our village, Mistress Sophie. Now, if it happened down in Swansea, where folks are about All Sorts of Mischief, I would be less surprised."

After she had checked her tears, helped by some patting from Agnes, Sophie went down to the sitting room. As she passed the drawing room at the foot of the stairs she sensed Émile was not in there, waiting for her to sing for him as though nothing had happened.

In the sitting room, taking a quick glance at herself in the gilt framed mirror, she thought that she still looked distraught, her eyes pink and swollen despite Agnes' bathing them in her remedy. The world seemed full of cures which didn't work.

She took up a baby's bonnet on which she was working for the Poor Box. She only took stitches in occasional bursts of activity as she sat, thoughts wandering unbidden into her mind like straying cattle, while she used her reason as a cowman to urge them along into a coherent group.

Feeling exhausted, Sophie went to bed early, putting the clove of garlic into the drawer on her bedside table. She slept on and off, waking now and then to sink back into a troubled doze, unhappy that Émile wasn't with her. Finally, she jerked out of a dream of something fearsome. She took the amulet from under her pillow, and stole through the adjoining doors to his dressing room.

Five minutes later, she sat on her bed in defeat, fighting back tears of jealousy and disappointment accompanied by lingering nausea brought on the smell of the cigar smoke and the burning amulet in Émile's room.

She preferred not to think about what that sick feeling might mean, but couldn't avoid thinking about those scratch marks on his ribs, surely evidence enough that Émile had sported with the savage Mistress Kenrick.

Her disappointment over Émile's destroying the amulet was the more bitter because she knew there only remained the Cure of the Charged Wine.

How could she ever get Émile to agree to being bathed in wine stored in a church? He would have jeered at such an idea even before, when he was desperate to find a cure. Now he revelled in becoming a monster.

Chapter Twenty-Two

AGNES WATCHED SOPHIE WRINKLE HER nose at the smell of the hot chocolate. "Nothing yet, Mistress Sophie? When you start feeling sick of a morning you will know for sure, and if so, you aren't to concern yourself about the baby as well as your other troubles."

Sophie thought that easy for someone else to say, and sipped the drink, which tasted more bitter than ever. "Agnes, with the excitements of the last days, it makes no wonder if I feel out of sorts."

Even so, Sophie admitted to herself that her bosom was tingling again. She whispered, "I tried to place the amulet under *Monsieur's* pillow, but he woke and burnt it." She didn't want to think about being pregnant at the moment. It would make her feel weaker, though for sure it added still more urgency to her quest for a cure, not only for him, but to ensure her developing baby (if she was growing one) would be human.

Agnes clicked her tongue. "Georges found his in his waistcoat pocket, and threw it out of the window. We may yet find it by the terrace."

"Agnes, how does Mr Kit?"

"For sure he must be getting better, as Mrs Kit smiled once this morning." Agnes smiled herself.

"I wonder how does poor Miss Morwenna?"

Sophie suddenly remembered what it was about Émile she had noticed in the small hours as subtly different (apart from the scratch on his side). For once, this change wasn't sinister. Surely, the freckles across his nose were more strongly marked this morning?

Émile was already in the breakfast room as Sophie entered and greeted her with only a slight edge to his punctilio. She wondered what was going on under his wavy fair hair, carefully disarranged as ever. His eyes, inhuman as they were, showed sadness mixed with the savagery and cunning.

Again, he didn't dismiss the footmen.

His coffee smelt even stronger to her than her hot chocolate earlier and she wrinkled her nose. Her own tea tasted as odd as the hot chocolate, and she only drank half a cup with her pound cake.

As Émile attacked his ham and eggs Sophie remembered how everyone had commented on his lack of appetite at Plas Uchaf at the time he was brooding over her supposed rejection. It was typical of his insensitivity as a half human that he ate his breakfast now with appetite. Besides, now she was his wife – enjoyed many times – and possibly coldness between them disturbed him less.

Sophie gazed out at the view over the garden leading to the fields and mountains beyond. It was a beautiful day with the wind sweeping clouds over a bright blue sky; every minute the mountains darkened to a purple tinge and then suddenly lightened with sunshine again.

She wondered how she would answer the letter from her friend – too far away now, up in Scotland to have been able to attend the wedding – suggesting a stay at Plas Planwydden.

Émile glanced up irritably. "What the Devil?" He strode to the door.

Then Sophie heard raised voices further down the passage. Lucien rushed in, breathing hard. "Monster!"

"Have you run mad?" Guto started towards him.

Émile smiled. "I take it you wish to leave us, Lucien? a pity; Mrs Kit will arrange things. *Madame* and I did enjoy your food."

Lucien, eyes almost starting from his head in his rage, pointed at him. "Food? You sate your filthy appetite in a different way – Monster! She has been bewitched –" He raised his arm to throw something. Émile was on him, seizing it.

The man struggled as Émile bundled him easily from the room, smiling amiably the while. "Lucien, you are a good fellow, but I cannot allow you to act out scenes from a Gothic novel in front of my wife, least of all at our *petite déjuner.*"

Sophie thought that unreasonable in one who had played out enough such scenes himself.

Lucien, bundled along in an iron grip, tried to free his hand to thrust the garlic into Émile's mouth. Émile cursed in French and kept Lucien's arm back easily, while Lucien struggled and ranted wildly, speaking too fast for Sophie to make out a word. They went out into the hallway in a sort of grotesque dance.

Even as Guto and Sophie rushed out, his eye temporarily caught hers in embarrassment. Meanwhile the other gawky footman – whom Sophie always thought looked even more uncomfortable than Guto in his livery – stood in ginger amazement.

Émile yelled, "Open the door!" Guto charged ahead of Émile and Lucien as they tripped down the hall. Near the door they fell over some item of furniture and it accompanied them as they fell through the door and rolled down the steps, smashing with a tearing sound as they landed on the bottom step.

Sophie winced. Émile leaped up cursing. He bent down to help up Lucien, who had landed underneath him, losing the piece of garlic. "Come back and settle matters when you have calmed down."

Lucian wrenched away his arm. "Monster!" he pulled away and limped away up the drive.

Émile limped slightly himself as he came back into the house. "These dietary recommendations thrust upon me become tiresome. Sophie, we must see about a replacement."

"Émile, I do hope you didn't hurt yourselves badly!" Even as she spoke, Sophie thought she sounded idiotic.

Mrs Kit, Agnes and Katarina appeared from somewhere. Sharp eyed Agnes shrugged and went down the steps to pick up the broken piece of garlic lodged under the boot scraper.

She smiled grimly, looking up at Émile. "No sense in wasting this. Is good riddance to him. He was a sneaky one."

Émile stalked off, turning up the stairs.

Sophie told Katarina, "Your tutor will be here soon, dear. To the library with you!" Over the last couple of weeks, Émile had increased Katarina's lessons and done away with her housework to the point where she was more a family member than part-time parlour maid.

Sophie turned to Guto. "Oh dear, is that nice stand quite broken?" He mumbled.

Mrs Kit came up. "The second parlour maid has taken herself off, Mistress Sophie."

Sophie sighed. They were indeed beginning to resemble the Kenrick household.

Georges stood at one of the windows in Émile's bedroom, watching Agnes and Sophie down on the terrace. "I hear horses."

Émile, sitting at his desk, listened himself. "I hear 'em myself now… Georges, I cannot write the words to my Cousin warning him. For all the world, it is as if an enchantment has been cast over me." He bit his lip, perhaps thinking of how the idea would once have appealed to Morwenna, and threw down his pen to join Georges at the window.

"Our little humans are about mischief." Georges said. "*Bien sûr,* they are searching for the amulet I threw from the window. Agnes was stooping over something just now; I hope she ain't found the thing."

"*Le Diable,* these girls are relentless. I could scarce believe it when I surprised *ma femme* advancing on me with that thing. Even touching it irritated my fingers."

"Beware your clothes. Agnes planted one in my waistcoat, my skin was crawling some while before I realised what it might be. I gave Katarina my mind. She was shameless, speaking of acting for my own good, like to some master as he brings out the whip."

"I must go to submit to the humiliation of Kenrick's orders to protect our humans, who weep and berate me, though I endure it for love of them. Doubtless *Madame* will suspend my will as before."

Georges sniggered. "You deserve no sympathy there. Such bubbies and *derrière* as *Madame* has!"

Émile ran his hands through his hair. "*Ma pauvre petite* must not find out! We haven't been married a month."

"*Le Diable,* maybe you ain't in a mood to speak on this, what with your worry over *Mademoiselle* Morwenna, but weren't it good, yesterday, when we took some from them floozies? It is torture to look upon these pretty necks. You talked about 'gentle persuasion'. It ain't working. Agnes will not endure me near her."

"*Vraiment*, my patience is become wearied by the freedoms these aggressive humans take upon themselves. *Les femmes* joining us is the best way to protect them from Those Others. Yet *petite* Katarina presents a problem, as it would be disgusting to safeguard her so. The idea of Kenrick getting his teeth into any more of them! It must not be."

"They defend themselves fiercely with them Superstitious Artefacts and poison."

"We know a way about that, as used by the *jeune fille* on you, and myself on Éloise."

Georges flashed his sharp teeth in a leer. "Of the girls working here only Agnes has a sweeter neck."

Émile looked indignant. "Keep your teeth away from her, Georges! But she will only take her cross off for me. Tomorrow, we –" He broke off, staring with dilated eyes out on the side lawn.

Georges followed his wild stare at Sophie and Agnes. Two whirlpools of light shimmered and swirled behind them.

———— ✦✦✦ ————

Kenrick snatched Sophie's hand even as the muted flash still brightened the sunlit bushes about her. His fingers, seemingly flabby, were stronger than Émile's. Before she knew it, his eyes had hers trapped while his voice dripped with oil. "My dear Madam."

She couldn't wrench her away gaze. Panic seized her as, unable to scream, she watched his eyes grow.

Arthur Williams moved towards Agnes, smiling, crooning to her in Welsh. With his reddish-fair hair and bright blue eyes, he looked the picture of a strapping, handsome, upright looking country servant. Agnes scrabbled wildly in her apron pocket. He winced and halted, looking disgusted.

There was something in Kenrick's eyes Sophie knew she must discover, even as she became aware of more flashing light and Émile rushing Kenrick and Georges rushing Arthur. Both came up against some invisible barrier, so that the force of their attack hurled them backwards and they almost fell.

Kenrick's eyes moved from Sophie, breaking the hold on her will. With a sob of terror, she stumbled backwards herself as he released her hand.

Kenrick and Arthur sniggered. Georges, eyebrows in his front curls, goggled in mortification, while Émile snatched Sophie and held her tight. She could feel his heart hammering against his ribs and she suffered for him again in his helpless fury and anguish.

Kenrick said, "For a clever man, you are slow to learn, Dubois."

Émile breathed hard and held Sophie for a moment longer, before pushing her in the direction of the house. "In!"

Georges was reaching for Agnes, but stopped, wrinkling his nose in turn. Kenrick giggled. "What a wicked little puss it is! She is proof against us all."

Émile seized her arm and pushed her after Sophie. "You too, girl."

Kenrick's eyebrows shot up. "You endure her stink bravely."

Reluctantly, Sophie and Agnes moved towards the house. Émile spoke hoarsely to Kenrick. "I can't serve you as I would for that attempt on my wife and maid, but I can tell you to take your experiments –" He broke off, looking astonished.

Kenrick spread his hands, speaking unctuously. "For shame, *Monsieur* Gilles, I was merely giving the little creature my condolences – whatever am I saying, Arthur? – I mean my felicitations. You call my word into doubt. For a certainty, you are become unused to the customs of gentlemen, save for Gentleman of the Road. I was in Llandyrnog on business, and about to leave my card with a message. Arthur, I ought to call in at that house near Denbigh where that healthy corpse was murdered – doesn't it make you sick to think on it – but it is out of my way." He and Arthur exchanged smiles.

Georges – longing to outstare Arthur, yet knowing the power of the experienced Man Vampires' hypnotic gaze – marched about in wild rage, cursing Arthur and Kenrick in French. He broke into English. "You filthy bastards!"

"Bastard yourself, Frenchman!" Arthur sneered. Georges bunched his fists while Kenrick clicked his tongue.

"We must attempt to control our lackeys, Dubois. I came to urge you to call at my little house as soon as may be. You scarce need me to tell you of the increase in the escaped power. We must to work betimes." He ran his eyes over Émile's face. "Mrs Kenrick would have me give you her kind regards. For some reason, the ladies like you well, despite those ugly freckles. Confess, *Monsieur*, there is something ridiculous about a vampire with freckles. "

Émile didn't react, but Georges muttered, "One as needs spectacles looks fool enough."

Kenrick took off his glasses and held them up for Georges' inspection. "Plain glass, fellow. I needed them as a human, and can't get out of the way of them as vampire. Until then, *Monsieur* Gilles. We tethered our horses ourselves, there being no stable hand to be seen. Have both the lads you stole from me deserted you already, the ingrates? Come, Arthur." He was gone.

Georges hit out at some of the swirling motes of dust. Émile paced about. He paused to say, voice unsteady, "Georges, it turns me sick to think how near a thing that was for Sophie. She was falling under his influence... Ah, boy, he is just left us." This last was addressed to Kenrick's ex-stable boy, who was trotting towards them, his face chalky.

"Sir, I couldn't warn you, I feared he might take me." Having hidden in a pile of hay, the boy had strands of it adhering to his hair like a caricature of a country bumpkin.

Émile ruffled his head, smiling, only his eyeteeth indicating his limited humanity. "Don't worry, boy, you were right to hide. Go and ask the cook for a treat – no, he is left us, ask Mrs Kit."

The boy ran off, and Émile turned to Georges. "Did you note, I couldn't finish when I was telling Kenrick to take his experiments to the Devil? For sure we cannot mention the Christian symbols, but it is coming to something if we cannot mention one whom we are rumoured to follow."

Georges, pacing about, hardly heard him. "Gilles, no man has ever treated me so!"

Émile gave him a weary smile. "*Alors*, women and children now treat us worse, Georges. It is time to assert ourselves before we are beaten down quite. A freckled vampire may be laughable, but a hen-pecked one makes for a true object of pathos. "

—⸾⸿⸾⸿⸾⸿⸾⸿⸾—

Sophie rushed to Émile as he and Georges, perhaps in deference to human feelings, came in through the side door. He took her in his arms and they breathed in each other's scent a while.

Agnes and Georges watched each other warily. She told him, "My garlic is gone. I suppose you put someone up to it? Is lucky the scent lingered and sickened Williams."

Georges looked guilty. "Agnes, I never thought that they would make an attempt on you in daylight!"

Sophie was still clutching Émile's shirt. "What did he say?"

"His usual drivel. I have no choice but to go, so no more on it, Sophie. Like Mackenzie, he penetrated Katarina's defences, and as Georges says, in daylight. I think she said our own presence here must weaken it. I don't want you out in the grounds save when we can take you from here on."

"But, Émile –"

"After that I have no choice, *chérie*. Promise me."

Sophie swallowed. "I cannot."

"I thought not." Émile smiled amiably. He took her wrist and drew her briskly along with him down the corridor. She could either resist, and be pulled along, or allow herself to be led. She berated herself again for leaving the clove of garlic Agnes had given her wrapped in a handkerchief in a drawer in her dressing room.

"Swine!" Agnes trotted after them. "Where are you taking her?"

"I conduct *Madame* to her sitting room for while I'm away. You can keep her company."

Besides her panic, Sophie had to struggle against her fury with Émile. As he led her up the stairs, she longed to slap his face. As they came to the room she said, "So I am to be a prisoner!"

His eyebrows shot up. "*Ma chère!* Only yesterday –"

"Yes, then you suggested I leave, knowing I wouldn't desert you. If you lock us in, we won't be able to escape should one of The Others come for us, and may they not be able to enter the house now, too?"

"I think they will still need invitation, and Georges shall be in calling distance throughout. I trust him to care for you as I would myself. Do come in, Agnes. I wouldn't have your little mistress lonely. Where is *petite* Katarina?"

Georges ushered Agnes into the room, closing the door behind them. Eyes sparking, she aimed the slap at his face Sophie longed to give Émile.

He jumped back. "Katarina is with the tutor till midday, having her head filled up with nonsense from books. I last spoke to her when I gave her my mind about planting them magic things on me. We supply *les femmes* with some of them silly novels to keep 'em happy."

"Perhaps '*The Mysteries of Udolpho*', Émile?'"

"Do I sense a gibe, *Madame* Dubois? You may also warble like a caged bird." He indicated the piano.

"Émile, this is beyond anything! Earlier, you accused poor Lucien of playing out a scene from a Gothic novel! You cannot keep me prisoner so. Whatever will the servants think?" In her outrage Sophie met his eyes. As she wrenched her gaze away, he laughed.

He came to whisper softly in her ear. "You cannot avoid my gaze forever, my pretty prude, nor will you want to. Your adorable throat has been well worth the wait, just as were certain other delectable parts of you. I refer, of course, to your knees and your toes, with which I am still besotted." He gave her chin a chuck of taloned condescension.

Now, instead of a treacherous flood of warmth, her insides turned to ice. "Émile, you gloat like a vampire Mr B*. It is too horrible!"

He laughed heartlessly. "*Alors*, you show a worthy *bourgeoise* concern for the opinion of the servants, Sophie, in asking me what they will make of this, but unless you cause a commotion, they will make nothing of your seclusion. I will say you are indisposed, and for sure you have looked a little pale these last couple of days. If I was a jealous vampire, I might become suspicious. Georges will only lock the door if you try and leave the room, so you can ring for service at any time."

"Women make water and so as well as men." Agnes remained earthy and practical.

"Georges will escort you to the closet, if necessary."

"Oh, how mortifying!" Sophie bit her lip, fighting back tears. "We are invited out to dinner tonight, Émile –" She broke off at a sudden twinge of nausea.

"I must send a messenger with our apologies. We shall the four of us have a cosy night in together. What books should you like? I am relying on *ma petite* to maintain some decorum before the staff."

Georges burst out suddenly: "Ah, *ma petite* Agnes, that ridiculous *retrousse* nose of yours melts me quite! I still love you for all you have treated me ill. Gilles Long Legs will bear me out; I have never been so besotted about any wench before."

Sophie was too busy struggling against the wave of sickness to note Agnes' expression, and heard her sharp retort as at a distance. "Then, help us!"

"That ain't reasonable, Agnes. You tried to force your so-called cures upon us, so there is no injustice in our forcing you in turn."

"We still wear our crosses, which burn you so!"

Émile smile amiably. "I think I know how we may free you of those religious symbols." He bent to kiss Sophie's hand, murmuring, "My *pauvre petite*, you look terrified! It will be the same with us as it was on our wedding night, I promise. *Au revoir, Madame* Dubois."

The two vampires lounged out.

Georges was soon back with some books. The one on the top was called, '*Twelve Reflections For a Proper Wife*'; Sophie supposed it to be an ironic thrust from Émile.

"When may we expect lunch?" Agnes asked.

"At the usual time, *bien sûr*." Georges' dark eyes glittered at the thought of the feast he and Émile would soon enjoy. He went out whistling, followed by Agnes' curses.

Chapter Twenty-Three

SOPHIE WENT OVER TO THE window and looked about. Agnes came and put her arms about her.

Sophie squeezed her in turn. Then, she put one finger to her lips, went over to her bureau, took out paper, pen and ink and scribbled quickly: '*Do not even whisper this, he may hear. I think we may safely escape through the window. Open it while I play.*'

Agnes, whom Sophie knew could read at least a little, frowned over it some moments and then nodded.

Sophie, heart thudding, sat down at the instrument. Without thinking, she began the first noisy song which came to her, one she sang as a child with her brother and sister, '*Frog Went A-Courting*'.

She didn't know whether the window would make a noise as Agnes drew it up, and sang as loudly as she could. She could detect no sound above the clamour of her music. Still, possibly Georges could even hear their breathing through it.

She finished and scribbled another message to Agnes. 'Tie up your skirts.'

She bundled up her own skirts and petticoats (the Dowager Countess would faint, had she known) as she went on to a rousing song from the opera by Mozart, *Don Giovanni, 'Il me Tradhita'* ('*I Still Pity Him*'). She wondered if Émile was still somewhere in the building, listening.

Then going over to the window, she climbed out onto the ornamental balcony outside. The cold wind buffeting her brought across the cries of the sheep from the surrounding fields. As she darted across the small balcony, willing herself not to look down, she dreaded equally its collapse and sharp vampire eyes upon her.

At the other side, she scrambled up the gentle slope of the roof to the window of the flower room, where she worked on her table centrepieces. snatching wildly at any hold, dreading these too might give way. So lucky how nobody but she had noticed the defective catch on the window, which would not lock, and that while always resolving to mention it to a staff member, she had always forgotten.

Agnes, behind her, started as the window squeaked softly as Sophie pushed it up. They paused, expecting Georges to appear. Nothing stirred in the room. Sophie opened the window some more and climbed inside in a swirl of lacy underwear. She turned about to help Agnes in.

Agnes winked at her and went to open the door a slit to glance up and down the corridor. She froze, and Sophie tiptoed over to look over her shoulder. Georges was standing at the end of the passage, leaning against the wall, smoking a cigar.

"Drat him!" Agnes mouthed at Sophie.

They waited while Georges enjoyed his cigar. Sophie had to fight nausea again.

Finally, he extinguished the stub and turned the corner. Would he soon notice there was not even the sound of breathing or a page turning inside Sophie's sitting room? Sophie pushed open the door leading to the middle staircase. Then they were scampering down it, as wildly as fleeing mice, not breathing, spines prickling, rushing on tiptoe. They dashed across the main hall to the front door.

"Ma'am?"

Sophie whipped about. Mrs Kit stood there. Sophie supposed she was ignorant of their captivity; no doubt if she stared disapproval it was at their running out without dignity or sufficient wraps. Sophie made some gesture at her and snatched at the front door.

Agnes bent down by the boot scraper. "Here's another bit of that garlic from earlier!"

The next moment they were running across the cold damp of the front lawn, making for the yew walk leading across to the back drive, their gasping breath misty in the chill air.

Georges was at the head of the stairs. "Dolly!"

"What ails you, Georges?" Mrs Kit seized him by the lapels as he rushed up to her.

"I heard *Madame* Sophie's voice! *Monsieur* Gilles didn't want them out, with Kenrick –"

"Kenrick, eh? You rogue, what are you and he about? Who did Lucien mean earlier, eh?" She slapped his face.

He shook his head in outrage. "I'd only take that from you, Dolly! Tell me where they went."

"*Madame* is your prisoner now, is that it?" Mrs Kit pulled out some garlic and stood between Georges and the front door, smiling grimly.

Georges drew back in revulsion; his form began to waver, only to reappear. This happened half a dozen times before he vanished.

Mrs Kit stood looking at the specks which swirled before dissolving. "Just wait until Monsieur Gilles comes back, I'll Give It Him Proper!"

———— ৩৫৩৫৩৫৩৫ ————

It was only when they were out on the lane Sophie and Agnes slowed their pace. "He must needs have heard Mrs Kit." Sophie wheezed, staring back. It seemed to her she was breathing differently, apart from being out of wind. At that moment she accepted she must be pregnant even as she once accepted she was in love with her grand relative. The possibility of a Semi Vampire baby was appalling, but she had an idea.

They trotted down the lane. "If only the local church was open." Agnes said. "The walk is over five miles round."

"It is lucky we didn't think to take off our shawls when *Monsieur* ordered us inside –" Sophie broke off at the sound of running feet behind them. Georges came round the corner.

"Get back!" Agnes brandished her small piece of garlic.

"Not again." Georges paled. "*Mesdames*, however come you outside? Did you climb down? I salute your courage! But if you insist on staying out, then I must be with you, and with Mr Kit abed that leaves Katarina and the others unprotected."

"We are only going to church, Georges. We will back betimes." Sophie tried to speak soothingly.

"Why cannot you pray at home?" He caught hold of Sophie's wrist, and as she angrily tried to wrench it free Agnes thrust the garlic in his face. He fell back, dropping Sophie's wrist, spluttering, knees buckling. They turned and scampered up the lane while he staggered some way behind them, cursing.

A peasant woman bent under a bundle of firewood passed them, staring. She looked particularly at Georges, still unsteady on his feet. She was the only person they met on the walk to Llangynhafal.

Once, Georges came nearer. "What of your promise to *Monsieur, Madame?*" He fell back as Agnes brandished the garlic again, demanding, "What then of his own promises?"

At last they came to the church. Agnes sneered, "Do you wish to come in with us, Georges?"

Sophie feared he might, to ensure they didn't escape via the back. Perhaps he couldn't enter, for he pulled a face and settled himself by the churchyard wall.

Inside the empty church, as they hurried over to the Count of Ruthin's pew, inhaling the church smell, Sophie uttered a desperate prayer that the wine would be there.

As Agnes triumphantly held up the bottle, Sophie said another of thanksgiving. Clearly, if anybody had noticed it, they didn't dare interfere with anything placed amongst the Count of Ruthin's possessions.

Sophie whispered, "We must pray now for this cure to work as the herbal seemed not to, or anyway, it worked not speedily enough for our needs. I did mention this wine cure once to *Monsieur*; I don't know how much notice he took or if he told Georges…Now, Agnes my dear, leave by the back, for you must put Eiluned first."

"Not again, *cariad*! Is putting her first I am in staying and fighting for a cure for them nice rascals as has become monsters. I wouldn't leave you,

and – " for the first time, Sophie saw Agnes blush, "I find I do care for that wicked Georges more than ever I thought that I could."

When they came out, Agnes stiffened. Georges was talking to an auburn haired girl standing by the wall, who resembled Sian Jones.

"So, Mair!" Agnes greeted the girl, arms akimbo. Georges looked embarrassed.

The girl evaded Agnes' gaze and bobbed to Sophie, who remembered that Mair Jones had been bitten and showed symptoms. Yet she had none of the alien quality now so evident in Émile and Georges. She turned to go, but paused to direct a torrent of Welsh at Agnes, who snorted.

They were all silent on the way home, Georges brooding behind Sophie and Agnes, while Agnes cast bitter looks at him as though she hadn't just declared her love for him.

"You have done well, Dubois." Kenrick was the one who smiled wolfishly now.

Émile stood, arms folded across his chest, looking infinitely sour.

Kenrick went on, "Tomorrow, all should be ready to put this into practice. It is a shame we cannot spend more time upon it, but you understand the increase of force better than I." He sighed heavily. "When we were callow young pups, following the lead of the late Count, we never thought what life held in store for us. You never make reference to those carefree past times we spent together with the Late Count, you, I and Lord Ynyr."

Something stirred at the back of Émile's eyes, but he spoke coldly. "What is there to say? Our paths diverged, leading us to pursue different types of investigation: I into law and disorder in revolutionary France, you into the myths of Transylvania and Lord Ynyr into a search for herbal cures."

Kenrick looked at him sharply. "Talking of which, I suppose that ungrateful kitchen wench dosed you well at the beginning of your change?"

"She did, but so ineffective has it proved I cannot believe it ever works. *Alors*, it is time I left. Until tomorrow, then." Émile turned to glance back at Kenrick, avoiding his eyes as ever. "As you assure me I cannot change my form, you must unlock the door."

Arthur, still following their every movement, sneered.

Kenrick went to unlock the laboratory door. "Earlier, you could brave that abominable stench from that wench's pockets strangely. That renders you the more suspicious in my eyes. Until tomorrow, then." He stared at Émile's face thoughtfully, and his expression turned to one of disgust. "I hate men of violence. Believe me, I have revelled even less in this enforced co-operation than you."

Émile went straight to where Ceridwen awaited him in the morning room. Resentment and surprise flickered at the back of his eyes as he opened the door, as though he wondered how he came to be there.

"My sweet ruffian, you are here as I ordered. *Viens ici salaud*! Now, come a little to yourself, as I like not the company of automatons. Lunch is on its way. Kenrick says the work progresses apace. Maybe this is the last time we shall enjoy each other. Then, perhaps you will return to your silly little wife. Or possibly not, if things work out otherwise. You do enjoy me, *Monsieur* Gilles, you cannot deny it. If nothing else, the light in your eyes and your touch gives you away. Answer your mistress like a good highwayman."

"I cannot deny I did the last time, but on the first occasion ..." He shuddered all over.

Ceridwen rose, lips pouting, and coming up to him, caressed his face. "As I said – and this is not a phrase I am given to using – I am sorry for that now, for you are rather a nice rake after all and a gentle lover."

He began to kiss her. They were still kissing when the man servant with the ill-fitting uniform scratched at the door. Ceridwen giggled like a playful girl as she pulled down her skirts and petticoats. "Don't fall over, *twpsin* (idiot*)*!"

The man breathed heavily as he set down the tray. Émile watched him expressionlessly and Ceridwen waved him away. "We will serve ourselves."

If these words put Émile in mind of intimate meals with someone else, he showed no sign as he opened the dish on the almost raw meat floating in pools of blood.

———

As Georges ushered Sophie and Agnes into Plas Planwydden, Mrs Kit rushed up with Mr Kit limping behind.

"So, you rascal!" She raised one hand. Georges seized it even as Mr Kit said, "Now, Dolly!"

"Get your dirty claws off me, you filthy vampire!"

"Filthy perhaps, but no more hitting me, Dolly."

"Mr Kit, I'm happy to see you a little recovered." Sophie spoke wearily. "Mrs Kit, I know you have had much to try your patience, but could I ask you to forebear a little longer?"

"Did you know all, Ma'am, you might not."

Sophie remembered Lucien's furious, '*You have sated your appetite*' and '*She has been bewitched*' and was suddenly certain Mrs Kit was referring to Éloise. Her knees went weak with sickening dismay and jealousy.

"When I see *Monsieur* Gilles he shall get a piece of my mind."

Mr Kit interposed here. "Now, Dolly, blaming them ain't fair. It's like blaming a man as has been taken by the law."

"Humph!" said Agnes. "Is times I have thought would be better for all had it been so."

"Do not say as much, Agnes!" Sophie thrust aside her jealousy and gave up any pretence at ignorance about The Rascals' past. "Mrs Kit, I know you are angry, but please don't confront *Monsieur* Émile when he comes in, I must speak to him firstly."

Mrs Kit snorted. "He needs his face slapping, and all…Why are you two loitering about?" This was addressed to Guto and Éloise, who were standing down the corridor off, watching the new drama.

Sophie avoided looking at this rival, who looked far too blooming to have lost much blood. Katarina came scampering up, and she took her hand. "*Monsieur* will come back weary from that long cold journey, and we must have some mulled wine awaiting him, Agnes."

———⌐⌐⌐⌐⌐———

What seemed an interminable time later, Émile – newly bathed – flung open the sitting room door. "Sophie, you wild creature, Georges says you and Agnes risked your necks climbing over the roof. How could you be so foolish?"

Sophie had spent the day fighting off an anguish of apprehension besides her two separate causes for jealous suspicion.

Her jealousy over That Woman was straightforward enough, inspiring Sophie to change into one of the new dresses Agnes had made up for her, a lovely mauve, which she hoped flattered her colouring. Émile having commented on her pallor, she thought she needed it. Agnes had helped further, by rouging her cheeks.

Her other jealousy was unaccountable, yet nearly as bad. She wanted to see Éloise's neck, and didn't know how to approach her without setting her into a panic, besides losing all dignity herself. She couldn't do anything about it now, for it was Éloise's day off. She had gone to the village, escorted by Guto, who fancied himself up to any confrontation with a human bat.

Now, Sophie noted the reluctant tenderness and admiration in Émile's eyes. "Yes, we did break free; it is awful being a prisoner. We went to church."

"Then came back, as docile as lambs to the slaughter? Something does not add up. Church, you said? Wait, my girl –"

They turned as Agnes came in with a tray with a jug of heated and spiced wine. "Yes, Émile, though of course you will mock. Why, thank you, Agnes dear."

Émile glanced from one to the other of them, eyebrows raised. Agnes put down the tray and lifted the jug. Even as Sophie dreaded Émile would refuse the wine, Georges was there in a display of sparks. "Don't touch that poison!"

"Thank you, *mon ami,* but I am not such a fool. So, *Madame ma Femme*, not content with your other tricks, you now intend to poison me!"

Georges said, "Idiot that I am! This is why they were so desperate to get to church! I sensed it as Agnes sauntered by me with the poisonous brew."

Émile jumped towards Agnes even as she flung half the contents of the jug over Georges. Georges let out a howl, clawing at his skin, and fell writhing to the floor, groaning a lot of incomprehensible French. "You have flayed me, *salope!*"

Sophie quailed, fearing he was badly scalded, but Agnes stood her ground. "That may work!"

Katarina stood at the door, hand to mouth, Guto behind her.

Émile lunged for the jug, but slipped on the wet floor. Even as he stumbled, Sophie snatched the jug from Agnes and threw its contents at him. She wasn't usually good at aiming, but the wine hit him full in the face, some even going between his parted lips, so he choked; it drenched the front of his hair, and splashed down his neck. Still choking, he fell to the floor, scrubbing desperately at his face and smearing the wine over his hands.

"I am sorry! I am so sorry!" Sophie found herself snivelling. Katarina rushed in to stare down at her hero in anguish.

Émile's inhuman eyes met Sophie's in speechless torment and rage. "Water!" he managed to pant at Guto, who stared in horror. "Quickly!"

"No! As you love him no, Guto!" Sophie cut in. Guto paused.

The Man Vampires' writhing agony horrified Sophie. It must have melted Agnes, too; her voice was shaking with repressed sobs. "We had to do it, Georges, but I am sorry!"

Georges seemed to be recovering slightly. He staggered to his feet and went over to Émile. "The burning will lessen directly. Let us to the pump."

Émile rose shakily, biting his lips. As his gaze raked Sophie, he looked as though it was taking all his self control not to slap her. "I will deal with you all later."

Georges drew himself up, the wine making ringlets of his longish, curly black hair. "You may be thankful, *Mesdames,* Gilles Long Legs and I have never yet laid hands on a woman."

Perhaps he realised how given their rakish history, there was something absurd about this speech. Anyway, after this attempt to regain some dignity and masculine authority, the Man Vampires staggered off towards the water pump.

Chapter Twenty-Four

FOR HOURS AFTER THE HOUSEHOLD at Plas Uchaf were asleep, Lord Ynyr sat up in the library, looking up information on the vampire legends.

Again and again, Lucien's unctuous voice sounded in his head. '*I believe Monsieur Émile is become a vampire...your Lordship knows what everyone says about Kenrick and his wife...*'

The Count read how there were Semi Vampires who have survived an attack, while those who die rise from their graves as the Vampire proper.

"Morwenna, it cannot be!"

He leafed through pages browned with age with desperate intensity, uncaring if his candle spilled wax on their pages, only thankful his librarian was back and had replaced the books about myths of Eastern Europe on the shelves.

All save the one Sophie took with her to Plas Planwydden.

At some passage, the Count would fling aside whichever book he was reading. "This is madness!" He would leap up and pace about the room, his normally calm grey eyes as wild as his Cousin Émile's.

A couple of times he went to Morwenna's room, where her old nurse took it in turns with Mrs Brown to sit with her all night.

He knew the Dowager Countess slept soundly, Dr Powell having prescribed laudanum drops as a sedative.

As always when he came into the sickroom, the women avoided his eyes. He gazed down at Morwenna in torment before coaxing her to take some of the herbal medicine.

"It is shameful poor Miss should be struck down, while wicked rogues flourish." Mrs Brown addressed her shoes. The Count knew who she meant, and he couldn't rebuke her.

As he went down the Long Gallery, the floor creaking under his boots, while outside the wind soughed through the trees and howled round the gables, he remembered his own outrage at Lord Dale's insistence the gang of highwaymen who robbed his carriage were led by '*That Scoundrel Émile Dubois*', masked, but recognisable by his eyes.

Thinking of Émile's household, of his extraordinarily democratic relationship with his disreputable valet, butler and housekeeper, Lord Ynyr suddenly realised the probability of this. All along, he had been blinded by his old love and admiration for his cousin.

Back in the study, he sat, his face buried in his hands, groaning, remembering the fear lurking in the back of Sophie's eyes as she asked where the books on myths of Eastern Europe might be; he recalled her nervousness as she distributed her farewell gifts of crosses to the staff.

The cross Sophie gave Morwenna soon afterwards was lying on the floor when they found her.

The Count groaned again as he remembered coming up to Émile as he knelt by Morwenna's bed, and catching his words, '*I so hate myself for this. Forgive me, ma petite.*'

He had thought Émile somehow believed that Morwenna contracted the sickness from him.

She has indeed.

He went back to searching the shelves, wrenching out volumes, throwing some on the floor, dislodging enough dust to shock *Madame* Blanch, until he found something which might be relevant.

It was lucky his late father had been fond of reading on myths.

No, it was particularly unlucky; for the late Count had introduced Kenrick to the legends of Transylvania, unconsciously inspiring him to seek out there the scourge now spreading through these villages. Perhaps he had killed his beloved first wife. Whatever may have happened, this second marriage seemed to the Count a loveless pairing.

For sure, Mistress Kenrick was a vampire herself! The day after the Lewis' Twelfth Night Ball (and Miss Lewis' inexplicable accident),

Émile went to Plas Cyfeillgar – hoping, of course, to satisfy his lust with Kenrick's wife – only to come back in a fever, rambling of an attack by a monster.

He was raving so when Lord Ynyr went to his room to offer him his herbal cure. Émile had told the Count to go to the Devil and take his herbs with him.

It was Émile himself who was going to the Devil.

Was his beloved cousin now a monster, capable of draining Morwenna's blood to satisfy his thirst? It could not be.

Lord Ynyr remembered Émile, cynically smiling at talk about the tales of vampires circulating in the villages, while Sophie shuddered. Thinking of it now, the Count could almost hate him.

Maybe the Vampire Émile had taken jaded pleasure in trapping his admiring poor relative with the offer to become his wife. Now he would batten on her until she became a monster, too. Yet, even as he thought this, some part of Lord Ynyr's seething brain admitted that even in his monstrousness, Émile appeared to be genuinely in love with Sophie. Probably, he couldn't help himself.

The Count muttered aloud, "Morwenna, I cannot endure to lose you, leave alone what must follow. I have never been a vengeful man before, but that monster shall pay for this."

What must he do? Who would believe him? Dr Powell? The Reverend Smythe-Jones? His own mother must doubt him. The villagers knew; but they were helpless in their fear and ignorance. No, he must act alone.

———— ✦✦✦ ————

Émile was shut away with Georges, refusing dinner, while Sophie was unable to eat any. Such of the staff who felt like dinner ate what the under cook had prepared for the dining room. These didn't include Agnes and Katarina, who sat with Sophie.

Mr Kit carved the roast and tried to jolly everyone along. He didn't succeed. Mrs Kit looked thunderous; Éloise, Guto and the others pushed their food about their plates, but the boot boy cleared his three times.

Mrs Kit rumbled like a volcano. "Disgraceful goings on..."

"Now, Dolly, later."

"I never thought I would see the day!"

"Dolly, please."

The others exchanged looks.

Sophie, Agnes and Katarina were supposed to be working on the Poor Box, but they hardly took a stitch.

Agnes was doing some jollying along herself. "From how those two howled, for sure something must happen. That wine wasn't really hot."

Sophie ran a hand across her eyes. "*Monsieur* Émile detested the taste of the herbs, yet they haven't cured him, or not properly, anyway."

Katarina was violently unpicking some work which yesterday had seemed good enough, but she now thought looked awful. "I'm not sure, Ma'am! His teeth are no longer so sharp."

Agnes said briskly, "I have a Good Feeling, but now is weary you look, Mistress Sophie, and I think you should lie down as *Monsieur* is sulking too much to take his dinner and you not able for yours."

Sophie sighed with relief when Agnes took off her stays. "I fear *Monsieur* may have bitten Éloise, Agnes. Mrs Kit knows as much, I'm sure." She bit her own lip as she admitted it. "Yet if he has, hopefully she has lost little blood, for she looks rosy yet. We must warn her about wearing her cross. I suppose as a safeguard we must start her on the herbs without alarming her, hoping they may work upon her, whether they do or no on the men."

Agnes' eyes flashed. "It could have been Georges bit her. I am going to warn the silly thing now, though I ain't seen her without her cross. At least tonight them Man Vampires is too put out to be breaking into Demonic Laughs and Slobbering at our necks."

"Agnes, if there any of the Charged Wine left over?"

"Near half, which I have safely locked up. For sure you are not thinking of dousing them rascals again so soon?"

"No, Agnes, but I think I should have a glass myself, just in case I am So*, and perhaps we should give one to Éloise too, though I think Katarina said that the herbs should be taken first. Bring the bottle up, and I shall keep it safe in my bedside cabinet."

Agnes nodded. "Is an excellent idea, Mistress Sophie. I'll bring it you directly. We cannot be too careful, though very likely it is not needed, for you know how since your wedding, long before you could show any symptoms of being with child, you have complained of your morning hot chocolate tasting strange? It is because I have been putting some of the herbs in it as a safeguard for you and any babies to come."

The soothing murmuring as he caressed Sophie was like the first time. Then she felt a chill of warning, lingering even as she melted.

"Open your eyes, *ma cher*." He kept insisting on this. Still, she took a long time wakening from her exhausted sleep. The two glasses of charged wine she had taken made her sleep the more heavily after the nausea and heartburn they caused had eased.

Seeing the savage green of Émile's own eyes, she tried to snap hers closed, too late. His gaze had already transfixed her. In the perimeters of her vision, she was aware of the shifting light of the guttering candles and the extinguishing fire.

"You bit Éloise!" Even as her brain became confused, she thought her whining note ridiculous.

"*Bien sûr*; only through your playing the coquette with me, Sophie *moi*. I only took a couple of mouthfuls from her, not enough to change her for sure. You are my walking banquet. No, *chérie,* keep those innocent blue eyes on me. They melt me quite, I do love you."

Now he was holding her fast and she knew her struggles to be hopeless, yet instinct forced her.

He went on, his tone condescending and gloating. "I cannot stay angry with you, though you subjected me to such agony earlier. I know you believe you act for the good of my soul, you little fool. *Alors*, these miserable religious convictions of yours shall no longer keep us apart, my praying little Goody Two Shoes."*

Again, even as his eyes grew, even as her thoughts slowed from their whirling, she somehow noted this was exactly like the Last Gloating Speech of the Villain of the Piece in novels.

There it would be followed immediately by his defeat by the forces of good.

There was no chance of that for her.

The candles and the low fire were burning normally again. He went on, "Undo the clasp of That Thing."

Now, she sensed the secret hidden at the back of his eyes. Her hands undid the clasp. He drew back a little, never relaxing his piercing stare into her soul. "Throw it aside, keeping it from me."

As her hands moved, she willed them to thrust it into his face. They ignored her, hurling the cross away. In the deadly silence she heard it fall.

"Now relax, *ma chère*. You know I love you." Her arms moved to lie quiescent at her sides.

She saw the secret in his eyes: it was herself, holding a blond baby.

She roused to one last desperate effort. "No, Émile! I am–"

He was talking across her. "Do not fear me, as I have often said, it will be as it is with the other. As then, all you need to do is trust me."

He was breathing fast, planting kiss after kiss on her bosom and throat, working himself up, tantalising himself in readiness for the final bite. But she had turned to ice.

As her senses sank, she made a disjointed prayer.

He bit. Horror overwhelmed her. There was no merciful oblivion of warmth.

He stopped. He lay drooping upon her, gasping. His eyes met hers again, but in mortification. "I cannot do it!" He might have been complaining of impotence, so outraged and humiliated was he. "I cannot do it! My only chance and I cannot follow through!"

Serves you right.

He muttered and swore in French, running his hands through his hair so that it stood up wildly. She noticed he looked rather nice like that.

"Tomorrow, I must have my strength – it cannot be I fast become human again! You devout meddler, what have you done?"

Unaccountably, she felt sorry for him.

He jumped up and was staggering from the room when he stopped to look back at her. "Sophie, make sure and find That Thing and put it on. You must be safe from the others."

He went on towards the door without a word of apology.

Sophie lay still breathless, not daring to hope he was right about becoming human. Then, suddenly, a memory pierced through her thoughts as a sunbeam breaks through the cover of rain clouds.

"*Viens ici, salaud!*"

That was the phrase *Mademoiselle* Charlotte had murmured –

looking shocked – in her dream weeks since. Sophie suddenly knew it to be a device Ceridwen Kenrick used to put Émile under her influence, no doubt to induce him to work with Kenrick.

Émile froze at her words and exclaimed in French. He turned to stare at her, and already there was something oddly automatic about his movements.

Sophie jumped up from the bed, but a wave of dizziness forced her to sit down again, blinking away the black swirling in front of her eyes. Meanwhile Émile stood where he was, as though waiting for orders.

She got up slowly and went to him, despising herself for starting to forgive him already. Close to him, she could see the glazed look in his eyes. "I free you of any ideas anyone has put in your mind while under the influence of those words." There was a stirring in his eyes, and she raised one hand to caress his face.

"How I would like to use it to order you not to go to Plas Cyfeillgar again, and to love me forever! I wish I was unscrupulous enough to do so, but you must act of your own free will. So I free you of those words. Come to yourself."

At once he shook his head violently. "Sophie?" He looked at her, puzzled. If she had half-expected an outburst of gratitude, she was to be disappointed; he remembered nothing and clearly wondered why he had turned back.

"How do you feel now?" she asked.

He looked outraged. "How do you suppose?!" He paused; perhaps he was trying to vanish in a burst of sparks. If so, he failed there too. He left ignominiously, on foot, again without a word of apology.

———✦———

Émile paced about his study while the candles burned in their sconces at either side of the mirror. He paused and stared down at the open book upon the desk. After some minutes, he paced again, breaking off to gaze at the book again. Sometimes a flickering came across the ceiling.

He spun about at a tap at the door. "Go away!"

The doorknob turned. "Let me in, it's Georges."

"Keep off, idiot!"

"Then I'll come in through the window."

Swearing, Émile flung open the door. "What do you want?"

Georges ducked under his arm. "Ah, you are about your funny work again."

"Stay out of this, Georges. I got myself into this and must get myself out of it."

"With me against them lot we stand one quarter of a chance, *n'est pas?* Without me, you stand none at all, and then what becomes of *Madame* Sophie and the others?"

Émile squeezed his shoulders. "You are all I would choose in a brother, Georges."

Georges' eyes glowed while he snorted. "We are in trouble, Gilles Long Legs. You weren't surprised I couldn't just appear in here because you cannot do as much yourself." He glanced down at his nails dolefully.

Émile sighed. "*Les femmes* chose an unhappy time to have their way with us. *Bien sûr*, now we cannot safeguard them by having our way with them."

"Never have we endured such treatment from women. *Alors*, tell me what you are about."

The flickering came back more persistently. "Think twice, Georges, for I go on a desperate venture."

The flickering intensified.

Sophie tried to hide her feeling of incipient nausea from Agnes' bright brown eyes, forcing herself to take sips of the odd smelling and tasting hot chocolate (which she suspected would have been distasteful to her even without the herbs). She must follow Émile to Plas Cyfeillgar today. Even apart from the sense of foreboding that drove her on to act today, tomorrow she might feel worse, and it is difficult to feel sick and brave at once.

"Agnes, *Monsieur* Émile made an attempt on me last night, and failed." For all the horror of their situation, Sophie had to smile as she remembered his humiliation.

"*Argol Fawr* (Good Lord) he was not the only one. Katarina was with me last night, though Georges didn't realise she was there, and I locked the door. Before now he has appeared and only my garlic has kept him out of my bed, but last night I heard him out in the corridor when I was half asleep, cursing and lamenting in French. For sure he tried to get in, and found he couldn't. They become human apace already."

"Have you seen *Monsieur* and Georges? How did Éloise take your warning? "

"I think *Monsieur* has said something to her, I don't know what, but she is taking the cure anyway and is angry rather than scared, talking of packing her box, but slow enough about it. I think *Monsieur* still locked in his study, and Georges may be with him. Mr Kit is up and drinking small beer in the kitchen, and is rude enough about what he calls bumpkins isn't it."

Sophie dropped her eyes, so Agnes wouldn't see in them her sudden dread that Émile and Georges might already be at Plas Cyfeillgar, for all her freeing Émile of the malign influence of the words given to her by Charlotte.

Sophie fondled the key in her nightdress pocket she had crept downstairs in the night to fetch, just in case Émile might leave orders for her to be kept inside. She wasn't going to tell Agnes about the key; if Émile had gone to Plas Cyfeillgar, then she would follow him alone.

More than her jealousy of Ceridwen Kenrick, more than anything, Sophie dreaded that having had his longing to change the past stirred by Kenrick, Émile would continue with this attempt, and so change the present in which they had come together and made this growing baby whom she was now confident would be fully human, and who might disappear too.

In Émile's dressing room on the cabinet where Émile often left her a funny or tender message in French (besides improving her riding and chess, he was teaching her French), Sophie found a note, in English save the endearment.

'Sophie Moi,

You do not need me to tell you how I love you, for all my savagery. Knowing it, please do not venture out today. I hope to be back for your English teatime.

Yours Always My Lovely Girl,
Émile.'

Lord Ynyr left Plas Uchaf before breakfast, riding through the grey morning down the foothills to Plas Planwydden. The sheep stared at him, and one challenged him with what sounded like, '*Merde!*'

That was exactly what the old Émile would have said about the gothic melodrama in which Lord Ynyr found himself.

The Count – usually far from devout – was praying.

The door was answered by the fat scoundrel who passed for the butler at Plas Planwydden. It was obvious from his battered face and black eyes he had been involved in a mill* recently. The Count drew back in disgust.

The ruffian was about to speak, but Lord Ynyr cut him off. "Is *Monsieur* Émile at home?"

"No, he is gone out." The Count realised that the fellow was looking at him commiseratingly. "Your Lordship, may I enquire how does Miss Morwenna?"

The Count found himself bandying words with a servant. "You dare ask me how your Master's victim does?! He is a blood sucking monster and the villain, having very likely murdered Miss Morwenna, will not face me."

"Did anyone else speak of *Monsieur* so, I would not stand for it, but Anyone who has been a Friend to *Monsieur* is a Friend of Mine." The ruffian looked regretful Lord Ynyr must be acknowledged as a member of this exclusive group.

"Perhaps he is about more mischief with his fellow vampires over at Plas Cyfeillgar?" The Count thought he saw confirmation in the man's eyes. "You disgusting fellow, most likely you are become one yourself!"

The man drew himself up, looking outraged, and began to speak, but Lord Ynyr whipped out his cross.

Instead of cowering back, gargling, Émile's butler looked bored. "I hope Your Lordship ain't got religion and come here to preach? But if you take comfort by it now, that is well enough by me."

Disappointed, Lord Ynyr had to admit that the man's teeth were normal enough. "Where is your Mistress?"

"Mistress Sophie is a little indisposed and seeing no visitors."

"I truly believe it! No doubt your monstrous master makes his poor wife a virtual prisoner in this disgusting nest of criminal vampires. I will waste no more words on you. But if *Madame* Dubois is by God's mercy still human, then I will ensure that she remains so!"

As he span on his heel, some detached part of Lord Ynyr's mind recalled Émile's reading out a part of '*Madoc the Magnificent or the Vampyre's Curse*' in which the hero Eugene made just such a speech. The Count's back prickled as he walked to the front door, reminding him how foolhardy he was to storm into this household alone.

The man was by him again. The Count thrust out his cross. Still unaffected by it, the criminal began, "You are wrong about *Monsieur*. That Kenrick –"

"Silence, you disgusting vampire's lackey!" The Count wrenched at the door and rushed down the front steps.

He had remembered the curio someone – it could hardly have been Kenrick – had brought the Late Count from Eastern Europe, knowing his amused scorn over the vampire legends. He must fetch it from Plas Uchaf before confronting Émile. Then he must bring himself to use it.

Chapter Twenty-Five

ENRICK SET UP THE CHANDELIERS, the mirrors and the books with the half visible images of the past.

Arthur stood lost in thought, fondling Émile's pistol.

"I pity you, boy." Kenrick said. "You dread Captain Mackenzie's call signifies he even now persuades my so-called wife to go off with him. There is no possibility of that while I hold out the hope of reunion with her dead infant."

Arthur said hoarsely, "I fear, Sir, you shall all be lost."

"Then so be it, I care not for the risk. The French ruffian will be here betimes to do the necessary calculations." He took off his glasses to polish and giggled. "Keep him covered; shoot if he tries any tricks. Also, it would be no loss if he should become stranded in another time stream, eh, Arthur?" He nodded conspiratorially, giggling again.

He went to the fire for a taper, and lit the candles in the chandeliers. "I must begin."

He started as a light began to play across the ceiling, and then to resolve itself into a series of pictures moving downwards. "It comes back uncontrolled again!"

Confused images were playing down the sides of the ceiling. Suddenly, Kenrick and Arthur were surrounded by a group of half transparent figures of Émile and Georges, seemingly in a fight, whirling and jumping about the room in a confusing, half formed crowd.

Arthur followed their movements, jaw dropped.

Kenrick raged. "From whence this –"

The store room door thudded open. Émile and Georges rushed out, knives raised.

Sophie, carrying some objects wrapped in a cloth, left via the locked side door two minutes after reading Émile's note, nauseated, knees shaking in terror that she was too late.

She trotted to the stables – expecting Georges to give chase at any minute – and told the groom she wanted to ride about the grounds. She fiddled as he prepared her horse. Then, at last she was riding down the back drive.

The weak February sunshine was breaking through the mist as Sophie made the seemingly endless ride along the lanes to the foothills of the Famau Mountain. Once she passed by a toothless old woman driving a farm cart loaded with turnips, who made a gesture of respect.

Married to the wicked *Monsieur* Émile as she was, Sophie supposed she should be glad the woman didn't make the sign against the Evil Eye.

She was frightened for herself, but even more for this future baby whose innocent blond head she had seen in her strange vision. She mustn't think of that, or she would run away.

Sophie sang, trying to keep her spirits up, as she tied her horse loosely by the gates of Ferrm Seren, the home farm of Plas Uchaf. Its main entrance was near the beginning of the level track leading to Plas Cyfeillgar. She wanted to leave a clue as to where she had gone. She knew this to be a forlorn hope.

She sang on as she walked the last quarter mile along the track down which they had flown in the sleigh in those far away days last Christmas. Then it had been snow covered. Now, the chill of the air held the first incipient warmth of spring.

As she went through the crumbling stone entrance of Plas Cyfeillgar, and the song of the birds turned to eerie silence, Sophie's heart plummeted and her limbs dragged. Still she sang, though the birds were mute.

She began on the aria from Handel Émile so loved her to sing to him, *'Ombra Mai Fù'*. She had always smiled at that, Dubois meaning 'Of the woods', while in the opera, Xerxes addresses his love song to a tree.

Then, as she came into the still, paved courtyard she sang as she never had before. She sensed she must warn Émile she was here, and to remind him of what there was between them, which he might well lose, if he went through with what she guessed he was about.

Perhaps it was already done. Yet she was still here, feeling the unfamiliar sensations which showed Her Condition. Still singing, she moved towards the side of the house, where a door stood ajar. That was sinister in itself. Still singing, she unscrewed the stopper of the container of wine, which also served as a receptacle, and filled it with shaking hands.

Ceridwen Kenrick appeared in front of her, as dusky, voluptuous and horribly beautiful as ever in a low purple gown. "Shut your mouth, you little bitch! What do you here? Get out, or I will destroy you!"

She was aware of Émile's calling as from a distance: "Sophie! Run! Save yourself!" Yet she knew she had not heard it normally.

She wanted to cower as the tall, enraged Woman Vampire dashed towards her. Instead, she threw the charged wine at her. Once again her wandering aim was true. The wine hit Ceridwen at the base of her beautiful long, curving throat. She screamed and fell to the paving stones, moaning, not like a monster, but like a woman in pain. "No! My baby!"

Those might have been Sophie's own words. Forgetting her fear she moved closer, exclaiming, "Madam, I would not have hurt you, if I could have so avoided. What mean you?" She dreaded this terrible creature might be with child by Émile too.

Ceridwen writhed as Georges and Émile had, tearing at the wine spilt on her skin, smearing her hands with it and shrieking, "I must get to her! I cannot lose her now! Ah, it burns…Don't just stand there, you idiot, fetch water!"

This last was addressed to a stout manservant in ill-fitting livery who stared at them from the side door.

"Where is *Monsieur* Émile?" Sophie called to him. He gave them an agonised glance, and turned and trotted back into the house. Sophie rushed after him and found herself in a chill, bright passageway with a tiled floor. A door leading off was closing. Sophie shouted, "Émile?!"

Though no shadows lurked here, the atmosphere almost crackled with threat. She whispered a quick prayer and clutched at her crucifix and the charged wine and the more prosaic cloves of garlic.

She heard a loud crash, and Émile shout another warning, and began to run towards the sound.

"Georges, recollect you, mon frère, we must pierce their hearts just as though we had stakes – hark at how I can use the word now – so they have no occasion to use their greater strength."

Gilles' words echoed in Georges' head as they hurled themselves through the door and their knives at the *salauds*.

Gilles' aim was perfection. The blade rushed to Kenrick's heart as though to a cosy home on an icy day.

Merde!

Kenrick plucked the knife handle from the air with the superhuman speed Georges had so relished in himself. There was to be no luck with fumbled catches for Gilles and Georges today, and *le Diable*, Kenrick even found time to shout a warning to Williams, who swivelled, so that Georges' own excellent throw came to nothing as the blade thudded into his left shoulder in a shower of blood.

Georges and Gilles snatched at their second blades.

Kenrick giggled, for all the world like a *jeune fille*. "Arthur, let us rip out these turncoat humans' entrails."

Georges had better sense than to take heed of insults in fights, yet that jibe shot rage and sensitivity through his threatened intestines. Pictures of Agnes and his family back in Provence flashed through his mind as he and *Monsieur* Gilles rushed through those other whirling, semi-transparent forms.

No possibility of another life as a full blown vampire now, thanks to those tender, relentless, interfering females.

Williams, the knife still his left shoulder, aimed his pistol at Gilles' midriff.

Time stopped for Georges, for all he knew of the difficulty in hitting a moving target.

Gilles didn't fall; the shot went wide. For sure those images whirling in between the *cochon* Arthur and his target must have confused him.

Georges and Gilles had practised moves amongst them; if they still found them distracting, their enemy must find them far more so.

Kenrick was on Gilles in a tiger bound, slashing at his eyes. Gilles whipped back his head, but Kenrick caught him with a shallow cut to the neck. Blood sprayed over their hands. Kenrick objected: "Damme, infected filth from your pox-ridden veins!"

Williams dropped the pistol, wrenched the knife from his shoulder and was through George's guard. Georges felt the cut as a thud at his guts – no proper pain as yet – and dodged back, feeling the blood come.

Perhaps it was a flesh wound merely. From the corner of his eye he followed Gilles moving backwards towards him with that *salaud* Kenrick following, chortling as he slashed at Gilles' abdomen in turn.

Gilles snatched his wrist as he moved, hurling him to the floor.

Kenrick's glasses fell from his pocket, one lens cracking. He was up instantly, now snarling like to some mad dog. He'd been fond of those spectacles, *après tout*.

Georges found himself in the air. The *cochon* Williams made to throw him across the room, but a boot in the face altered that plan. Georges joyed in the blood and tears flowing down that face before the floor rose up to meet him. Now he could only fight to get air into his lungs.

Gilles was on Williams' back, wrenching his head and yelling to Georges, "The heart!" Georges yearned, helpless as an infant. In that frozen instant, he saw Gilles' eyes widen as he glimpsed Georges' belly which for sure was bleeding freely.

Kenrick sprang, knife raised to sink into Gilles' back. Anguish dimmed Georges' own eyes even as he sucked in air.

As if summoned by the original, one of the images of Georges was between Kenrick and his target, confusing him. The blow glanced down Gilles' arm, slashing through his sleeve and cutting into the flesh in a spray of blood which added to the gore congealing on the floor.

Williams flung Gilles off. His knife came at Georges again and missed. Gilles pulled Kenrick down by the legs. There was a *mêlée* of bodies, then Gilles was up and keeping them both off Georges through will alone, feinting and dodging.

Georges wheezed in more air. Kenrick's and Gilles' knives clashed and they lurched to the side.

Williams was momentarily still before Georges, his arms spread wide, offering an opportunity so wonderful it seemed to Georges it was pure longing that propelled him to his feet to slam the blade straight – he believed – in to the heart.

Blood sprayed them all, drops splattering as far as the walls. The bright blue eyes dilated, their look turning inward as if someone was telling Williams an all important secret, while the ruddy face turned chalky white. Georges wrenched out his knife in another surge of blood accompanied by a piece of flesh.

Somehow Williams was still on his feet, grappling with Georges for his knife. He yet had the strength to hold Georges fast while Kenrick lunged for Gilles' intestines again.

Gilles leapt back and slipped in one of the pools of gore, going down backwards. His knife sank into the floor and as Gilles tried to wrench it free, it snapped.

Still the *cochon* Williams kept Georges rooted to the spot as they grappled, their hands slipping in their combined blood.

Kenrick launched himself on Gilles, but Gilles seized his arms, hurtling Kenrick over his head in a wrestling move. Kenrick thundered to the floor behind Gilles with a crash like a carriage overturning, but rolled to the side and was up instantly. Gilles moved backwards with Kenrick prancing after him, gurgling like a wench ripe for a tumble.

Arthur drooped; Georges hurled himself free, springing towards Kenrick and Gilles as Gilles sank down to his knees.

Kenrick moved in. "Now I'll rip out your entrails as should have been done long since at Tyburn."

Émile whipped a knife from his boot. It thudded Kenrick's chest, hurling him backwards in a fountain of blood.

Pretty work, Gilles! That was worthy of Marcel Sly Boots himself.

Blood pulsed from Kenrick's mouth. He spoke in a wet wheeze, his voice somehow penetrating the gore, "You disgusting cut throat from the gutters of Paris."

Perhaps he considered the gutters of Paris to be inferior to those of London.

Kenrick sank down, his eyes glazing.

Gilles spoke in gasps. "You were dead from the moment you threatened my wife. Don't fear for your own."

Kenrick let out a last wet gargle and his eyes became as empty as the broken glass in the spectacles lying nearby.

Georges and Gilles panted. Gilles came to examine Georges' stomach wound. "A gash merely...That was a close one, Gilles."

Émile mopped the blood from the wound with his handkerchief, looking hard at it. "Yes, a flesh wound, else I never could have forgiven myself." He began to bind up the wound roughly, using his torn cravat. "That was disgusting butchery enough. I would have spared that fellow Arthur Williams, had there been another way."

"I wouldn't." Georges said. "It was he killed the woman in the village for his sport. I heard he was after Agnes in the other way at one time, but it wouldn't have been fair to kill him for that. *Bien sûr*, I never thought we'd come out of that alive, as we went into it with our strength gone."

Gilles sighed. "Thank you, *mon frère*, for joining with me against such odds."

Georges' heart glowed. He said, "I like to have your freckled face about, to set off my own good looks."

"Remind me to retire from violence, Georges."

The half materialised figures were disappearing, yet the other light grew in strength.

"You timed that well, *Monsieur* Gilles. Them sums came in useful for once."

Gilles glanced about as a strange silver and blue light that began to play about the room. The candles burned fiercely and the air seemed charged.

In a sudden bright glare Mistress Ceridwen was with them, fairylike in her beauty, the skirts of her purple gown and her loose black hair swirling in her hurry. Her eyes widened as she saw Kenrick's bloody, sprawled body.

"Don't look, *Madame!*" Gilles started towards her.

"*Monsieur Gilles* is ever the gallant scoundrel; he even tries to protect his taskmistress. Ah, I see you have killed him." She gazed without expression down at Kenrick, and then looked over to where Arthur's remains lay sprawled and the gore on the floor. She clicked her tongue. "Poor Williams, he has not a nice body now. You are both covered in blood yourselves." She sniffed happily.

Georges saw Gilles wince in horror even as he did himself. Yet, they had been like her only last night, longing to drink the stuff.

The widow patted Gilles' cheek. "I sense you are human again. How unfortunate that little scrub has ruined you both. You and this handsome accomplice must somehow dispose of the bodies."

For once, Georges paid no heed to a compliment from a pretty woman, for Gilles was indicating the flashing lights. "I must stop this, this bodes not well. We must find the key to leave and soon, Georges."

Her expression was one of gathering resolution. "No. It had to be today. I will not be gainsayed."

"The power is far beyond our control. It would be madness, *Madame*. I could not permit you." Gilles started towards the candles.

She shrieked: "*Viens ici, salaud!* Stop! I order you to keep on with the work!"

That was no way to persuade a man to do your bidding, and to be sure Gilles looked startled.

She screamed again, "*Viens ici, salaud*! Obey me!"

"Calm yourself, *Madame*, this avails you nothing." Gilles seized the candle snuffers. Mistress Ceridwen caught his injured arm. "How comes this about?"

He flinched his arm away and she froze suddenly. "I hear singing."

Certainly, no living creature sang at Plas Cyfeillgar.

Gilles caught hold of her, listening too.

"Can it be your insipid female human? Leave me go, I shall deal with this!"

Eyes widening, Gilles tightened his hold. She screamed in rage again, then was gone in a whirling flash.

Now Georges' human ears caught the voice. Gilles rushed to the locked door and hurled himself against it. It held. All about the laboratory, the lurid glow throbbed and swirled.

As Georges ran to join him in throwing himself against the door, Gilles was roaring in desperation, "Run, Sophie! Save yourself!"

———❧❧❧———

Émile and Georges, smeared in blood and wildly dishevelled, came rushing down the passage towards Sophie. Behind them, flashing through a door drooping on its hinges, pulsated strange, silvery blue light.

Émile seized Sophie, and her relief at having the wiry, lanky, beloved body in her arms once again was so overwhelming she could ignore the gore. She stroked his face with one hand, still clutching the wine with the other, sobbing with relief. Then her eyes widened as she fully took in his blood soaked state and the stiff way he held her. "Émile, how badly are you hurt?"

"They are but flesh wounds, Sophie."

She sensed both Émile and Georges were surely fully human once more. In Émile's slanty, light green eyes – lit by tenderness for her – there was no lurking inhumanity.

Georges moved to block the way as Ceridwen Kenrick rushed up to them, her neck, the bodice of her dress and the front of her hair stained with the charged wine Sophie had thrown on her, her eyelashes damp with tears. She screamed a combined accusation and demand: "That insipid creature has freed you!"

Georges had hold of her, but she had enough strength left to break free and thrust past him towards the laboratory.

"No!" Émile shouted. Letting go of Sophie, he dashed after her.

Georges followed Sophie as she rushed through the doorway, still clutching the bottle of charged wine and the garlic, her eyes seeking for Émile in the dazzling, pulsating light.

She saw the mangled, blood soaked bodies of Kenrick and Arthur, the dreadful pools of spilt blood all about, and could only feel a stab of relief it was they, not Émile and Georges, who lay dead.

"Sophie, stay out!" Émile barred her way. She seized him with one hand as he shouted a warning to Ceridwen.

The lights flickered; pictures whirled across the ceiling. Ceridwen ran to one of the books and tore through the pages with one hand, while she seized a small magnifying glass with the other. She stopped searching and passed the glass over one page.

A substantial Georgian house appeared amongst the flickering on the ceiling, and Ceridwen stared at it, panting. She moved towards it into the centre of the pulsating pale blue and silver light. The scene reflected in the mirrors had moved to the nursery. A baby girl appeared there and on the ceiling, crawling and cooing on a rug.

All the while the colours throbbed, and now Sophie could hear a high, vibrating whine in which she sensed more danger.

Émile pushed Sophie backwards through the door and leapt towards Ceridwen just as she was wrenched still further towards the intense light in the middle of the moving images, directly by the largest mirror where the flames on the candles in the chandelier now blazed a foot high.

She stumbled, her arms reaching out to the baby in the images above. A burst of sparks and a flash made her body luminescent. She screamed, falling to the floor. The crawling baby girl was gone. The candles fizzed out, the smell of wax mingling with the stench of spilled blood.

Sophie started forward even as she heard the horrified gasps of Agnes and Katarina as they came up the corridor behind her. "Arthur?" Katarina sobbed, while Agnes said, "There now, don't look!"

Émile and Georges leapt forward, but now it was Georges' turn to slip in one of the congealed pools of blood which smeared the floor. As he fell Émile jumped into the fizzing lights, pulling Ceridwen clear and staggering with her dangling, unconscious body towards the group by the door. Georges jumped up to help him, wincing as he touched her. As they tried to lay her down, they had to struggle to free their hands from her.

She was dying. Sophie sensed it at once. Her face was ghastly, her body oddly disjointed and shrunken, her skin strangely loose and shapeless, as though it – like all of her body – had been wrenched out of shape. She seemed torn, yet she did not bleed.

Sophie knelt down just outside the doorway by her while Georges drew Agnes and Katarina towards him, Katarina reaching out to pat Émile too as though to reassure herself he was alive.

Sophie put down her wine and took Ceridwen in her arms – she could feel the prickling of some force even now lingering about her. There was no point in making an attempt to save her body. "Madam, please, look to the light beyond. It is all about us. Oh, do look for the light."

The great dark eyes with those sweeping lashes were the only feature unchanged, save in their expression. All their hardness was gone as they fixed on Sophie without hostility or recognition. Sophie found herself – incredibly – sobbing, dreading for the light to go out of them. She was aware of Katarina kneeling by her.

She pleaded for Ceridwen to turn away from hate and cruelty, using the most practical advice she could. "Look to the light; don't expect darkness." Indeed, Ceridwen's eyes took on an expression of wonder, but what she saw, she could no longer tell anyone. Her pupils were dilating. The great eyes emptied.

"May she find peace." Sophie whispered. Then she looked at all that remained of the arrogant Man Vampires Kenrick and Arthur, sprawled in their own blood on the floor, while nearby the lenses of Kenrick's broken glasses caught the swirling lights. "And they, too."

It was a great comfort to her now she believed in a Creator of infinite mercy; that Lucifer and his demon host waited bored in an empty hell until such time as they chose to turn towards the light themselves.

Sophie could not understand why she cared so for the death of a woman who had treated both herself and Émile so cruelly. Convention held she must hate a rival who had made Émile unfaithful after less than a month of marriage. Perhaps it was seeing the woman's longing for her lost baby.

Émile was kneeling behind Sophie, fondling her hair with soiled, bloody fingers, while she revelled in his touch, not caring how blood smeared he was.

He was staring into the room, and Sophie saw the candles were out now, but the flickering continued. Émile said, "To safety now, *mes chères,* the power builds again."

Then, suddenly he froze, releasing her hair, and stood up slowly. She knew what was happening even before she followed his gaze.

Émile's siblings stood close to one another, next to the sparkling, threatening, broken chandeliers and mirrors. They seemed to be partially in this time and partially in another. They were relaxed, not confused. Rather, they seemed to be assured messengers.

They were the ages they must have been at the time their *Château* was razed, but they looked at Émile as he came to them with an empathy far beyond their years. They didn't seem to see the broken bodies of Kenrick, Ceridwen or Arthur or to see Sophie and the others either. They seemed unaware of Émile's bloody state.

Émile moved towards them as one in a trance again. Sophie was in terror of what he would do, for she could see the *Château,* imposing and unburned, flickering on the ceiling, reflected in the broken mirror. She tried to call to him but her throat wouldn't open. She seemed frozen; for that matter, so were they all save Émile.

She might lose him now, for what if he could go back in time with them – if that is where they were? – or did they come from beyond?

Bernard was as grand as ever in his finery, yet somehow more approachable. Charlotte was blonde and slight, as she had been as the child who had befriended Sophie. Like Agnes, she exuded a combination of bossy common sense and spiritual awareness. Small Marguerite, brown haired and alert, somehow resembled Katarina, as Émile had said.

Émile was with them, trying to embrace them all at once, then seizing Marguerite and picking her up, while the others crowded about him. Charlotte was kissing his face and Bernard was hugging him.

They could move, though Sophie and the others were frozen.

"Idiot!" Sophie could hear Charlotte's voice, though her lips didn't move, as in dreams. "You are supposed to be clever. Cannot you see how things are? You have a brother and sisters once again, a wife and a family to come. It is time to let us go."

She said – or rather, communicated – something else. What it was, Sophie could never recall, though she sensed it was something even more important.

Émile turned his head; his eyes met Sophie's.

The candles flared up again and colours burst down from the ceiling. Émile gave Marguerite a kiss on top of the head and handed her to Charlotte, whom he kissed too. Then he seized them all in a last embrace. He threw himself free. He was back with Sophie and she could move and speak again as she caught hold of him.

The flashing light increased. The figures of Émile's siblings were dissolving – were gone. Émile and Georges were bundling Sophie, Agnes and Katarina back through the door. Émile paused to push Ceridwen's body back inside. The corpses were illuminated by the pulsating, throbbing violet light. Émile kicked the door shut and pulled Sophie and Katarina to one side, trying to wrap himself about them, while Georges did the same with Agnes. There was a thrusting at the door as if a monster hurled itself against it, while the floor shuddered beneath their feet.

None of them said anything. Émile released Sophie and Katarina, but Georges went on holding Agnes and she kept her arms tight about his neck. It seemed that she was willing to overlook his being a ruffian just as she ignored the blood smeared all over him.

As domineering as ever, Émile put Sophie and Katarina back and shoved open the laboratory door. As he stood looking, Sophie and Katarina crept up to peep round him.

The bodies of Ceridwen, Kenrick and Arthur, the mess of blood and the equipment were all gone. Émile's duelling pistol had gone too. A couple of scorches on the flooring and an overpowering smell of burnt wax were all that was left of the time travelling schemes of Goronwy Kenrick, Ceridwen Kenrick and mile Dubois.

Émile had Sophie in his arms again, adoring her with his human eyes, his freckles as obvious as she could wish. "Sophie, you brave girl, to come here. I would not change you for the world, and I do not care if that is a *cliché*, neither. I can see now what a monster I have been, though through much of it, I moved as in a dream. Ah, but there are the other things too. How can you ever forgive me?"

She put her arms about his neck. "Do you know, I believe I can."

After some more passionate kissing, he turned to give Agnes and Katarina a different sort of kiss. "You mad girls, following too."

Sophie smiled on them. "We have all risked ourselves here for each other. Gracious, for Katarina to see such horrors!" She was anxious at the shocks she had undergone herself, but took comfort in her female relatives' whispers that a de Courcy never miscarried. "Émile, we must tend to these wounds; Georges, you still bleed."

―――⊙⁄ℛ⊙ℭ⁄ℛ⁄ℛ⊙ℯ⁄ℛ⊙―――

Georges, always the dandy if only sometimes the valet, had brought changes of clothing for himself and Émile, should they survive to need them. Émile and Georges washed at the laboratory pump and went back into the storeroom to change.

Emile searched about. "Luckily for me, Williams carried only one of my pistols, Georges, which vanished in the explosion. I cannot find the other, neither. I will look far to find a set that suit me so well."

"I recollect me you said you wished to retire from violence, *Monsieur* Gilles?"

Sophie, Agnes and Katarina waited in the laboratory, holding onto each other and glancing about nervously, Katarina still sniffing over Arthur, while Sophie patted her hand. "I know, dear. It is all such a waste."

Agnes found some old sheets in the storeroom and wrapped the soiled clothing up in it, tearing up part of the rest for bandages. Georges climbed stiffly out of the window and threw the bundle down the dry well shaft outside.

Sophie hoped nobody was watching. Certainly, all this while there had been no sign of the staff. Katarina led them all to the kitchens. Here, they found the remains of Kenrick's household in a silent group.

Émile told them there had been an accident in the laboratory, with Kenrick, Ceridwen and Arthur Williams vanished in a strange explosion, whilst he and Georges were been injured.

Kenrick's staff must have overheard some of the noise. How far they believed the story of the accident, Sophie didn't know. None showed concern at the disappearance of Kenrick and Ceridwen, though they murmured sadly in Welsh over Arthur. They broke out in English about their wages due.

Émile cut this outcry short by assuring them that he would pay them. At this, the man in the grotesquely ill fitting livery managed a smile, but a little kitchen maid – Katarina's replacement – burst into tears.

Agnes, questioning her, learned she was scared of not finding other work. Émile spoke to her kindly, offering her work at Plas Planwydden.

She cheered up at once, but Katarina bit her lip in jealous fury. *Monsieur* Émile was only allowed to rescue one kitchen maid from Plas Cyfeillgar, herself.

Sophie, though her legs still felt like jelly, surprised herself not only by noticing Katarina's outrage, but by being able to deal with it. She took her hand. "Katarina, you are become as a sister to *Monsieur* Émile, not a maid. Did you hear what *Mademoiselle* Charlotte said?"

Katarina stared. "The blonde lady? I understood her, but what language did she use, *Madame* Sophie?"

"Perhaps she didn't use one." Sophie smiled. "But you must try and be kind to this poor girl, who has probably been ill-used, even as you were." Katarina nodded grudgingly. She suspected this kitchen maid was not besotted with her own hero, but already disposed to worship Georges, with his flashing dark eyes and rascally winks of reassurance.

The man in the ill fitting livery accompanied them to the stables to borrow a couple of horses. There were no shadows in the hall. As they came out into the gardens, a blackbird sang.

This seemed to Sophie to serve as a good an epilogue for the story of Kenrick and his associates as any.

Chapter Twenty-Six

THEY WENT HOME SLOWLY, ÉMILE and Georges stiff from their gashes and bruises. Sophie sat in front of Émile on his mount, delighting in his nearness and wondering how he handled the big horse so easily with an injured shoulder. He patted her now and then as if reassuring himself she was truly there.

Agnes drove the cart she had come in with Katarina, but the horse wandered as she kept on exchanging looks with Georges, who had even raised no objection to her driving.

They stopped outside Ferrm Seren to untie Sophie's mount from the gates, where she still waited, undiscovered. Georges then rode her.

Émile said, "*Mes chères*, I will tell you what happened, going into as little of this morning's brutality as I can.

'We knew we could not lay hands on our fellow monsters. Kenrick had assured me how as more advanced bloodsuckers, they could use firearms against *arrivistes* such as ourselves, and when I was in the laboratory they always had me covered with a pistol. Yet I had been able to cut Kenrick when throwing a knife to him when he first took my weapons, and I laid my plans accordingly.

'When we realised that we became human apace last night, we knew we could fight them hand to hand, but knew also we must lose half our strength, while having no idea if we were yet human enough to use stakes – harken, *ma chères*; I can say that word again. Our ability to visit uninvited availed us nothing, given we would never be able to break in without their hearing. Before, surprise would have been our main hope; now it was our only one. Do not blanch, Sophie *moi*, we are here yet, though why you should wish it, after our recent behaviour, is a mystery.

'I knew the physical form could travel back in time from how I retained that necklace you gave me, Sophie. I managed to affect it for myself only once, and that was but momentary. Now at the last, even as I despaired, I found a way about the problem of being drawn back betimes from a journey. I used Kenrick's ideas to create a link with Kenrick's laboratory. Georges and I travelled back in time by a couple of minutes, arriving in Kenrick's laboratory before dawn.

'We retained our memories throughout, as for various reasons I thought probable in a trip transporting us backwards through so short a period of time. We waited in the storeroom, Georges meanwhile disabling the lock sufficiently so we could not be trapped there. Had they come in, we would have had to fight them without the minor distraction I arranged through a crowd of our own forms appearing half materialised. It was an idea I worked upon after those visitations from poor Tom and *nos amis* from our smuggling days…Such a turn it gave me, when I heard your singing, Sophie, my foolishly brave wife!" He broke off to caress Sophie's back with his new, blunt nails.

"I can only guess at what happened when *Madame* used the time warp. Believe me, I did not intend that accident. For sure, I think it *Madame's* carelessness created the time warp firstly."

Sophie gazed at him adoringly. "It was so like you to try to save her." Then she sighed. "In making her human again, I suppose indirectly I killed her."

Agnes said briskly, "She was ruined, poor woman, from that man's ill usage. Better off dead and ready to start again."

Sophie had long since gathered that for Agnes, death was a transient state, but the others looked puzzled.

They rode on in silence. Sometimes Émile or Georges looked about suspiciously. Sophie supposed that if she felt that someone was watching them, it was a lingering effect from the atmosphere of Plas Cyfeillgar.

They were rounding a corner in the lane only a quarter of a mile from home when Lord Ynyr came on them.

Sophie's first, incongruous, thought was that she had never seen him looking so lively and handsome. His grey eyes were flashing, his colour high.

"Cousin!" Émile was delighted.

A changed Lord Ynyr glared at him. "Dubois, you scoundrel! You monster!"

Émile's mount tossed its head and eyed Lord Ynyr's Boris as if planning to emulate its late master's old habits in taking a quick nip.

Lord Ynyr's gaze fell on Sophie. "Madam, I am sorry that I have to say what I must before you. But can you have been spared, living in a den of vampire criminals? Dubois, I see you and your man have been in some sort of brawl."

Sophie felt Émile's sigh. "Ynyr, I owe you an abject apology for failing to take you into my confidence. It was that led to Morwenna's danger. Yet you would scarce have believed me had I told you the truth. Yes, Georges and I were vampires – part vampires according to Katarina – but we were routed by these matriarchs with herbs and a final dousing in charged wine. Do tell me how Morwenna does, for –"

"I cannot believe a word you say, Ém – Dubois, or any of your claims. You truly are a smiling villain! You are capable of anything; you have trapped your poor wife nicely and cared not if you killed poor Morwenna!"

Émile did some eye flashing himself. "We have just served Kenrick out for his threats to Sophie and the others and his attack on Morwenna."

The Count looked confounded a second. "You turned on your accomplice? For such he was, Dubois, do not try to deny it. Still, I suppose such perfidy all fits with your former career as highwayman."

"Oi! We was honest rogues!" Georges was outraged.

Agnes' bosom heaved, while Katarina tried to follow the quick speeches, looking outraged herself that anyone could speak so to her precious *Monsieur,* vampire though he may have been.

Even through her growing sense of alarm, Sophie was conscious of an equal sense of waste and sadness. Ceridwen Kenrick, her baby girl, Kenrick, his wife, Arthur, Émile, his siblings, Morwenna, the other victims – why had any of the dismal saga of destruction and love gone astray had to happen? But the purpose of suffering was supposed to be a problem beyond human understanding.

"I was an unwilling accomplice, Ynyr. Sophie and the others being human, he could use them as a threat to force me to carry out his wishes while his fellow watched me like a turnkey. But we laid our plans and he is gone."

"That is not all, Sir!" Sophie burst out. "I know that Mistress Kenrick had power over Émile through putting him in a trance."

Lord Ynyr hardly spared her a glance. Émile told her, "Get down, *ma chère!*" "No!" she hung on to him, guessing now that Lord Ynyr had a pistol. Émile tried to put her down. She clung on to him while the horse began to plunge. As Émile struggled – hampered by his gashed shoulder – to stop it rearing and to keep Sophie from falling under its hooves, Georges leaped on the Count from his own mount. They fell to the ground and rolled there while Agnes and Katarina screamed.

The fall winded Lord Ynyr, enabling Georges to wrench the pistol from his inner pocket. He jumped up, cursing.

"Don't shoot, Georges!" Émile bawled, jumping clear of the horse, holding Sophie despite his injured shoulder, so that he nearly dropped her. He pushed her backwards. "Stay back, Sophie! Georges, let me handle this!" He rushed towards Georges and Ynyr.

Agnes screamed, ""Mackenzie!"

Captain Mackenzie was by the hedgerow over a hundred yards down the lane, aiming his pistol at Émile. He wore nondescript clothes, but with his strong build, dark curly hair and handsome features, he was no less striking.

Émile turned and shouted, "Mackenzie, it's me you want, let me get clear of these others." He started towards Mackenzie. Mackenzie levelled his pistol. Sophie rushed after Émile, the shot rang out and Émile dropped, the blood welling through the side of his frockcoat.

Sophie knelt beside him, dreading a chest or abdominal wound.

"That saved Your Lordship the trouble!" Mackenzie's cry shook exultingly.

Émile's horse bolted towards Plas Planwydden and Lord Ynyr's ran into the hedge in its panic. The horse harnessed to the cart plunged. Katarina and Agnes jumped from the cart, falling to the ground. Sophie's placid mare only stirred nervously.

Georges fired on Mackenzie with the Count's pistol, but the

silver bullet missed. He rushed towards Mackenzie, but the Captain disappeared in a burst of whirling specks.

Lord Ynyr staggered up to grab the reins of the panicking horse, saving Katarina from its plunging hoofs.

"Émile!" Sophie sobbed, taking him in her arms while the blood spread out over the side of his frockcoat. "Is it bad? Can you speak?"

"Away from me, he may shoot again!"

"No! Where are you hurt?"

Agnes and Katarina joined Sophie in kneeling by Émile. "How can we staunch the bleeding?" Sophie was undoing his coat, her mind running automatically on torn petticoats.

The Count staggered over, one eyebrow split and bloody, to kneel by Émile too. "Cousin! Oh, no, Émile, you are human!"

Georges was back. "Out of the way, let me see."

Émile bit his lip and muttered, "I bleed like a pig, Georges, and deservedly. It was unforgiveable in me to let him sneak up on us so. Sophie, I forbid you to worry, it is nothing. Yet, make me a happy scoundrel by telling me that you forgive me for all the sorrow I have caused you."

"Oh, Émile, how can you even think to ask me!" Sophie sobbed, as splashed with blood, she fought along with Georges and Agnes to staunch the flow from the wound in Émile's side. He knew more about it than she, and she followed his instructions with desperate faith.

Katarina sobbed aloud and Émile told her, "No more, *ma petite*. You have not your handkerchief."

Sophie wailed at Émile as he began to pass in and out of consciousness: "Émile, you must live! I love you too much to lose you!"

Georges tried to rally them both. "*Monsieur* Gilles is too much of a rascal to succumb to a little gunshot wound like that. The ball's not too deep. Go for Dr Powell, Count. No time to waste."

For the first time in his life, Lord Ynyr took orders from a servant. He rushed for his horse, whose tack was still tangled in the hedge.

Dr Powell was expected home within the half hour. The Count galloped back to the others, cursing himself.

He felt as guilty of Émile's danger as the demented Mackenzie. Hadn't he brought the pistol loaded with the silver bullet half decided to shoot Émile himself? Certainly, he made the distraction which enabled Mackenzie to creep upon them. He was sure now that Émile had been telling the truth when he said it had been Kenrick who attacked Morwenna.

In his agony of remorse, the Count even forgot his former outrage over Émile's making Sophie live among his ruffianly cohorts and the highwayman rumours. He forgot almost everything but how he was now in danger of losing his favourite male cousin as well as his love Morwenna.

They brought Émile, pale from loss of blood, back to Plas Planwydden in the cart.

Mr and Mrs Kit at once took charge, Mr Kit meanwhile cursing his bruises for keeping him away from the confrontation. The Count could only find their familiarity with gunshot wounds a relief. Mrs Kit was confident of a 'Sure as Fire' method of stopping the bleeding involving ice and Georges rushed to the ice house.

She spoke briskly to Émile, slapping his face until she got a mumbled response. "Now, I know what I am doing, Mistress," she told the outraged Sophie. "With respect, don't interfere." She forced more brandy between his lips, and crossly sent Agnes to make Sophie tea, while Katarina sobbed and tried to think of some herbal cure.

Her method worked. The bleeding slowed.

"That is more like it." Mrs Kit said, her tone as indignant as if Émile had been losing blood through carelessness. "You is never going to pass out again? Stay with us, you are neglecting the company. I don't know, I tell you I am still of a mind to pack our boxes and making for home, where it is nice and quiet. Nobody told me of the goings on in Wales, and I am shocked, *Monsieur* Gilles. Not as if you have not caused a lot of the trouble yourself, what with One Thing and Another I Won't Mention."

"Not another word. Mrs Kit!" exclaimed Sophie, stroking his head. "Oh, Émile, can you hear me? Is it very agonising?"

"*Monsieur* Gilles?" Lord Ynyr asked vaguely. "His valet calls him so, too." He realised he must be in a state of shock to be speaking to this vulgar, unfeeling woman.

"So did lots of folk." Mrs Kit looked at Lord Ynyr as if he knew nothing.

Perhaps she was right, for as she looked at Émile the Count saw the combined fear and tenderness in her eyes.

Marcel Sly Boots and Felix the Professor seized the bemused and swaying Émile to right him, chuckling in sympathetic recognition.

Émile looked round, dazed. There was a window, and outside the light was bright, and there was birdsong, too, but no scenery visible. They were in the living room of his old lodgings with Françoise's Gránd-mère. The ginger cat washed itself by the door.

Marcel Sly Boots was shaking his head. "That looked bad, Gilles Long Legs. We didn't like seeing it. When they dig them slugs out, it do hurt. So we brought you here for a little visit."

"Here." The Professor handed Émile a cup. The others laughed, for the Professor had a thing about the healing qualities of boiled water. They had always teased him about it. When they came back cut up from fights, and Françoise fussed and pestered them to let her bathe their wounds, the Professor insisted she boil the water first.

She did, under protest. "But this is Seine water, Monsieur Felix, than which these Parisians say there is nothing better in the world, certainly not that horrid boiled water."

Émile gulped down the water, looking astonished to find himself so thirsty. The Professor nodded solemnly. "That will soon put you to rights."

Émile roused to embrace one while patting another on the back. "I never thought to see you again!"

Marcel Sly Boots nodded solemnly as he clapped him on the back in return. "Gilles Long Legs, I was watching when you got that Kenrick as quick and clean as I could have done myself. I am proud of you...Here." He handed Émile a cup of wine.

Émile drank it straight off too. "I had the best tuition from you."

The Professor looked uneasy. "Now, less of that violent talk. Old Kenrick couldn't help being a vampire bat or wolf thing no more than Gilles here." He glanced out of the window and hurried to open the door. "Alors, here is a surprise!"

Françoise came in smiling. They all rushed to kiss her. When it was Émile's turn, she hugged him extra tightly. "Gilles Long Legs, I never had time to thank you for giving me the money so we could have our farm." She shook her head. *"All I could do was light candles for you."*

He pinched her cheek. "So you did marry your old sweetheart? Give me another kiss while he's not here to be jealous then, ma petite. It was kind in you to strive for my soul, and I have proved a dismal ingrate, for only yesterday I was in a fair way to becoming a monster. Still, what chance does a rogue have against these religious women?"

She glanced about, puzzled. "Sure this is not purgatory! What mean you, about monsters?"

He laughed. "Keep lighting those candles, Françoise, ma chère, and include these reprobates, too."

Felix shook his head, smiling. "This may not be purgatory, but poor Gilles Long Legs was in purgatory only now when they were digging out that shot."

Françoise winced. "That is horrible, Gilles, but how came this about?" She started. "That's my man rousing me from my doze, I must go. I'm so happy to see you all again —" She was gone, and they all smiled after her.

Émile said, "It is good she did marry her sweetheart."

"Yes. Proper upset she was, when you didn't come back. We all thought you were dead, especially when we heard you were last seen with Southern Georges. She kept saying, 'Poor Gilles Long Legs, I never said thank you for the money.' We had our work cut out to keep her quiet about the money in front of her grasping Grànd-mère. We packed her off a couple of days later, still taking on about you: 'He was so sweet'."

Émile laughed. "Nobody called me so before."

"We were all upset." Felix nodded solemnly. "Then I'm sorry to say I made a little mistake, which cost Sly Boots dear."

Here, Marcel Sly Boots turned from looking down at something invisible to Émile. "Never mind, Professor, it were only a Tactical Error." He liked the sound of that, and he repeated it thoughtfully, before turning to grin at Émile. "Long Legs, who would have thought you were an aristocrat? Just like one of us, you were, and we can't think of you as this grand Émile Dubois fellow what was raised in that Château with dozens of servants." He bowed ironically.

Émile gave him a shove. "Less of that! I'm always Gilles Long Legs."

"To think of Southern Georges being a friend of yours all along!" Marcel shook his head. "You kept that quiet. I had to laugh, seeing him in that

lackey's get up, waiting on you." Then, *he shook his head sadly. "But you should have told us about them sending your Mère et Père for the chop. We would have helped you. Any family of yours is family of ours, eh, Professor?"*

Felix nodded solemnly, his moustache tremulous.

Émile smiled. "Listen, you were friends, and I hated lying to you. But if you knew about me, your necks would have been in danger, as Georges' would have had he kept with me. Stopping the tumbrel would have been madness, with you for the guillotine yourselves before you knew it."

The others laughed as at a great joke. "I always say, a short life, but a merry one." Felix the Professor no longer had those terrible shadows under his eyes, and he hadn't coughed once. He glanced down, as if looking through the floor, and added, "We ain't got much longer; Gilles, your poor Madame Sophie is sobbing her heart out. She thinks you won't come back from this one."

"Sophie! Ma pauvre petite! How could I forget?!"

"You did find her again, after all." Marcel Sly Boots sighed. "I do like a bit of romance."

Felix nodded. "She'll keep you in order; les femmes look as though the butter would not melt in their mouths ever do."

"I have to go." Émile's form wavered.

They laughed. Marcel said, "That's what you said that other time. Be lucky this time, eh, Gilles Long Legs? Au revoir."

Georges was pouring brandy in Émile's mouth, while Dr Powell slapped his face. "He's back. I thought we had lost him."

Lord Ynyr looked nearly as pale as Émile. He had never seen shot dug out of a wound before, and he didn't intend ever to see it done again. Everything seemed distant and his legs felt weak, so he dreaded he might disgrace himself by fainting. If, while they held him down, Émile had groaned and writhed, the Count knew he would have screamed himself.

"Hold your noise!" Georges said, for Katarina was sobbing as she held the basin of bloody water for Dr Powell while Éloise was hiccoughing as if she had no suspicion Émile had been as delighted to see her blood as she was appalled to see his.

In her own bedroom, Sophie was almost bawling, while Agnes sniffed as she poured her tea.

"I don't want that, Agnes! It tastes strange. I think you right about my condition. Oh! Maybe it will be all I have left of poor Émile! Ah!"

"There, now, *cariad, Monsieur* will live to do more mischief yet and you will have a whole brood for sure. I saw this baby on the cards back when I did that first reading when you first came to Plas Uchaf, and I saw the young men from abroad, and the black magic and all the rest of it, and now there is no doubt he will be fully human."

"Oh! Ah! It is my fault entirely for stopping Émile from being a Man Vampire."

"Oh, nonsense! We had to cure him." Agnes hurried over to answer the door.

Dr Powell smiled at Agnes and addressed Sophie in the reassuring voice she knew to be professional, but trusted anyway. "I think he will do, *Madame* Dubois. He's a very strong young devil."

From the way he had sent her to rest and not witness the gruesome removal of the shot from Émile's side, Sophie wondered if Agnes might actually told him her mistress might be pregnant. Certainly, she was capable of it.

———— ✦✦✦ ————

Captain Mackenzie sat in the laboratory. He didn't weep, having long ago forgotten how, but his heart felt as though it would burst.

The stout, hard faced serving woman who had opened the door to him (he went in for that unnecessary civility here) – triumph glowing in her eyes, clutching her cross – had told him of Kenrick, Ceridwen and Arthur's end and of the strange impact from the laboratory which had seemed to shake the building.

"Vanished, Captain Mackenzie, all three." It was only her fear of him which prevented her from saying, 'Good riddance'. She added sourly, "Not that Frenchman; his wife and half his household came here too."

Mackenzie thought with luck Dubois would die of a festering wound if not from blood loss; he must have been as human as Mackenzie had heard him assuring the Count for the shot to wound him as it had.

"We are all packing up, now, Sir, and going to close the house. Will you take the keys? I am sure I don't know who else is to have them. Mr Kenrick didn't have any relations alive that I know of."

Mackenzie held out one hand from the keys. He went to the laboratory.

The door was unlocked, and the embers still glowed in the grate. He glanced about, tormented by the insane hope that he might hear Ceridwen's voice. Of course, nothing came. The woman had spoken of a type of explosion, yet the windows were intact, with the only signs of heat a couple of scorch marks upon the floorboards.

Yet, there had been some extraordinary force at work; an overturned chair near those marks had been warped strangely, legs bent but not broken, while the branches of the chandeliers were distorted.

Obviously, violence had been done. He saw from odd splashes of blood still smearing the walls there must have been a desperate fight. Someone or something had cleaned up the mess.

He was sure Dubois had tricked the others somehow. Mackenzie hated all Frenchman as a matter of course, and would have believed the worst of him even if Ceridwen hadn't taken him as her lover, low robber as he was. Odd, that such a fellow should have come together with Kenrick over that time travel obsession they all had in common.

Of course, Ceridwen had been happy to draw him in the time-honoured manner. She adored savagery in a man. Dubois' career as bandit, smuggler and highwayman fascinated her. Murderous brutality was what she so enjoyed in Mackenzie himself, until he had been foolish enough to show his love for her.

She had love for only one, of course; her dead baby.

She never would behave rationally about that. He had pointed out to her if only she came away with him, they could have children enough if she wished. They would have made bloodthirsty household, perhaps, but a cheerfully robust one.

But she wanted her dead baby, and only that baby, and insisted on remaining with Kenrick in the desperate hope he would be the means of reuniting them.

Kenrick, with all the amazing beauty of Ceridwen before his eyes, was equally blind to his present possibilities of happiness. He longed for that dowdy little woman in the picture behind the curtain in his study, and nobody else.

Absurd there should be talk of his deliberately killing his first wife! She had died falling downstairs, running away from one of his biting fits. A bathetic end, not unlike the one which happened to the floozy Mackenzie had picked up in Chester the day he'd walked out on Ceridwen, resolving to leave her for good. As if he hadn't made that vow dozens of times, always returning for more humiliation.

How would he get through all those years to come without Ceridwen? He wouldn't take care of himself and he might have the good luck to be killed in action if something pierced his heart. If not, then a Man Vampire could exist for perhaps two hundred years.

Later, when the door opened, Mackenzie knew it was an accomplice of Dubois' even before he saw him.

He knew a murderously loyal man when he met him; he wouldn't have risen through the ranks to Captain otherwise. He had predicted that either the fat fellow or the dark one who chased him earlier would come to kill him. He cared little for the outcome of the fight. Still, he would fight; it was his nature.

It was the almost cherubic looking man with the black curls like a water spaniel, smiling broadly.

He hurled his knife even as Mackenzie snatched for his, only to be dazzled by a burst of light. As Mackenzie's eyes cleared, he found himself looking into Ceridwen's slanting black orbs.

Georges, temporarily blinded by the flash, staggered backwards, bracing himself against the force wrenching him into the pulsating light after Mackenzie. The struggle seemed endless to him, yet could not have lasted for more than half a minute.

Then the lights were gone, and Mackenzie and Georges' knife with them. "*Merde!*" Georges stared about wildly and went on aloud: "That was more than his turning tail. I think he's gone like them others. I think I got him, but now I can't make sure and kill him for Gilles."

——————

The Dowager Countess dropped her embroidery, which may or may not have been in a Sad Tangle. Lord Ynyr couldn't tell and didn't care. "Émile badly shot? And by Captain Mackenzie? Surely you are misinformed, Ynyr! That sort of thing does not happen hereabouts. You bring me such a tale as this in return for my happy news Morwenna is rallying!"

Lord Ynyr sent Mrs Brown for the smelling salts. He saw her smile as she scampered away. He hoped that it was a lingering smile over Morwenna.

"I am sorry, Madam. The man is clearly deranged. Dr Powell is hopeful." Lord Ynyr didn't remind her that he had been hopeful until twelve hours before the Late Count's death.

The Dowager Countess was so anxious that she insisted on coming to see Émile in the squalor of his sickroom the next morning.

Dr Powell was been there, along with a Sophie almost as pale as Émile himself, and Agnes, relieving Éloise and Katarina. Émile, rambling and wild-eyed, had seized the Count's coat sleeve. "When I heard her voice in that accursed place, it was worse than anything I have known. Ynyr! There is too much delay – they have been for Morwenna already –"

Dr Powell came over to the Dowager Countess with his most soothing manner. "Your Ladyship must not be too anxious. This is as strong a young fellow as ever I have bled."

At this, Émile's fever bright eyes flashed (but only in a human way). "I'll see you damned before you get your teeth in my neck! It was bad enough with That Woman."

"He is delirious quite, Madam." The doctor ushered Her Ladyship from the dismal scene of bloody bandages and draughts.

Clearly, the absurd stories that were going about in the villages must have been preying on *Monsieur's* mind, though it was the first time Dr Powell had heard himself named as a vampire; ironically, along with the missing Kenrick couple and Arthur Williams, *Monsieur* himself was usually named as the most likely suspect.

—⁂—

"This is getting to be a habit with me, *chérie*, and dull enough for you. You did not marry me to become my nurse. Wicked Gilles Long Legs was at least robust."

Émile – though pale and haggard enough to satisfy even Mrs Brown, could she have seen him – had made such good progress since coming out of the fever* following his gunshot wounds that Sophie felt she could soon concentrate on her own internal discomforts.

For all that, she found time to pray every night for Ceridwen, Kenrick, Mackenzie and Arthur. Georges had disappeared after Dr Powell had extracted the shot from Émile. Agnes told Sophie that while Lord Ynyr had started proceedings to arrest Mackenzie, he had apparently vanished. Sophie thought she knew why.

She was as happy not to know the details as she was not to know those of Ceridwen's relations with Émile.

She had merely asked him to forgive the tormented woman. He had pulled a face. 'I would do much for you, Sophie; that is asking a good deal. Still, I will try.'

Some things were better left alone. Mackenzie had sometimes behaved as a fiend, but that was not his fault, any more than it had been Émile's, or even Kenrick's.

At the moment, though Sophie felt too sick to dwell on such thoughts. Over the last few days, she had made several hand-to-mouth dashes from Émile's bedside to the basin she kept for the purpose in the dressing room. Now she felt on the verge of another. It being morning, she was at her sickest. She had been hardly able to touch the mint tea that Agnes brought her and could only respond to Émile's banter with an uncomfortable smile.

Just then, Georges came in from the dressing room. Sophie caught a whiff of the cigar he must have enjoyed earlier. Her stomach heaved; snatching her hand from Émile's grasp she dashed into his dressing room, beginning to retch even before she gained it.

Agnes was following her, when Émile stopped her. "I become worried about *ma petite*, Agnes. Her stomach trouble becomes worse. It is she who should be in bed, being waited upon."

"No getting up yet, *Monsieur* Gilles! I think Mistress Sophie is Well Enough Under the Circumstances."

With male obliviousness, he looked puzzled. "You mean all the worry I have given her?"

"No, although I do not suppose it helps. But she might have Interesting News for you." Agnes put such a wealth of meaning into her tone and glance that even a male couldn't fail to understand. As she went into the dressing room to Sophie she saw Émile looking first startled and then gratified.

He beckoned to Georges. "Is Mackenzie still at large, for I fear for *ma femme* and the other women?"

"You ain't going to like this, Gilles. As you know your cousin as magistrate signed the warrant for his arrest, but he ain't been seen? I went back to the Kenrick place after him, finding him in the laboratory. Even as I threw my blade, the flashing came in front of him. He disappeared into it and I near did too. There was something different about it from when it pulled us in."

Émile swore. "Devil take it, it ain't over, then. I so wanted to kill him myself for making those threats to the girls. So that force lingers, Georges? This is not happy."

"I think there to be nothing there now. I was back a couple of times, in case the old man staying there had seen anything of him, and all was still. I think he's gone like them others."

"I would we had been able to dispatch him, Georges, and that instead of lying like a helpless baby here I could explore any lingering influence there."

"I know you will find nothing, so do not annoy us all by rising before you should. I have happy news; Agnes has agreed to marry me. Incredibly, I find that is what I want more than anything."

"Georges, I am delighted for you, though she is far better than you deserve."

"Even as adorable *Madame* Sophie is far too good for you. My only criticism of your lovely Madame Dubois is all the praying over us. Why cannot these women leave an honest rogue be? But I have promised Agnes I will reform, so that old – mother of hers will us have Eiluned. And my only complaint about Agnes is she is too superstitious. I would like to set fire to that Tarot set of hers." Georges dug in his pocket and drew out the shot. "The Doctor dug this out of you. What think you of that?"

Émile whistled. "I did notice his doing so, Georges. Alors, I deserved to have some of my own blood spilt after my wild lust for that of women."

Georges shook his head. "Now I shudder to think on how we slobbered after their necks."

Émile looked disgusted too. "What a business, eh, Georges? Life was tame in Paris, Boulogne and Hounslow Heath in comparison. We have been villains enough, and lucky enough to escape Tyburn, let alone stakes in our gizzards. It is high time we made some effort to become respectable citizens – comparatively. *Ma pauvre petite*! I feel I must spend the rest of my life grovelling to her for the sorrow that I have caused her, and we owe those redoubtable females endless thanks for fighting us so magnificently to make us human again."

"For sure we do. *Alors*, it all worked out for the best, though you and I went to the Kenrick place cursing at losing our vampire strength for the coming fight, let alone Kit. *Alors*, it seems when *Madame* is recovered somewhat you will be having a private conversation, so I will withdraw." Georges made his mocking bow.

"My *pauvre petite*." Émile smiled. "We will not tell the ladies of how Mackenzie disappeared in the hope that matters are truly over."

"Especially not *Madame* Sophie now...I will tell you a secret. I fell down on my knees to Agnes quite as abjectly as you did to *Madame,* as that is what they like." Georges gave a patriarchal sigh.

Epilogue

Dubois Court
Buckinghamshire
England
October 1795

"WHAT SHALL WE CALL HIM, Sophie?"

Sophie and Émile watched entranced as the baby sucked frantically at her nipple.

His downy head was very blond – as in that premonition that she had had – a six pound boy.

They stared in wonder at the way his ten fingers and toes wriggled as he suckled, as overwhelmed by this miracle as if babies hadn't been doing that since babies began.

It was amazing how new he was, how completely free of the past, how intensely he lived, oblivious of anything that had gone towards his making, the happenings of Provence, Paris, Plas Uchaf and Plas Planwydden, let alone Plas Cyfeillgar. He was so obviously, reassuringly, toothlessly human, too, for all his father's having been only half so when his life was started.

Agnes' Tarot cards (returned to making accurate predictions after the Kenrick adventure) had reassured Sophie about that as had the Charged Wine and the herbs she had taken, yet she had always had a tiny doubt about this baby's full humanity until now.

Émile stroked Sophie's cheek. "My brave girl made little enough fuss in giving me this prize, so Agnes tells me. I made more. Georges and Mr Kit dosed me with brandy."

Sophie had given her word about the baby's name. As Georges would have said, 'Honour is Honour'. She answered Émile's query about the name stoutly. "Bernard or Armand, as we agreed for the first boy." She didn't like either name.

She was not all that fond of the name Marguerite either, for the first girl, though she liked the name Charlotte. She knew a girl would be next. Agnes said so (just as she said that this baby and her own coming baby would be boys) and once again her Tarot set was Never Wrong.

At the moment, though, Sophie felt too battered to dwell on what went towards making another baby.

Émile went over to the windows, which gave a view over the sunlit carriage entrance of Dubois Court. Out there, Katarina (now a sort of adopted younger sister for them both) was playing with Eiluned and some of the kitchen kittens.

Outside Sophie's bedroom door, Agnes was telling Georges about the wonders of the new arrival. Sophie hoped she was praising Mistress Sophie's courage as much as Émile had. Mrs Kit and Agnes both said it had been an easy first birth. If so, she was happy to escape a difficult one.

Sophie and Émile had made the journey down to Buckinghamshire and the incredibly grand Dubois Court by easy stages, following their household from Plas Planwydden some weeks after Sophie's sickness had reluctantly left her. Before leaving, she was able to enjoy Lord Ynyr's and Morwenna's wedding breakfast as she hadn't Agnes and Georges'.

By then, Miss Morwenna and Miss Lewis were long been cured of their other symptoms. That is, Sophie and the others supposed poor Morwenna to have suffered from vampire symptoms. She'd been too ladylike to say. Still, during her recovery, Katarina had supplied the Charged Wine for her and for Miss Lewis, and the cure had presumably been as quick as it had been with Émile and Georges.

They had all sheltered the Dowager Countess from the truth. Lord Ynyr and Katarina distributed cures, while gradually the fear in the villages faded away. Everyone seemed happy to blame the vanished Kenrick and Captain Mackenzie for every unpleasant happening in the area since ten years before they came to it, including the recent bad harvest.

The Dowager Countess had pointed out at length to the recovered Émile the moral of the Kenricks' disappearance following on from those Mischievous Experiments.

He had smiled imperturbably. "You are fully in the right, *Madame*. Yet, given his unpopularity, it seems ungrateful of the people to blame him for his own disappearance."

The Count and Émile were now as friendly as ever, though once, when a neighbour was holding forth about hangings and floggings for criminals, Lord Ynyr had looked uneasy, while *Monsieur* Gilles smiled imperturbably through this, too.

By the time of the Count's wedding, Sian Jones had been bursting with pride over her lusty baby boy.

"That is very kind of you, Sophie." Émile now said hoarsely, his back still turned. "But you must choose his second name yourself. John, if you like, after your father and brother?"

"Gilles, then."

At that, he turned about in astonishment, his eyes still damp. "Whatever you wish, *ma chère* – but why?"

"Because I love *Monsieur* Gilles Long Legs entirely." said Sophie.

THE END
Lucinda Elliot 2012

You can read more about this and other writing by the author
on her website http://sophieandemile.wordpress.com/

Notes

'THE LIGHT OF OTHER DAYS' A quote from the 1815 poem of that name by Thomas Moore, (1780-1852). The first verse is: -

Oft in the stilly night
Ere slumbers chain has bound me
Fond memory brings the light
Of other days around me;
The smiles, the tears, of boyhood years,
The words of love then spoken
The eyes that shone, now dimmed and gone,
The cheerful hearts now broken!
Thus in the stilly night
Ere slumbers chain has bound me
Sad memory brings the light
Of other days around me.

Chester: The County town of Cheshire, England. At that time, a busy port.

Plas Uchaf: 'Highest Hall' in Welsh.

Famau Mountain: Mountain in Clwyd, North Wales UK.

Brighthelmstone: At this time, Brighton was a tiny fishing village known by its full name.

Enemies of the State: Numerous aristocrats and others were held as enemies of the state during The Terror, many being guillotined. *Monsieur* and *Madame* Dubois have engaged in political intrigue.

Plas Cyfeillgar: 'Friendly hall' in Welsh. Of course, anything but.

Committee of Public Safety: The Jacobin government disapproved of formal address modes, but policing such a thing must surely have been difficult, especially in a time of national emergency.

Levée en masse: In April 1793 the revolutionary government, faced with attempted invasion to restore monarchical power in France by Austria, Spain, Prussia, Britain, Piedmont and the United Provinces, issued a directive calling on all unmarried men under 25 to enlist in the military, and imposed quotas on areas. Evasion and desertion were high.

Tyburn: The gallows near Hyde Park where many highwaymen and robbers ended their days.

Clarissa: A moralistic novel written in 1748 by Samuel Richardson, in which the virtuous heroine is pursued and eventually raped by the rakish Richard Lovelace.

St Nicholas' Day: Traditionally the day for giving presents, celebrated on 6th December. Later this became part of the Christmas Day festivities.

St Asaph's: Small town sized city in Denbighshire, approximately three miles inland.

Natural philosophy: There was no term for what is now called 'science' at the time; authors have to improvise; some years later, Mary Shelley used this term in '*Frankenstein*' for scientific processes.

Ombra Mai fú: Famous aria from Handel's 1738 opera '*Xerxes*' addressed to a tree.

Challenge him: That is, challenge him to a duel.

Name his friends: That is, name his friends as seconds in a duel.

Lascia che'io pianga: Aria from Handel's 1711 opera *Rinaldo* in which the innocent heroine mourns her misfortune in being captive to her enchantress rival.

Pamela: Moralistic novel (1747) by Samuel Richardson in which a virtuous servant girl resists the improper advances of her employer, so that eventually he proposes.

Llandyrnog: Village in Denbighshire, approximately three miles from the Famau Mountain.

St James: The Royal residence at that time.

Comte de Sade: Marquis de Sade (1740-1814) founder of modern sadism.

Admitting to the 'de' wasn't exactly discreet: The aristocratic names 'de' etc were officially frowned on in Revolutionary France.

Too fierce to wear breeches: The *sans culottes* wore trousers rather than breeches, and were invariably portrayed as semi naked ruffians in the British press of the time.

Too controlling: A husband was considered to be entitled to dictate his wife's reading at the time, and Lord Ynyr defers to Émile as Sophie's fiancé.

Plas Planwydden: 'Plane Tree Mansion' in Welsh. Synchronicity, as in the song, *'Ombra, mai fù'* which is special for Émile and Sophie, Xerxes addresses that aria to a plane tree.

Sister Harriet: Sisters-in-law were called 'sisters' at that time.

Cat O' Nine Tails: A savage whip used for punishment in the Royal Navy at the time.

Front: A fringe of false curls.

Altitudes: A cant slang expression for 'drunk'.

Bully: The term of the time for 'ponce'.

Mountebank: People who sold quack remedies at fairs.

Drawn: A reference to the unspeakable method of execution in fact reserved for traitors, hanging, drawing and quartering, where the person was hanged and then cut down whilst still alive to be drawn, that is, disembowelled, the entrails then being burnt before the person's eyes before final dismemberment, the quartering.

On her promotion: That is, seeking social advancement.

Blue-stocking: A term of contempt for an obviously intellectual woman.

Gentleman of the Road: Highwayman.

Mr B: The lecherous master in Samuel Richardson's 1747 novel *'Pamela'*.

Mysteries of Udolpho: Gothic novel by Ann Radcliffe (1794) in which the heroine is imprisoned in a castle, surrounded by brigands.

So: A term of the time for 'pregnant'.

Goody Two Shoes: An old expression for an excessively virtuous person, origin unknown, but further popularised by the anonymous book '*The History of Little Goody Two Shoes*' (1765) featuring an exemplary girl.

Mill: A fist fight.

Fever: Any wound at that time was invariably followed by an attack of fever.

5121020R00208

Printed in Great Britain
by Amazon.co.uk, Ltd.,
Marston Gate.